NICHOLAS DANE

MELVIN BURGESS

HENRY HOLT AND COMPANY

**SQUARE
FISH**

An Imprint of Macmillan
175 Fifth Avenue
New York, NY 10010
macteenbooks.com

NICHOLAS DANE. Text copyright © 2009 by Andersen Press Limited.
All rights reserved. Printed in the United States of America by
R. R. Donnelley & Sons Company, Harrisonburg, Virginia.

Square Fish and the Square Fish logo are trademarks of Macmillan and
are used by Henry Holt and Company under license from Macmillan.

Square Fish books may be purchased for business or promotional use. For information on
bulk purchases, please contact the Macmillan Corporate and Premium Sales Department at
(800) 221-7945 x5442 or by e-mail at specialmarkets@macmillan.com.

Library of Congress Cataloging-in-Publication Data
Burgess, Melvin.
Nicholas Dane / Melvin Burgess.
p.   cm.
Summary: When his single mother dies of a heroin overdose, fourteen-year-old Nick is
sent into England's institutional care system, where he endures harsh punishment, sexual
abuse, and witnesses horrors on a daily basis before emerging emotionally scarred but still
alive. Loosely based on "Oliver Twist."
ISBN 978-0-312-55146-9
[1. Coming of age—Fiction.   2. Orphans—Fiction.   3. Sexual abuse—Fiction.
4. Child abuse—Fiction.   5. Emotional problems—Fiction.   6. England—Fiction.
7. Great Britain—History—Elizabeth II, 1952– —Fiction.]   I. Title.
PZ7.B9166Ni 2010   [Fic]—dc22   2009051779

Originally published in the UK in 2009 by Andersen Press
First published in the United States in 2010 by Henry Holt and Company
First Square Fish Edition: April 2013
Book designed by April Ward
Square Fish logo designed by Filomena Tuosto

10   9   8   7   6   5   4   3   2   1

AR: 5.2 / LEXILE: HL810L

IN MEMORY OF CHRIS HAYWOOD

CONTENTS

NICHOLAS DANE

1
MURIEL'S LITTLE TREAT

Nick Dane lifted his head and stared blearily at the doorway. There was music blaring through, light flooding in. It sounded as if he was in the kitchen but he could have sworn he was still in bed.

His mother appeared. "Come on, wake up, I want you out, I've work to do," she bellowed cheerfully. She headed back down the stairs toward the kitchen. "I'll make you some porridge with cream and Goldfish syrup," she called over her shoulder.

She'd called it that ever since he said it himself when he was three. One mistake: a lifetime of pain.

Nick looked at the clock.

"Bloody 'ell," he yelled in outrage. "It's only eight bloody fifteen. There's hours!"

"I have work to do," she yelled from downstairs. Nick rammed his head back under the covers, but he knew he'd never get to sleep now. He was too cross. Eight fifteen! He had another half an hour. What was she on?

"Turn the radio down!" he yelled. Why was it so loud? It was Adam Ant, music for morons. Then he realized it must be the radio in her bedroom to make so much racket up here. She was trying to *irritate* him out of bed.

"Get up and turn it down yourself," she yelled, so he got up, slammed the door so hard the room shook, and went back to bed. No one was going to separate Nick Dane from his zees. No way.

Pause. Footsteps on the stairs. The door opens. The soft approach. "I've got an essay to hand in, I'm late. Come on, Nick. Please?"

He stared at her. "I'm in bed," he explained, as if to a child. A flicker of irritation crossed her face. They stared at each other, mother and son, for a long moment. Then he relented.

"Mum," he groaned, giving in. It was blackmail, it really was. She'd been studying for years now, trying to improve herself. She could do with improving. There was a good job at the end of it. Nick was hoping she'd make enough money to keep him in the style to which he wanted to become accustomed.

Muriel trotted back downstairs. Nick lay listening to the music for a while, then pulled the covers down. It felt cold. He pulled them back up. It felt warm. Bed was so good, it was a shame you had to fall asleep and miss it.

A few minutes later Muriel appeared in the doorway again like an overgrown pixie, with her dyed red hair and her lime green gown, baring her yellow teeth at him and trying to be cheerful.

"Come on! You promised. I'm not going till you're up."

"I've got nothing on."

"I won't look. Not that there's much to see, from what I remember . . ."

Nick looked alarmed and she instantly regretted her joke.

"Only joking, I know it's a monster," she said.

"Shut up! Close the door, then."

It was a deal. She closed the door and Nick tipped himself out of bed, pulled on his pants, and crawled to the loo. It was too early. Every morning of his life was too early. Life began at about one in the afternoon, everyone knew that.

Muriel stirred the porridge and made a cup of Nesquik milkshake. Her big boy, but he still had his sweet tooth. Nick walked in, with his school trousers on and his shirt undone. Lean, short for his age, but broad shoulders and good muscles. Fourteen years old. It was amazing watching him grow. He was a man—well, on the outside, anyway. He grunted at her, sat down, and started pouring the milkshake down him in long, thirsty gulps. Muriel struggled briefly, trying not to remind him not to drink all the milk first, because that would leave no room for breakfast, but as usual she couldn't help herself. Nick glanced sideways at the kettle and ignored her. The milk dribbled down his chin. He tipped the glass back to let the last few drops trickle down and put it down with a bang.

She swallowed her irritation. Nick was one of those kids—the slightest hint of being told off and he was off in the other direction. Infuriating! Just like her when she was his age.

She didn't want a row this morning. Neither of them were at their best first thing.

She decided to horrify him out the door. She started dancing around the kitchen, waving the spoon in the air, to the music on the radio.

"Karma karma karma karma karma chameleon, you come and go, you come and go—oh-oh-oh."

Nick stared at her as if she'd just turned into a pink blancmange, and she was suddenly overcome with giggles. She clutched the edge of the table, put her wrist to her forehead, and rocked with silent laughter.

"You're bonkers," Nick told her. "You don't even like that song."

"Karma karma . . ." she started again.

"Right, that's it, I'm off," said Nick, jumping up. See? It worked. Like magic. "I'm too clever for my own good," she thought to herself as he ran back into his bedroom and collected his bag.

"Eat your porridge," she told him.

Nick paused in the hall. "No twattin' about, then?" he said.

"No twatting about," she agreed.

He came back in, lured by the irresistible Goldfish syrup, and stood next to the breakfast bar, spooning it down him and talking with his mouth full.

"What's up with you this morning?" he asked her.

She smiled ruefully. "Exam hysteria. Jailhouse rock. Stir crazy," she said.

"The exams aren't for ages."

"Essay. I'm late. The last one wasn't good enough, I have to step up my game."

Nick grunted. Typical. Muriel had blown school, left early,

and gone straight on the dole and to a life of idle pleasure. Then she had Nick, went clean, got bored, went back to school, and discovered it was easy. She amazed herself. She never even knew she had a brain. All those years at school, she'd been no more able to concentrate than grow a tail, and now, suddenly, thirty years old, she could devour whole books for hours on end without so much as a glance out the window.

"Another thing for Muriel to get addicted to," said Jenny, her only friend from the old days. It was true. Anything under an A and she became unbearable.

Once he was settled back in, Nick took his time. He went into his bedroom again, and she found him back lying on his bed. By the time he was on his way a second time he was only about five minutes earlier than normal.

He slammed the door and stamped off, his bag over his shoulder. She watched him walk along the road. Who knows, she might have confused him so much by getting him up early that he might actually end up at school by accident. It didn't take much to make Nick walk the other way. He was hanging out down at the flats or playing football on the common, or smoking cigarettes or spliffs down behind the mill as often as he was in lessons.

He was a bad lot, her boy. Too good-looking, too bright—one of those kids who found it all too easy. Friends, school-work, girls. Leadership qualities, they said at school. The trouble was, he wasn't so much a role model as a ringleader. If there was trouble to be had, Nick wouldn't just be in it, he'd be trying to get everyone else in it as well. He had more than his fair share of charm, just like his dad. He was going to need it if he didn't get his finger out.

And he was loyal. That was his saving grace. Once Nick decided you were one of his, he never let go.

Muriel waited by the window until he disappeared around the corner before going back into the kitchen and getting the gear out from inside the washing machine. It was becoming harder and harder to find somewhere Nick wasn't prepared to go, but the washing machine was one place she could be sure he'd leave alone.

The kettle was still hot from her tea and she had the works prepared in a moment. She wanted to feel warm and cozy, so she turned the gas fire on and kneeled on the rug in front of it. She wrapped the belt around and pulled with her teeth until the veins popped out—little highways to pleasure.

It was the first time in ages. She'd been as good as gold for months. Well, years, actually, except for occasions like this. You were allowed the odd treat, weren't you? Amazing chance, Mo having a brother just around the corner on Lime Road. She couldn't believe it when she saw him walking past the newsagent the day before. He was staying overnight. Nice of him to drop it off for her on his way back, too. Seven in the morning didn't often see Mo out of bed, she bet.

Dangerous, though. Far too convenient. The last thing she wanted was a dealer just around the corner. Yesterday morning it had been two bus rides to get to his place. Now he even knew where she lived! Shit. But he was only rarely around this way to see his brother . . . maybe it would be all right . . .

Three or four times a year. Why not?

Muriel knew she really ought to wait for Jenny to come around, but she couldn't wait. She pushed the needle into the vein and closed her eyes. Heaven ran into her arm. There was nothing on earth like it.

She sighed and leaned forward until her head was resting on the floor in front of her knees, her arm stretched out before her and the needle still in the vein. Bliss overwhelmed her, and she stopped breathing. She was in exactly the same position an hour and a half later when Jenny called around for a little bit of bliss herself and, hearing no answer to her knock, peered through the curtains and saw her lying flat out on the fireside rug. She rapped on the pane, then started shouting. She put her shoulder to the door and bruised it, and had to rush around to get a key off old Mrs. Ash from next door. When they got inside, the thing that struck her was how Muriel had cooled on one side and was hot on the other, where the gas fire had been toasting her.

Mrs. Ash rushed around, ringing for the police and making Jenny a cup of tea, but what was the point of rushing now? Jenny looked anxiously at the bag of heroin on the floor next to her ex-friend. Oh my God! How hard it was to sit there and ignore it. She could pop it in her handbag and walk away . . . But Mrs. Ash must have seen it. She couldn't risk it.

Anxiously, she began going through her pockets and handbag to make sure there was nothing dodgy in them, even though she didn't think anyone was going to search her. That would be heartless, she was being paranoid . . . but paranoia doesn't mean to say they're not out to get you. Best be sure.

Mrs. Ash came back in with a steaming cup and stood next to her, staring at the corpse on the floor.

"I never knew, I never knew," she kept saying. "Did you know?" she asked Jenny.

"Years ago," said Jenny. "We both did. This was . . ." She began to crack up as she spoke. So unfair! When she thought of all the things she and Muriel had been through together, to OD now, when weeks and months went by without either of them using. To have her life snatched away just when she was making something of herself. All the time, she'd been this genius and none of them had even guessed. And now she was nothing, just this lump of cooling meat that looked like her on the carpet. It made Jenny feel sick to look at her.

At least Nick hadn't come home to find her like this. And then she thought—Nicholas! What on earth was going to happen to him now that Muriel was gone? My God. He hadn't got a soul in the world.

2
JENNY'S HOUSE

Nick didn't go to school that day. It seemed a pity to waste getting up early on being bored. Instead, he intercepted his best friend, Simon, tapping on the window as he ate his breakfast. They picked up Jeremy farther on, and that was the three of them, cronies since they started at school ten years ago—longer, because they used to play together even at nursery. They'd been friends for as long as they could remember.

They went in for registration to get their names down, then snuck out before lessons began. Jeremy's mum worked all day, so they hung out there, as usual. They made instant coffee and drank it in front of breakfast television. Nick caught up on his beloved zees on the sofa. They watched a few videos—there was an almost complete collection of Looney Tunes cartoons, which they'd been watching for years but still always passed the time with a few laughs.

Then they got bored. The trouble with skiving off school was there was never enough to do and you always got bored. But at least it was boredom you were in control of—not like being pinned behind your desk at school, going out of your mind and not able to do anything about it.

At lunchtime they ransacked their pockets for change and scraped together enough money to buy some cigarettes. They smoked a couple in the park, then went back and spread the rest of them over the afternoon, in front of the telly and playing cards. The last one got handed around, and they sucked the smoke in deeply, pretending it was a joint and that they were getting off their heads. The funny thing was, it worked—they all ended up feeling stoned.

"It must be the deep breathing," said Simon.

That was all. Just hanging out. Talking, sitting about, not doing anything. And it was boring and nothing happened, but you know what? It was great. For Nick, there was nothing on this earth better than hanging around doing nothing with your mates.

At four o'clock he went home and found Jenny sitting in the front room with a small, plump, neatly dressed woman he'd never seen before.

"Hi," he said. He looked around. "Where's Mum?" It was at that moment his heart started beating like a terrible drum, as if it knew everything already.

"Nick," said Jenny, and stopped.

The well-dressed little woman stood up and held out her hand.

"Ah'm Mrs. Batts. Baaatty Batts," she said in a long, slow, northern accent, stretching out her "a"s so far, it was almost funny. She sounded like a sheep. Nick smiled at Jenny, but she shot him such a ghastly look the smile faded on his face. Mrs. Batts smiled back, thinking he was enjoying her feeble joke. Nick nodded at her and looked around.

"Where's Mum?" he said again.

What could Jenny say? She's at the morgue, Nick. She's gone to Heaven. She's with those she loves.

That certainly wasn't true. The only two people Muriel had loved were standing right there in that room.

So she just blurted it out.

"She's dead, Nick. I came 'round and found her," she said, and burst into floods of messy, snotty tears. She took a step toward him, but Batty Batts got in between them and took her in her arms. Jenny didn't hug her back but stood there, weeping helplessly with one hand on her face and the other hanging by her side, while the little woman stood and patted her. Nick just stood there and watched.

"Ah'm soo sorry, Nick, Ah'm soooo, soooo sorry," intoned Mrs. Batts over her shoulder.

Jenny's tears proved the truth of it, but he couldn't believe it. He wanted to run around calling for her—people didn't just die! But the word *dead* was so final, it froze him to the spot.

"What happened?" he said.

". . . an accident," blubbed Jenny.

"How?" he begged. Jenny shook her head, and Mrs. Batts looked at him and shook her head too, as if to say, Now isn't the time, as if it were some adult thing, something too personal to say to him, even though of all the people on earth, he was the one with the right to know.

"It'll take a whiiiile for it to sink in," said Batty Batts to Jenny, glancing at Nick. She let Jenny go and both of them sat down. Nick stood there, not knowing what to do, until

Jenny pulled herself together, got up, and gave him a big hug.

"It's mad, Nick, it's just mad, isn't it?" she whispered. She squeezed him tightly and then went off to make some tea while Batty Batts patted the sofa next to her.

"Nooow then, Nick," she said. "This must be a terrible shock fer you."

Nick sat down next to her. "She was all right this mornin'," he said.

"Death aaalways comes as a surprise," bleated Mrs. Batts, shaking her head. "Our loved ones aaalways leave us before we're ready." She laid her hand briefly on his arm and pursed her lips. Nick nodded. There was nothing he could say. He had no idea if anything she said was true. This was his first experience of death.

"Nick, Ah knoo this might not seem the time, but we're all very concerned about your future," went on Mrs. Batts in her long-drawn-out way, glancing at him. "And Ah doo need t' ask yer a few questions. Ah need to knoo something about yer wider family. Can yer tell me anything about your faarther?"

Nick shook his head. He hadn't heard anything about his dad for years, didn't even know where he lived. Mrs. Batts began to go through a list of possible relatives. Grandparents? He had a gran in Australia. Did she have an address? Not as far as he knew; they hadn't heard from her in years. His mum fell out with both her parents years ago. Her dad was dead, he thought.

"They were 'orrible," said Nick. "She wouldn't want them 'ere, anyway."

"At where, Nick?" asked Mrs. Batts.

"The funeral," said Nick.

She glanced at him warily. "Oo noo, this isn't about the funeral. This is about your future, Nick," she intoned. Nick stared at her. Something about the way she was looking at him made him realize what this was all about.

He was on his own. He was fourteen years old. Who was going to look after him now?

Answer: No one. He knew it at once. Muriel had always said they only had each other.

Batty Batts carried on. Aunts and uncles? His mum had been an only child.

"I think Mum still has an uncle somewhere," he said.

"Oh?" Batty Batts looked expectantly at him, her pen poised over her notepad. She looked so eager, Nick felt almost sorry for her.

"I never met him. Mum 'asn't seen him for years."

"Is that the pie man, that one?" asked Jenny, popping her head through the door.

"Yeah, think so," said Nick.

"Pies?" inquired Mrs. Batts.

"Maggie's Pies and Pasties. You know." Nick shrugged. "Gran's brother. I don't think Mum ever even met 'im. He ran away from 'ome when he was small. She always 'ated her family. So do I," said Nick. Not because he'd ever met any of them, but out of solidarity with his mum.

Batty Batts looked surprised. "Next a kin. There must be some next a kin. There must be someone who'll take care of yer."

"I'm not livin' with anyone."

Mrs. Batts pulled a rueful face. "There must be someone," she repeated.

Jenny appeared at the doorway with the tea. "I told you, she was on her own, just her and Nick, wasn't it, Nick?" she said, coming in. "And me," she added, glancing reassuringly at Nick. Batty put her notebook down.

"Well. That's not taken for graanted like next a kin, you see. Ah. Tea," she said brightly.

"Tea, Nick?"

"Where's my mum now?" he asked abruptly.

The two women glanced at each other. "Well. She'll be at the morgue, now, Nicholas," said Mrs. Batts.

"But what happened?" Suddenly he needed to know.

Mrs. Batts put her hand on Jenny's knee to stop her saying anything, and looked straight at him. "There'll be an auutopsy. There's always an auutopsy in case a sudden death. They'll have the answers, Ah expect."

"Was it a stroke or a heart attack or somethin', was it?"

". . . we'd better wait for the results before we speculate."

Jenny stood over them with the teapot. Nick looked appealingly at her. She ought to tell him, she knew she ought to—get it over with for him. But she couldn't. It had been something no one else knew, just her and Muriel for so long, she couldn't break the habit of secrecy in front of one of the kids.

"How many sugars?"

"Two." He stood up suddenly. "Where was she?" he demanded.

Jenny nodded across the room. "On the rug. There."

He walked over to the place, conscious of the two women watching him. He eyed them sideways and they turned away and started talking between themselves. He bent down and touched the rug.

Here. She died here. She lay here, dead.

"The fire was on," said Jenny. "Maybe she was feeling cold."

There were no stains on the rug.

"It wasn't . . . was she . . ." he began. He didn't know anything about death of any kind. "Did it hurt?" he asked.

Jenny shook her head. "She looked very peaceful," she said. "She didn't suffer." Suddenly, Jenny had to suppress hysterical giggles. Suffer! "Hope you enjoyed it, babe. The biggest hit of all," she thought to herself.

Nick got down on the rug. Behind him, Jenny and Batty Batts got up and left the room. He could hear them talking in low voices in the kitchen. He thought about his dead mother lying there. He thought about their cross words that morning and about her dancing across the floor to Boy George. He tried to squeeze out a tear for her, but he couldn't. It wasn't real yet. He wanted to go into the kitchen to Mrs. Batts and Jenny and shake the answers out of them—how, why, when? What for? He wanted to ask to see the body, but he couldn't bring himself to do that either. Was it sick to want to see your mother dead?

So he just kneeled there, and looked at the fire, and waited to see what was going to happen next.

A few hours later, Nick found himself standing in the sitting room of Jenny's little house in Middleton. He hadn't been there for years, since he was a kid, and now he felt too big for it, like some kind of outsize freak, with his grief on his head like a great tall dunce's cap. The boy with no parents. Jenny's two kids sat eating their Weetabix in their jim-jams and watching telly. Grace, the older at nine, studiously ignored him. That suited him. The last thing he wanted was any conversation. He knew exactly what she'd want to ask.

"What's it like to have no mother?" she'd say. It was a question Nick would have liked to ask as well. So far—he could tell you this without fear of contradiction—so far, it was crap.

The little boy didn't look curious. He looked scared. Jenny bent down to him.

"What's he want?" he asked in a loud whisper.

"He doesn't want anything," Jenny whispered back. "He's just going to stay for a bit, that's all."

"How long's he staying for?" asked little Joe.

"I don't know. Eat your Weetabix, Joe, and don't stare."

Joe was only five, but he'd already had enough of great big blokes coming to his house and getting upset. Jenny's choice of boyfriends was famously hopeless. Nick wasn't exactly helping, bless him, sitting there, staring at the TV with a face like he'd seen a ghost, not saying a word.

As soon as the kids were fed, Jenny chivied them upstairs early amid wails of protest with the promise of extra stories. Nick could do with a bit of time to himself down there. He hadn't had a second on his own since he'd found out. Give him a chance to get his head around the fact that poor Muriel was gone forever.

"You're having my bed tonight," said Jenny when she came

down after more than an hour of stories later. "I'm not having you sleeping on the couch. There's no room with Joe and I can't put you in with Grace, can I?" She smiled. "A girl that age needs a bit of privacy." She sat down next to him. "I can't believe it," she said. She pulled a handful of damp tissues from her sleeve and began to weep. Nicholas stared at her, watching the tears that should have been his.

"What's going to 'appen to me?" he said.

"Like I said, you can stay here as long as you like," said Jenny.

"There's no room."

"We'll make room. The Social'll find out about your dad or your granddad . . ."

"I don't know them," exclaimed Nick. He jumped up. "I can't live with people I don't know."

"We'll see. The important thing is, you can stay here for as long as it takes. For as long as possible, as far as I'm concerned," she added.

Nick sat down. He began to leak tears. "What's possible?" he asked. "What's that?"

Jenny put her arms gently around him. "Oh, Nick, darling, don't. You don't have to worry about that now. You know me and Muriel, we were like that, two peas in a pod. We always shared everything. You're staying here, OK, Nick? OK, darling?"

Nick tried to relax in her arms. "Thanks," he said. "Thanks."

She nodded and let him go. "Right, that's that, then. Now, I'm starved, I bet you are. Fish and chips, what about it?"

"Yeah."

"Shall you go or shall I? I'll go, will I? You can babysit. See? I've got it made—a live-in babysitter! I never had it so good."

"Yeah, right."

Jenny went out for fish and chips, and they sat together on the sofa eating them. He was starving—he finished all his and most of her chips as well. As they ate, he asked her again about what had happened.

She was dreading this—having to tell him that his mum had died of a heroin overdose. She'd put her foot in it right at the start by telling him it was an accident. It had just blurted out of her. She was always such a gob. She thought he was bound to want to know what she meant by that, but as luck would have it, it seemed as if he'd forgotten and remembered only the social worker talking about the autopsy.

"What do you suppose 'appened?" he asked her, popping chips in his mouth. "She was too young for an 'eart attack, weren't she?"

Jenny didn't flicker. It was another chance to tell, but she still couldn't bring herself to do it. "Poor thing," she thought, "he's got enough on his plate for today." Tomorrow was soon enough to find out his mum had been using in secret all these years, and died like a junkie, with a needle in her arm.

"Whatever happened, she was too young," she said.

"She was just lying there, was she? Just fell down dead?" She looked into his eyes to see if there was a hint of doubt there, but he was just chomping on his chips, trustful as the day was long.

No. She didn't want to tell him now. It was too soon.

"I don't know, Nick," she said firmly. "We'll just have to wait and see."

Let him down gently. And her. She needed letting down gently as well. "Boy, oh boy," she thought. "What a mess. What a big, enormous fucking great mess."

3
BACK HOME

Nick slept a deep, seamless, dreamless sleep that night in Jenny's bed, which was cleaner, warmer, bigger, and far more comfortable than anything he could remember. When Jenny crept in to see him at eight in the morning, he was stretched out with one hairy leg sticking out from the covers, an arm flung up, his head to one side, the very picture of relaxation. She stood in the doorway holding a mug of tea, admiring him. He'd been a kid only yesterday, and now look—like a young prince. Maybe he *was*, in his dreams.

She didn't want to wake him up now to all his sorrows. She closed the door and tiptoed out. Let him sleep. He'd been plunged into a world of shit, and he hadn't hit the bottom yet, not by a long way.

She had an appointment with Mrs. Batts at two, to discuss the options. What was to be done with Nick? Jenny had insisted the day before that, of course, he would stay with her for as long as he needed to.

"Dorn't be too quick abaht it," Mrs. Batts had advised. "You have a young family of your own t' think of. There aare other options, even if his dad and grandfather don't want to commit."

"What, you mean adoption?"

"Well, that's unlikely at his aage," she drawled. "But some of the children's homes are very good these days. Times have changed a lot since Oliver Twist. They provide a safe 'ome, discipline, people his own age, good food. They'd keep him busy. Keep his mind off things. Ah've been thinking about Meadow Hill." Mrs. Batts dusted her skirt with a professional air of satisfaction. "Tony Creal, the deputy head, is an inspiraational figure to many of the boys there, particularly for those whose faarthers haven't been all that much in evidence, like our Nick. A wuunderful man. Very dedicated. He has a *huuge* amount of experience dealing with difficult young people."

"Difficult?" said Jenny. She knew Nick was a handful, but difficult? In the mouth of Mrs. Batts, it sounded so official.

She looked kindly at Jenny and smiled. "Ah speak from experience. Teenagers are a nightmare. Nick seems like a nice boy, but Ah wouldn't wish even a nice teenager onto a young family like yours."

It was so, so tempting! She and Muriel had always promised each other they'd look after the other's kids if anything happened, but Jenny had to admit, if Nick did happen to prefer a home, it would be handy. There wasn't a lot of room in her house—that might be sorted out, of course, especially if the Social paid up—but there was still little Joe to worry about. The way he'd been looking at Nick yesterday, you'd have thought Nick was going to eat him.

It was her own fault. The usual. A bloke. All her troubles came from blokes. How come all the lovely ones turned out to be shitbags? No matter how hard she tried to discover someone who liked gardening, say, or cooking; or just conversation, they always turned out to have a secret vice. Weeks would go by and then she'd be woken up at three in the morning with some vile drunk banging on her door, who just the day before had only wanted to stroke her hand and read passages of his favorite books to her. Or she'd discover works in the bathroom cabinet, or bottles of vodka in the attic, or a bag of cocaine the size of Bolivia in her handbag just as they were going through customs on the way back from their holiday in Spain.

The last one, Bob, had been particularly lovely. All he had to do was smile and her insides turned to custard. He was funny, generous, and kind. A carpenter, a good one, he could get work whenever he wanted. He'd even played with the kids at first. But he did that thing, he got drunk, started to feel sorry for himself, and then he got angry.

You wouldn't know it was the same man. One minute he was weeping beer fumes into her arms, the next he was smashing the place up. *Bang!*—down with the kitchen cupboards. *Wallop!*—over with the TV. The first time it happened, she was so scared, she'd run upstairs to hide with the kids, which had been a stupid thing to do, because of course he'd followed her up into the room and started up there. The kids screaming, her trying to calm everyone down and not knowing who was going to get it next—her, the kids, or the window.

The next day, he'd been so mortified she'd forgiven him. It had gone on for six months before she banished him. He'd begged, wept, raged, come banging at the door in the middle of the night, and once, he even turned up at school and tried to pick up the kids, the bastard. Then he'd found someone else and vanished overnight. By then, little Joe was wetting the bed, bullying other kids at school, whining, fighting, and lying.

It was into this unsteady emotional construction that Nick had arrived to add his own seesaw heart. Nick was a charming, likable lad in deep trouble through no fault of his own. On the other hand, he was also a rampant, raging, hormonal, skiving, lying, recently orphaned, and frequently furious teenager. There was trouble ahead, how could it be otherwise? Especially once he found out what had really happened . . .

The next morning, it was a wet bed for Joe, the first for weeks.

Jenny hurried Joe and Grace through breakfast while she got herself ready. She worked part-time at a community center, doing a bit of secretarial, a bit of organizational, and a bit of drugs counseling. She was going to study and get qualifications in a few years' time so she could do more counseling and project work, earn some decent money. Like Muriel . . .

Before she left she wrote a note for Nick, telling him to help himself to whatever for breakfast, and that she'd be back at twelve, in plenty of time for the meeting with Mrs. Batts. Her plan was to let him know then how his mum died, before the meeting.

She chucked the dishes in the sink and ran upstairs to do her makeup in the bathroom mirror. Her own face looking back at her made her pause for thought. What a mess! Gear, she thought—it made you feel so good. You lay there feeling wonderful even while death himself was creeping in through the windows. Now look. Her beloved Muriel. They used to say how they'd live together when they were old ladies and keep each other company. Now Muriel would never be old.

"You bitch, you left me," she thought. She was suddenly furious. Funny how you could have feelings and you didn't always know where they came from. And another thing—she was scared. Now, what on earth was there to be scared of?

Scared of Nick, came the answer.

"Don't be stupid, he's just a kid," she told herself.

"What are you looking at?" She turned around to see her daughter scowling at her watching herself in the mirror.

"Come on, let's go," she called, and got the day in motion.

When she got back at twelve thirty, the house was empty. There was a clutter of cereal, spilled milk, and cornflakes on the work surface. The cornflake packet, which had been half full, was empty. The milk was all gone. She found the bowl itself on the settee. Of Nick himself, no trace remained.

Jenny tidied up with a sinking heart, crunching cornflakes underfoot. Please God he hadn't gone back to Ancoats. If he had, please God he didn't meet anyone who knew what had happened to Muriel, which would be anyone within about five miles by now.

But he didn't have any money. He was scarcely going to walk that far, was he? Unless . . . Jenny picked up the change mug she kept on the kitchen windowsill, out of reach of little hands.

Empty! There'd been more than a fiver in there. The greedy little bastard had taken the lot.

"He's stolen my money," she thought. "He's only been in my house for less than a day and he's eaten all the cereal, drunk all the milk so I can't even have a cup of tea, covered the floor in cornflakes, and pinched a fiver off me." And now there he was, back in Ancoats, finding out what a shit she was for not telling him at once how his mum had died—and doing it on her money!

"Wait till I get my hands on him," she thought to herself. But at the back of her mind was the thought that maybe, by now, he'd be thinking the same thing about her.

Nick had woken up suddenly when Grace banged the downstairs front door behind her. His eyes sprang open as the door thumped, and he lay there for a moment wondering where he was and why he had such an odd pit of anxiety in his stomach. Then it all came back in one sudden rush, and he was bereft.

He went downstairs and got some cereal, which he ate in front of the TV. After he'd finished it he sat and watched for a while, but then he began to go mad. There was nothing of his in this house—his books, clothes, tapes, everything was still at home. He was confronted with a day of emptiness, a stranger in a strange house. He wandered into the kitchen to find some money. He had some of his own at home, he was sure of it. Or there'd be his mum's purse and stuff. Whose was it now, if not his?

He went straight to the mug on the windowsill because Muriel used to keep her change in the same place right up until he got big enough to reach it and spend it. He knew as soon as he lifted it up, it was more than half full! Gold!

He rifled through it. A bit under three quid. Enough to get him to Ancoats on the bus, buy some snacks or sweets, some chips for lunch, perhaps. He ran upstairs for his jacket with his front door key in it, and then straight out the door, without even noticing Muriel's note on the kitchen table asking him to be there when Mrs. Batts came around at two.

It was about half past nine by the time he got off the bus in Ancoats, but with his feet back on his own patch, he wasn't so sure what to do. He didn't want to go home—he didn't want to think about that. So he went around to Jeremy's house to see if he and Simon had taken another day off. The house looked empty, but it always did—skiving off wasn't something you advertised. He spent quite a bit of time peering around the corner and trying to look in the windows, before someone came out of a house down the street to watch him and he walked off.

He wandered around a bit, bought a Mars, got fed up, walked back to Jeremy's house, and boldly knocked on the door. It was answered by Jeremy's sister, Amanda. He saw her peer through the curtains at him from the side of the bay window before she went to the door. She stood there, her big eyes sparkling at him.

"Nick, I'm so sorry," she said, and without warning flung herself at him and gave him a hug so big, it startled him.

Of course, the news about his mum would be all around everywhere by now.

Amanda was a year younger than Nick, and for years she and her friends and Nick and his friends had been playing together, hanging out together, and more and more these days, going out together. In a few years, they'd start sleeping together as well. Some of them already were, although neither Nick nor Amanda was among the precocious few.

Amanda was off school for the morning to go to the dentist.

"Two fillings," she groaned. She ran around making coffee nervously. She'd never met anyone in Nick's position before and didn't know how to deal with it.

"At least I get the morning off," she said.

"Me, too," said Nick.

She looked at him and laughed nervously. "Yeah. You could have the week off, I reckon."

"The year," said Nick.

"It's awful. No one had any idea." Amanda's eyes twisted up to his. Nick was pretty much the last person at the school not to know that his mother had died with a needle in her arm— but she was scared to ask him directly. What if the rumors were wrong? She didn't want to be the one to tell him tales like that were being spread about when he'd just lost his mum.

And Nick didn't ask. The looks he'd had from Jenny and Mrs. Batts and now from Amanda could all have been put down just to the death on its own, but in his heart he knew there was more to come, and he didn't want it. So nothing was said. Amanda handed him his coffee.

"Let's drink it in the front room," he suggested.

"All right, then." But she felt unsure as she led the way. The sofa was snogging territory. Was it all right to cop a snog when his mum had just died? And was it all right for her to let him?

Sure enough, they sat down, and after a little chat, Nick's hand crept out and touched her leg. "I could do with another hug," he suggested slyly.

How could she say no? She reached out for him. "Just a hug, then."

They put their arms around each other, and kissed. She leaned her head on the back of the sofa while his hand pushed the bottom of her blouse to one side to touch the skin on her waist. She was expecting him to go further, but he just put his arms tightly around her, buried his nose in her neck, and sniffed wetly.

"Oh, my God," she thought, "he's crying." It was just the hug he wanted after all. She put her arms right around him and gave him the biggest love she had in her.

After a long moment, Nick pulled back and wiped his nose on the back of his hand.

"I don't know what's going to happen now," he said in a strained voice.

"Where are you staying?" she asked.

"Jenny. Friend of Mum's."

"What about your family?"

Nick dashed his hand angrily to one side. "I don't have any."

"What, none?"

"None."

Amanda had four aunts, six uncles, two granddads, three grandmas, one great-grandmother, and more cousins than she knew about. She couldn't imagine how you could end up with no one.

"You've heard of the seventh son of the seventh son?" said Nick bitterly. "Well, I'm the only child of an only child."

"Wow." She shook her head. "That could be tricky," she said thoughtfully.

"Jenny's putting me up."

"What's it like?"

Nick shrugged. He didn't know what to say. He had no idea what it was like at Jenny's, he hadn't had time to notice.

He slid his hand behind her back. "Another hug," he begged.

Willingly, Amanda took him in her arms, but this time his hand crept up to her breast. Nick had been thinking— alone, in an empty house with Amanda? It was a pity to miss a chance. Amanda was a bit disappointed that he wanted that after all, but she was ready to offer him whatever kind of comfort he needed—within reason, of course.

It was universally acknowledged that Nick Dane was a bit delicious.

Somehow he swished her down so that her head was resting on the arm of the sofa and she was flat on her back with him half on top of her.

"That was quick," she said.

Nick smiled and kissed her. For another moment she just lay there, letting it happen, enjoying the long kisses and his hands on her skin. Then she suddenly sat up and pushed him off.

"Oh, is that the time, I have to go," she said, although she'd lost all track of time. Nick sat up looking dazedly around for the clock. She went into the kitchen and found that she really was late, and started rushing about collecting her bags and books—she was going straight on to school afterward. Nick followed her about the house woefully.

"Can't I stay here for a bit?" he asked.

She stared at him. Didn't he have a home to go to? But she wasn't sure if he did anymore.

"Not too long," she said.

"No," he said. "Just a bit."

Amanda hurried out the door. Before she went, she kissed and hugged him. "You're still gorgeous," she whispered to him.

"I still have me," he said, nodding. It was what his mum used to say . . . "Whatever happens, Nick, you always have yourself."

"You'll be all right, then," she told him. She kissed him again and left. As she walked down the road, she shook her head. Amazing. Just a couple of days ago, Nick Dane seemed to have it all; now he had nothing. It just went to show: some things were so much a part of you, you just took them for granted. Perhaps she'd give her mum a hand around the house tonight, just to show her that she appreciated her for being there. She shook her head again and ran down the road to catch the bus.

Another door banging, thought Nick, as she left the house. He went to lie on the sofa awhile, for the want of anything else to do, and stared at the ceiling. He tried to sleep, but he couldn't settle. Jeremy was at school, Amanda had said, and if Jeremy was, so was Simon. There was nothing to do here. So he did what he'd come for. He went home.

The house would be no different, he told himself, but in his mind it had already died, just like his mother. He walked along the road self-consciously, hoping that no one would spot him, and he almost made it, too—he actually had his key in the lock when old Mrs. Ash from next door jumped out on the pavement, dressed in her pink apron and fluffy slippers, as always. Her youngest grandson gave her a new pair every birthday. Her hair was always in a pink-rinsed perm, which he thought made her look a bit like a poodle. The pinkish-gray curls were too thin these days to really hide her ears, which stuck out and drooped slightly with age. She was as kind as anyone they knew, but that didn't stop her from being a nuisance. She was at home all day on her own with nothing to do and she was as nosy as a puppy.

It was an old-fashioned thing from the days when half the street belonged to the same family. Thirty years ago there were dozens of Ashes within a stone's throw of her house, but they'd all flown off one after the other. Only Evelyn Ash was left, but she still liked to know who was who and what was what. She'd have done almost anything to find out your business, or to help you, for the simple reason that you lived nearby.

Before he knew what was going on, she had him sitting down in her kitchen eating double egg on toast and drinking strawberry Nesquik, which had counted as a treat for him in her eyes since he was three or four.

"Your poor mum," she said, sitting opposite him with a cup of tea. "I were shocked. I don't know how she kept it all together. Who'd have guessed?" She shook her head and looked at him with big, blue, pitying eyes. "And no relatives!" It was something she could hardly comprehend, having so many herself. "Well, Nick, there'll always be a place here at my table for you, you know that."

Nick forked up his eggs. Who'd have guessed, Mrs. Ash had said. No one had any idea, Amanda said. Who'd have guessed what? No one had any idea of what? Not him, that was for sure.

He was getting fed up with not knowing.

He took a swig of his milkshake and waited.

"You know I let Jenny in?" asked Mrs. Ash. Nick nodded. "Awful!" she went on. "Just kneeling there in front of the fire. She looked like she was praying, except for that arm stretched out." She shook her head and her eyes filled up at the memory of it. "I'll never forget it," she exclaimed, fidgeting in her sleeve for some damp tissues. She blew her nose and peered over the tissue at him.

"We tried the school, but of course you weren't there," she scolded, and smiled wanly. "Your mum would have been furious."

Tried the school? It was all news to Nick. The feeling that he knew far, far less than he should have was beginning to overwhelm him.

"So what do you think she died of?" he asked.

Mrs. Ash froze mid-blow. "You don't know," she stated. Then her mouth dropped slightly as she realized that she'd just more or less told him that she did.

"What don't I know?" insisted Nick. He tensed himself up as if waiting for a blow.

Mrs. Ash did her best to think quickly. "Was she . . . a diabetic, your mum?" she asked desperately.

"No."

"No." Mrs. Ash bit her lip. "She stopped taking sugar in her tea a few years ago, that's all," she pointed out.

Nick thought about that for a second, then looked at her expectantly.

". . . medication of any sort?" quavered Mrs. Ash.

"Was she ill? She'd have told me if she was ill. Wouldn't she?"

Mrs. Ash sighed dramatically and looked from side to side as if some form of escape route would suddenly appear. She was in it up to her eyebrows.

"Oh, lad, Nick, oh, Nick lad, you poor boy, oh dear, Nick!" she said, and taking refuge in the only direction open to her, buried her face in her apron and started to sob.

Nick sat still and waited.

"Oh, Nick, there were a needle in her arm, that's what it is," she wailed suddenly. "She were lying there in front of the fire on her knees wi' her arm stretched out and a needle sticking out of it. I don't know what it was, Nick, I've got no idea." She peeped out at him over the top of the apron. "It were heroin!" she exclaimed, and burst into tears again. "Oh, Nick! The police were searching your house yesterday from top to bottom, they pulled the whole place to pieces, it were awful. Oh dear, there, Nick, I've gone and blurted it out and it were never my place. How will you ever forgive me? Oh, Nick, I'm so, so sorry!"

Nick sat still, listening to the new information quietly. So that was it. His mother was a junkie. Jenny had known it. Mrs. Batts had known it. Amanda had known it. Mrs. Ash knew it. And if Mrs. Ash knew it, so did everyone else.

The only one who hadn't was yours truly.

Nick was furious. But he had this quality, which was to serve him well in the months to come—he always managed to think of something to do. Even when the world was falling to pieces around him, he could whip up a plan and act it out. Now he reached across the table and touched Evelyn's hand.

"No, it's all right, Mrs. Ash. I knew all about that."

Her old face, red and wet with tears, peered out over the apron. "You knew? All the time?"

"I thought she'd packed it in, though. You know Mum. She never tells me anything." Nick smiled. He made a good job of it, under the circumstances—good enough to fool Mrs. Ash. The apron came down.

"It's not the sort of thing you talk about," said Nick helpfully.

"Addiction is a terrible thing, Nick. I've seen it all before. Alcohol, mainly. A nephew. A niece—two nieces. At least one brother, perhaps two. Do you remember Frieda?"

But Nick was in no mood to share stories of family tragedy. He'd had enough information for now. He pushed back his chair and got up.

"Thanks, Mrs. Ash. I've got to go. I just called 'round to pick some stuff up."

"Oh, you're staying with Jenny? She was a good friend to your mum. She was so shocked, poor dear, I thought she were going to collapse, she were that upset. I thought she might be coming 'round to have a share—you know, of that stuff. But she swore she never knew a thing about it. Oh, it's a terrible thing, addiction. It turns people against their own family. It turns good folk into liars and thieves." She nodded and rubbed her face. "Jenny'll look after you, dear. At least you have her."

She saw him to the doorstep and watched as he went down her path and up his. He fitted the key in the door and stepped inside.

Nick's first impression when he stepped inside his house was that it was too clean. The front room looked as if it had been freshly hoovered. Not only hoovered, there were no papers on the floor. The TV glinted, the coffee table had a shine on it. Even the windows were clean. The place had a funny smell . . . polish, wasn't it?

Evelyn said the police had been around and searched the place. Nick had a sudden bizarre vision of a constable in his uniform and helmet running around with the vacuum and a can of Pledge. Did they do that after they'd searched a place? Really?

He went to the loo, which smelled of bleach. In the kitchen it was just as bad. Where had all the clutter gone? The surfaces were clear, the table wiped until it shone, and the stove looked as if it had never been used to cook so much as a boiled egg.

He opened a drawer and looked inside. But where had the hoover bags, dishcloths, and tea towels gone? Eventually he found them under the sink. Gradually, he realized that everything was in a different place. The earthenware jar on the windowsill that used to hold the wooden spoons now held the newly rinsed dried flowers that used to be a dusty decoration in the green vase on a shelf, which itself now held a packet of half-used incense sticks.

Nick wandered from room to room in confusion and despair. His house was no longer his.

He began to search through the house. He went through the kitchen first, looking inside the cupboards and shelves, sorting through the stacks of postcards, letters, and bills that had gathered over the years. He poked inside cups where old buttons, corks, brass hooks, nails, twine, and other bits and pieces that might one day come in useful had been stored. It just got weirder and weirder, because it was all in the wrong order even on that level—the buttons in different mugs, the papers in different stacks. It was as if some evil pixie had taken hold of his life, shuffled it up, dropped it on the floor, rearranged it, and handed it back to him in some kind of odd disguise.

What was he looking for? He had no idea. His mother hiding in the cupboard, perhaps, or some reminder of the life that had so recently been his. Clues—information about who his mother really was—a needle, a packet of white powder, the address of the dealer who had killed her. Instructions from her about what to do next. Dear Nick, go to this address, where you'll find money, a home, and a spare mother. I love you, Mum.

But Muriel's words had stopped forever. No more nagging, no more begging, no more love.

He tore through the house, searching, searching, searching. He wanted to find a million pounds, a magic wand, a ring with three wishes attached, a spell, a dream come true. He wanted to find some way out of the nightmare that was rapidly closing over his head. From room to room he ran, from his bedroom to his mother's, to the kitchen, to the sitting room and back again, over and over, all so tidily disordered, all so familiar and twisted out of shape. He looked everywhere, but there was nothing there to find.

At last he stopped in the middle of his mum's room, seething in rage. What was the point? What did it matter? In a fury he kicked out as hard as he could, straight into the door of the wardrobe. There was a crash as the wood splintered under the blow. What did it matter now? There was no one to care.

He stood and stared at the splintered wood.

"Sorry, Mum," he said. Could she hear him? Was she watching still—seeing him, hearing him, unable to reach him? He caught sight of himself in the dressing table mirror.

"Nicholas Dane," he said. "Nicholas Dane." Even his own name sounded fake. Everything he did was fake.

The place was a mess; he couldn't bear it any longer. He left, and went to catch the bus back to Jenny's. There was nowhere else to go.

4
DINNER

Jenny was hoping that Nick had just popped out for sweets or a magazine or something, but by the time Mrs. Batts came at two, he was still gone and they had to discuss his future in his absence.

Mrs. Batts was not happy when she heard about the money.

"Stealing soo sooon," she said. She shook her head sadly.

"It's not exactly stealing," said Jenny defensively. "It was just the spare-change pot."

"He knooos better and you knooo he knooos better," scolded Mrs. Batts. "If any of mine had done that, they'd have what for."

"Have you got teenagers, then?"

"Ah don't actually have any of my own."

"I see," said Jenny pointedly.

Mrs. Batts looked sideways at her. "But Ah've got a huuuuge experience of young people in the course of my work. That's why Ah have the responsibility of having to make recommendations about the welfare of young people in the position of Mr. Nicholas Dane."

Jenny looked closely back. "As I said, he can stay here for as long as necessary. Muriel was my best friend."

"Of course you're *involved* in the decision-making process—that's why Ah'm here. But you not being family, like, we 'ave to decide what's best for you, a single mother . . ." Mrs. Batts paused to let that sink in. "With two young children on a low income . . ." She paused again. "And what's best for Mr. Nick himself, a fourteen-year-old boy, with a record of nonattendance at school, in the event of his mother dying of a heroin ooverdose. Do you see, dear? What's best for you aaall."

With a sharp pang, Jenny realized that Little Mrs. Batty Batts, with her long-strung-out funny voice and her neat little smile, was a wolf in sheep's clothes. "You could make my life a total misery," thought Jenny. She'd think twice about telling tales on Nick in future.

"In that case I'd like it down on record right now that I want Nick here. I'm the closest thing he has to family. I have a job. I have a good attendance record, even if he doesn't, and excellent references. Just for the record."

"It all goes down on the record." Mrs. Batts smiled. She paused to write something in her notebook, while Jenny cast her mind back. What had she said to Mrs. Batts yesterday? How much had she told her about her worries about Joe? She'd been so upset . . . she couldn't really remember what she'd said.

"How did little Joe react to Nick last night?" asked Mrs. Batts, as if she'd read her mind.

"Oh, it was great. Nick played cards with him for over an

hour," lied Jenny serenely. She had her own weapons up her sleeve.

Mrs. Batts nodded. "That's good," she said. "I want to be suure that your desire to look after Nick isn't just an initial reaction. It's the soort of thing people do when someone near and dear paasses away. They say what seems to be the right thing and then when it comes to it . . . ooh dee-ar! Commitment, you see—it's half the struggle. Whoever takes Nick on, they may have to be in it for the loong teerm, if no one else comes forward."

Jenny quailed inwardly. "That's me," she said, firmly.

Having shown her teeth, Mrs. Batts got back to being friendly.

"Don't get me wrong, Jenny," she said. "Ah'm not at all against Nick living here with you and yours. A family is always the best option—so long as it works. Ah've been in touch with his school and, ooooh, he's an 'andful by all accounts. Ah need to be sure that you knooo what you're taking on before considering aaaall the options very carefully. What if it didn't work out? That would be the very worst thing for Nick himself. He needs something staable now more than ever. The last thing we want is it not working 'ere for him and then he has to go to the home anyway, when it'll be more like a failure than if he goes straightaway. Now, 'ave you told him how she died yet? How did he react?"

"I haven't had a chance to tell him yet," confessed Jenny.

"But he'll find out at school, won't he?"

"He's not actually at school."

"Where is 'e, then?"

"I'm not sure just at the moment," said Jenny through gritted teeth.

"Oh dear!" said Mrs. Batts. "Jenny, it's not a good start. You 'ave to be firm with him. It would be better if there was a man about the 'ouse to help out, of course. I mentioned Tony Creal at Meadow Hill, didn't Ah? A lot of the boys do very well under him. Very caring—but firm. There's no mucking around at Meadow Hill." She nodded at Jenny, trying to impress on her how very good Meadow Hill and Mr. Creal were. "What do you think? I could pull a few strings, if you like." She smiled.

"I'm sure Nick would be better with me," said Jenny firmly. "He's used to a single-mother situation. And you know what men are like, Mrs. Batts. You can't trust any of the bastards, can you?"

Jenny grinned, although it was only half a joke. But she'd said the wrong thing again. Mrs. Batts looked horrified.

"Oooooh, nooo, not all of them, Ah can assure you. No, no. If that's your experience, Jenny, it's not the usual one, that's all Ah can say. Anthony Creal. My own husband. Oh, no, they're not all like that."

Jenny groaned to herself. She wasn't doing very well. "Just a figure of speech," she apologized.

A little more conversation revealed that Mrs. Batts was going to be writing up her report and her recommendations the next day. In an attempt to rescue the situation, Jenny invited her around for a family meal that evening.

"You can see for yourself," she told Mrs. Batts. "I'm not saying it'll be perfect—Joe will take a while to get used to things, and as a family, of course we have the usual little difficulties that other people have . . ." She tossed her head and laughed to indicate how fond she was of life's little trials . . . "But we are a safe house, and we care, Mrs. Batts. That's the main thing, isn't it?"

Mrs. Batts was delighted to accept. There was nothing like a look at the inner workings of a prospective family to give you an idea of what was what.

Jenny planned her dinner for six thirty that evening. A proper meal at the table was an unusual event in her house. Feeding time, as she normally called it, tended to be sandwiches or fish fingers, that sort of thing, eaten on laps in front of the TV. Not the sort of thing Mrs. Batts would consider proper, she was sure. Not the sort of thing a proper family did.

"The family that eats together, stays together," she'd explained to the pudgy social worker as she let her out the door. She'd heard someone say that once. Say what you like about Jenny—she was an accomplished liar. Mrs. Batts was completely taken in.

Jenny spent the rest of the afternoon running about, trying to get things in order. She borrowed a recipe book from Hilary down the road, who was known to cook meals. As she flicked through it, she rang Ray, her latest, and commandeered him as Man about the House.

"The children are very fond of him, in an uncle-y kind of way," she'd told Mrs. Batts earlier. "He can't do enough for them. He does DIY as well," she promised, getting carried away. In fact, Ray just about passed the basic test for a man, which she had formulated long ago; a knob, a job, and a hobby. (He collected First World War medals and worked as a clerk in the same office as Jenny.) At most other things, he was pretty useless.

"He's not the man of my dreams," Jenny had once explained when Muriel expressed doubts about Ray's general manliness. "But at least he's not the man of nightmares, either."

Ray was delighted. It was the first time she'd ever invited him around for a family meal.

"Are you grinning?" she asked him suspiciously.

"No," insisted Ray. In fact, his face was riven in two by his happy lips.

"The thing is to be firm. She wants a man about the house. That's you."

"Man about the House," whispered Ray to himself.

"What? Are you whispering to yourself again?" asked Jenny suspiciously.

"No!"

"Remember, Nick is upset," cautioned Jenny. "His mother's died. He's a teenager."

"A teenager, yes." That was bad news. Teenagers were scary, especially the boys. They hung around in gangs on the streets, trying to intimidate you. They were angry, hormonal, aggressive, and unpredictable. Like an old woman having a three-year-long period, as his mother had once explained to him. Nasty.

Ray gathered himself up. "You can count on me, Jenny," he told her firmly.

He put down the phone and did a dance around the flat. He hadn't had a girlfriend since he was sixteen, when Teresa Downey had let him take her out to the pictures three weeks in a row. He'd hardly been able to believe his luck when Jenny, lovely Jenny—not the most gorgeous but certainly one of the most lively girls in the office—had agreed to an after-work drink and then dinner. Things had been on the up and up ever since. And now—invited for a family dinner! It would be Meet the Parents next. Before long, she'd be asking him to move in. Man about the House! Yes, yes, yes! He was on his way to getting a life at last.

Ray rushed upstairs to get changed. He'd promised to go around early to help Jenny with the dinner. He knew very well that he represented the safety option for her—nothing wrong with that. It was up to him to show that safe could be sexy as well. As he dressed, he thought about what she'd asked him to do.

"Be firm," she'd said. He could do firm. He'd seen other people doing it all his life. You had to refuse to back down and you had to interrupt people. Easy.

Still . . . a teenager! He found that very intimidating. This was one occasion when he needed all the help he could get, which is why he popped into the pub on his way over for a swift half and maybe a scotch to toughen him up for the test ahead. He wasn't a drinker—never had been. But a little Dutch courage surely wouldn't go amiss.

Ray might not always rise to the occasion, but at least she could rely on him not to start a fight, reflected Jenny. Her main worry was little Joe, still shaken up from the traumas of the last man who'd been a regular at the house. She was somewhat relieved when she picked him up from school. He was strutting about like a little cockerel and perfectly full of himself about having a big boy staying at his house. What had happened was he'd started talking about it at school. It could have gone either way—his mates were half inclined to tell him horror stories about being bullied by their own big brothers, but in the end, they settled down into a good bout of boasting. How their brothers played football like gods, had loads of mates, helped them with their home-work, even.

Jumping on the bandwagon, and with nothing true to say, Joe started inventing boasts about the things Nick did with him. They played football together. Nick told him jokes and offered to beat people up for him. Then, the killer—Nick's mother had just died. Wow! How cool was that? For a while, Joe was the center of attention. Maybe Nick wasn't such a bad thing after all.

Then, the icing on the cake, one of his friends had invented a little rhyme going, "What's the game, Nicholas Dane?" They'd been repeating it all afternoon, and for some reason, it had become funnier and funnier as going-home time ap-proached, until now it was utterly hilarious. Joe only had to think about it and it made him want to burst out laughing.

He came walking in the house with his hands in his pock-ets, whistling tunelessly.

"Where's old Nick?" he asked, and giggled to himself.

"He'll be here later," said Jenny. "Why? What's so funny?"

"Oh, nothing," said Joe airily, and he sniggered again. Jenny considered her son as he sat down in front of the TV. She'd been wary of telling him that Nick was coming to live with them, but seeing him now, she was inclined to take a chance. If she could get him on her side, well . . .

"Would it be nice having a big brother?" she asked.

"Oh, yeah!" exclaimed Joe enthusiastically, and he almost fell over laughing.

He was in such a good mood, Jenny decided to take the chance, and she explained exactly what was going on to Joe and Grace as they had an early evening sandwich in front of the TV.

"Why does he have to live here, though, Mummy?" Grace wanted to know.

"He has nowhere else to go. He's my best friend's son. I'd expect someone to do that for you as well if anything happened to me."

Grace had a think about it.

"Does that mean you're going to be his mum?"

Jenny thought about it and nodded. "In a way, yes."

Grace nodded.

"Good girl. Joe?"

"No probs." Joe nodded and got stuck into his sandwich. He finished it, sniggering to himself every now and then. Then he and Grace watched TV for a while, before she sent them upstairs to change, to play, or, in Grace's case, to do her homework.

Jenny opened the freezer door and stared at the frozen pies, fish fingers, peas, and oven chips that made their usual evening meals, trying to work out exactly what it was Mrs. Batts would consider a proper family meal. It was probably meat and two veg of some sort, or a big salad, but the thought of Joe and Grace's outrage at having to eat anything healthy made her quail. The only time they ever ate veg willingly was with a roast dinner, when it was all soaked in lashings of gravy.

A roast! That was the answer. OK, it was Wednesday evening, not the day for it, really, but it was a big, nourishing meal. With veg.

Jenny turned to the cupboards. The house was vegetable-less and it was already five o'clock. That left her an hour and a half to make a full roast dinner, including shopping. It could be done, just—if she rushed like a madwoman.

Jenny tore a frozen chicken out of its wrapper, stuck it in a low oven, and rushed like a madwoman out of the house and down the road to the shop to buy a cabbage. As she ran, she sent up a quick prayer. All this effort depended on one vital ingredient over which she had no control: Nick himself. She'd rung both his school and his house, and had no answer from either. Please God—make him come home!

She was so concerned about making sure she impressed Mrs. Batts, she utterly forgot that she still hadn't got around to telling him how his mother had died.

Upstairs, as Jenny tore down the street like a tornado, Joe played with his Transformers and kept his ears out for the front door. Now that he'd got over the initial shock, Joe was looking forward to Nick being here. He wasn't a man at all, really—he was a kid, like him, only bigger. They could do things together. Best of all, at last he'd have an ally against his evil big sister. It was just so cool.

The door opened and Grace came in. She watched him on the floor turning the Transformers inside out and back again for a while, then she went to look out the window into the garden below. She and Joe were the result of two separately failed relationships on Jenny's part, and she'd been just about Joe's age when her new baby brother arrived. She got on all right with him now, sort of, but she could still remember her fury at the callous way her new brother had stolen her mother's attention away from her and had never, to this day, properly given it back.

Grace watched a cat walking along the wall at the end of their yard. She glanced over her shoulder at Joe playing on the floor.

"Joe? Don't you mind sharing your mummy with Nick?"

"I want to have a big brother."

She looked back down at the yard as if it were full of interest, gripped internally by a fever of malicious greed for mothers the world over.

"She loves him as much as she does us, and she's not even his mum," said Grace.

Joe said nothing. Love wasn't something he'd thought about, but now that she mentioned it, it did seem a bit much.

Grace glanced over at him again.

"I know what she died of."

"No, you don't."

"Yes, I do. I heard her and that woman talking about it."

"What, then?"

"She was poisoned."

Joe thought about it. It seemed unlikely.

"No, she wasn't."

"Yes, she was."

Joe shook his head. Grace stared down at him and went on to stage two.

"Do you want to know a secret?"

"Yeah?" Joe pretended to be fascinated by his toys again, but he was all ears. He adored secrets. They always seemed so much more true than things people just told you . . .

"Do you promise not to tell?"

"OK."

"I heard him talking in his sleep."

Joe's eyes turned as big as saucers.

"And do you know what he was saying?"

"What?"

"He was saying that now he'd lost his own mummy, he wanted ours instead."

Joe's eyes turned as big as soup bowls.

"And he said that if he couldn't, he was going to kill her, just like the one before!"

Joe's eyes turned as big as dinner plates, fell out of his head, and rolled under the wardrobe, where the dead spiders lived.

"Don't forget, you promised not to tell!" Grace left the room and skipped along the landing to her own bedroom. No way was she going to share her mum with some ugly tall boy just because he was too stupid to keep his own. Of course, she'd get found out—Jenny would extract from Joe what she'd said, or something like it, and then she'd get done. And then she'd have to get Joe again and she'd get done for that, too. But hey! It was one way of getting attention. She felt better already for it.

It was six o'clock. Ray should have been there an hour ago. The roasties were browning nicely in the pan, the guests were due to arrive at any minute, and there was still no sign of Nick. Jenny was actually getting worried about him now. Suppose something had happened? What if he'd done something silly? She didn't know whether to ring the police or just keep her fingers crossed and hope for the best.

She looked outside. It had started raining. Where on earth was that boy? She felt helpless, anxious, and scared. Was this what it was like looking after teenagers?

The doorbell rang just as Jenny was about to take the chicken out of the oven. She rushed downstairs hoping for Nick and opened the door to find Ray and Mrs. Batts sheltering from the rain, standing uncomfortably close together in the porch. She ushered them down the hall to the living room, chatting brightly. Being a smoker herself, who had asked the whiskey bottle for a little help just as Ray had that evening, she completely failed to notice what had been only too apparent to Mrs. Batts, standing so close to him in the porch. Ray stank of ciggies and whiskey, the result of an hour at the Stag down the road.

Ray followed her through and stood behind her. "How's it going?" he whispered.

Jenny turned around and glared at him. "Where were you? You said you'd come and help."

". . . got held up," said Ray.

"Well, don't stand there," she said. "Go inside and make small talk. Tell her what a nice family we are."

"I'll see to it," said Ray, tripping over the mat as he went back. Poor Jenny hadn't time to notice—she was too busy. Why on earth had she picked a full roast dinner? She'd even done Yorkshires—no one ever did Yorkshires with chicken. Roasts always made her panic.

Jenny took the chicken out of the oven, decanted the roasties into another dish, and popped them back in at a higher heat to crisp them up.

Then she put the baking tray on the hob to make the gravy, poured boiling water on the cabbage, and shoved the plates in the oven to warm.

A pause. She lit a fag and poked her head around the door to see Ray also smoking, and shouting to Mrs. Batts about family values.

"But you don't smoke," she muttered to herself. She watched curiously for a moment longer, but before she could do anything, the bell rang.

Mrs. Batts watched suspiciously as Jenny hurtled past and ran across to answer the door before anyone else got there. There was Nick, damp with rain, his eyes shining.

"Nick, thank God you're here, thank God," she gibbered. "Listen." She grabbed him by the arm and pulled him in, her voice sinking to a conspiritorial whisper. "I found out today it's not up to me if you stay here, we have to convince Mrs. Batts. I've invited her 'round for a meal to show her how normal we are. You have to help me! OK?"

Nick nodded. Jenny gave him the thumbs-up, took a deep breath, and led the way through into the front room. Everyone looked at him expectantly.

"Well!" exclaimed Jenny. "Isn't this nice?"

Dinner didn't last long.

It was quickly apparent even to Jenny how drunk Ray was by the way he poured about half a liter of gravy onto his plate and had to fish his potatoes out with exaggerated care to stop it slopping over the edges. It looked like he was eating a plate of soup. Shortly after, she realized that Joe was sulking furiously by the way he kept pulling faces at her across the table and glaring at Nick. Grace had her look of wide-eyed innocence on—a sure sign that she had been involved in some terrible machination, usually involving Joe.

Mrs. Batts was leaning away from the fuming Ray and trying not to wince or glare, which was doing some odd things to her face. Nick seemed to be the only normal person there. In fact, he was far from it. He felt like a mushroom—kept in the dark and fed on shit. The tight-lipped dinner-table conversation was making him feel as if his head was going to explode. If he'd had a room, he'd have run up to it and wept.

He ate the food in silence, put his knife and fork down on his plate, turned to Jenny, and said in front of everyone:

"Why didn't you tell me that my mum died of an overdose?"

Jenny turned to stare at him with a potato halfway to her mouth.

"You still haven't told him?" asked Mrs. Batts incredulously.

"He was late . . . it was . . ."

"I found out from Mrs. Ash next door. It's fucking outrageous."

"There's no need for language like that," snapped Mrs. Batts primly.

"You've all been lying to me like Muppets."

"Muppets don't lie," pointed out Joe.

"I'll handle this," said Ray.

"You weren't here when I got back at lunch today. How could I tell you when you're not here? Didn't you read my note?"

"How come everyone else in Manchester knows what happened to my mum and no one tells me?" Nick snarled. Jenny winced. "And what about you, what were you doing 'round there, anyway? Were you going to have some as well?"

"No!" insisted Jenny indignantly.

"You and her were always going off together."

"Don't speak to your mother like that," demanded Ray, pointing a stern finger in Nick's face.

"She's not my bloody mother!" yelled Nick.

"Not yet, anyway," whispered Grace in Joe's ear.

"I think we all need to calm down," began Mrs. Batts. Nick jumped to his feet. As he did so, he banged the table and Jenny's water fell into her lap. She shrieked and leaped up.

"Now look what you've done! She's only trying to help!" exclaimed Mrs. Batts, jumping up to Jenny's rescue.

"She's a lying cow," yelled Nick, reeling around the table in an agony of distress. He was trying to get upstairs to weep, but as he pushed past, Ray rose unsteadily to his feet.

"Don't you dare leave this table without asking," he roared. He stepped forward to deal with the situation, but tripped over the leg of his chair, lurched forward, and fell into Nick, wrapping his arms around him in an effort to stay upright.

"Ray!" howled Jenny.

"Get off me!" yelled Nick, and shoved him violently backward.

"Fight! Fight!" screeched Mrs. Batts, mistakenly thinking Nick had attacked Ray and unconsciously echoing the cries of the playground. Joe burst into tears and started to try to make his way upstairs, but was stopped by his sister, who pinned him to the chair by grabbing hold of the back of his jeans. She calculated, correctly, that his howls of fear and distress would better serve her purposes here at the table.

Ray tumbled backward. As he went down he swept his arm across the table, knocking his dinner plate, the salt, and the gravy boat after him.

It was pandemonium. Joe wriggled free from Grace's grip and ran howling upstairs in floods of tears.

"Typical. It happens every time," observed Grace succinctly to Mrs. Batts, and she wandered upstairs after her brother.

But Mrs. Batts had already seen enough. Her unfailing

social instinct warned her it was time to leave. She stood up and took her coat primly off the back of the chair. It had gravy stains on it, she noticed. She looked around for Nick—there was no way she could leave him here in this madhouse. But Nicholas Dane had already gone.

5
MEADOW HILL

The police came for him at his own home around lunch-time the next day. He hid in his room when he heard them banging, but when they started to knock the door down, he went to let them in.

They took him straight to Meadow Hill Assessment Centre.

Nick's first sight of Meadow Hill was the grand steps leading up to a pair of imposing stone pillars framing the door, glimpsed between the rhododendrons and sycamore trees that lined the winding drive. The bushes were all in flower, so they drove up through a forest of purple blossom, dappled in bright May sunshine, into a cracked tarmac car park in front of the house. It looked more like a church than a home. The front door was big enough to admit giants. The two policemen who had picked Nick up led him up the grand but decaying steps.

"There, you're the Lord of the Manor now," one of them said.

"Better than where you came from, eh?" said the other.

Nick followed them in anxiously. He asked them if Jenny

knew what was happening to him but they just shrugged. "We're just taking you where we were told to," one of them said.

He was left inside with a fat black woman in a trouser suit, who signed for him and then sat him down in her office with a biscuit and a glass of cola, while she rang through to see if the head was ready to see him. Her call made, she sat opposite him and watched as he ate and drank. He'd eaten nothing since his dinner the night before—just a chunk of cheese he'd found in the fridge at his house that he'd eaten in bed before he went to sleep.

"How'd you come to end up in a place like this?" the woman, whose name was Dilys, asked him. "Don't answer, I have your notes here. I know everything about you. Mum died. Things not too good. Well, you're going to have to make the most of it. Do as you're told and keep your head down. It's going to take a little time to find your feet in a place like this. Maybe you're going to have to take a few knocks. Tell me, Nicholas," she said, tipping her head back and looking at him across her plump cheeks, "do you know how to be invisible?"

Nick shrugged. It didn't sound like the kind of question that required an answer.

"Because you have to learn to be invisible here," she told him, shaking her head. "And don't rely on getting rescued, either. Who's going to want to foster a great big brute like you? Your pretty face won't help you in here. On the contrary. So. You have any family nearby, then, Nicholas?"

"They're all in Australia," said Nick defensively.

"Well, it's not like a family here," she scolded. "I don't

think there's a soul in Meadow Hill who knows what a family is really like."

Nick swallowed his cola and said nothing. Dilys picked up her pen and got back to flicking through the papers on her desk for another few minutes until the phone rang. She answered, then took Nick off to meet the headmaster of Meadow Hill, Mr. William James.

Bill James was a wide, pale man with soft pink ears that stuck out like mug handles through his thinning, shoulder-length hair. He had tired, puffy brown eyes. The skin beneath them was so dark it was almost black. He was sitting well back from his desk, dressed in a scruffy black suit, dandruff on his shoulders, drinking instant coffee and dusting biscuit crumbs off his sleeves when Dilys delivered Nick to him. When he got to his feet and came around the desk to shake hands and introduce himself, he revealed an enormous waist. The headmaster must have weighed nearly three hundred pounds.

Bill James had been the headmaster of Meadow Hill for more than twenty-five years. He was a campaigning man, a reformer. He firmly believed that there was no such thing as an evil child, and that even the worst of them could be turned into useful adults. His motto: "Every child deserves a fresh start."

He settled himself back down behind his desk and looked at the boy sitting on the other side. Nick was pale and dirty and his face was red and slightly swollen on one side. He'd been in a fight recently. The usual sort of thing. Good-looking lad. Light brown hair, blue eyes. Trouble. He could see it coming. Funny thing, it was the pretty ones who were often the most trouble.

He welcomed Nick and began his introductory speech.

"Meadow Hill," he told Nick, "is the end of the road. We take care of boys that no one else will. They all come here. Juvenile delinquents, runaways, ne'er-do-wells, bullies, and orphans. Outside of these walls, a great many bad things happen, as I'm sure you know, and a great many perpetrators of those bad things end up here in my care at Meadow Hill. And every one of them arrives at a level playing field. We're all equal at Meadow Hill. Every child has the opportunity of a fresh start. I have to say, though, Nicholas, not many of them take up that chance. Very few. Just the odd one, occasional escapees from a life of crime. Nicholas," he said earnestly, peering hopefully at him from over his reading glasses, "I want to ask you—do you think you'll be one of them?"

Nicholas was confused. "I haven't done anything, sir."

Mr. James smiled grimly. "No one has ever done anything, in my experience." He flicked through the notes on his desk. "Mother," he observed. "Heroin."

Nick stared sullenly at him.

Mr. James sighed and waved a hand at the window.

"Tell me, Nicholas. What do you see out there?"

Nick followed the hand. "Nothing, sir."

"Trees," prompted Mr. James.

"Trees."

"Trees, sir."

"Trees, sir."

"The darling buds of May. It's a fresh start. Away from the streets and the drugs, away from the inadequate parent . . ."

"She wasn't inadequate."

"Ah. Perhaps a good parent would have been a little more careful with the care of their child, don't you think? But the good news is, Nicholas, that a life on the streets with no solace but cheap drugs is no longer the limit of your horizons."

Mr. James lifted his eyebrows and stared across at Nick, waiting for a useful response. Nick scowled. "I haven't done anything, sir," he said again. The fact was, he liked the streets. He liked the drugs, too, when he could get his hands on them, although all he'd ever really tried was a bit of weed.

Mr. James shuffled his papers. "I don't think I'm really getting through to you, am I?"

"Fuck you, Mr. James," Nick replied. But not out loud.

"I'll be honest with you, Nicholas. We can't offer you a mother's love here. That has been taken from you. What we can do, however, is offer you an education of sorts, plenty of exercise, and a secure home. There's a lot of boys would give a great deal to have that—although precious few of them seem to end up here," he muttered to himself, half under his breath. "So, Nicholas! Make the most of us, and we will make the most of you!"

Mr. James went back to the file.

"Good at school. No weaknesses, the report says. Wonderful—a boy with no weaknesses! An all-rounder. Marvelous. But!—what's this? Attendance, awful. Ah. No weaknesses—but without the gift of hard work." He shook his head. "I never met a truant who didn't regret it in years to come," he remarked. "But it's hard enough teaching you boys geography, let alone wisdom. Well, there'll be no skiving off here. We have everything here on site—home, school, play, all in one place." He smiled across the desk. "No escape. Nowhere to run off to! And no stealing, either. There's nothing here to steal!"

He leaned back and laughed at his own joke—which was, sadly, pretty nearly true.

Mr. James picked up a telephone and asked for a lad to be sent up. He sat and waited, smiling vaguely and twiddling his thumbs. After a few minutes there was a knock on the door.

"In," hooted Mr. James. The door opened and in came a pale, slight boy, a year or so younger than Nick, with a head of wavy blond hair.

"Oliver, this is Nicholas," said Mr. James. The two boys looked at each other cautiously. "Take him to Mr. Toms, will you? He's to be settled in. Keep an eye on him. I think he might need a bath."

"Will do, sir," piped Oliver. Mr. James dismissed them, and the blond boy led the way out of the office and back into the grounds.

After the two boys left, Mr. James sighed and straightened the papers in Nick's file. He didn't feel optimistic about the lad's chances. A bad age to lose your mother, even if she was a junkie. He offered a fresh start, yes—but the material he had to work with was far from fresh. In fact, by and large, it was pretty rotten. Only the dregs came to Meadow Hill.

They were undereducated from years of skiving off, underfed from years of poor food, they'd been set bad examples, been badly cared for, and had no respect for anything, least of all for themselves.

"I haven't done anything, sir," muttered Mr. James to himself. Hadn't been caught doing it yet, that's all. He'd seen and heard it all before. Well, you could take a fish to water but you couldn't make it swim, as his wife always said.

He looked at his watch. Two o'clock. There were a few more files on his desk he could profitably look through, but they could wait. Or his deputy, Tony Creal, would deal with them for him.

He squeezed himself out of his chair and walked the short distance back to the headmaster's residence. He tried to stay optimistic about his work here at Meadow Hill, but it was hard, not least because he knew that he had failed in what he'd set out to do when he first arrived as a young headmaster—one of the youngest in the country—from his previous place in a children's home in Northumberland. He and his wife, Janice, had worked wonders there, everyone agreed. Feted, admired, promoted. His glory days. A faraway young and slim Bill James had transformed the lives of a number of boys. He had taken in the wretched and sent them away full of hope. Kindness, firmness, a good teaching staff, respect—it had worked wonders.

But not here. Meadow Hill was a mire. The boys in Manchester seemed so much worse. Nothing he did made any difference. The badness was so ingrained in them that sometimes he almost believed that the fighting, the lies, the vandalism, the violence, the stealing, the dirt, the sheer lack of manners and self-respect in these boys went all the way back, not just for hundreds but for millions of years. They had evolved like that, from lying, stealing little fish into lying, stealing little frogs, to lying, stealing little rats and finally into the lying, stealing little bastards that they now were—a loathsome, criminal underclass, bred to torment him.

But that was depression speaking. They were just boys—there was good in all of them, if only it could be reached, and it was Mr. James's personal failure that he hadn't done so. The fact was, shortly after they had moved here, his best friend and ally, his inspiration and right hand, his partner in optimism, had fallen foul of misery herself. Janice had become depressed. A series of miscarriages had started it. Lost babies—she hadn't been able to bear it. Only to be expected, a dip—but it went on and on and on and on and on. That which had once been so bright had been darkened, he thought.

Truth be known, Mr. James was not far behind his wife. Most of his time these days was spent caring for her. If it wasn't for his deputy, Tony Creal, he would certainly have had to leave.

Not for the first time, Mr. James blessed his good friend. The man was an inspiration, tireless in his optimism. He could still see the good, even though Mr. James had lost his own vision somewhere down the long years of trying to raise his darling Janice from the twilight of the soul into which she had sunk.

Mr. James swayed through the garden gate and disappeared

from sight of the rest of Meadow Hill behind the high privet hedge that girdled his house. Inside he closed the front door quietly.

"Janice? You all right?" he asked.

A muffled voice drifted down from upstairs. It sounded like it was saying OK, but he knew it wasn't true. Still in bed. He sighed. Another bad day.

Ponderously, he made his way upstairs and opened the door to a darkened room. A sad-looking little heap stirred under the duvet.

"Have you had any breakfast, my love?" he asked.

"Not hungry," croaked a flat voice. His heart sank. He walked to the wardrobe, opened it, and took out a bottle of pills.

"A pillular breakfast this morning?" he suggested with a wan smile.

Janice's head appeared and nodded. Thank God for Valium. He was always trying to get her off it, but whenever he did, she only got worse. Once, after three days off the stuff, she had actually left the house and wandered around the grounds in her dressing gown, looking, apparently, for the way out. The boys had had a field day.

She would already have taken her prescription, but on days like this, it wasn't enough. Fortunately, he had a private supply.

Janice popped her little helpers. He bent down to kiss her—his love had never wavered, even though his care had become so perfectly poisonous. Depressed Janice James certainly was, but worse than that, she was a Valium addict. Her husband's constant attempts to take her off it produced alarming withdrawal symptoms, which resulted in him overprescribing, which in turn made it worse. Unknowingly, he kept her in a constant state of depression and anxiety, from which she would have recovered all on her own years ago, if simply left alone.

Bill James swallowed a few pills himself and took off his trousers—what a relief! The belt hidden under his pullover dug in. Then he went downstairs to cook lunch. Sausages. There was a good butcher in Northenden where he always bought them—he got through several pounds a week. He always made enough for Janice, even though on days like this she rarely ate more than one or two. He'd probably end up finishing them himself.

He stood in front of the stove, a fat man with no trousers on, cooking sausages on the stove. He climbed the stairs slowly, carrying a tray with tea and the sausages on it; she managed a couple and he finished the last himself before getting into bed with his beloved. He cuddled her from behind. Her hand crept around to hold his. Embracing like this, front to back, still in love despite all the pills, all the disappointments, and all the years, they both drifted off to sleep.

As the headmaster was making his way toward his house, the blond boy led Nick across the worn grass to a square brick building a hundred meters away from the old house, hidden behind the trees. Nick was a good head taller than the younger boy, who bobbed along in front of him, his blond hair bouncing in the breeze, like a fluffy seed head being blown across the ground.

"What you here for, then?" Nick asked him.

"Crap mother," said Oliver. "What about you?"

"Dead mother," said Nick. Oliver flashed Nick a sideways look. Nick snorted, the blond lad giggled, and suddenly they were both laughing. Nick would have liked to stop to talk, but the other lad carried on and he had no choice but to follow.

"Someone's always watching," explained Oliver.

"How come you're not at school?" asked Nick. Oliver flashed him another sideways glance. "I get let off," he said.

"How come?"

"I run errands for Mr. Creal."

"That's good, then."

Oliver didn't reply. "What's it like here?" asked Nick.

"Bloody awful."

Nick started to laugh again, and the boy shrugged and smiled wanly. "Just do what you're told and it won't be too bad," he said.

Nick pulled a face. He'd never been very good at doing what he was told.

The boys drew up to the front door of a smaller brick building built onto the side of the main one. Oliver paused at the door. "They beat you up like a man," he explained. He looked at Nick for a moment, then turned and knocked.

There was a long, long pause before the door was opened by a balding man, short enough to be looking them straight in the eye but powerfully built. He stood there with a bottle of milk in his hand, watching them.

"New boy, sir," said Oliver.

The short man looked at Nick and lifted his chin.

"Nicholas Dane," said Nick, supposing that was what the man wanted to know.

A look of immense surprise spread over the short man's face. "Oh! We're friends, are we? Already? How nice for me. Do you want to come in and watch telly, Nick? Fancy a beer later on, do you, mate?" He smiled mirthlessly and thrust his face right up to Nick's. "What do you think my name is, Dane?"

"Sir," guessed Nick.

The short man nodded. "And don't forget it. Take him 'round to Mrs. Stanton, get him kitted out, Brown," he said, still staring hard at Nick but obviously talking to Oliver. "Show him what's what."

"Yes, sir."

Mr. Toms nodded and strolled back into the house. Nick realized he'd been holding his breath, and let it out in a rush.

"Jesus. What's up with him?"

"He's always like that," Oliver said. "Must be constipated," he added as an afterthought. Nick stared at him in surprise and laughed. Oliver had a sense of humor—maybe he was going to like him.

Nick followed Oliver around into the main body of the brick building.

Downstairs was one big room divided into two by a folding partition wall. Each side housed fifteen boys; here they ate, watched TV, cleaned their shoes, played games, and spent their free time. On special occasions the partition was pushed back, so the whole hall could be used. Behind a door at the back of the building was a stairway leading up to a single long corridor that ran the length of the building. There were two bathrooms, one at each side, with three baths in each, and separate lavatories. The dorms were behind doors on either side of the corridor, a series of rooms each housing five or six beds. The whole floor smelled of pee and disinfectant.

The boys on each side of the partition were governed by separate house parents, who lived in flats built onto each side of the building; it was Nick's luck to have Mr. and Mrs. Toms. Their job was to look after the boys outside of school hours—organize their activities, discipline them, tend to their problems and general care. Behind the building was another built-on flat, where the house wardens lived, another married couple whose job it was to take care of the building and look after such stuff as laundry and the various physical needs of the boys who lived there.

There were three such houses in the grounds, plus the big house, where another group of boys lived, and which also housed the administration block and the flat belonging to the deputy, Mr. Creal. Also on the site was the school, a small building kept solely for the children of Meadow Hill.

Oliver led Nick around to the back of the building where the Stantons, the house wardens, lived. Mrs Stanton issued him with his school uniform, school shoes, and bedding.

"Are you a bed wetter?" she wanted to know.

Nick stared. "I'm fourteen," he said.

Mrs. Stanton looked tiredly at him. "You'd better say now if you are. You'll have Mr. Toms to see to you if you wet the mattress." Nick just gaped at her. "It's nothing to be ashamed of, you'd be amazed at how many of them do," she said. Nick shook his head and remembered the smell of pee and disinfectant that had filled the top floor.

"It's all out in the open in a place like this," she said, shutting the cupboard doors. "Now then—anything else you need?" she wanted to know.

"Something to eat?" said Nick immediately.

Mrs. Stanton looked surprised, but she went inside and came out shortly with a couple of sandwiches. "It's jam," she said, giving one to each of them. "Dinner's not for another hour, it's out of my own stores."

Nick thanked her. She stood and watched them eat for a moment, then asked Oliver, "Where are you supposed to be?"

"Inside, waiting for the others."

"Go on then," she said. Oliver led the way back to the main building, and they stood in the doorway, eating their sandwiches. When he'd done, Nick was still ravenous. He felt in his pocket, where he still had a pound left from the money he'd taken from Jenny's windowsill.

"Any shops?" he asked.

Oliver stared at him and shook his head.

"We're not allowed off the grounds," he said.

"No one'll spot us," said Nick. Oliver lifted his hands in a gesture that indicated that only a madman would do anything like that. Nick shrugged. He was thinking that despite his sense of humor, Oliver was a bit of a wimp. Instead, they went upstairs, where Oliver showed him the bathroom and the dorms, and the lockers at the top of the stairs for him to stash the uniform and other stuff in.

"Why's it not in our bedrooms?" asked Nick.

"So's people don't wander around getting their things out at night," said Oliver.

"It's like a bloody dogs' home," said Nick. "How often do they take us for walks?"

"They don't let us out," replied Oliver. Nick looked closely at him; Oliver looked back. Nick was just beginning on a very steep learning curve.

They hung around a bit, not really knowing what to do. There was an enormous TV in the big room on the ground floor, but apparently it wasn't turned on until after school. Nick wanted Oliver to show him around outside, but Oliver wouldn't go.

"Not allowed in the grounds without a prefect about," he explained.

Instead, Oliver led him downstairs and they sneaked out behind the house and hid among some elder trees and shrubs growing out of a neglected flowerbed. Oliver went off with his odd, fluttery run, leaving Nick crouching uncomfortably among the trees. He reappeared quickly enough, and led the way deeper into the thicket, where there were a couple of old buckets turned upside down to sit on. Oliver produced from his pockets a bag of wine gums, two Mars Bars, a packet of ciggies, a box of matches, a pack of cards, and, tucked down the back of his trousers, a magazine.

"Tit mag," he hissed, dropping it on the ground.

Nick seized the magazine and flicked through. It was wall-to-wall girls—some of them very naked indeed. He didn't know much about life at Meadow Hill but he could already guess that this was treasure indeed.

"Where'd you get this lot from?" he asked. "Not your mum," he guessed.

Oliver hushed him. "Whisper," he said. He ripped open a Mars Bar. "Haven't seen her for years," he said.

"Mate?"

"Friend of mine, yeah," said Oliver.

They sat quietly for a while, eating the sweets. Then they lit up the cigarettes and sat there smoking.

"You've got it really sorted here, haven't you?" said Nick. "How long you been in for?"

"Since I was about five," said Oliver. "In and out of care," he said, repeating a phrase he'd heard social workers say so many times in his presence.

They exchanged stories, although Oliver hadn't got much to say, except that his mother hadn't wanted him, and that she'd stopped even coming to see him some years ago. Nick, now that it came down to it, didn't want to say much about his story either.

They flicked through the mag together, read each other particularly funny sections out of the readers' letters section, and then turned to cards.

"Do you know snap?" asked Oliver.

Nick was surprised at his choice of game, but said yes. They played a few hands then turned to other games, and in this way passed a pleasant hour. At that point, someone blew a whistle, and soon after, they heard a man shouting instructions.

"That's school done," said Oliver. "We'd better get back before we're missed."

Oliver was in the same building as Nick, but on the other side of the partition. He didn't want to come in, but stepped just inside the door so he could point out the prefects who kept order in the place when Toms wasn't about.

It was like being plunged back into the past. Inside there were fifteen boys kneeling in a row polishing their shoes on newspapers spread out on the floor. They were all really going for it—scrubbing with a brush, even spitting to help bring out a shine. Nick couldn't believe it. He'd had to wear black shoes at school, but they never got polished from one term to the next. The boys turned their heads to look at him, but no one stopped polishing.

"That's Andrews, with the black hair," whispered Oliver, pointing out a tall, rangy boy glaring at them. The other prefect was a burly lad called Julian, with a soft, red rubble of acne all over his cheeks.

Oliver fled, leaving Nick to his own devices. He stood there uncertainly for a moment, unsure. The boys were all watching him out of the corner of their eyes, so he walked self-consciously across to the dark lad Oliver had pointed out.

"I'm to see you," he began.

"New boy," stated Andrews, getting to his feet. He nodded down to Nick's feet, clad in his old trainers. "Have they given you your gear?"

"Yeah, upstairs," said Nick.

"Get your shoes down and clean 'em up, then," said Andrews. "Get on with it, we're half done down here." He kneeled back down to his work, leaving Nick to find his way upstairs to his locker. By the time he got back down, the rest of the boys had finished and he had to stand aside on the stairs as they made their way up in their socks, to stow their school things in their lockers and bring down their day clothes. Downstairs, Andrews made Nick polish his shoes till the wrinkled old leather shone before he was allowed to go back up and change back into his trainers. Downstairs, the TV was turned on for half an hour, at which point Mr. Toms himself appeared, and got the boys busy putting up the trestle tables they were to eat their dinners on.

Nick was grateful for the food, but it was pretty grim—pasty fish fingers, lumpy mash, and peas the color of cheap green paint. It was eaten in a lively chatter, with Toms waiting impatiently for them to finish, walking up and down and nagging the boys to get a move on.

The plates were cleared and carried through to the kitchen behind the building, where a group of boys washed them. The tables were folded up and put back against the wall. Then it was time for sports, two hours of it. Nick had an hour on the football pitch, and then another hour in the gym.

Nick liked his sports and he was happy enough for a while, running about and not thinking. After sports it was showers, and then the TV was turned on again. By then, Nick was too tired and disoriented to do anything but sit in a corner and stare until bedtime. They were all under the covers by half past nine, in a draughty, narrow, uncarpeted dorm with a full-size snooker table at one end and a row of beds down each side. There were sniffles and tears among the coughs as the boys, aged from thirteen to sixteen, settled down, and not all from the smallest ones, either. Nick noticed none of it. He lay down on the narrow little bed, closed his eyes, and was asleep before they'd even turned the lights off.

Nick hadn't just lost his mother. He'd lost his entire life. Music, books, videos, his clothes, even, except for what he arrived in, had all been left behind, like dreams that vanish in the morning. His friends, the people who had made his life worth living, Simon and Jeremy and Amanda and the people he'd known at school. All gone.

And he hadn't just lost his past, he'd lost his future with it. None of his hopes and ambitions had come along with him, if he only knew it. His dreams weren't going to come true now. There had been talk of university, but the school Nick was to attend the following morning did not produce anyone fit for that. When the light died in Muriel's eyes just a couple of days ago, the light that shone on Nick died, too. He had been propelled into a world of poverty and fear of which he had no conception.

His new life began in earnest the following morning.

6
MR. TOMS

In the morning, Nick was jerked awake by an earsplitting whistle that made him leap up and look around in alarm. Mr. Toms was standing in the doorway in a tracksuit with a sports whistle around his neck.

"Up you get, you little toads," he shouted. "Up, up, up!" He left and went to the next dorm, to repeat the good news there.

All around, the other lads were rolling around and groaning, before crawling out of bed and stumbling rapidly off. Nick sat up in bed. It was freezing. He pulled a blanket around him and watched in a daze as the other boys rushed around him. Already they were coming back and without any delay started getting into their school clothes and folding up their pajamas neatly. After that, they stripped down their beds, and began making them again from scratch.

It was too early. What about his zees? The previous night, Toms had told Andrews to show Nick the ropes. But Andrews had only just crawled out of bed. He was leaning on the windowsill looking out at the day and scratching his arse while another boy made his bed for him, and Nick was scared to disturb him.

Nick needed the loo—that was where everyone had gone running off to—but everything was happening so quickly. They were all back already and busy making their beds. Nick tried to copy them but it was coming out all wrong, so he plucked up courage and went to ask Andrews if he'd got it right.

Andrews looked at the bed in horror.

"Didn't anyone bloody think to help him? You twats . . ."

He rushed over to get it sorted. The bed had to be made with hospital corners—grubby sheets folded over like paper, neat as an envelope. Andrews fell on the bed and ordered one of the other lads to get on with Nick's pajamas, while Nick was sent off to get himself ready, feeling like a fool and wondering what was so urgent.

He'd left it too late, that was the problem. A moment after he got back in the dorm, Toms reappeared in the door and blew his earsplitting whistle again. The boys dropped what they were doing and made a dash for the snooker table. They arranged themselves around it in two rows, three on each side, backs to the table, with their neatly folded pajamas balanced on their outstretched hands. Andrews hustled Nick into place and helped him get his clothes in a pile. Nick twitched; the pajamas tumbled. He caught them and hurriedly refolded them as best he could. He caught a brief glimpse of Andrews's agonized face staring helplessly at the tangle of his clothes before Toms blew the whistle again and everyone froze.

Nick was anxious, but more bemused than anything. He had no idea just how wrong his pile of clothes was, or how bad his bed looked, or what that would mean.

Toms walked up to the snooker table and removed one of the cues from its rest before going over to inspect the beds. He paused by Nick's, then came to walk down the line of boys, like a general inspecting his troops.

Toms hated this part of the morning. Whether it was all neat and present and correct affected his mood for the whole day. He was already in a bad mood, having had to look at a bed made by a moron. When he got to the culprit, the new boy, he could hardly believe it. The boy half smiled at him—as if he had anything to smile about. His clothes looked as if they'd been folded up by a monkey.

Andrews opened his mouth to speak.

"Shut up," barked Toms. He lifted his hand and stirred the air, with a circular motion of his finger. Obediently, Andrews took a step forward, holding his arms out straight ahead of him. Toms lined himself up to one side, held the snooker cue down with its tip on the floor under Andrews's hands, paused a moment to get his aim just right, and then swung it up in a vicious arc through the air. There was a hard crack as the wood hit Andrews's wrists, the clothes were flung all over the room, and the prefect collapsed to the ground with a high scream, tucking his hands under his armpits.

No one moved a muscle.

"I didn't mean . . ." began Nick.

"Shut up, new boy," said Toms.

On the floor, Andrews was gathering together his clothes. As he got back to his place in the line, he gave Nick a truly poisonous look.

Toms left the room. He didn't need to punish Nick; he

knew that would be done for him. The boys scattered and Nick backed off to his bed—he knew what was coming. If the staff behaved like that, what could you expect of the boys?

Andrews came straight at him and swung a punch. And Nick being Nick, even though he was almost a foot shorter, swung one back. That was Nick—never say no to a fight. He had a secret weapon, too. He was fearless. Go for the biggest bugger first, take no prisoners. It meant he got his face punched in from time to time, but no one ever picked a fight with him lightly.

Andrews wasn't expecting it. Nick caught him right on the side of the face and stepped back. Nine times out of ten, a bully stops when they know you'll fight back, but Andrews wasn't a bully—he was a thug. He grabbed Nick by the front of his shirt, slapped him hard around the side of the head, and shoved him to the floor. He swung a kick, but Nick was like rubber—he literally bounced back on his feet.

The red mist came down. Nick lost it like this sometimes. He let out a yell and went for Andrews like a madman. Andrews was so surprised by his fury that he fell backward before him.

Nick was on him at once. He grabbed Andrews's hair in both hands and started banging his head on the floor. When Andrews knocked his hands away, he started slapping and punching his face. Andrews had actually begun to cry for help, when suddenly an irresistible force lifted Nick right up by the back of his trousers and flung him through the air. He landed in a heap against the wall, but was back up in a second and ran in for more, like a fool—straight into the furious figure of Mr. Toms.

Nick was like a madman, he even prepared to go for Toms. Toms simply reached out his hand, seized hold of the hair on top of Nick's head, held him still for a moment while he stopped struggling, before lifting his head so that he was standing up straight. Then he punched Nick in the stomach as hard as he could.

It was like a kick from a horse. Nick was fourteen, tough and wiry; but Toms was a grown man, and a strong one. As the wind rushed out of him, Nick could hear Oliver's words in his ears the day before: "They beat you up like a man." He'd thought it was the usual exaggeration, but here it was, just as he'd said. Not detention or even the cane. A violent blow to the stomach. Beaten up like a man.

Nick doubled over like a reed. The punch had been right in the stomach when he wasn't expecting it. His whole body went into a seizure, his lungs stopped working and he started writhing and thrashing on the ground, desperately trying to snatch some air. The pain was incredible, but far worse was the terrible panic that overwhelmed him, because he was so completely unable to breathe. Toms came to stand over him, shouting something, but Nick couldn't make it out. His ears were roaring.

Toms stooped down and hauled him to his feet by his shirt. "Breathe, you silly twat, breathe!" he yelled, and let him go. Nick fell straight back to the floor, thrashing and banging like a fish out of water, still unable to get so much as a sip of air.

Toms began to look worried. The last thing he wanted was a hospital job. But although Nick was badly bruised, Toms hadn't ruptured anything, and gradually he managed to get his breath back in little sips. Within a minute or two he was crouched on the floor, on his knees, almost in the same posture his mother had died in, clutching his stomach and rocking to and fro.

Toms was furious—as much at the shock he'd given himself as with the breach of discipline. The new boys did sometimes require a knock or two to get them into shape, but he rarely found little scraps like this punching the lights out of one of his prefects.

He shoved Nick onto his side with his foot. "I've got my eye on you, and that's something you aren't going to like, you ugly little piece of shit," he bellowed. He looked at Andrews. "Fucking pathetic," he sneered. "Beaten up by a kid. Wanker!"

Toms left the room, and as soon as the door closed, Andrews went straight over to Nick and carried on where Toms had left off. He stood over him and kicked him several times in the head and kidneys for good measure.

"You get me hit again, I'll kill you," he hissed. "You fight back to me again, I'll get him to do it." He jerked his head in Toms's direction. He put his foot in Nick's face and ground it in. Then he bent over him. "Get cleaned up. Breakfast is in fifteen minutes. If you're not ready, you'll get more of the same again and so will I. And if I get more, you're dead. Understand?"

Nick nodded and sobbed. He had never felt so humiliated

in his life. He could hardly walk, his stomach was a ball of pain, his face was swollen where Andrews had kicked him. He hauled himself to his feet and staggered to the toilets to splash water on his face. Somehow, he managed to be ready with the others, waiting on the landing for the whistle, so they could file down in a crocodile to the hall below for breakfast.

The year was 1984. No one who had thought about it for long believed that beating kids was going to do anyone any good, but inside Meadow Hill the violence went unchecked. In some of the homes it worked well enough. There were plenty of people willing to work long hours for low pay to help the kids. But when it went wrong, as it had in Meadow Hill, there was no inspection and no accountability. The staff could do as they liked.

The only training Mr. Toms ever had was in the army. He had fought very bravely years ago in Korea, but the only technique he had ever been given to sort out human problems was discipline. It was a simple fact that if you hit a difficult kid often enough and hard enough, the problems disappeared. Of course they didn't really go away—they just went underground and a few years later the brutalized victims would start making their presence known elsewhere in the country, reemerging and filling up the prisons in the form of addicts, thieves, bullies, murderers, and rapists.

Outside, Nick's mates were hanging around in their New Wave hairdos, smoking weed, cheeking the teachers, watching their parents clean up after them, punking it up on a

Saturday night and listening to Adam Ant, Depeche Mode, or The Clash. Inside, you could be hospitalized for folding your clothes badly. Toms thought of it as "teaching the new boy the ropes," which basically meant picking him up for every little infringement of the rules he might make. The rules were countless at Meadow Hill, but if there wasn't one handy, Mr. Toms just made it up. Of course the new boy was messing up all the time.

The other boys were used to new lads getting this treatment. For some of them it meant it wasn't their turn anymore, and they were more than happy to see Toms's attention turn to Nick. Others liked to join in. There's always someone who wants to please the biggest, toughest kid by following their example, and Toms was the biggest kid by far. To this, Nick responded as he always did—by fighting back. As a result, he upset the pecking order. In Meadow Hill, the pecking order wasn't about clothes or good looks or wit and how cool you were or how good at sports—it was plainly and simply about how tough you were. Nick had showed himself a fighter by having a go not only at Andrews, but even at Toms. As a result, every kid in the home who fancied himself with his fists lined up for a go.

The first fight came at the first chance—during break. A lean, tough-looking boy pushed over to him and started shoving him backward.

"Who are you looking at? What do you want?"

"I wasn't . . ." began Nick, but the boy wasn't there to listen. He shoved Nick in the shoulder so he staggered backward.

"You're a little twat, aren't you? Staring at me. Eh?" Another shove. It didn't take much. It never did with Nick; he had a temper about two microns long. With a cry of rage, he hurled himself at the boy.

Next thing he knew he was on the floor with a foot going into his ribs. He tried to get up, but was kicked back down—*bang bang bang.* In the end, all he could do was curl up into a ball and wait for it to finish.

There were two more at lunchtime. He won one of those, lost the other. If he managed to get going, he stood a good chance because he just went completely ape, but if they were quick, like that first lad, he was lost.

There was more trouble after school on the sports field. By then, it had become a game. Nick had raised his head too high, too fast. He had become a target.

By the end of his first day he'd had four fights. Toms was completely vindicated in his assumption that Nick Dane was trouble. Four fights! What more proof do you need?

That evening, before dinner, Nick got his punishment. Toms took him out of the main hall with the two other lads he'd been caught fighting—the others had got away with it—and Andrews. He did them first. It was the cane, six strokes each. They were tough lads who could take a punch without a whimper, but Toms had all of them, even Andrews, screaming in pain. He made them wear their gym shorts while he did it and Nick was terrified to see the blood show through by the end of it. Blood? He was a kid being smacked for being bad. How did blood come into it?

Toms sent the other boys out before he had a go at Nick. From the hall there were cheers as the boys entered. Toms looked down at him and nodded his head.

"Your turn, son," he said. Oddly, he was at his kindest at these moments. Nick bent over with his hands on his knees as the other lads had and stuck his behind out. "It's always worse to start with, but once you get to know the ropes you'll find it easier," Toms told him. "And I'll tell you what. If I see you trying, I'll go easy on you, OK?"

Nick could only nod.

"But today you haven't tried. You got caught fighting twice, Dane. Not good enough. Those boys got six for having one fight. How many do you think you should get?"

Nick couldn't even answer. It was all he could do to keep his legs from trembling.

"What's two sixes, boy?" yelled Toms suddenly.

"Twelve, sir," he croaked.

Toms didn't reply. He swished the cane to and fro a bit, then landed the first one.

Nick had promised himself not to make any noise, but he couldn't help himself from yelping. It was agony. Toms waited in between each blow for him to compose himself. The first three he spread out, but the fourth he deliberately aimed where the first had landed. Nick screamed with pain, and on the fifth, involuntarily put his hands back and caught the cane on his wrists; so Toms delivered that blow again. After six, there was a longer pause before it started again. He stopped at nine.

"Now get out of my sight," said Toms. He stood leaning

against a table with his arms folded while Nick got himself together, wiped his nose, and made for the door.

"They're all the same, the tough ones," remarked Toms behind him. "They all come in here smirking and they go out crying like girls."

Nick went through the door, swallowing his sobs. He was expecting jeers on the other side, but they never came. He got a bigger cheer than any of them, even from the lads who'd been fighting him a few hours before.

"Let's see if he's a sergeant or a corporal," someone shouted. Nick was rushed and overwhelmed. He began to flail about to fight them off, but there were too many of them. They meant no harm, though. They grabbed his arms and legs and pulled down his shorts. Everyone bent to have a look at his backside.

"He's a bloody general!" someone shouted. Another cheer went up. They let him go. Nick pulled up his shorts and staggered off to a corner to collapse. His shoulder and back were slapped as he went past.

"Well, done, mate!"

"Nine stripes on your first day—it's a record!"

"General Dane, eh?"

Nick nodded and tried to grin, but he could hardly speak. Then the whistle went, and he joined the rest of them in a crocodile onto the football field.

The attack from Toms gave him a break from the boys—he was left alone for the rest of the day. But it wasn't over by a long way. Andrews still had a lesson to teach him. He was twice the size of Nick, but perhaps he was wary now, because he got some friends to help him. They crept out of bed and came on him in his sleep. One of them pinned his hands above his head, another put his hand over his mouth, another held his legs while Andrews punched him in the stomach, just where Toms had got him that morning, five or six times.

"That'll learn you not to mess with me again," hissed Andrews in his ear. They held him down for a while longer, clamping his mouth shut while he heaved and struggled silently, before they let him go. Nick doubled up in bed, rolled over and vomited onto the sheets.

And next day, the fights started again.

For the next few days, Nick wandered around in a daze. Why was this happening to him? Because his mother had died. Each night, he wept. Each morning, Toms found an excuse to bring the snooker cue down on his head, or across the back of his knees, or to jab it in his stomach. All he wanted to do was get through the next hour without another fist, another kicking, another caning. The only break he got was during lessons at school or after a caning, when all enemies briefly banded together in a celebration of their stripes.

School itself was a joke. One of the teachers' idea of a lesson was to sit them down, put a tape recorder on playing hideous country-and-western songs, put his legs up on a desk, take out a book, and leave them to it. The only time he got up was when someone made too much noise, in which case he took him into the corridor and beat him. Not everyone was so bad, admittedly. In some of the classes there was even the chance to learn something, but it was pretty basic. Nick was well into his studies for his O levels when Muriel died. Here, no one did any exams at all. It was taken for granted that even if they were on offer, no one was going to pass. The only lessons that did any real good were woodwork and metalwork. In the expectation that the best the boys could hope for was trade, the workshops were actually rather good.

The only face Nick knew in the whole place was Oliver, but since he was in a different class and dorm, he didn't get to see much of him. With the kind of attention Nick was getting, he would have understood if Oliver stopped bothering with him altogether. But the younger boy still found time to come and talk with him in the playground, and sometimes he'd pop over to Nick's side of the hall after school. Admittedly, he was never to be seen when there was a fight going on, but Nick couldn't blame him for that—there was hardly anything of him. He was more like a dandelion seed than a boy, the way he floated and bobbed around under his shock of blond hair.

The fact was, Oliver was unpopular himself, but somehow he managed to get away with it. He seemed to have a knack of avoiding trouble, work, or exercise. The other boys sometimes called him names, but by and large, he was left alone. Even Toms seemed to take no notice of him. Nick couldn't help noticing that when Oliver was around, the trouble seemed to stop for a while at least.

There was always a supply of chocolate, magazines, and sweets, but oddly, no one ever tried to take them from him.

They just left him and Nick alone to get on with it. Once, about four or five days after he'd arrived, Oliver turned up with a pack of cards in his pocket with nudes in some very revealing postures on the back of them. Nick was amazed.

"Where'd you get this stuff?" he cried.

Oliver smiled and shrugged. "I guess I'm just lucky," he said.

"You bloody are 'n' all," said Nick. "That's you. You're a good luck charm, you are."

"Am I?" asked Oliver shyly, peeping at him from under his hair.

"I never get into a fight when you're around. I can't normally move without someone having a go at me. See? Good luck!"

"Just call me lucky," said Oliver proudly. "Snap," he added, proving the point by winning the game.

Oliver obviously didn't want to reveal where he got the stuff from, and Nick reckoned that was his business. But whenever he saw Oliver's blond head bobbing toward him among the other lads, his heart always rose up a notch in spite of his troubles.

But day after day the violence went on. Mostly, the boys managed to avoid getting caught, since that meant the cane, but with so many fights, Nick was bound to get caught from time to time. That first week he suffered twenty-four strokes. His backside was literally raw. No sooner had he scabbed over than he got another dose. It became a game with some of the other boys to creep up behind and kick him. He spent the breaks leaning up against the wall to protect himself.

Nick was exhausted. He barely thought about the mother he'd lost such a short time ago. That was from another world, another life. It had all died with her. He was a prisoner of war, a refugee, too tired, too scared, too busy trying to find his way to have any feelings except fear and relief. His ribs hurt; he was black and blue all over them from countless kickings. He had a black eye swollen up as big as an apple, a busted lip, loose teeth. He was limping from where someone had kicked him in the ankle. He was a mess.

He was so dazed, he'd lost his sense of time, but it must have been about a week after he first arrived that he finally got into some really serious trouble with the other boys. It happened like this: he'd got so used to people attacking him, that he'd started lashing out more or less at once, without asking any questions. At least it meant he got a blow in quick and a chance to scare his attacker off. But Nick had no idea about the politics of Meadow Hill, and finally, more or less by accident, he knocked down Steven Morris.

At the time he hadn't thought anything about it. When Steven poked an arm into his face he didn't stop to see how big this latest attacker was, or even if he really meant to hit him. Next thing, Steven was flat on his back with Nick sitting on his chest and his fist going up and down on his face—one, two, three, four, five times—before he was plucked off by a couple of other lads, worried for the safety of both boys.

"You're dead now," one of them whispered to Nick. It wasn't a threat; it was a prophecy.

Steven was a couple of years younger than Nick. He was always picking fights, and tough enough—but no one ever fought him back if they could help it because of his brothers. The Morrises were the biggest, hardest clan in the whole of Meadow Hill. There were three of them in at that point and another two coming up in other homes around Manchester. You didn't mess with the Morrises. It was just too dangerous. In another five or six years, they'd be running rackets around the streets of Salford, and in another ten, they'd be one of the hardest and most violent of the Manchester gangs. Already, they ruled Meadow Hill. No one ever touched them. You weren't fighting with just one person, you were fighting the whole clan.

Nick flattened Steven at break. The brothers caught up with him at lunchtime.

The first Nick knew of it was the usual—someone standing suddenly in front of him, shoving him in the chest and shoulder.

"You picking on my little brother, are you? Do you know who I am?" Shove, shove, shove. Nick went back three times, then, as always, his temper blew. He was living in a red mist. He flew at the lad in front of him but he never made contact. His legs were kicked away from under him, he went down with a thud on the tarmac on his side, and that was it. All three of the Morris brothers were around him, with little Steven dancing around to get to his head and face, and the heavy black school shoes going bang bang bang against his ribs, his head, his neck, and his face.

He could taste the salt blood in his mouth within a few seconds. The Morrises ruled the roost from sheer violence. Within a few seconds, he was already unable to defend himself. His head was lolling on his neck and banging from side to side from one boot to the next, a ball on a short rope, as blow after blow after blow landed home. Other boys around were starting to yell at them to stop, because this wasn't a fight; it was turning into a maiming.

Then it was over. Nick saw nothing, just vaguely heard the feet run off. He tried to move but his limbs weren't doing what they should. Someone was shouting near him, a man.

"I saw it, you three. You better run, Michael Morris. And you, Steven and David. You're going to have me to answer to now." There was a pause. Nick managed to crawl onto all fours, blood dripping out of his mouth and from the end of his nose. He raised his head and tried to get a look at his rescuer through a haze of blood, mucus, and tears.

It was a tall, thin man. He was wearing a sandy-colored suit that matched his pale chestnut hair, peppered with gray. He spoke in a soft Geordie accent. He had an alert, intelligent face, and he was bending over Nick with his hands on his knees, looking very serious indeed.

"Up you get, Dane. You lads, help him to his feet. Go on."

Nick was dragged upright. The tall man looked at him for a moment, then tossed his head.

"Right, can you walk? You're coming with me. You two, give him a hand and the rest of you lads get on with whatever you were doing. And tell the Morris brothers they're going to have a long appointment this evening with Mr. Harvey."

He turned and led the way out of the playground, with Nick limping behind him, helped along by two other boys, and into the big house itself. Inside, he sat Nick down on a chair in the hallway while the other two lads were dismissed. The man sat down next to him and introduced himself as Tony Creal, the deputy head at Meadow Hill. Once Nick was a bit steadier on his feet, he told him to get up and led the way up the grand stairway, up to the first floor.

7
TONY CREAL

It had been a fine old house once, Meadow Hill. The staircase was as wide as the average sitting room, curling elegantly up to a high landing. Once, the boards had been stained and waxed and laid with woollen rugs, the walls papered with costly designs and lovely paints. Now Mr. Creal led Nick down a dirty long corridor that smelled of stale cabbage and dust, with dark brown linoleum underfoot and walls painted dull green to waist height and then a dirty, shiny cream up to the ceiling. They turned a couple of corners, and eventually came to a cheap-looking modern door.

Mr. Creal took some keys out of his pocket and turned to look at Nick.

"Nicholas Dane," he said, with a wry little smile. "Mrs. Batts was telling me about you."

Nick nodded.

"Batty Batts," said Mr. Creal. Nick watched him closely but didn't respond. It sounded friendly, but how did he know it wasn't a trap?

Mr. Creal shook his head and smiled his bright little smile. "Right, Dane," he said. "Where we stand here, it's Meadow

Hill Assessment Centre for wayward boys. Behind that door, it's my flat. On this side," he said, nodding at the floor, "I'm Mr. Creal or sir, and you are Dane. Not Nicholas, not Nick— just Dane. But!" He lifted a finger in the air and raised his eyebrows. "Behind that door, two steps away, you turn suddenly into good old Nick again. As for me, I'll tell you my name when we get there. Deal?"

"Yes, sir," said Nick, cautiously.

Mr. Creal smiled again, put the key in the door, and led the way inside.

It was a house, it was a home—it was the real thing. There was carpet on the floor, a settee, armchairs, books, a TV. One thing that struck Nick after only a week in care was how so much of it was covered in cloth. The chairs, the floor, the lights. Nick stood there staring at it. It looked weird. It looked . . . normal.

The tall man held out his hand. "Tony Creal. Pleased to meet you," he said. Nick stood there, oozing blood and spit, and stared at the proffered hand. Mr. Creal raised his eyebrows and nodded. "Go on," he said encouragingly. "It's not a trick. Promise."

Nick took the hand and shook it. "Nick Dane," he said.

"Fantastic! Right." Mr. Creal spread his arms. "Here we are. Make yourself at home. What'll it be, Nick? Tea, cocoa? Coffee, cola? Well?"

"Cola? Thank you. Sir," suggested Nick, still not sure he wasn't being lured into some awful trap.

Mr. Creal held up a finger. "In here, my name's Tony. Just Tony. Remember! OK?"

Nick looked at the man standing in front of him, smiling brightly, with his perky manner and bright eyes. He looked nice, but he wasn't sure his mouth would form the word *Tony*.

Mr. Creal laughed. "You'll get used to it. Right, you have a look around while I get some coffee on." He made for the kitchen, but paused at the door. "Put some music on," he said. "The tapes are over there." He nodded to a corner and went through to the kitchen.

Nick looked around him, aware that he was dirty, bloody, and unpleasant in this clean place. He limped over to the music cabinet. There was a shelf with rows of albums and tapes, all arranged alphabetically. On top of the music center itself was another stack of tapes that looked familiar. Nick picked one up, turned it over. It was his. He looked at the ones in the stack. They were his, too.

Mr. Creal came back into the room carrying a steaming mug and a glass of Coke. "Mrs Batts asked me to look after them. Not much use leaving them back in your old place— it's going back to the council, I'm afraid. I can look after them for you. Don't worry, I'll keep them safe. At least you can listen to them from time to time up here. Do you want to put one on?"

Nick shook his head. "No, sir . . ." he mumbled; then he remembered he was supposed to be calling the man Tony, and paused in a fright, thinking he was going to get punished.

Mr. Creal looked at him and put down the drinks. He put both hands on Nick's shoulders and guided him to a sofa and made him sit down. "Not easy, is it?" he asked, sitting down next to him. "These places . . ." He waved his hand at the window and Meadow Hill in general. "Underfunded, badly staffed, used as a dumping ground for all the dregs society can dig up. We're all ghosts and orphans here, Nick. But it won't go on forever and there are things I can do to help make life a little easier in the meantime. Now . . ." He reached over and got the Coke. "Drink this. First thing is to get you sorted out. Then we can think what we can do to make life a little better."

Mr. Creal went back into the kitchen and came back with a plate of chocolate biscuits, which they shared. He didn't ask Nick to speak much at that point, just talked to him about his own day, what he'd been doing—a story about the toilets not flushing, and it turned out to be some lad whose mum had brought him in a cake and he'd hidden it in the cistern in a plastic bag from the other lads, but the bag leaked, of course, and every time anyone flushed, the loo filled up with what looked like the most disgusting dirty water. Gradually, Nick began to relax.

"How's your day been, then, Nick?" asked Mr. Creal quietly.

Nick shrugged, as if he was going to do a typical teenage "Dunno." But he wasn't going to get away with that here. Slowly at first, but then more and more quickly, out it all came. The fights, the beatings, the violence . . . over and over and over again.

"It's illegal, isn't it? Mr. Toms, I mean . . ." asked Nick.

Tony Creal pulled a face. "In theory. But these places, Nick. Once you get sent here, people just forget about you. The police are just pleased to have you lot off the streets, they're not going to help you out. As far as they're concerned, the kids who come here are the scum of the earth—the criminals of tomorrow. And very often, they're right." He nodded. "You need to be careful. There's some very unpleasant people here. Unfortunately, some of them are on the staff." He leaned back and roared with laughter at his own joke.

As they talked, Mr. Creal was glancing at Nick and smiling to himself. Finally he began to laugh. "Tell you what, come and have a look at this." He took him by the arm and led him into the bathroom, where he stood him in front of the mirror.

"Look at that," he said.

Nick looked. In the mirror there was the most amazing-looking beast. His nose was bleeding, his eyes were swollen, his face was black with dirt, half red, and half blue with bruises. His lips were fat, there was blood in his mouth—he looked like . . .

"You look like you've spent a few months being interrogated by the IRA," said Mr. Creal. "Tell me, where does it hurt the most? No, don't tell me—your backside."

Nick smiled weakly. Mr. Creal bent over the bath to put the plug in and turned the water on.

"I'd get you to show it to me, but I don't suppose you want to show me your arse at this point, do you?" He stood up, wiping his hands and laughing. Nick giggled, slightly hysterically, just from the sound of a staff member at Meadow Hill speaking like that.

"When was the last time you had a good soak?" he asked.

Nick shook his head. He couldn't even remember. Mr. Creal took down a bottle from the windowsill and tipped it in. The water began to foam.

"You have a good soak while I rustle up something to eat. OK? Go on, in you get."

He closed the door and left him to it. Nick got his clothes off and gently let himself down into the bath. The hot water stung his cuts and bruises, but he settled back into the foam, let out a long sigh, and closed his eyes. Ahh . . . bliss. He wondered if he ought to take this break from the violence by thinking about his mother, but he couldn't. The water was just too warm . . . it was sheer ecstasy . . .

When he opened his eyes again, Tony Creal was standing by the bath with some clothes over his arm.

"I thought you'd drowned, you didn't answer," he said. He put the clothes on a chair. "These are yours—I've got a few of them from Mrs. Batts. Food's ready. I've put your old clothes in the wash. Come on, it'll get cold."

Nick spent the rest of the afternoon at the flat. Mr. Creal patched him up himself, dabbing his various wounds with iodine, claiming he'd done first aid and was better than the home nurse, anyway, who was a sweet thing but had no training. He fed him steak and oven chips and ice cream and Coke, put him in front of the telly, and let him sleep for an hour after lunch.

He woke him up at three with a sandwich in time to get back—"Or Mr. Toms will put in a complaint and we'll both get into trouble." Nick ate his sandwich, drank some milk, and then Mr. Creal sat him down to give him the lowdown.

"What we need to do, Nick, is get you out of here," he said. Mrs. Batts, apparently, had been trying to get in touch with his family in Australia. She'd managed to find his grandmother, Muriel's mother, but she'd made it very clear she didn't want anything to do with him.

"I haven't seen her for twenty years. Why should I want to look after her brat?" she'd said.

The only other family was the great-uncle at Maggie's Pies. Mrs. Batts had written a letter, which had apparently been forwarded. They were awaiting a personal response.

"That'd be all right," said Mr. Creal. "Maggie's Pies are everywhere. You'd be rich."

Nick didn't think that was very likely. "What about Jenny?" he asked. "She wanted me to live with her." He'd been thinking a lot about that. It had seemed awful at first. Now, the thought of staying with Jenny was sweet heaven.

Mr. Creal nodded. "Mrs. Hayes didn't do herself any favors when she invited Mrs. Batts for dinner. But she's a canny lady, Mrs. Batts, and she realizes it may have been a case of trying too hard rather than not enough. Leaving you with Mrs. Hayes didn't seem like a good option at first, but Mrs. Batts is beginning to think it might be the right thing to do after all. Mrs. Hayes—Jenny—is on the phone all the time, apparently, trying to get you back. But these things take time. You're in the system now. It's not like she's related to you. There are procedures, forms, all sorts of things. Committees. It's not up to any one person. Mrs. Hayes is going through the procedures, but it will take time. And Nick—I have to be honest—there's no guarantee that she'll succeed."

Nick looked so glum, Mr. Creal put his hand gently on his back. "But that doesn't mean to say it won't happen, just . . . well, don't pin all your hopes on it. What we *can* do is arrange a visit. We don't have visits on site but you could go to stay with her for a weekend, perhaps. Would that be good?"

Nick was unable to speak. He nodded his head.

"You know the system for visits?"

Nick did. It was a points system. Three points, you could go home one weekend a month. Six points, two weekends a month. Nine, three weekends, and if you got full marks, twelve, you could go home every weekend. Nick, of course, had none.

"I'd be minus if Toms had his way," he complained.

Mr. Creal nodded grimly. "Right, well, I'm giving you three points right now, so if you can hang on to those, you know you have a visit in three weeks. It's the best I can do. If I give away too much, Mr. Toms will complain to Mr. James, and then I'm in trouble. Mr. James might think of it as favoritism, and he doesn't encourage that. Quite rightly, I think. Still. Better than nothing, I suppose."

Three weeks seemed an awfully long way off. "I'll be dead by then," croaked Nick. Mr. Creal laughed and told him so long as he had his sense of humor, there was hope.

"I know you shouldn't be in here, Nick," he went on. "I'm going to do my best, but you have to understand that there's a limit to what I can do. Mr. Toms is your house tutor. I can overrule him as deputy head, but not all the time, and discipline in his house is up to him. It's a shame I was away when you arrived or I might have been able to swing it for you to go to one of the better masters. It's because you turned up with a black eye. Mr. James always puts the fighters in with Mr. Toms. But one thing—have you heard of the Flat List?"

Nick hadn't, and Mr. Creal explained. It was a plan of his own to give some boys "the chance to see a bit of ordinary home life," as he put it.

"It's for some of the more sensitive boys who might benefit from it," he said. "The head is right behind it, so the likes of Toms can't do anything about it, however much they hate it."

Three or four times a week, Mr. Creal pinned a list of names to the notice board in the school. The boys named came to his flat in the evening after dinner to watch TV, play games, chat, listen to music, and generally relax.

"I don't let just anyone in here," said Mr. Creal. "Most of them would just take advantage. But I think you're different from the others, Nick. Now, I'm not promising anything— you've got yourself a bad name very quickly, and I can't give treats to one of Mr. Toms's lads if he thinks you don't deserve it. The fights have to stop. I know, I know—it's not your fault, but that's the way it is. You see that? Good lad! You stay out of trouble and I can be a good friend, as you can see. I just need your cooperation."

Nick didn't see how he could avoid getting picked on, but he agreed to try. But now it was getting late. Soon, the crocodile would be forming outside the school. It was time to go back to hell.

Mr. Creal led him to the door. Nick looked around the flat before he left.

"It's the only place fit for humans," he said.

Tony Creal looked at him in surprise. "You're a bright lad, aren't you?" He laughed. "Fit for humans—very good. Very good." Chuckling, he led him to the door and opened it. He pulled a face.

"Back to the farmyard, Nick. I'm sorry," he said. "Hang on, though . . . I'm forgetting. Wait here . . ."

He went back into the room and came out a moment later with a bag full of goodies—chocolates, sweets, a packet of ciggies. Nick looked at him and smiled. Now he knew where Oliver got his stuff from.

"Thanks," said Nick. It had been great. He took a breath and walked back out of the world and into the home.

8
DAVEY O'BRIAN

Nick was terrified that the Morrises were going to go for him again, especially since Creal had had them flogged until the blood ran.

"He don't look the sort to do that," said Nick to Oliver a few days later.

"He doesn't do it," said Oliver. "He hands them over to Harvey to do it."

Mr. Harvey turned out to be another of the house tutors. Oliver pointed him out a while later—a tall, gangly man, with a dully bald head and eyes as black as beetles, dressed in a skinny teddy-boy–type suit.

"He don't look like much," said Nick. It was true—Harvey was long but thin. He didn't look as if he could do as much damage as Toms, for instance, who was tubby, but strong.

"Look at his arms," said Oliver. Nick saw what he meant at once. Harvey's arms were really long. When he used the cane, he curled his arm back around behind his head like a piece of rubber hose and spun on his heels as he brought it down. The wounds were like whiplash.

"Blood on the first stroke. No one wants it from the Chimp," said Oliver.

"Bloody hell," said Nick.

Despite such a thrashing, the Morrises didn't take it out on him anymore; they seemed to feel they'd done what they had to. God knows it was enough. He ached from head to foot for days after. A couple of them threatened him, just to make sure he didn't try it on with Steven again, but that was it.

Perhaps it was the influence of Mr. Creal, perhaps it was just that Nick had fought his way to a standstill, but the fights began to slacken off as well. He knew which lads to avoid, and the other lads knew whether to avoid him. He'd made his mark and found his place. Life got easier. And then something else good happened. During the shower after football one day, for the first time since he arrived, Nick spotted a face he knew.

It was Davey O'Brian.

The O'Brians were a huge clan. Davey's mum and her two sisters and all their twenty-odd kids lived in three houses all within a stone's throw of one another in Poplar Road, not far from where Nick used to live. There were ten kids in Davey's house alone, living there in a pack with their mum and dad. His parents were both more or less permanently drunk, and as a result, the kids were in and out of care all the time. They rarely went to school, but spent most days wandering around Manchester, begging and stealing. Every evening, they went back home and handed over their takings to their mum and dad, who would pocket the lot, take it down to the pub, and drink it all away, while the kids went back out the door look-ing for their tea. They'd steal anything and were banned from every shop within a mile, but the odd thing was, it never occurred to them to steal from their mum and dad. It was partly fear, but they were a loyal crew, the O'Brians, even though everyone in the family hit everyone else, from their dad hitting their mum down to the smallest tot kicking sleeping cats off the wall, if she could get close enough.

Nick and Davey had been friends, on and off. Davey was a little older, but shorter than Nick, who was on the short side himself, and just as ready to stand up for himself if need be. Together, they made quite a team.

Davey was always coming and going—now Nick knew where. They'd always got on well. Davey knew every scam going and Nick was always up for trouble. Since he hadn't been banned from all the local shops and no one knew him for a thief, Nick had been very useful to Davey. He'd keep a shopkeeper busy while Davey crept in on his hands and knees and filled his shirt with biscuits, cakes, and other eat-ables. It had been fun—until he got caught, and his mum found out what he'd been doing. He'd been grounded for a week, and when he got out, he wasn't so keen on the stealing. For Davey it was a matter of getting himself fed, but for Nick it just wasn't really worth it. But they hung around together from time to time anyway, just because they were mates.

In the showers, they caught each other's eye but Davey was talking to someone else, and Nick didn't break in. It felt a bit odd, being naked, introducing yourself, and anyway, he'd been long enough at Meadow Hill to know that just that could lead to a fight, unless you were one of the in-crowd, which he certainly wasn't.

He didn't have much of a chance to talk to Davey that day. Everyone seemed to know Davey and he was always surrounded. In the end, Nick got fed up waiting for a chance to get Davey on his own, so he went up when Davey was talking to a couple of other lads during break at school the next day.

"So this is where you keep disappearin' to," Nick said.

Davey smiled sheepishly and shrugged. He was aware that some of the other lads were watching him, and they weren't too impressed.

"Nah, I got sent here from Boulders." Boulders was another home. "I kept runnin' off. I'm high security, me." He laughed at his own feats. Nick smiled.

One of the other boys butted in. "What's it to you, anyway?" he wanted to know.

"Leave him, Case," said Davey. "I know 'im, he's OK." Davey nodded at the other two lads, who nodded back. Nick nodded familiarly at them too. They didn't look as though they liked it, but they left it alone anyway.

"So what are you doing in 'ere?" Davey wanted to know. "You with yer posh mum and all?"

"She's not posh," began Nick, but she obviously was to Davey. So he just told him.

"She died. Heroin overdose."

"No! 'Eroin? 'Er?"

"I never knew aught about it. Came home one day and the place was full of the Social. I don't 'ave any family—so that was that."

"Bloody hell. Who'd have thought that? Nick Dane in care. Bloody hell. And I'm in 'ere because me sister died, I reckon."

Nick remembered Davey's sister Kath. The O'Brians were a close lot, but Davey and Kath were inseparable. She was a few years younger than him and Nick, but she was up for anything they did. It drove Davey mad, because he was the one who'd get into trouble if she got caught. She never did, though. She could dodge so fast, no one could touch her. Sometimes, she'd do her robbing by dashing into a shop, running along the aisles grabbing what she wanted, and then back out, with people falling over themselves and one another trying to catch her, and no one ever able to lay a finger on her.

She had a terrific imagination as well, always thinking things up.

"Look at that man over there," she'd say, picking someone out in the park or walking down the street. "'E's a murderer, I know it!"

"You can't know that, Kath," Davey would say.

"I can feel it comin' out of him. Look at his eyes. How cool he is. You'd never know, would you, just to meet him on't street?"

By the time she'd finished, Nick would feel in his bones that he was looking at a man who'd killed his own wife or his daughters or done something else terrible.

"He's looking! Run for it!" she'd yell, and they'd all go haring off down the street, squealing with laughter and fear. She had a real gift for stories, did Kath.

She died like this: there was a block of flats, Glorianna Buildings, on the way into town. Davey and Kath had discovered that if you wedged your foot in the lift doors in between floors, the safety system would kick in and the lift would stop. Then you could force the door open and climb up on top of the lift. It was easy, and not dangerous because the lift was between you and that breathless, terrible drop to the bottom of the lift shaft all the way down in the basement. The great thing was, on top of the lift there was a separate control panel. Once you switched it to override, you could use the control panel to make the lift do whatever you wanted.

"You'da loved it," said Davey. "We used to wait till someone got in and we'd trap 'em in it. You could make that lift do anythin'—take 'em to the wrong floor, stop 'em in between floors, all sorts. They went barmy! We got one old dear in there for over an hour. She had to pee on the floor. Then when we let her out, someone else came in and she wrinkled up her nose and blamed it on the kids. Old bag, serve her right."

But one day, disaster had struck. Davey was in the lift and Kath was up on top, so he never saw what happened. Something hit her—the counterweights maybe, he never knew. By the time he looked up, saw blood coming down from the roof of the lift, lovely little Kath was already dead.

Just to make it worse, his parents blamed him. "When me dad came home he leathered the life out of me. I was in a home within a week. And I bin in ever since."

"Maybe they just thought your mum wasn't lookin' after you properly again."

Nick regretted it as soon as he said it, because he didn't want anyone to criticize his mum—why should Davey? But Davey just shrugged.

"Nah," he said. "If that was the case, we'da all gone. This time, it was just me."

Nick was appalled. Another disaster! But at least it made him feel that he wasn't alone.

"How long 'ave you been in?"

"Months. They keep moving me around. See, Davey O'Brian's too much for 'em!" Davey grinned and stabbed his thumb into his chest. "I keep doing a runner, dun I?"

"Back home," said Nick.

"Yeah, back 'ome. Me brothers and sisters sneak me into their rooms, and I've got this friend who puts me up—in return for a few jobs." Davey winked and smiled. He always had a scam going.

"So how come you're back in?" asked Nick.

"Same as always," said Davey, his face falling. "As soon as me dad finds out I'm back, the bastard shops me to the cops! Me own dad!" He looked at Nick with wide eyes, as if he couldn't believe his bad luck. "And 'e's the one as always says how we O'Brians have to stick together. Yeah, us O'Brians, so long as it's not me." Davey looked so stricken, Nick laughed at him, and Davey grinned again. "He's a bastard," he said fondly.

"You gonna do a runner here, too?" asked Nick.

"You bet. But it's a bummer here. Really hard to bunk off here."

"How come?"

"Prefects, innit? And fences. It's a bloody prison camp, 'ere."

It was true. Since he had nowhere to run to, Nick hadn't thought about it, but he had noticed the perimeter fence, which was a good eight feet high, curving in at the top. You could get over it if you had the time, but the prefects were everywhere. Whenever any kid was out of the building, at games, on the way to and from school, the prefects were there watching. During the day they patrolled the fence, at night you were locked in. At Meadow Hill, you never got to spend any time on your own.

"And the staff are all the most evil bastards on earth," pointed out Davey.

"What about Creal?" said Nick. "He seems OK."

"Creal? It's him that keeps you in here. Him and his little bum boys. Creal's a bastard. They're all bastards."

Nick laughed. That was Davey all over. If you were in authority, you were a bastard. It didn't matter if you were a cop, a social worker, the mayor, the prime minister, or the local vicar. You were on the wrong side—bastard, by default.

"Creal's been all right to me," he said.

"'As he?" said Davey. He looked at Nick and shrugged. "That's your business. A few treats, innit? Don't forget, though, he might wear a suit and a tie, but he's still a copper, and remember . . . ?"

Nick remembered—the O'Brian chant. They repeated it together.

"All coppers are bast-ards!"

The two boys laughed, and around them, other lads looked

around and laughed too. Nick was delighted. He and Davey— and Davey knew everyone. Things couldn't help but get better now, surely?

He was right—things were getting better at last. The first week had been hell, but now Nick was becoming part of a little group. It was the first stroke of luck he'd had for ages, and he had another one straight on its heels. Davey got put in with Toms too, and they ended up in the same dorm.

Getting a new friend never meant to Nick that he had to get rid of the old ones. Davey wasn't all that keen on Oliver at first, and really accepted him only because Nick was immovable on the subject. Oliver was too much of a goody-goody, always being given treats and favors. Mr. Creal in particular seemed to like him—he was on the Flat List almost all the time, and he was always being given time off school or sports or whatever.

Davey moaned at Nick and teased Oliver about being Creal's little bum boy same as everyone else, but he had to accept it.

"I'd do the same for you," said Nick, and they knew it was true. That was Nick—once you were one of his you stayed one of his, even if you were teacher's little pet. Davey got used to it. He was always keeping an eye out for his young brothers and sisters back home, and he accepted Oliver like that—as someone to be taken care of. But he never liked him much.

9
THE FLAT LIST

So life at Meadow Hill went on—early mornings, school-ing that didn't even try to teach you anything, sports every evening, getting beaten, trying to avoid getting beaten. Every now and then Nick saw Mr. Creal around and about the grounds, but didn't have a chance to talk to him. A couple of weeks went by, and he was beginning to think he'd been forgotten about when Davey came running up to him in the corridor at school.

"Nick, you're on the list! How 'bout that?"

Nick ran to see. There he was, on the Flat List, just as Mr. Creal had promised, for that same evening—him, Oliver, and another lad called Mick Flynn.

"You bum boy!" exclaimed Davey.

Nick couldn't believe his luck. "Wonder why he picked me?"

Davey laughed. "I can't think. Hey, see if you can nick some ciggies for me, will you?" Davey loved smoking. He'd do almost anything for a cigarette.

Nick went around the rest of the day on a high, he was looking forward to it so much. He couldn't help laughing at himself, though. He was getting a night of TV and ginger-snaps, and he thought he was going to heaven. How things had changed . . .

That evening, Nick, together with Oliver and Mick, changed into their regulation pajamas early and put on the tatty dressing gowns hanging up among the lockers for expeditions of this kind. Nick thought they might at least have let them wear their own clothes. He moaned about it to Oliver as they gathered outside before making their way to the big house, but Oliver just shrugged.

"Creal says," he muttered.

All in all, Oliver didn't seem all that pleased that Nick was coming along on one of his nice evenings out, which was a bit mean, Nick thought. Didn't want to share, he supposed. But he couldn't blame the younger boy all that much, even though it irritated him. Sharing out his sweets was about the only bit of leverage Oliver had at Meadow Hill.

Andrews took them across on the short journey from the house to Mr. Creal's flat.

"What's up, we can find our own way," said Nick.

"Yeah, over the fence," said Andrews. He jerked his head and led the way across the grass. They followed, looking like a row of ghosts from an old comic book in their baggy jim-jams and tatty brown gowns. Mr. Creal met them at the main door, dismissed the prefect, and led them up the stairs himself.

He paused outside the door. "You look like a trio of scarecrows!" he said, smiling at them. The boys laughed a little self-consciously. Tony Creal lifted the key in the air. "Right—you can say good-bye to the pleasures of Meadow Hill for a little while. Just remember—what goes on out here is what goes on out here, and what goes on in there is what goes on in there. And never the two may meet!"

He winked, opened the door, and waved them in.

There was a plate of sandwiches on the coffee table, plates of nuts and crisps, and a cake on a table in the kitchen for later. It was friendly and ordinary, that was all. And it was great.

"*The Sweeney*'s on, we can watch that in a bit," said Mr. Creal. "Now get stuck in, you lot! Stretch or starve, that's the way it is here."

They chatted, watched telly, munched nuts, ate sandwiches and cake, then played cards for a while. One moment they were being treated like hardened criminals, the next, they were sitting on the sofa eating Battenberg cake and sipping hot cocoa. Surreal—but wonderful. Already, Mr. Creal had found a way into Nick's heart. He was his only link to what he thought of as real life, his only lifeline back to the real world.

After *The Sweeney*, Mr. Creal offered around some cigarettes. Flynn, who claimed that he smoked forty a day on the outside, sucked them down like mother's milk, and Mr. Creal had to get another packet before the evening was out. Then they drank some beer. Flynn got overexcited and started gulping it down and had to be put on rations, but it was all friendly. They all got tipsy and soon everyone was telling crap jokes and roaring with laughter.

The only fly in the ointment was Oliver, who wasn't his normal jokey self, but looked sulky and uncomfortable. Mr. Creal did his best to cheer him up, but he just sat there all night looking glum, until Nick was sick of him. It was his only chance in weeks to relax and enjoy ordinary things—why should Oliver spoil it by being miserable?

"Don't mind him," said Mr. Creal. "Everyone gets like that in this place from time to time. Even me," he added, slightly wistfully.

"Yeah, but not tonight," said Nick.

Mr. Creal pulled a face. "You can't always tell when sadness is going to call, can you, though?"

It sounded too deep for a night off. There was time enough to be miserable some other time, as far as Nick was concerned. But he found out that Mr. Creal was right soon enough. It happened at the end of the evening, when they were playing some music. Nick had put on some of his own tapes, but it wasn't one of his that got to him. It was ABBA—"Dancing Queen," a stupid song.

It was Christmas back home, after the presents had been opened around the tree. He'd bought his mum ABBA's album and this song was on it. She was doing a daft drunken dance around the sitting room to it, with an enormous vodka and orange in her hand, warbling, "Dancing queen . . . only seventeen," while he wailed at her to stop that terrible racket.

He'd got a Walkman that year. He remembered opening it around the tree and his mum stooping to kiss him . . .

The memory took him completely unawares and pierced him like a glass shard. Stricken with horror and loss, he panicked. Standing there in the middle of the room with the music blaring away, caught between the past and present . . . He felt tears coming up and he knew he was going to blub.

"Nick, we need some more Coke." Mr. Creal was at his shoulder, guiding him out of the room. "Oliver, that's too loud, turn it down, please. Nick, you come with me . . ."

He guided Nick out of the room, down the corridor, and into the bathroom. "I know," he said. He patted him on the shoulder, and suddenly, in a fit of sympathy, hugged him tight to his chest. He held him a moment while Nick struggled with his tears, then stepped out of the room and left him to his grief.

Ten minutes later, when Nick came in with a washed face and another four-pack of Coke, no one seemed to notice that he'd gone. He nodded to Mr. Creal in thanks and sat back down. He smiled weakly at Oliver. It was true. Sorrow could catch you when you least expected it—even when you were in the middle of a good time. Sometimes, perhaps, especially when you were in the middle of a good time.

By ten thirty, Mr. Creal was getting anxious.

"Mr. Toms," he said, pulling a face. "I keep telling him that I'll make sure you lads are safely in bed without him having to worry about it, but he still insists I get you back by ten thirty, and look—it's already gone past. Sorry, Nick, you'll have to go. Oliver, Mr. Albans on your side doesn't mind so much, you can stay a bit longer if you like. And you, Flynn. Nick, can I trust you to make your own way?"

Nick pulled a face. No one ever wanted to be first to bed. Just his luck to get Toms! But he went quietly enough. As soon as the word *bed* was mentioned he started yawning. He wasn't used to staying up so late. Mr. Creal saw him to the door.

"I can trust you to find your own way back? Of course I can!" He smiled. Before Nick went, he slipped one of those paper bags into his hand.

"Safe home," he said. He waited outside as Nick went down the stairs and waved as he turned the corner out of sight.

Nick made his way back to the dorm as promised. The prefects were waiting downstairs for him and waved him up.

"Bum boy," jeered Andrews as he climbed the stairs. Nick didn't care. He'd had the best night for years—that's how it felt. He had a bagful of goodies—he'd give a packet of cigs to Davey tomorrow. He got into bed, sighed deeply, pulled the covers up to his chin, and fell fast asleep.

10
THE PIE MAN

Jenny was devastated. Nick, in a home! How could she have allowed such a thing to happen? What would Muriel have said? It was awful. Depressing. So depressing that she'd taken to her bed for a day. But then she pulled herself together as always, and hauled herself up. Pausing only to dump Ray forever, she rang Mrs. Batts to arrange a visit, and discovered to her amazement and horror that visits were forbidden.

"Forbidden? You're joking. What is it, a prison camp or what?"

"Now, Mrs. Hayes, Meadow Hill is a hiiighly respected instituution," insisted Mrs. Batts irritably. The visiting rule was unfortunate. Strictly speaking, Meadow Hill was an assessment center rather than a home, and in theory, no one was supposed to stay there for more than a few weeks before they were moved on. The no-visits rule was originally put in place after a number of ugly scenes, when parents had traveled miles only to find that their child had already been moved on. For them, only good behavior could give them a glimpse of their families.

Mrs. Batts explained the rules as patiently as she could, but Jenny's outrage was undiminished.

"I shall complain to the head. I'll complain to everyone I can. My MP," she snarled. "He's just been orphaned, Mrs. Batts, and you're telling me I can't go and see him?"

"Visiting points are given out easily enough. He'll be out for the weekend if he behaves himself."

But, of course, the weeks went by, and no Nick, no news of Nick, not even a letter from Nick. Jenny made it her business to start badgering Mrs. Batts for news, for a visit, and for another chance to have him live with her.

"One-paarent families aren't reeeally the thing, Mrs. Hayes, are they?" she'd pointed out. "There's no man in them."

"I'd have thought that was an advantage," muttered Jenny.

"In your case, maybe that's true," muttered Mrs. Batts back.

"But I'm the only thing Nick has," insisted Jenny. "Don't you think it's harsh for a boy to lose his mother and then everything else along with it? Home, school, his friends, everything? At least here he could attend school like he used to."

"*When* he used to," said Mrs. Batts. But Jenny had made a good point. Mrs Batts's admiration of Meadow Hill was really an admiration of Mr. Creal, who was both a formidable organizer and had the charm of an angel—he put her in a flutter every time she saw him. And so dedicated to those boys! He hardly ever had a word to say against them, even the most vicious of them. And the hours he put in—his own time, too. No effort was too much for Tony Creal where those boys were concerned.

It was difficult to believe that Jenny had anything to compete with that level of commitment. But she was persistent, you had to give her that. And the point about school and friends was well put.

Single-parent families very rarely got permission to take on a difficult teenager like Nick, but it wasn't impossible. Mrs. Batts could have fast-tracked it if necessary. The trouble was, Nick was getting on so well at Meadow Hill.

"He's taken to it like a duck to water," Mr. Creal had told her. "Really—the routines seem to be just the thing for him. Working hard at school. I'm thinking of sending him out to do some O levels. I'm sure he's capable of them if he keeps this up."

Well—what could you say with a recommendation like that? Mrs. Batts didn't say an outright no to Jenny, but things were going to have to take a severe nosedive for her to ignore that kind of advice.

Friends and well-wishers were one thing—family was another. Family had rights, and responsibilities, too, and Mrs. Batts was putting most of her efforts into that direction. It cost a fortune to provide for the facilities at Meadow Hill. Why should the state pay for Nick when half his family was swimming in gravy? The trail in Australia had gone cold, but she was having better luck with the pie side, as she was now calling that part of the investigation.

"Those bloody pies!" exclaimed Mrs. Batts to her colleagues at work. And "I'll get to the bottom of those pies if it kills me." Or "Pies, pies, pies, my life is full of pies." She had a sense of humor, did Mrs. Batts.

It turned out that Muriel was the illegitimate daughter of one Daniel Moberley—Dirty Dan, as Mrs. Batts called him. Dirty Dan had kept up an affair with Muriel's mother Sarah for years, right up until his wife found out about it when she discovered a dry cleaning bill for a number of very posh frocks that she knew nothing about. Dirty Dan had been faced with an ultimatum—ditch the bitch or face an expensive divorce.

Sarah had responded to the crisis by getting pregnant. Dan, however, was more interested in money than love, or children. The wife was the cheaper option, and he'd gone for her, leaving Sarah with a baby and little else. Not only that, but the first two weeks of motherhood convinced her conclusively that she didn't like children. Very soon she came to blame the round-eyed little girl, watching her like a goblin from the cot, for all her woes. She lived in a state of perpetual warfare with her daughter for fourteen years, until Muriel ran away from home. Sarah jumped at the first chance of escape, and immigrated to Australia, where she continued to live without any apparent interest in her offspring from that day forward.

But the Moberley family was still in existence, although they no longer had anything to do with Maggie's Pies and Pasties. Nick's grandfather was dead, but a couple of his children still lived on, including Michael Moberley, who had inherited the family pie firm and subsequently sold it, living off the proceeds very nicely ever since.

When Mrs. Batts rang Michael Moberley he was not in any way astonished to discover that he had relatives that he knew nothing about—he knew his long-deceased father better than that—but he was curious. One of his father's old lovers in Australia? No surprise at all. A nephew from his dead half-niece in Manchester? He never knew.

He was disgusted that the grandmother wanted nothing to do with the boy, though.

"Not even a letter from her for the lad? Not a phone call?" he asked.

"Nothing, Mr. Moberley. She was really quite short with me on the phone as well."

"Sounds as if she would have made a good match for Dad. He was a right bastard, too."

Michael told Mrs. Batts he'd have a think about it and put down the phone. He felt sorry for the boy whose mother had died and who, if not for a chance of birth, might have been safely and comfortably educated at the expensive private schools his own children had gone to when they were growing up.

He made a few phone calls. Discussed it with his own children and talked to his brother, John, about it. John took after their dad and he didn't give a toss. Michael's children agreed with him, however. No one wanted to actually take the boy on—Michael was too old for that sort of thing and the rest of them had busy lives, children of their own, careers and so on—but they were well off, and there was no reason why they couldn't help out in some other way . . . slowly introduce this boy into the family, maybe. Even schooling, perhaps? Something, anyway.

As a result, Michael Moberley rang Mrs. Batts a few days

later to arrange a trip to Meadow Hill, to discuss the case with Mr. Creal, the deputy there, and see exactly what he might be able to do.

Tony Creal was in his office ready for the appointment, and watched out the window as Michael Moberley pulled up the drive and into the weedy car park. A bloody big Rover. Money. The door opened and out stepped the man himself, dressed in a well-cut suit. More money! Amazing. Money didn't often put in an appearance at Meadow Hill. Who'd have thought it? Mr. Creal watched closely as a middle-aged man strolled across the tarmac to the grand front steps and lightly walked up them. Funny, how well-dressed people always seemed to stroll. Or they strode purposefully. It probably wasn't possible to shamble in a good suit. The cloth wouldn't let you.

Sitting opposite him a few minutes later, Mr. Creal wasn't so sure what to make of his visitor. He'd been thinking businessman, loads of money, tailored suits and shirts, expensive cologne, trim, right-wing, help-those-who-help-themselves sort of thing. Here was the posh suit all right, but it wasn't one of those city things, and the man in it was unshaven. There was no whiff of expensive cologne, no shiny handmade shoes, just a pair of trainers. Michael Moberley was smoking roll-ups, his hair was around his collar, but he still, somehow, managed to carry an air of being expensively brushed, dressed, washed, and powdered since the day he fell gracefully from his mother's womb onto the fine linen sheets that had enwrapped his life from that day to this.

"Record producer. Packed in the pies years ago. I even went vegetarian for a while."

"I quite like a pie myself," admitted Mr. Creal.

"Take my advice, never eat a pie unless you see what goes in it. Or a sausage. I was in pies for years; I never eat pies. I won't eat arseholes."

"Ew," said Mr. Creal. "I'd have thought that would make them rather chewy. Maggie's Pies are always very juicy."

"Even an arsehole gets tender if you boil it long enough," observed Michael Moberley; and they both giggled like schoolboys.

"Everyone's going to get ill from eating that sort of stuff one day, trust me," said Michael Moberley. "I got out of pies originally because—well, to be honest, when I was young, all my mates were making pop records, designing the inside of classy London houses, and shagging starlets, and what was I doing? Trying to source the cheapest arseholes in Europe. Recycled meat slurry doesn't have quite the same ring to it as rock 'n' roll, does it?"

"The music business? Is it lucrative?"

"More lucrative than pies," admitted Michael Moberley. "Even I made money and I'm crap, really. You can make a huge amount of money, but people do know how to spend it. I was one of those. A spender. But you know what? At least mass-market music isn't as bad for you as mass-market food. I'd listen to my pop songs but I was never prepared to eat my own pies. Which tells its own tale. Now then." He crossed his legs and got down to business. "I believe you have a nephew of mine here?"

"Nicholas Dane." Mr. Creal shuffled the papers on his desk. "Mrs. Batts says you knew nothing about him at all?"

"Amazing, isn't it? Not a thing. Do you mind?" Michael Moberley took out a tin and started to roll himself a cigarette. A habit acquired from a misspent youth smoking wacky baccy, as Mr. Creal rightly supposed. "My dad was a bit of a lad. Well, that's one way of putting it. A bit of a bastard would be another. He gave my mum a hell of a time—and me. Hard but fair, I think they call it, but I can't see what's fair about having the shit knocked out of you by someone twice your size. He whacked me and he whacked my mum and I expect he whacked this lad's granny as well, when she was with him."

Michael lit his cigarette. "So I'm curious," he said, speaking around it and squinting over the smoke. "I used to think, you know, how unlucky I was when I was younger. With a dad like mine. But now look. Easy job, easy money. And this poor kid, he could so easily have been where I am and instead what's he got? Mum on drugs dies in a council flat, no one to look after him, bang, disappeared into care. Shit, isn't it? So, basically, I'd like to do what I can for him. I dunno. A boarding school, perhaps? Decent education? I can't give him a family, it's too late for that. But I can help out with money, maybe . . . what do you think, Mr. Creal?"

"Tony, please."

"OK, Tony. Now, how do you think he'd get on with that?"

Tony Creal stuck out his lip thoughtfully. "That's very generous of you," he said. "It's not often that people want to take an interest in what is, after all, a fairly distant relative."

"I'm his uncle Michael, innit?" said Michael, and he grinned. Tony Creal noticed how he had a couple of teeth missing to the side, one above, one below. Drugs, he thought. He'd read somewhere that they were bad for the teeth and gums.

"To tell you the truth, though," he went on, "I'm not sure how well Nick would adapt to boarding school—unless you can find a very special one, of course."

"What, special needs, is he?" asked Michael Moberley, frowning and tapping his ash onto the carpet.

"Well, if you could call needing to have a few heads at hand to kick the teeth out of, yes."

The smile vanished. "Teeth? You what?"

"I'll be quite honest with you. The boys who come here aren't all that great to start with. They've all had pretty hard lives at home. Then they get sent here, taken away from everything they know—often for very good reasons, but still. Mr. James, our head, likes to offer them a second chance, but the kind of problems we get—well, sometimes it's hard for the boys to leave their pasts behind. That's certainly been the case with Nick."

"In what way?"

"I'd have to say, he's been very difficult. He's been in a fight pretty nearly every day since he got here."

"Well—but doesn't that mean he's in trouble? Psychologically, I mean?"

"That's one way of looking at it," said Mr. Creal grimly. "As I say, you're very generous. You could say that about any form of violence. Your father, for instance."

Michael Moberley looked away. "I suppose you could."

"But I'm beating around the bush. Make no mistake about it—Nick is a very violent young man indeed. Some of these boys are like land mines, I promise you. I'd be just a little bit careful about putting him in with some well-bred young fellows just at the moment."

"What? Do you think he's . . . what?"

"Dangerous? To be frank, it'd be like putting a fox among the chickens. Not that he'd be there long—he'd be off as soon as the going got tough, I daresay. As I say, unless you can find somewhere very special. And somewhere to put him up when he gets expelled or runs away."

"Do you think he would?"

"I know he would."

"Couldn't he come back here?"

"This is a state institution for people with nowhere else to go. If you take him out, he would be your responsibility from then on."

"Bloody hell!"

"Nicholas is a dangerous young man, but we also think of him as being very highly at risk. They run away, fall in with some very bad types. Drugs, violence. We run a tough ship here, but not like out there." Tony Creal jerked his head at the window. "There's a lot of nasty types preying on young lads like Nick. If he ran away, you have to ask yourself what's in store for him. Murder, prostitution, addiction . . ."

"I wasn't expecting this," exclaimed Michael Moberley. "A boarding school's out of the question, then?"

"At the moment, yes. Of course, things might change. We're

equipped to deal with these kinds of problems at Meadow Hill. The staff here have a great deal of experience in dealing with difficult young people."

"Dear oh dear, I wasn't expecting this."

Mr. Creal cast a grim look at the man opposite him. "When you look at the boys in here, Mr. Moberley, you see the murderers and rapists of tomorrow."

"Jesus."

"Nick's been in the Secure Unit . . . let me see . . ." Mr. Creal flicked through the pages of an imaginary report. "Five times. One lad suffered two broken ribs at the hands of our Nick. Another had to spend two days in hospital having treatment to his eye—there was a chance he'd lose the sight in one of them."

"My God!"

"There are signs that he's just beginning to settle down. I have to say, though, Mr. Moberley, I really don't think it would be wise to uproot him again just now."

Michael Moberley sat there chewing his nail, caught between wanting to be good, and wanting to avoid the kind of trouble the monster Tony Creal was describing would bring to his pleasant life.

"So he's a complete thug, then, you say?"

"Really, yes. You'd never guess it to look at him, though," added Mr. Creal, looking up. "Butter wouldn't melt. Thing is, he always picks on the smaller kids, so there's never a bruise on our Nick. Quite a bit of native cunning, in that sense, anyway."

"A bully? Well, sod that, then." Agitated, the other man got up and paced up and down. "It sounds like a total disaster. I've no idea what to do now!"

"A suggestion?"

"Please!"

"Leave him here for now. This is the best place for him. We have an enlightened head and, unlike a lot of institutions, we do have programs to try and help boys like Nick. He is showing signs of responding. Firmness and kindness, firmness and kindness." Mr. Creal nodded firmly and kindly. "He's had very little of either in his life. They do pay off. Who knows? Maybe in a year or so, he'll be more able to accept the sort of help you can offer him."

"Right. Well, that sounds about right. So—can I see him before I go?"

Mr. Creal shook his head firmly. "We never allow visits on site—I know, I know," he said, seeing an objection forming. "It's the rules, and there are very sound reasons for it. Anyway, he's in the Secure Unit right now. It would totally undermine our regime. If he improves, maybe he can come and see you."

"Dunno about that," muttered Michael Moberley. "We'll see. Nothing I can do in the meantime?"

"Well, if I can speak on behalf of the home for a moment . . ."

"Please do."

"Nick is one of those lads who could do with a few extras. Counseling, perhaps, to help him come to terms with the loss of his mother? Since you ask . . . If you can provide funds, a little toward that sort of thing . . ."

"I can do funds. It's about all I can do, but I can do funds." Relieved that things were getting down to the simple matter of cash, Michael reached for his checkbook. "To the home?"

"To the home would do fine. Write it out to Meadow Hill Special Funds. That's the account we use for special needs provision. Which is what this is."

Michael Moberley bent his head and scribbled.

Mr. Creal beamed. "This will be a great help, I promise you."

Their business over, the two men parted. Mr. Creal showed the other down to his car and watched him drive off. "A boarding school—for one of these lads! What a bloody waste of money," thought Mr. Creal as he made his way back upstairs. Back in his office, he looked at the check. Five hundred! Fantastic. He'd pay it in this afternoon. Meadow Hill Special Funds strikes again, he thought. He'd opened the account years ago for occasions just like this one, which cropped up from time to time. It had nothing to do with the home, of course, and there was only ever one beneficiary—himself.

He picked up the phone and rang social services.

"Mrs. Batts? Tony Creal . . ."

"Tony, how are you?"

"All the better for hearing your dulcet tones, my dear . . ."

"Sooo—what was the pie man like?"

"Rich, vain, and selfish. One of those pop music types. Probably on drugs. The thing he was most concerned about was whether the newspapers might find out."

"Oh. Some sort of celebrity, is he?"

"I've never heard of him, but he seemed to think he is. But as far as the Dane boy is concerned, we can forget it. He wasn't remotely interested. Wouldn't even offer any cash help—although he has enough of it, if the car he was driving was anything to go by."

"What a shaaame!"

"It's how the rich stay rich, Mrs. Batts."

"I suppose. And how is Nick? Still doing well?"

"Very much so. He's made friends, he's working hard in school. I'm really very happy with him."

"Is he due a visit? That friend of his mother, Jenny Hayes, is making herself a riiight paaain about it."

"Not yet. To be honest, there's still the odd fight. Don't say anything about that to her, though, I don't want to spoil his chances for later on. But he does have a very short fuse and when he blows, he blows. I believe you've seen some of it yourself."

"At dinner, yes, but I don't really think he can be held . . ."

"Not responsible, no, after what he's been through. But maybe you haven't seen him at his worst. I've seen him inflict some real damage on other boys quite a lot smaller than himself. I'll be honest with you, Mary, it's not so much Nick that worries me—it's Mrs. Hayes's own children I'd be more concerned about."

"Oh dear!"

"I know—it's very much at odds with how he is most of the time, so I don't think it's a permanent thing—but I wouldn't risk it, not yet."

"A bully."

"I'm afraid so."

"Well. You're always soo good about those boys! Proogress is being maade, that's the main thing. You will keep me up to daate on this case, won't you, Mr. Creal?"

"I'll certainly do that," he promised. And after a few more pleasantries, he put down the phone.

Job done.

11
PAYBACK

By the end of June, Nick had been in Meadow Hill a little under two months and he still hadn't managed to earn enough points to get him a home visit. Mr. Creal kept giving them to him, but then Toms kept taking them away.

"Rivalry," Mr. Creal told him. "Toms is just a big kid. He knows you're one of my favorites, he knows I'd stop him if he beat you too much, so he takes your points away instead."

The whole points system was used as a form of punishment, and they never went to the kids who needed them. Oliver had the full twelve, had had them forever, but he had nowhere to go. He hadn't heard from his mum in years. Even the Christmas and birthday presents had dried up by this time.

"I've got somewhere to go and they won't give me any," Nick moaned.

"Yeah, fancy that," said Davey.

Davey had six points, but no one expected him to keep them for long.

"They know I won't come back if they let me out of this

misery pit," he said. "You watch—they'll all be gone as soon as the visit comes near. They always find some excuse."

Davey had been planning his breakout since he arrived, but he'd run off so many times, the prefects never let him out of their sight. He was forever trying to get Nick to come with him, but Nick was still putting his faith in "dear Tony Creal," as the other boys called him. Every time he saw him, Mr. Creal gave increasingly optimistic reports of how close he was to getting a visit, or how Jenny was working her way through the procedures.

Davey was unimpressed.

"You don't wanna believe a word he says," he said.

But Nick didn't see it like that. As far as he was concerned, Mr. Creal was the only decent thing in the place.

"What about you, Oliver?" he asked.

Oliver shrugged. "He likes you, so why would he send you away?" he said, which Nick thought was a bit odd. As if Mr. Creal was going to go to such a load of trouble just to keep some kid near him!

Davey shook his head. "Jobs for the boys, innit? I reckon they get paid per head in these places, that's why no one ever gets out. You wanna come with me, mate, I tell you," he said. But Nick shook his head.

"I can't anyway. I'm like Oliver, I got nowhere to go," he said bitterly. A visit was one thing, but after that, what? Why hadn't Jenny got in touch with him? She seemed to have abandoned him altogether. His only hope was that something was going on behind the scenes. Until he lost all hope of that, he wasn't going to go outside the law. That would make him . . .

"An outlaw." Davey grinned. "Great!"

Nick shook his head.

"A twat," he said.

"I could sort you out," insisted Davey. "Friend of mine."

"Creal says . . ."

"Creal!" Davey rolled his eyes. "You'll wait forever if you wait for dear Tony Creal. Yer better trusting my mate Sunshine."

"Who's he?"

"Someone who'll give us a few jobs and a roof if we do all right. Hey, what about you, Oliver? You gonna do a runner with me?"

Oliver, who had been sitting on his haunches at their feet, looked up and shook his head with a smile. It was a tease, really. Everybody knew Oliver was going nowhere.

"I'm no good at running."

"Yeah." Davey contemplated him for a moment. What on earth would Oliver do on the outside? He couldn't run, got into a panic at the slightest thing. No good for nicking . . .

"I know," said Davey. "We could dress you up as a girl and put ribbons in yer 'air and flog you off to lorry drivers as underage totty. They'd pay a bloody fortune."

"Right," said Nick. "Then when they find out he's not a girl, it's too late!"

They all laughed. Oliver got up and did an impression of a girl giving the come-on, and they hooted some more. "Or I could flog my arse down Canal Street, where the homos hang out. I'd make more money like that. Make a fortune, I reckon."

"We could be your pimps," said Nick, and they laughed again.

"Seriously, though, mate," said Davey to Nick. "You don't wanna wait for dear Tony. You might be in his good books now, but it won't last. Someone else'll come along, wern they, Oliver?"

Oliver nodded grimly.

"He's been OK so far," said Nick.

"So long as you give him what he wants," said Davey.

Nick shrugged. It sounded like the usual O'Brian anti-everyone-in-charge stuff. Nothing more was said.

Later that week, Nick's name appeared for the second time on the Flat List.

"That's twice in two weeks," said Davey. "Don't forget my ciggies, will you?"

Nick grinned happily.

"You look pleased," said Davey wryly.

"Why should I mind?" asked Nick in surprise. It was a treat. Who minded being given treats?

"I wouldn't have thought you were the sort," said Davey, pulling a face.

"He's not so bad," said Nick. "You lot! Just because he's in charge don't make him bad."

Davey shrugged. "If you can get some cigarettes out of it, I don't care what you get up to."

It was the same crew as before—Flynn, Oliver, and Nick. They met outside, as before, and were led up by Andrews as before, in their dressing gowns, to be met at the door by Mr. Creal. There wasn't much on the box this time, so they watched videos and ate nuts and crisps. Afterward, Mr. Creal got out a pack of cards and they all sat around the coffee table drinking cola and playing games—brag and pontoon for pennies that Mr. Creal doled out from a big jar. Flynn wanted to teach them all poker and got very pleased with himself and self-important, teaching them all how to play. It was fun. The stacks of pennies went up or down, and for a short while you could forget where you were.

At the end of the evening, Nick was expecting to get sent back early again but this time it was Oliver and Flynn who got sent home, and him who was asked to stay on.

"You don't mind, Nick, do you?" said Mr. Creal. "We need to have a little chat."

That sounded ominous. Nick sat on the sofa and watched Flynn and Oliver leave. As Oliver closed the door behind him, he cast an odd look back at Nick. Their eyes locked for a moment, then Oliver looked up to Mr. Creal, who was standing behind him. For a second, Nick was certain that something had passed between the two of them, but then the moment was past. The door closed.

"Just the two of us, now, eh?" Mr. Creal came and sat down next to Nick on the sofa. His voice sounded funny. He sat a bit too close. Nick could smell him, his aftershave, the soap powder on his clothes, the cigarettes on his breath. He shuffled slightly farther away.

Mr. Creal took out a cigarette and lit it. He seemed nervous.

"I've got some news, Nick," he said softly. "And I'm sorry to say it ain't good." He pulled a face.

"Sir?" asked Nick.

"I had a call from a relative of yours. The pie side, Mrs. Batts called them. They're not interested. I know, it's disappointing, but it can't come as any surprise." He paused and shrugged sympathetically. "Sorry, Nick. It's no go."

"But what about Jenny . . . Mrs. Hayes? She's a better bet, isn't she?"

Mr. Creal held his cigarette close to his face and bent his head to one side, in a pained gesture. "That's not going too well, either, Nick. You know Mrs. Batts had her doubts about it. No man in the house, you see. Those two kids she has got are a handful, apparently. The little boy has problems . . . the girl is very willful, getting into trouble at school. In the end, the social services have said no."

Nick stared up at him. "But you said . . ."

"I know! I know. I had such high hopes. I didn't know those kids were so unstable. Mrs. Batts put in her report just yesterday. She turned her down."

Nick couldn't believe it. Somehow, he'd managed to convince himself that this couldn't be. Here at Meadow Hill, the rest of his childhood? No mother, no one to care for him? Just stuck here until he was sixteen, getting knocked around and then booted out on the street?

"Then I'm . . . I'm just here, then," he said.

Mr. Creal put his arm over Nick's shoulder. "I know, Nick," he said. "It's hard. But this is your home now."

It was a bitter blow. Nick felt like crying. "But that's not fair," he mumbled, trying hard to keep the tears out of his voice. "Isn't there anywhere else?"

Mr. Creal suddenly took him in his arms and buried his own head on the boy's chest, as if overcome with sympathy.

"Nick, Nick, don't," he whispered. "You have to be brave." It was uncomfortable and really quite weird being so close, but Nick wasn't thinking about that. He was thinking that his whole life had just ended. He was thinking about his mother. She was the one who was supposed to look after him. Where was she now that he needed her? She'd gone, gone forever, and left him like this.

His tears were winning the struggle, and he wiped his eyes on his dressing gown, which was awkward, because Mr. Creal was holding his head tightly against his chest, his eyes closed, shaking his head and patting his knee. Now he raised his head and pushed Nick's head against his own shoulder.

"It needn't be so bad," he murmured. "I can help. You can come up here from time to time. It's nice up here, isn't it? You like it here?"

"Yes, but . . ."

"It's not home, I know. I wish I could offer more. All I can do is offer a few nights, a few games of cards. A little comfort . . ."

As he spoke, Nick was aware of Mr. Creal's hand on his leg, creeping upward.

"Don't cry. It breaks my heart when you cry," murmured Mr. Creal. And now there was no mistaking it. His hand moved higher still. Nick froze. Was he . . . ?

Mr. Creal's grip on his head tightened sharply. He leaned over, pressing his whole body against Nick's, swung his leg over his and moved his hand up the final few inches, so that he was cupping him in his hand. Nick was so shocked he froze.

"Don't be scared, Nick. We all need a little comfort from time to time," said Mr. Creal. And his fingers began working.

"Sir, sir," whimpered Nick, horrified, frightened, and embarrassed all at once. He tried to push the hand away, but Mr. Creal's grip on his head tightened until it hurt. Short of fighting him off, there was nothing to be done.

"Don't fight me, Nick. Ah, there we are," crooned Mr. Creal. The fingers worked more urgently. "See? It's nice," he murmured as, against his own will, Nick began to stiffen. "Oh, yes, you've done this before, I bet. Haven't you?" he hissed in his ear. "There . . . there. Yes . . ."

It was horrible, but Nick felt utterly unable to help himself. Mr. Creal bent his head against him, pinned his legs down tight, and worked him in his hand. It was all over soon enough. Mr. Creal released him and wiped his hand on a tissue from his pocket. He told Nick to go into the bathroom to clean up, which he did in a kind of daze. Words began to move in his head. "Sucking up to an old bloke like that," Davey had said. Did he know? Was this what he meant?

Nick stared at himself in the mirror. He could have fought back, he could have kicked the old sicko in the crotch and run for it. Instead, he'd just let him. How weak he was! He might as well have given him permission.

His reflection looked sickly at him in the glass, as if he were a stranger to himself.

Back in the front room, Mr. Creal had changed into his own dressing gown, and for a horrible moment Nick thought he was going to ask him to return the favor. But that wasn't coming—not yet, anyway.

"I'm off to my bed and you're off to yours," said Mr. Creal. "Here—look. For you!" On the coffee table was an outsize bag full of goodies—cigarettes, chocolate—more than Nick had ever seen. "You've been a good lad tonight, you took it very well," said Mr. Creal. "I hope you appreciate what I've done for you. We all need a little comfort, Nick. I can see you're a boy who knows what side his bread's buttered on, eh?" He laughed and clapped Nick on the back. Then he stepped forward and took him in a hug. His lips brushed Nick's cheek.

"Good night, sweetheart," he murmured. He pushed Nick gently toward the door and patted his bum behind him as he left. "I'm just looking forward to my turn, now," he said.

Then Nick was on the stairs and on his way down. At the bottom, Andrews was waiting to escort him back. He wasn't being trusted tonight.

As they walked back across the dark grounds, Nick heard a slight noise behind him. It was a dark night, everything was in shadow, but he could just make out a slight figure bobbing along toward the main door and up the steps. It was Oliver, going back to the flat to say his own good nights to dear Tony Creal.

"Pair a sick little bum boys, you are," remarked Andrews casually as he led Nick into the house. Nick turned and made his way back to the dorm. In bed, he lay very still. He'd been tricked, used, and humiliated. He felt filthy with it. Sleep was a long time coming that night, but before it did, his shame turned to something else. Hatred. A deep, poisonous loathing began to possess him. Curiously, though, the target wasn't Mr. Creal. It was himself.

12
REVENGE

Nick awoke suddenly the next morning. His eyes snapped open. Everyone was still asleep. He lay there very still, not moving.

A minute later, the whistle blew.

"Oi—where's my ciggies, then, eh?" said a voice. It was Davey, loud and happy.

Nick bent down and pulled out the bag of goodies that he'd flung there last night. He'd been paid, he realized.

"Here." He chucked a pack of twenty Embassy over and turned away.

"What's up with you?" asked Davey.

Nick turned to glare at him and half opened his mouth. But what could he say? That he'd let Creal wank him off? His feelings were so strong and so complicated, there were no words to describe them.

"Balls," he growled, and turned away.

Anger is a strange snake. You don't always know where it comes from and you never know where it will strike. It wasn't the fact that Mr. Creal had touched him up and made him come that made Nick so angry. It was because he'd been

tricked. Creal had pretended to be his friend. He'd lied, promised, bullied, and bribed to get Nick to the point where he'd
let him have his way, quite against Nick's own will. He
didn't understand how it had been done, but he knew it had
been done, and the worst thing about it was the way it made
him hate himself.

Tony Creal had been playing this game for years and he
knew exactly how to get what he wanted. He'd taken Nick at
his lowest ebb—let him suffer and then thrown him a line
and fondled him while pulling it in. Somehow, his manner
suggested, Nick had brought it on himself. And he'd enjoyed
it, too, hadn't he? It felt good. That's the kind of person he
was—a dirty little whore.

But already as he made his way downstairs with the other
boys, Nick's self-hatred had begun to morph into another
stage of betrayal—rage. A slow-burning but steadily increasing fury had begun slowly to possess him. Once again, the
target was not the source of his betrayal. In his mind, it began
to seem to him that Creal had not been alone in his seduc-
tion. Oliver had helped plan the whole thing—sharing out
the goody bag, being his friend, all so that Mr. Creal could
get him where he wanted.

Oliver knew all along. Why hadn't he said? Because he
was in cahoots with dear old Tony Creal.

But of course that wasn't the real reason Nick was angry
with Oliver. The real reason was simpler, and darker. Nick
needed someone to take it out on. Mr. Creal was big, and
Oliver was small. That was all it was.

———

All that day Nick lived in a daze of despair and rage. His hopes had been raised only in order that they might be dashed. It seemed that there was no escape unless he turned into what Oliver had become—Creal's little creature, running his errands, doing him favors—and God knows what that might entail, although he could guess what was coming next.

Davey, of course, knew exactly what had been going on at the flat the whole time. He'd done the same thing himself from to time when he was smaller. He wouldn't do it these days, but he'd never blame anyone for getting a few ciggies or sweets just by letting some old geezer squeeze his parts. So long as it didn't go too far, turning into a little pet like Oliver, where was the harm? His only reaction had been surprise that Nick seemed to like Creal despite it—but who was he to worry about that, either?

Davey knew at once something had changed. All during lessons, Nick sat and seethed, hardly able to speak to anyone. When he did speak, it was in a flash of fury.

Davey had seen it before, he knew what was coming. Nick was suddenly at the end of his tether and he was going to blow. It was just a question of where, and when, and to whom.

During lunch, he grabbed hold of his friend and gave him a shake. "What's up with you? What 'appened last night? You're going to get yourself done the way you're going on."

Nick pushed him away and turned his acid gaze onto him. "Do you know what goes on up there?" he demanded.

Davey's eyes slid away. Everyone knew what went on up there—it was just that no one ever talked about it. Then he looked back. "It's none a my business what you get up to up there," he hissed, angry himself. He calmed himself down. "Nick, no one's going to blame you for getting a few extras the easy way. You got to get what you can in a place like this."

Nick snorted in disgust and pushed him away. Davey followed after him but the conversation was over. He couldn't get any more sense out of him.

It was just a matter of time.

Davey knew about the sex, but he had no inkling of the kind of manipulation Creal used, or how it made you feel. Oliver, however, knew only too well. He saw the way Nick was looking at him. He knew what lay behind those dark eyes, and he kept his distance.

If only he had managed to stay out of the way for a day or two until Nick cooled down, all might have been well. But it didn't work out that way.

It was early evening—sports. Oliver, as usual, was let off and spent the time weeding in the vegetable garden. Meanwhile, out on the pitch, Nick was in trouble again. The prefects were like a pack of hyenas, they could see that he was in danger of losing it and had started to pick on him—teasing him, winding him up, tackling him harder than they should have. The games master, Mr. Peake, took pity on him and gave him a break by telling him to go and bring some spare footballs from the cupboard. As Nick trudged over to the sports hall he saw a small blond figure running around and going into the loo. Nick glanced over his shoulder to check that no one was following him, speeded up his step, and followed Oliver inside.

It was as silent as the grave in the toilets—Oliver must have spotted him. Nick pressed the doors to the cubicles until he found the locked one, then he went and stood on the toilet next door. There, sitting on the loo, looking up at him, face as white as a sheet, was . . .

"Oliver," said Nick.

He went around and pushed the door through with his shoulder and stood there watching coldly while Oliver pulled up his pants and began to weep. Curiously, so did Nick.

"You never told me."

"I thought you knew."

"You bloody little liar." Nick clenched his hands and stepped closer.

"Let me through," squealed Oliver. He tried to push past, but Nick had his shirt in his hand. He shoved him up against the wall.

"And all the time he was giving it to you right up the arse, wasn't he? You little bum boy. Wasn't he?"

Oliver didn't answer. He buried his head in his arms and began to wail.

"Mercy!" he begged. "Mercy! Mercy . . ."

"You like it, don't you?" rasped Nick. "That's it—you like it. Don't you? Don't you?" Oliver knew the time had come. Desperately, he tried to push Nick aside and escape, but he was cornered. Nick simply flung him to the floor, and lifted his boot.

Afterward, he remembered very little of it—just a picture in his mind of the little body curled up on the floor and him kicking and stamping, kicking and stamping. He remembered how, once or twice, he had bent down to shake his victim, almost as if he were trying to waken him from his nightmare. Fortunately for both of them, Oliver's cries for help had been heard and the other lads arrived to drag him off. It wasn't easy. Nick was possessed. All the sadness, the injustice, the violence, the abuse, everything that had happened to him since the day his mother died translated itself into this terrible attack on the wrong person. Twice he broke away and went back to relaunch his attack on the injured boy.

It wasn't until the prefects turned up that they got him off. Andrews and another lad hauled him backward and dealt him a vicious blow to the kidney that had him heaving on the floor. They dragged him out of the cubicle. They were furious. Nick had done Oliver some real damage and they'd get into serious trouble for letting it happen on their watch. They got him down among the urinals and gave him a serious kicking themselves, but Nick hardly felt a thing. All he could hear was what Oliver had been shouting at him over and over again during the attack . . .

"I don't like it!" he had screamed. "I don't like it, I don't like it, I don't like it," over and over again.

If there was one thing Mr. James loathed, it was bullying. There were plenty of fights at Meadow Hill, but this was a particularly severe one. A much bigger boy on a younger, smaller one. Reports had to be made. The Dane lad could very easily be charged with assault, if not actual bodily harm—if not grievous bodily harm itself. His victim had been so badly beaten that he'd had to be sent away to the local hospital. More reports! The whole thing was incredible.

If there was one thing Mr. James loathed more than bullying, it was reports of bullying. That sort of thing was absolutely not to be tolerated at Meadow Hill.

The boy had been left to stew in the Secure Unit for a day and a half and fed on bread and water. His only visitor had been Mr. Creal—if anyone could make him see sense, it was Tony Creal, but according to him the villain was far from repentant. He had actually threatened Mr. Creal himself. Unbelievable. Not with violence, of course—he wasn't so stupid as to attack someone bigger than he was—but with accusations.

"He's a cunning one," Tony Creal had said. "He's saying he's sorry about the boy he beat, young Oliver Brown, but I can't say I see much sign of real repentance. He's just parroting, I'm afraid. But he did threaten to accuse the staff of just about every form of abuse under the sun if we took things any further."

"Abuse? Here? What sort of thing?" asked Mr. James. He shook his head.

"Violence from the staff. Sexual abuse as well, he says . . ."

"Of course he's just making it all up."

"Yes, of course. But he could cause a lot of trouble. You know how mud sticks."

"And the police sniffing about as well," groaned Mr. James. They'd had the devil's own job convincing the police that they could deal with the little beast on the premises. The inspector on the case had made it clear that if anything like that level of ferocity occurred again, charges would have to be made.

"That's the very last thing we want," agreed Tony Creal. "Think of the paperwork . . . Think of the damage to our reputation . . ."

Mr. James peered through his glasses at the lad standing in front of him. It made him feel physically sick to look at him—although, to be fair, it might have been because he'd neglected to take any of his wife's little blue pills this morning. The Valium was a steadfast friend in difficult days, but it did make him feel woozy, something he couldn't afford when he had police inspectors, social service directors, and God knows who else insisting on speaking to him on the phone.

Nicholas Dane. A monstrous villain, if ever he saw one. The lad was bruised from head to foot from all the fighting he'd been involved in over the past few weeks. Almost every day, apparently. Mr. James snorted in disgust. He wasn't even any good at fighting, judging from the color of his face.

"How much younger than him was his victim?" he asked the two prefects who were standing guard over the monster.

"Two years. Just a little lad, sir," replied Andrews, who of course was only too delighted to help Nick into trouble. "A good lad, too, sir. Everyone likes Oliver."

It was such a lie, Nick turned to stare at him, but Mr. James swallowed it whole.

"What an incredible thug you are, Dane!" he exclaimed. "A bully and a coward. Vile, Dane. You are vile. You've let me down, you've let the home down. You've let this lad Brown down and, most of all, you've let yourself down. Look at you," he went on. "You were offered a fresh start and now this. And this lad was a friend of yours, I believe. Incredible." He looked at the report on his desk and shook his head. The Brown boy had a cracked rib and a broken nose, among other things. What a mess! Mr. James glanced anxiously at the two prefects standing behind the miscreant. He hoped they would be enough to hold him if he went berserk again. Animals like this—you never knew when they would go mad . . .

Now what? The Brown boy had gone to hospital. A report. The Secure Unit. Another report. The police. A third report! Reports everywhere—and guess who had to read them? Mr. James. Three reports for one incident. It was paperwork gone mad. At least he could rely on his friend and right-hand man, Tony Creal, to write the wretched things. The reputation of the whole home would suffer because of this one nasty little thug.

"Well?" he demanded. "What have you got to say for yourself?"

He didn't expect any reply. Boys like this could hardly speak, usually. The most you could expect was an adenoidal grunting. But to his surprise, this one proved to be positively voluble—but in the most disagreeable way.

"I want to make some complaints, sir."

"Complaints?" Mr. James gazed around the room in amazement, as if he expected the furniture itself to recoil in horror. He'd been warned this would happen, but he was still amazed. After what he'd done, the boy wanted to complain! The barefaced cheek of it took his breath away.

"I know what I did was wrong, sir, but there are things going on you should know about."

"This is unbelievable. What sort of things?" demanded Mr. James, before he could stop himself.

"Mr. Toms, sir. He beats the boys up with his fists. And he uses a snooker cue. Surely that's wrong, sir. And Mr. Creal . . ."

"Mr. Creal? You have a complaint about Mr. Creal? Have you any idea how respected that man is?"

"He—he tried to interfere with me, sir."

"What?"

"He tried . . ."

"I heard you!" roared Mr. James. He looked anxiously again at the boys standing behind him. This would never do.

"Not only that, sir, but he has boys stay in his flat late at night, when we should all be in bed, sir. That's not right, is it, sir?"

"Right. I've heard enough of this . . ."

"But can't I make a complaint, sir . . . ?"

"You have just committed one of the most violent acts that this home has ever witnessed. If you were a few years older, you'd undoubtedly go to prison for it. Do you really think anyone is going to believe your pathetic attempts to cover yourself? Making unfounded accusations against a respected member of staff . . . a man renowned for his care and dedication . . . a man always ready to do his bit . . . a man . . ." Mr. James, who had been working himself up into a greater and greater frenzy of anger as he spoke, finally choked on his own rage and ground to a guttural stop. He took a sip of water from the glass before him to try and calm himself down.

He'd heard these kinds of allegations before. Dirt-slinging for the sake of it. It was always the lowest little toads who tried it on, and it was always the most respected members of staff they tried it on with.

"Now is not the time for complaints by you, Dane," he announced. "Now is the time of punishment. When your punishment is over, you can complain then, if you like. But let me tell you this. Let me tell you! No amount of complaining will alter your situation one bit—not one little bit. All you're doing is making things worse for yourself. I have no doubt these ridiculous complaints will fade away, just as they always have done with other boys before you. And I warn you, Dane—listen to me! I warn you! If you do see fit to try and carry this nasty little plan of yours through, trying to soil the reputation of a man who has done nothing but good to you and hundreds of other boys who have passed through this establishment, it won't be him who'll suffer. Your horrible little story will show itself for what it is—a web of deceit and lies, designed with no other purpose in mind but to take the heat off your own precious person. It won't work—do you hear me, Dane? It. Won't. Work. In fact, it will go very ill for you. I do not take kindly to unsubstantiated complaint-making. Understand?"

Nick understood perfectly.

"As for now, you will be kept in the Secure Unit for two weeks. You will be flogged. I shall recommend twelve. You will be flogged again the next day and the next, for three days. If at the end of that period you wish to complain, you may ask to see me. And let me tell you this. If you do ask to see me, you'd better have some very good evidence. Do you understand the word? Proof. Facts. Because if you don't, what's going to happen to you now will be like a bloody picnic. Understood!"

The boy said nothing more, just gaped at him like the village idiot. Mr. James waved a hand and the two prefects marched him out.

Disgraceful. That was where you got from being kind to that sort. He'd spoken to Mr. Creal about having boys up to his flat before now. Some nasty little piece of work was always going to try and make capital out of his kindness. But to a man like Creal, whose commitment Mr. James could only wonder at, such accusations were part and parcel of the job.

He'd have a word with him about this one, just so he'd know what he was up against.

Mr. James sighed shakily as the door closed and put his head in his hands. He could so much be doing without this just now. His wife was currently going through one of her good spells—that's what she called them, anyway. He didn't. Admittedly she got up and did things—but the things she did! Loud music, dancing in the garden, running about in her dressing gown, barely covered up. The boys loved it, of course. They thought it wonderful that the headmaster had a madwoman for a wife.

Mr. James walked to the window and waited until the prefects had led the criminal away before he went downstairs and made the short walk through the grounds to his house, to see how his wife was getting on. As he turned the corner through the gate, he gave a gasp of horror and broke into a fat, wobbly run. There, for all to see, perched on the front-room windowsill wearing only her nightie, was Janice. She'd opened the top light to the window and was trying to wave at someone to attract his attention. As he wobbled up the path, Mr. James caught sight of Ben Jollie, the groundsman, standing by his barrow and staring at her blankly.

"I'll take care of it, Jollie," he gasped. Thank God he'd remembered to lock her in. The last time he'd forgotten to lock up, he came back to find her wandering around the grounds in her nightie, telling the boys she was being kept prisoner against her will and encouraging them to escape with her.

It looked as though she was trying to climb out through the window. As soon as she saw him running toward her, she jumped down from the sill and ran off into the house. He fumbled with the front door key, and burst in to find her standing behind the door with the poker in her hand.

"Stay away from me," she commanded.

"Janice, darling, what's wrong?" he pleaded.

"I demand my freedom," she quavered in a high treble. "You've kept me prisoner here too long. It has to end. Bill, I demand you let me call the police and give me back my freedom."

Mr. James sighed. She'd been withholding her medication again. She did it from time to time, hid her pills under her tongue, spat them out when he wasn't looking. And then went mad.

He sighed, locked the door carefully behind him, and, with one eye on the poker trembling in her hand, began the long business of talking her down.

13
THE SECURE UNIT

The Secure Unit was a small room on the ground floor at the back of the main house, with one small barred window high in the wall, well out of reach, a thick door, and a tiled floor. It was furnished with a bed, a table, and a chair. Its supposed purpose was to house very vulnerable children, those at high risk of absconding and running away into dangerous circumstances. In practice, at Meadow Hill the Secure Unit was for punishment. Inmates were kept there in solitary confinement.

From time to time, a visiting social worker expressed surprise that the Secure Unit looked so much like a prison cell, and it had to be pointed out that the kind of boys who had to be put in there (for their own good) were often so violent that even the table and chair had to be replaced on a regular basis. That much was true. After a week or so of nothing to do and no one to speak to (unless, as in Nick's case, it was being taken out to be beaten once a day), most boys went through a period of rage before depression took over. At some point, they'd almost always turn their attention to the only things around that they could affect in any way at all—the table and chair, which they duly smashed to match-wood with every sign of satisfaction.

In defense of Mr. James and other members of staff, it should be said that most of them lacked the imagination to work out for themselves what havoc days on end with no company and nothing to do can work on the human psyche. They would have been most surprised to know the levels of despair felt by the boys left in that place for any length of time, although they knew enough to make sure there were no belts, ropes, or knives left in the room. Self-harm and even suicide were known things at Meadow Hill, particularly in the Secure Unit. No one wanted any repeat cases.

For a while, being locked away was something of a relief to Nick. Away from the constant threat of violence that hung over the home, he was able to relax for the first time in weeks, to think things over and even find a little time to mourn his mother. It was only after a few days that the long, black night of the soul settled on him.

The first day, waiting for his interview with Mr. James, was positively helpful. He'd soon come to his senses. First and foremost, he was horrified at what he'd done to Oliver. He'd completely lost control. It had been a moment of the blackest despair, the removal of all his hopes and the realiza-tion that he had been fooled. The one man he thought of as his protector was anything but. Even so, it was no excuse, and by the time he was marched in for his interview with Mr. James, Nick was in no doubt that the main culprit, alongside himself, was Tony Creal.

He knew exactly what he was going to say to the headmaster. By the time he left, he knew that he was wasting his time. No one was ever going to listen to a word he told them about this matter ever again. It was then, sitting alone in his cell, waiting day after day for the terrible beatings the head had ordered for him, that the darkest despair began to descend.

The first thing Mr. James did, once he got Janice dosed and in bed and his own head full of Valium and gin, was to ring up his deputy and tell him what the boy had said.

"You need to be more careful, Tony," he slurred. "Taking little shits like this one into your flat with no one else there. It's asking for it. Of course they're going to try and use it."

"I'm not thinking of myself," said Mr. Creal.

"I know, I know. The trouble is, Tony, the trouble is—well. You're just not a very good judge of character."

Tony Creal put down the telephone and sat for a while at his desk. His feelings at that point were more hurt than angry. Perhaps the head was right. Of course he was aware that he had manipulated the situation, but somehow, he always managed to convince himself that it was all for the best. Jenny Hayes was no sort of a carer—Mrs. Batts had said so herself. As for the pie man, with his druggie history and his money, the boy would have been in the most terrible danger. Money and drugs were a lethal combination to boys of his kind; it would have been tantamount to abuse, letting him go off with someone like that. As for boarding school, the boy would have been a fish out of water. No good at all . . .

Meadow Hill had its faults, of course; but against the Toms and the prefects and so on, there were people with heart—Tony Creal himself, for example, taking care of you, watching out for you, getting close to you. Helping. There was nothing like a close, loving relationship to get you back on the straight and narrow, whatever age you were. Society might not share his ideas on the nature of that love—well, society was wrong. He'd helped countless boys. The fact that he shared himself with them—gave himself to them, you could say—might be unprofessional in a strict sense, but in fact there was no evidence at all that it did them any harm. None that he'd seen, anyway. On the contrary, he firmly believed that the boys he gave the most to put the most back in.

All this he had done for Nick Dane, and what was his reward? The boy had turned on him. He'd helped him, offered him comfort, put himself on the line. Trusted him. And he had been repaid with betrayal.

"What does he want?" he muttered to himself. "My whole bloody soul?"

As the day went on, his anger grew, but later it began to be mixed with pity and a certain amount of understanding. The boy was upset—it was understandable. Of course, it was unforgivable that his pain should come out in the form of violence, or that he should betray someone who wanted only to help him, to love him. But he had come to Meadow Hill much later than most of the other boys. Obviously, the idea that he was stuck there had cut deeper than Mr. Creal had believed it would.

"I should have moved more slowly," he thought. After all, the boy had lost his mother. His heart was bruised. He should have been more cautious before trying to get so close to him.

He'd have to pay Nick Dane a little visit and see what could be salvaged.

The beatings were given by Mr. Toms, so it could have been better and it could have been worse. At least it wasn't the Chimp. Three nights, three beatings. Even Mr. Toms balked after the second day at giving him another twelve, and he got only eight on the third day. The worst thing about it was, it was the only thing that happened each day. There was nothing else to think about. By the time the beatings came along, after school at five o'clock, Nick was almost ready to run out and beg for it.

Mr. Creal waited for the beatings to end before visiting him. He wanted to show him that he was still prepared to be his friend, in spite of everything. He did everything he could to make him see reason—really emptied his bag of tricks at the boy's feet. He reasoned, promised, wept, and begged. He opened his heart, but all he was able to inspire was disgust.

He was there for nearly an hour and in all that time, Nick made only one promise to him.

"I'm going to get out of here," he said. "And when I do, I'm going straight to the police."

Mr. Creal waited another few days before he went to pay Nick his second visit. Love was one thing, but only a fool sits by while his life is destroyed. To drive the message home, he took a couple of colleagues along with him. One of them,

Mr. Jameson, was the math teacher at the home's school. The other, Nick had not seen before, but Mr. Creal made sure before they left that evening that Nick knew he was a policeman.

They came in the dark of the night. The first thing Nick knew about it was when a flashlight was switched on and he awoke to see the men standing around his bed.

"Telling tales, Nick," scolded Mr. Creal, smiling and shaking his head. Someone above him leaned down and pressed his shoulders into the bed. And then the lesson began.

There are no details necessary for that night's work. There were three men in the room with him, and it was rape. Nick's ordeal lasted an hour. As the door closed behind his visitors at the end of it, Tony Creal poked his head around the door for a parting shot.

"We'll see you tomorrow, Nick," he whispered fondly.

Every night after, Nick went to sleep not knowing if this would be another night like that one. It made the nights long, you can believe that. Creal and his friends fully intended to pay Nick another visit before he was let go, but as it turned out, they never did. Over the next three days one or other of the three had some engagement or other, and the day after, Mr. James had a letter from Mrs. Batts.

She was under pressure from two fronts. First, Michael Moberley had written to her, asking to be kept informed about the boy's progress. Simply by asking, he was helping Nick. There was a wealthy eye on him, and that in itself was enough to make the social services cautious. At the same time Jenny had stepped up her pestering in an attempt to win Nick back, and the social worker had felt obliged to take the unusual step of asking Mr. James directly if Nick could be granted a home visit, just to see how things went this time.

Of course, in the light of recent events, Mr. James felt unable to grant her request—but all the same, he was alerted that people outside the home were interested in the fate of Nicholas Dane. He knew nothing of Mr. Creal's midnight visit, of course, but even so, two weeks in the Secure Unit and three doses of twelve strokes were a severe punishment indeed . . . and so Mr. James decided it was expedient to cut short Nick's punishment.

They say that rape victims divide their lives into two parts— before and after. Rape is the line that turns you from one person into another, from fearless to fearful, from relaxed to anxious, from hero to victim. The secret of recovery is to lose the fear—to stop being a victim and become yourself again.

Some people find pain sticky. They try to rub it off but it just gets on their hands. The more they wipe and scrub, the more it seems to spread, like treacle on their skin. Others cope better. They lick the sore place, and the wound shrinks and heals to a neat little scar that hurts only when they press it directly.

A lot of things can affect it. How well equipped the past has left you, for one thing.

Davey O'Brian, for example, had been abused for as long as he could remember, by his mum and dad and older brothers and sisters to start with, and then by various house tutors, teachers, policemen, and other figures who had held authority over him. It was mainly violence. Davey was a tough-looking lad, not unattractive, who moved like a terrier and was so full of energy, you could have lit a small town off him for a week if you could have found a way of wiring him up. But he didn't have Nick's good looks, and the likes of Tony Creal left him largely alone. Even so, he could have told a tale or two, if tales of that kind had been something the boys discussed.

There was one home he'd been in where the tutors used to come into the dorms to pick which boy they wanted that night, two or three times a week. Davey being Davey, he'd learned a few tricks to put them off. As a five-year-old, he already knew to save his toast crusts from breakfast, chew them up, and spit them onto his bedcovers at night, so the men would think he'd been sick and leave him alone. Or he'd pick up the piss pot from under a bed and pour it on his sheets.

"Don't touch him, he's a pissy pants," the men would say, and they'd pass on to the next bed.

Davey had his share—but he had something else: his family. Nine brothers and sisters, God knows how many cousins, aunts, and uncles. The ten children in the O'Brian crew fought like dogs among themselves but let anyone try to batter an O'Brian outside the family! You'd be torn to pieces. They had nothing in the world but one another, and they stuck together every bit as hard as they fought together.

Davey had the street, too. People knew the O'Brians for miles around and there was always someone who'd keep an eye out for the little ones and part with a jam sandwich, or take them in to bathe their wounds. It wasn't enough, of course. The prisons were going to be full of O'Brians for years to come, locked away for stealing, mugging, drinking, snorting, injecting, armed robbery, even murder in one case. But some of them got through, two or three—with a little help from their brothers and sisters, and a few sympathetic faces among the families who lived nearby.

Oliver, at the other extreme, had no one. His troubles had begun when he was raped by his mother's boyfriend when he was three years old. A neighbor who made a little extra cash as a childminder found out about it when Oliver had to go to the loo and she found bruising around his bottom. All might have been well even then had his mother reacted differently, but she had been unable to accept that her lover was a rapist.

Over the next month the rapist controlled Oliver with lies and threats—that his mother hated him and would leave him if he made her unhappy, by, for example, telling her certain secrets. But despite all his bluster and cunning the truth eventually came out when the little boy began bleeding. The boyfriend fled when Oliver's distraught mother insisted on taking him to the hospital, where the doctors confirmed repeated buggery.

It would be nice to think that repentance and atonement followed discovery, as it does in the good old story books, but as we've already seen, life's not always like that. Not just the knowledge of what had been done to her innocent, but her own part in it made the little boy hateful to his mother from that day on. She did her best, but his inability to trust her was met with increasing anger from her, until at last she became fearful of her ability to look after him and Oliver went into care for the first time.

The fact that the people who ran the homes in those days were left pretty much to their own devices didn't mean that they were all bad, but it was just Oliver's luck to go into a small home in Didsbury where the two wardens and a janitor were of the same tastes as Tony Creal. They took full advantage in enjoying the pretty little boy over the next few months. The fact that he seemed to know what was expected of him only helped them feel better about it.

"He's obviously going to turn into a homo," one of them joked. "So we might as well make the most of it before he gets there." His rapists were both staunch homophobes. Boys, in their eyes, were not the same thing as men.

As for the truth of Oliver's sexuality, who knows? Along with so much else, they'd taken that from him as well.

There followed long years of going into care, back home, into care, and back home. Some of the homes were good, some bad; but the damage had been done. Every time Oliver came back he was harder to control and more hateful to his mother and to the little sister who soon followed. Eventually, despite his mother's desperate efforts to make him love her again, he became dangerous.

What she didn't know was that he did still love her. Every night he wept for her all alone, every minute of every day he longed for her. But he could not show it anymore. If he could have told her what happened in the homes, she might have understood at last, but his abusers had cast the spell of silence on him, by making him believe that he deserved it, that he wanted it, that it was all his fault. To tell her what had happened would be to tell her what a dirty little monster he was. When he tried to utter the words, his throat swelled, his tongue turned thick, he gagged on shame and humiliation.

So, in the end, love was not enough. Her new family was suffering and she decided she could not deal with him anymore. The home visits stopped. Oliver was offered out to various foster families. He was a pretty boy, the sort of lad many mothers might want. But of course they fared no better. At the age of eleven, he was transferred to Meadow Hill, where the good Mr. Creal welcomed him with open arms, and gave him the only protection and kindness he had ever known. By the time Nick came to make friends with him he had turned into the broken little blond rag we know, with nothing to get him through other than the ability to acquiesce to anything that was asked of him, and the remains of that wicked sense of humor that had met Nick Dane on his first day.

It would be stupid to say that Nick was one of the lucky ones after what happened to him, but the fact was, however dangerous his present and however uncertain his future, he had a solid past behind him. Muriel hadn't been a great mother, but she hadn't been a bad one either. He'd had fourteen years of love and support from her, and that was fourteen years more than most of the other kids locked away at Meadow Hill. If her little trip to paradise hadn't turned out to be permanent on that fateful morning, he stood every chance of turning out pretty right. As it was, Nick Dane was a tough lad. Damage had been done, and it had gone deep, but it had been done to a healthy heart.

In the long, lonely hours and days in the Secure Unit, there was a great deal of misery and despair. Never again was Nick to feel so alone, so hopeless, or so helpless. But for the first time since his mother had died, there was remembering as well.

"Don't let the bastards get you down," Muriel used to say to him when he was having a bad time at school. And "Don't be like them." That was another Murielism. Nick was used to not listening to his mum's advice, but now, for the first time since he was small, it really seemed to have a message for him. In the long hours alone waiting for Mr. Creal to come back and pay him another little visit with his jolly friends, it sang around the vault of Nick's head over and over again.

"Don't be like them." Because the ogre has two ways of destroying you. He can eat you—or he can turn you into him. Either way, he's won. When Nick attacked Oliver, he became one of them—like Creal and Toms and Andrews and all the rest of them. He had become a bully and an abuser.

He was a rogue always, Nick Dane, but a bighearted rogue and a loyal rogue. When he attacked his friend he had broken the golden rule of his own heart. We all have our gifts; friendship was his. Without his friends, without loyalty, Nick was nothing. In his darkest hours, he saw not Tony Creal leering over him, not the arms of his attackers holding him down, but Oliver's face at the end of his boot.

"I don't like it, I don't like it!" the younger boy had cried. As if, in his heart, Nick didn't already know that. All he wanted to do when he got out was to make it up to him.

14
THE PLAN

On the seventh day Nick was escorted back to his house, walked in, and went to sit against the wall on his own. After a short pause, Davey came over and stood by him.

"All right, mate?" he said.

"All right," said Nick.

There was a pause. Davey sat down next to him.

"See anyone in there?" asked Davey.

"Creal and a couple of his mates," said Nick. He looked away and Davey looked away. Nothing more was said; and so Nick joined the ranks of the silent. It wasn't just the violence or the humiliation. Creal had made him feel dirty deep down inside. All he wanted to do now was forget—never talk, never think, only forget.

"Tell you what, though, mate," he said. "If you're still up for it, I'm ready to run."

"Too bloody right," said Davey. And that was it. They were going to take their futures into their own hands. It was just a question of deciding how, and when.

"And Oliver," said Nick.

Davey looked sideways at him. "Oliver what?"

"Oliver's coming with us."

Davey didn't even have to think about it. "You're off your twist," he said. "He was only being friends with you in the first place to help Creal get at you. You can't trust the likes of him."

Nick shrugged. In his bones, he believed that if you trust people, they repay you with trust. That was how he operated, and that was that.

It wasn't going to be easy. A long time ago, Oliver had learned not to trust people. What were friends? In his experience, they were people who wanted something. Once they got it or stopped wanting it, they stopped being friends—it was that simple. Nick had been his friend, and he had turned out like all the rest. Worse, if anything. Oliver had taken many beatings but none as severe as the one Nick had handed out. He was not likely to make such a mistake again.

When Nick approached him for forgiveness, he turned his back. When he approached him again, he turned his back again. On the third attempt, he looked straight past Nick's face and said, "If you come near me again I'll make sure you get more of what they gave you before."

He saw Nick's face sag, saw him glance anxiously from side to side as if they had been overheard and everyone knew about his shame. He nodded and walked away.

It worked—for two days. Nick chewed his lip, swallowed his pride, recovered, and went back to try again. He caught up with Oliver in the school corridor one day.

"I didn't know what was going on," he said. "Creal promised me he'd get me out and then he said I had to stay here.

I was in a state. He's the one I was angry at. I'm really sorry. Come on, let me off. I'm your friend."

"You're not my friend," said Oliver.

"Yes, I am. And there's nothing you can do about it."

Oliver shook his head and walked off. Nick left it. He'd said his piece and he was prepared to say it again if necessary, but for now, he was happy to have lodged his arrow.

Getting out of Meadow Hill wasn't going to be easy.

There were two ways of doing it, according to Davey. One was Bunker's Lane. This was a cobbled lane behind the main building, all rutted and ankle-deep in mud, running with water half the year. It ran half a kilometer through an area of tangled, boggy woodland to the outside. It was a favorite escape route—hence the name. That whole part of the grounds was out of bounds. The nearest the boys ever got to it was when they made their way to school in a crocodile every morning, and got within a couple of hundred meters of it.

A lad named Terry had tried it, just a couple of days past. He'd taken off without a word just as they passed the entrance to the lane, and managed to get a lead of ten or more meters before the prefects saw him. A great whoop went up—the call to hunt—and the runners set off on his heels. Terry was a good runner, but not good enough. He was hoping to lose them in the thickets, but they caught up with him there instead, which was bad luck because there were no staff there to call them off. He was a mess by the time they brought him back—bloodied nose, black eye, limping, his ribs a mass of bruises.

They didn't like runners at Meadow Hill. It looked bad on reports.

The other way was to break out of the dorms. The door to the stairs was locked every night, and up on the second floor there was no question of jumping out the dorm window. But there was another window at the head of the corridor, which overlooked the roof of Toms's flat. If you could get out of that, you could jump down onto the roof, from that onto the grass, and then away.

The good thing about it was, you had the dark to hide in. The bad thing about it was that the window, which was a big, tall one, had been screwed shut years ago. You had to smash the glass to get your way through it and then go pounding across Mr. Toms's roof. By the time you hit the ground, not only had you woken Mr. and Mrs. Toms from their much-needed beauty sleep, but half the home was out of bed ready to run you down.

And you had to do it all in your pajamas. Toms made sure their clothes and shoes were locked up for the night.

"So what?" said Davey. "We'll just 'ave to nick some on the outside, weren't we?"

The night run had a better chance of success, he reckoned, but fewer people tried it because the consequences were so severe. Breaking the window was vandalism. Mr. James hated vandalism almost as much as he hated bullying. If you got picked up by the coppers, you could get done for criminal damage. That was one thing; but if Toms got his hands on you, heaven help you. Literally, the blood ran for weeks on end at the smallest excuse.

That's why Bunker's was more popular.

"But I reckon that's wrong," said Davey. "Bunker's is too risky, the prefects can always run faster than you. Through the window is the only way, mate. Trust me."

They shook. The night run it was.

15
THE NIGHT RUN

The plan was to wait for lights-out at half past nine, then lie awake until everyone went to sleep; then to lie awake even longer until the staff were all in bed—you could hear them moving around, and you could see the lights from Toms's flat from the window of Davey and Nick's dorm. Then they were going to wait for another hour or so, to make sure all was quiet. Only when there had been no noise for some time would they get up.

"Once we get out of the building, we should be OK," said Nick. Their main enemy was the creaking floor and the squeaky doors. Rumor was, Mr. Toms had told the janitor never to oil them so they called out a warning. The smashed window would wake up everyone for miles, of course. They'd have to clear the frame and get out past the jagged teeth of glass before the prefects had time to get out of bed and run the few yards along the corridor to get them—no easy matter.

They chose Friday night. With the weekend beginning, there would be fewer staff on duty the next day, the streets and roads would be busier—it gave them a better chance, they reckoned.

At bedtime, the usual. A splash of tepid water for a wash, teeth, into the regulation pajamas. Into bed, and the lights turned off. The boys in the dorms scratched and grumbled like dogs as they settled down. There were whimpers and tears as people remembered those they loved, and if they were lucky, who loved them back, on the outside.

"Shut up crying," someone shouted. Sleep didn't take long; the boys were exhausted. The breathing in the dorm became slow and heavy, but Nick lay with his eyes open, staring at the ceiling. Around the building he could hear footsteps on the bare boards, doors closing, and keys turning as the staff retreated back to their own houses and flats. Then, the long wait.

Nick did everything he could to stay awake, but it was hard. He sang songs in his head, tried to remember his mum and friends on the outside. He was so tired. The two hours' exercise every day, too little food, the constant stress of avoiding another beating left them all exhausted. And the bed was so warm . . .

He didn't dare move around, or toss and turn. Andrews slept in the same room, and although the prefect was known to sleep like a rock, Nick didn't want to risk making any noise.

Slowly, slowly the hours passed. A couple of times, he did actually fall asleep, but some dream woke him up. He'd lost all track of time. How long had he been out? Outside, there was still a strip of light coming through the window at the end of the building. Toms's light, still on. He must have dozed off only briefly.

"Jesus!" groaned Nick to himself. That meant it was only eleven or twelve at the latest. He felt like he'd been lying there for an age.

More long seconds, more long minutes, more long hours. Trying not to roll over too often and attract attention, waiting for the moon to creep up the window and over behind the house. It darkened further. Then, a wind blew up—he could hear it in the trees—and the night darkened again as the moon went in. It began to rain, patterings on the window to start with, then harder. The wind increased some more, and before long it was heaving at the trees and shoving at the windowpanes and roof above him. Nick huddled down in his blankets. What a night! And how long before he was out in it, with nothing to wear but his pajamas?

It'd put the prefects off, though. They weren't going to be keen to be out tracking him and Davey down in weather like this.

The strip of light shining through from Toms's window went out at last. Another few weeks seemed to pass by. Someone got up to close the window—the rain was getting in—and he had to wait still longer again.

More long minutes. Another hour, maybe longer. It had been quiet for ages.

It was time to go.

Nick sat up and looked around. No one stirred. He put his foot on the cool boards. How different it all was at night—so quiet and still. But not safe. Nowhere in this place was ever safe. He could be beaten till he bled just for getting out of bed.

He stood up. Silently as a cat, he padded across the floor and stood by Davey's bed. He looked down. Davey was flat on his back, snoring lightly. As Nick watched, though, his eyes opened, and he winked.

Nick jerked his head sideways. They tiptoed out of the dorm and into the corridor.

It was game on.

It was so dark in the corridor they could barely see, and they didn't dare turn the light on. They groped their way toward the pale rectangle that marked the window at the head of the stairs and looked out. It was almost as dark outside. All they could see was the wind wiping the rain on the other side of the dirty glass.

Nick took a deep breath. It had all been done in silence. Now they had to break the glass. He turned his attention to the fire extinguisher a couple of meters along the corridor.

The fire extinguisher had been there for years. Every now and then some new kid would let it off. It was never an old hand. They knew life just wasn't worth those kinds of games, because the thrashing that followed was always beyond belief. The staff would have loved to get rid of it, but the local fire officer was a stickler for the rules, and the extinguisher remained. Over the years, it had been through the window maybe half a dozen times, and there was nothing anyone could do about it.

"Ready?"

"Do it!"

With a grunt Nick shifted the extinguisher out of its cradle and walked with it to the window. He hefted it up above his head—it weighed a ton—paused, and then hurled it through the window.

The noise shattered the sleeping night, like Satan himself was breaking out of hell. The heavy metal cylinder crashed down in a hail of shattered glass and pounded onto the flat roof below. In his bedroom, directly beneath, Toms jerked up out of sleep with a shout and snarled at the ceiling. Davey let out a whoop of pure joy. Behind them, the shouts and yells of stirring boys began.

The face of the window was full of jagged teeth of glass. Davey was already on it. He'd wrapped his arm in his dressing gown and began shoving at the glass to clear the way.

"Go, go, go!" he yelled. Seconds had passed, but behind them there were footsteps on the boards. Nick jumped up onto the sill and stepped over the daggers of glass still attached to the frame. Something caught at his thigh as he lowered himself but there was no time to worry about that. Davey stepped out after him and they paused a moment on the sill. Under them, it was pitch-dark—they couldn't even see the roof down there.

"There they go!" someone shouted.

"Go," gasped Nick. The two boys turned around and slid down, hung by their hands from the sill a second before letting go, one after the other like ripe fruit, and dropped down onto the broken glass on the roof beneath. The glass caught at their feet and cut them both, but not badly. They scurried to the edge of the roof and paused again. Another drop. They had no idea if they were going to drop onto soft earth, rosebushes, plants, stone, or canes down there. The light came on over their heads. Nick looked around to see people gathering at the window just yards away; there was no time to worry. Again, they reached down, hung, and fell—thankfully onto wet grass.

They were up as soon as they landed and running like dogs. The rain had slowed to a drizzle for them. There was a shout. They looked back and saw someone had already got a leg over the sill; but then their pursuer paused. It was a wet night, the frame was still full of razor jags of glass. It was Julian, one of the other prefects. He didn't want to get wet, he didn't want to get cut, and he could see what Nick hadn't yet realized—the streak of bright red blood down the back of his pajama trousers.

Nick slipped on the wet grass; it hurt like hell but he was up again, running as fast as he could to get out of sight into the trees, following Davey's pale figure limping rapidly in and out of the bushes, slipping and slithering on the wet grass, falling, getting up, going down again. There was mud and water in his eyes; he couldn't see a thing, had no idea where he was.

Suddenly Davey was flung backward onto the grass. He'd hit the fence in the dark and bounced back. Nick jumped up and clawed on to it. Davey thudded beside him, gripping the wire as well as they hauled themselves up. They paused at the top to look behind them and held their breath to hear what was going on.

The world went suddenly still. Their pounding hearts were surrounded by the quiet of the night, but back at the house someone was banging. It was the prefects, Julian and Andrews and the others, still inside, banging at the doors. They lacked the heart to chase the lads out through the window and across the field of broken glass they'd left behind on the roof, and were waiting for Toms to come with a key to let them out the easy way. For once, the locked doors were serving the boys.

The wind blew; it began to rain again. They were alone in the refuge of the desperate prisoner—foul weather.

They dropped down, already safe, and ran. Within a few yards, they could hear traffic. They were back in the world—the cold, dark, wet, rainy world. The only question was—whereabouts?

"No idea, mate," said Davey.

A few minutes later, they were hiding behind a bush, looking out at a road. Every now and then a car went past. Opposite them was a row of houses, all in darkness apart from a couple of outside lights, illuminating the rain. Both of them had cut their feet on the glass on Toms's roof, and Nick had a nasty cut on his backside. It was still bleeding as he crouched in the bushes, and, despite the cold, it was beginning to hurt badly.

They were cold, soaked to the skin, with nothing on them against the wind and chilled rain except their thin charity pajamas.

Which way to go?

Both of them were from north Manchester. This was south. Their hope was to slip away out of sight, creeping along the backstreets and through the parks, till they found some way of working out where they were and how to get home. In the middle of the city. In the dark. Dressed in their pajamas . . .

It had seemed like a good idea at the time.

"We can't stay out in this, no way," said Davey. "We're going to catch our deaths."

They glanced at each other and hissed with laughter at the phrase. How often had they heard it before? It was always nonsense, but not anymore. Their body temperatures were steadily dropping. The cold was creeping into their core. Already they were moving slowly, like old men or worn-out insects. They had nothing waterproof, nothing warm, nothing dry.

Was it possible to die of exposure in the middle of Manchester? In summer?

"Look at all those houses," groaned Davey. "All warm on the inside . . ."

"And all freezing cold on the outside," chattered Nick, his teeth going like a snare drum. If they didn't find a way out of the rain and into something warm, they could die like kittens left out in the rain.

They had a whispered conference. They might as well have been on a mountain in a blizzard as in Manchester in the middle of July. Their feet were bleeding, Nick's backside was bleeding—he couldn't feel a thing again but that was only because he was so cold. They had no cover, no shelter, and they were getting colder and colder and colder. They'd been free less than an hour and they were desperate already.

The rain, which had slowed down for a while, started up again. The wind blew. They were literally turning blue.

"We gotta break in somewhere," said Nick. "Nick some clothes or something. Anything!"

But which house? They were all asleep, but the boys knew how little it would take to wake them up.

They gave up and ran on, just for something to do. Then, at last, they spotted a church. Just the thing—at least they'd get shelter there. They ran across the road toward it, through the tall wooden gate and up the path, to the high arched door—which was locked. They shook the lock and ran around trying to find a way in, but the place was totally secure against anyone who needed shelter. All they could do was take cover from the wind and the rain in the porch.

"Thanks, God," growled Davey. He leaned against a wall, wrapped his arms around himself, and shook his head like a dog in an effort to get some heat into his bones. He nodded at the graves lying in the grass in front of them. "They're warm enough down there, eh?" he said.

"Yeah, well, if we don't get warm soon, we'll be finding out for ourselves. Come on." Nick pushed himself off the wall, but Davey held back.

"Wait a bit, I need to rest," he moaned. "It's out of the wind anyway."

"This is no good. We have to get warm." Nick rubbed the back of his hand. It was going numb with cold.

He was getting scared.

They wandered out through the dripping graveyard and found themselves on a main road, although there was little traffic about at this time of night, in this weather. There was a row of shops—a fish and chip shop, a hairdresser, a news-agent, a corner store. They decided to try to break into one of them, and hid themselves in the shadow of the churchyard wall while they cased the shops and tried to decide which one offered the best chance of getting in.

"And which one has the best chance of some grub once we get in," said Davey.

At first, they thought maybe the chippy. They were so cold their brains weren't working, and it took them a minute or so to realize that there wouldn't be any fish and chips at this time of night.

"Unless you want raw fish and potatoes," said Nick.

They were deciding between the corner shop and a news-agent when a taxi pulled up outside. The light came on inside. A couple sitting in the back paid the cab, jumped out into the rain, hauled some cases out of the back, and dashed into a door among the shop fronts. A moment later, a light went on in one of the flats above the shops. Behind them, the driver just sat there, staring at the rain, doing nothing.

The boys were trapped. If they left the shadows under the wall, they'd be spotted.

"What's going on? Why doesn't he go?" demanded Davey. They couldn't do anything while he was there. They hun-kered back against the wall and waited for him to leave. As they watched, the rain began to beat down harder than ever, sheets of it blowing across the road, bouncing back off the ground in a fog of spray.

The driver had dropped off a fare he'd picked up at the airport, and now he was stuck for what to do. There weren't going to be many fares wandering about at this time of night. It was two in the morning—Friday night, but not many were going to be out looking for a taxi in this rain. He was thinking about going home. He sat in the cab and pulled out his takings. Not a lot. He sighed. It was either back to the airport and sit in the queue with every other driver who had the same idea, or he might as well call it a day and go back home to bed.

He tapped the wheel and stared out into the rain. His wife would be disappointed with the little bit of money he'd made. So was he. He put the radio on and leaned back in his seat. Maybe the rain would stop. He'd wait for the downpour to lessen at least, and see what he felt like then.

Across the road, Nick and Davey squatted down in dead leaves under the privet hedge and argued it out.

"We could ask him to take us to my mum's," Davey was saying. "She'll pay at the other end. She can't say no, can she?"

"He'll say no."

"We can ask."

"He'll report us, they'll know where we are."

"They know we're around here anyway. We can leg it if he says no."

Nick looked across at the taxi. It wasn't a very good idea, he knew that. But what else could they do? The taxi driver didn't look as if he was going anywhere in a hurry. If they ran he'd see them anyway. It looked warm in there—nice bright light. The driver was just sitting there. It was so tempting.

He was so cold his teeth had even stopped chattering. They had to do something.

"Go on, then," he said.

Davey stood up and led the way onto the road.

The taxi driver saw something out of the corner of his eye, looked up, and squeaked in surprise and fright. A pale figure was floating across the road toward him in the pouring rain— literally floating, its feet a few inches off the ground. And—oh my God—it was coming straight out of the churchyard! A ghost? An angel from the Lord? What was it? Another one appeared out of the bushes behind the first one. They were both bearing down on him . . .

Mary, Mother of Jesus. Oh. My. God.

He crossed himself—something he hadn't done in the fifteen years since he left school—and fumbled at the ignition. He was on the verge of driving off when he realized that they weren't apparitions at all; they were boys in their pajamas. Bloody hell! That was almost as bad. Boys, dressed in their pajamas, floating across the road in the middle of the downpour? He peered down at their feet suspiciously. The rain was spattering off the road so hard, it bounced back up and formed a dense mist. In the dim lamplight, with their pale, drenched faces and hair, and their pale, drenched clothes, they really did look like a pair of ghosts.

Suddenly, he laughed.

"Bugger me!"

They were wetter than anyone in pajamas he'd ever seen. Drenched. They were turning blue with cold, just like corpses. One of them, the smaller one, made it to the car, leaned down, and peered hopefully in through the window. He looked like a drowned rat. No, decided the driver—not a rat. A pig. He was an ugly little beast.

He wound down the window.

A moment later the two boys were squeezing in the back. The driver had put down some magazines to try to keep his seats dry and clean—he'd noticed the blood down Nick's backside, not to mention the bits of stick, dead leaves, mud, and other debris stuck to their feet and pajama bottoms from running about in this lot. The world outside was made of mud, and these two seemed to have most of it sticking to them.

"I was on me way back anyhow, I might as well. You're on the run, I can see that. Don't blame yer, don't blame yer—me brother was in one of them places, he'd have done a runner if he could, but he had a twisted foot, he was lame, see, couldn't get away. His mates did, some of 'em. All ended up back inside, though."

"Th-th-thanks," stuttered Nick. The driver had turned up the heater, and waves of warm air were rushing past them. Now that they were reheating they were starting to shiver again.

The driver laughed at his chattering teeth. "Thought you were a pair of bloody angels come to tell me to change my ways. Christ, that's a relief. Mind you, you'd have been ghosts before long if you hadn't met me, eh? What a night to do a runner! Here—keep those seats clean, all right? My customers don't pay for a dirty arse. So—your mum'll pay, you reckon? Well, why not. Not that she'll be pleased to see you, eh? You have to be a right pair of scoundrels or you wouldn't be in there in the first place, would you? But she'll see yer, anyway. Family, innit? Right then—where to? Hello—what's this?"

A car had pulled up alongside. Someone got out, turned up their collar against the rain, and ran through the puddles over to the waiting taxi.

Nick and Davey peered anxiously through the window, but in the dark, through the wet glass and the rain, they couldn't make out who it was.

The figure tapped on the window. The driver opened it and a brown face with a combed red beard peered inside.

Their hearts sank.

"Oh dear. Caught red-handed," said the man. He looked at the taxi driver. "I'm afraid you've got a pair of runners here, driver."

"Well, I never," said the driver. He looked over his shoulder, pulled a face at Nick and Davey, and shrugged.

It was Alex Jones, the local scoutmaster. He ran a group at Meadow Hill once a week. Nick and Davey weren't in it—they weren't well-behaved enough. Mr. Jones wouldn't have known the two boys by sight, but he recognized the pajamas.

It was the most ridiculous bad luck for Nick and Davey.

Jones had been driving back late after visiting his father in Sheffield; filthy weather over the Snake Pass, he got held up for hours by an overturned truck. He was only a mile or so from home when he saw the two boys getting into the taxi dressed in their pajamas.

Alex was a decent-enough man. He knew Meadow Hill fell short, although he had no idea just how short. If he had, he would have been helping them rather than catching them. As it was, he had only one option—to take them straight back.

The captured boys stared at him as if he were some kind of beast smiling at them through the window, but they made no attempt to get away. They were freezing cold—when he touched one of them on the shoulder it was scary how cold they were. They could catch pneumonia like that. They were both bleeding, as well. They looked like escapees from Broadmoor, rather than a pair of kids trying to get out of the local children's home.

"Look at the state of you!" He nodded his head at his car, parked just across the road. "Come on, boys, I'll take you back. Not really the night for an escape bid, is it?" He smiled at them as kindly as he could, opened the door, and waited for them to get out.

He felt even more sorry for them when he got them back. They'd had to break a window to get out, and Gerald Toms didn't seem at all happy to be knocked out of bed to get them sorted. No doubt they'd get the flogging of their lives for it. Well, maybe they deserved it, but it was hard to see them dripping and shivering, blue with cold, bleeding, in the grip of Mr. Toms, who, as Alex well knew, had all the compassion of a pair of tweezers.

"Don't be too hard on them," he said. "They've been through enough already, by the looks of them. They need a hot bath before anything else, or they'll catch their deaths."

"Oh, they'll get a bath all right," replied Mr. Toms. He stood with his hands placed protectively on their shoulders as he watched Mr. Jones get into his car and drive off. He squeezed until they both winced.

"You little bastards," he murmured, as he turned them around and led them into the house. "You're going to suffer for this," he added.

"We'd already worked that one out," said Nick, and he was felled with a blow to the ear.

Mr. Toms was a man of limited intelligence and imagination—in fact, he was a man of limited pretty well everything, except cruelty, of which he had an abundance. He'd never have thought of such a clever idea on his own if Mr. Jones hadn't put it into his head for him, nor would he have carried it out at that time of night himself—he had a warm bed with a warm wife in it waiting for him just meters away. He gave the orders to Andrews and Julian to carry it out. And he was confident they would carry it out in the spirit in which he intended it, too, since it was going to keep them from their beds half the night themselves. They were already in trouble for letting these two get away. You could bet they weren't going to be soft on them for that.

Mr. Toms did as Alex Jones had suggested—gave the boys

a bath. He stayed long enough to supervise the running water, watched them strip and get in. He went to bed feeling very pleased with himself. Funny! Clever, too! So clever and so funny, it gave him a warm glow as he snuggled up to his large, soft, warm wife and chuckled to himself as he dozed off.

To say that Nick and Davey were cold would be an understatement. The cold had gone through their skin, into the muscle, and through to their livers, their stomachs, their hearts, and their bones. When Mr. Toms ran the baths, they were both amazed, and so overwhelmed with gratitude that they'd thanked him pitifully. It only slowly dawned on them what he was doing when Andrews had tried to turn on the other tap.

"Turn it off," ordered Toms. That was the hot tap. They were getting a bath, all right—but it was freezing cold.

Mr. Toms stood and watched them get in before he left.

"You're very welcome, boys," he said as the water closed around them like the cold hand of death. They both immediately began shivering violently. Toms went off to bed leaving Andrews and Julian sitting on the edges of the baths watching them turn first red, then blue, then pale blue, then white.

"It's like watching sunrise over the Arctic," said Julian. At one point Davey tried to get out, flapping slowly like a dying fish with no strength at all in him, but they just pushed his head under till he gave up. They left them in there for fifteen minutes, and when the time came to get them out, they had to help them stand up.

Once they were out, the two prefects amused themselves by flicking wet towels at their bare bodies. The boys tried to twist and turn to get out of the way, but they were too cold to move properly and soon they were covered in bright red marks. At least they didn't hurt so bad, their skins were so chilled. They were refused pajamas, but thrown towels, and then sent off to bed before they were properly dry and had to curl up naked under the thin covers, still half wet.

They lay there for ages, huddling the blankets around them, trying to get warm. Very, very slowly the heat seeped back into their icy flesh and chilled bones. Gradually the violent shivers that wracked them died away.

Nick felt a sneeze coming on—only to be expected, really. He sneezed three times, like a cat, and fell asleep.

When he awoke again it was still dark, and he was still cold. He looked around in alarm—what was going on?

It was Andrews, prodding him awake.

"Up you get," he growled.

"What?"

"Up."

Across the dorm, Julian was hauling Davey out of bed, too.

"What's up?"

"You are. Get up, go on, hurry."

Nick crawled miserably out of bed, stiff and exhausted. The prefects marched them down the corridor back to the bathroom, where the baths stood full of water. Davey looked at Julian, appalled.

Julian winked. "Apparently you're still not clean enough. Ain't that funny?" he asked innocently.

"In you get," said Andrews tiredly. "I'm going to batter the pair of you tomorrow for this," he added, as if he'd do it now, but just couldn't be bothered.

So it happened all over again. This time, straight from bed, the water felt colder than ever. Nick paused halfway in—he just couldn't bring himself to do it—and Andrews pushed him right under so he gasped and sucked down a lungful of water. He held him under for a good few seconds before letting him back up for air. He lay there, thrashing weakly, until the cold took him and he just lay still.

Andrews took a packet of cards out of his pocket, and the two prefects sat down on the floor and began to play brag for matchsticks.

After five minutes, Davey began to cry, a thin sobbing. It was just so miserable, so depressing, so cold. Neither of them had anything left, no fight, no strength, no warmth. Once he was off, it got to Nick as well and he started up. They lay there, the pair of them, side by side in two identical baths and wept like babies.

"Oh, don't start that," moaned Andrews. He and Julian rolled their eyes at each other and dealt again.

"You can pack that racket in, you've another ten minutes yet," Julian told them irritably.

But the boys had reached an all-time low and couldn't stop. Toms had stumbled on just the right torture to break them. They were cold, they were exhausted, they had failed in what they set out to do. It felt as if they would never be warm again.

The game of brag went on, and the two boys lay there and cried, until at last they got so cold that the tears dried up and their eyes began to roll in their heads.

This time they were more supported than carried back to bed. Once more they were left to fall asleep, and once more they were woken up and dumped back in the icy water—freshly drawn, since water from the pipes was colder than water left standing. This time they had to be dragged back to bed and were dumped between the sheets still wet, since they hadn't had the strength to dry themselves. Mercifully, this time they were left there until the whistle blew to wake them up the next morning.

They were sent to school despite the dry, hacking coughs that had developed overnight, and snuffled and sneezed their way through the day. And not the colds, or the cut feet or even the nasty gash on Nick's backside saved them from the official punishment, which came that evening—the flogging.

Toms laid in with more gusto than usual, if anything, to make up for the broken window and the extra work, not to mention being dragged out of bed in the middle of the night twice, just because these two jokers wanted to walk. They got twelve each. They both wept and howled after the first three. As usual it was done in the room behind the hall so that everyone could hear.

When they got back into the hall, no one said anything

about the screams. Same as always, the boys had to bare their backsides to see if they were a sergeant or a corporal. When Nick showed his, they fell silent.

"Better get the nurse to have a look at that," Nick heard someone say, and then he fainted.

16
THE INFIRMARY

It was a disaster, but one good thing came of it. Overnight, the sore throats spread down into the boys' chests, and they woke the day after their caning with blazing temperatures. Toms sent them to school as usual, but the teachers weren't having it and sent them back with a note. Result—they got a call from the local doctor, who prescribed antibiotics and a few days off, lying in the infirmary, being taken care of by the legendary Nurse Turner.

The infirmary wasn't really an infirmary, and Nurse Turner wasn't really a nurse. It was just a room with a few beds in it put aside for sick boys, and she was the wife of one of the housemasters. It was a bit of a joke, really, but she was a kind woman and couldn't do enough for you while you were there. The Turners were the best of the house tutors at Meadow Hill, and if Nick had ended up with them instead of Toms his would have been a very different story.

It was great. There was a telly, provided by the Turners, that you could watch all you liked. Nurse Turner spent the day trotting to and fro, carrying trays with various treats piled up on them. In a place like Meadow Hill, it was next door to heaven.

Nurse Turner was an odd-looking woman, with a wide, wobbly smile, dazzling bright blue eyes, too much makeup, and hair puffed out at the sides, which for some reason made her look rather like a toothless elephant bearing down on you as she came in with yet another trayload of squishy cake, rice pudding, or ice cream. She was nearing forty, but she still had a magnificent figure, so the boys spent half their time pretending to lust after her and half the time pretending to be appalled that she might actually be trying to get off with them. She wore short skirts and blouses not exactly plunging, but low enough to give them an eyeful when she bent over the bed with her tray.

It was a great few days. The thought of how furious Toms would be that their misdeeds had given them all this time lying in bed, eating ice cream, and trying to look down Nurse Turner's cleavage, made it all the better. Endless TV, board games—it was pure bliss. Davey reckoned it was worth the cold baths and the flogging just to get the time off.

"You never cut your arse open," pointed out Nick, shifting uncomfortably in his bed, which made Davey roar with laughter. For some reason, he thought Nick's arse wound, as he called it, was hilarious.

The only disadvantage was, they weren't allowed out of bed and no one was allowed to visit them, so once they got their strength back and their temperatures had gone down, they started to get restless. Whenever Nurse Turner caught them out of bed, it brought the day they would be sent back closer and closer.

They did get one visitor, though. To Nick's amazement and horror the door opened one day and in walked Mr. Creal. He looked just the same as normal, with his black suit and his blond-gray hair and his V-neck jumper, with his bright smile and his crinkly eyes, like someone's favorite uncle.

"Boys!" he exclaimed when he saw them, sounding as if someone had just given him a bowl of particularly juicy trifle. "Making the most of it, eh? All tucked up like a pair of little toads in the hole," he added. He behaved exactly as if he were Nick's best friend still. He brought them treats—bottles of Coke, chocolate, and a couple of bottles of beer, which he slipped down under the covers next to Nick as he sat on the side of the bed.

"Don't tell Mrs. Turner," he said with a wink. "And don't drink it all at once. I know what you boys are like."

Nick edged as far away from him as he could, terrified that he might start to try to touch him up, or even worse, start referring to what had happened in the Secure Unit. That night had given Mr. Creal a strange and terrible power over Nick. He felt that just to mention what had happened would destroy him utterly, and he spent the entire time Creal was there terrified that he was suddenly going to talk about it.

Already, Nick had learned never even to think about that night, but he couldn't stop his feelings. The memory came to him when he was helpless, tired, or in his dreams, and he'd wake up yelling and screaming. He'd woken Davey more than once in the infirmary since they got there. Just being this close to his abuser gave him the shakes—literally. His hands were quivering like leaves.

He hated Creal like he'd never hated anything before in his life. The worst thing about it was that Creal made him feel so helpless.

What on earth did he want? They were in their night-wear—in bed. It seemed obvious, but in fact, Mr. Creal never touched him. He knew better than to sniff around for favors while there were two of them. He put his hand on Nick's forehead to see if he had a temperature and smiled sympathetically.

"I heard that bastard Toms was his usual brutal self," he said. "If I could do anything . . ." He shook his head. "But these people, they're a law unto themselves."

Then, to Nick's disgust, he started feeling sorry for himself. He got all sad and doe-eyed about how he could be such friends to the boys if only he didn't have to be in charge all the time, how tired he got of his role in the home, how his job got in the way.

"I may seem popular to you," he told Nick, "but I'm lonely, very lonely a lot of the time. If it wasn't for boys like you . . ."

It was an amazing performance. How could he feel sorry for himself, after what he'd done?

There were threats, too. "Don't try running away again, boys," he said. "You know what can happen, especially you, Nick. Don't you?" And he smiled at him and bared his teeth, and dared Nick to say either yes or no. He seemed pleased when Nick was unable to answer.

And promises. "You need to knuckle down and get on

with life here. I can help. I can make your lives a great deal easier." And he patted Nick in a familiar way on the leg.

By the time he had gone, Nick was shaking with anger, fear, and shame. If he didn't get away, he would have to deal with Creal again sooner or later, that much was obvious.

He had to escape. There was no choice.

They couldn't try the night run again. Every time it got broken, the window got boarded up with inch-thick plywood screwed to the wall, and no way was that coming down in a hurry—at least until the next fire check, when the fire officer would insist. That left Bunker's Lane, and very few boys made it out down Bunker's. Really, there was only one way it could work. They needed a bribe. Something to get the prefects on their side.

"Fags," said Nick. It was a known fact that almost all the prefects would do anything for cigarettes. That's how things worked at Meadow Hill. Ciggies, beer, chocolate, and girlie mags. If you had a constant supply of those, you could do anything.

"I can't get enough ciggies for myself, let alone that lot," declared Davey.

"Then we'll just have to work out how to get some more, won't we?" said Nick.

They racked their brains but they couldn't think of anything. If you got home visits you could smuggle some fags in, but that wasn't likely—they'd lost any points they might have got for about a thousand years. They could have used the beer Creal gave them, except they'd drunk it before they even had time to think about that. Nick tried to drop hints to Nurse Turner that some cigarettes would go down well, but she was scandalized.

"Cigarettes? With a sore throat? In the hospital? It's ice cream or nothing in here, my lads!"

They had to think of something else. It was a pity they'd fallen out with Oliver. He always had loads of ciggies.

"Creal smokes, dun he?" suggested Davey. "You get back in with him, you can 'ave some away."

Nick gave him a look. Davey didn't press it.

They sat there and racked their brains some more. They were going to have to steal them, that was obvious. Their best chance, they realized, was while they were here in the infirmary. Dilys, the receptionist, smoked; so did Creal, who had his flat in the same building. If they could only get out, just for a single hour, they could surely pinch some ciggies from somewhere.

As luck would have it, though, they'd run out of time. Nurse Turner came to see them the following morning with Andrews, to tell them they were better. They were to get their things together. They were going back to school that same afternoon.

17
THE NEW BOY

It looked as though Nick and Davey were just going to have to keep their eyes open and wait for a chance to present itself, either to pinch the ciggies or perhaps to find a way to sneak off to the fence when no one was looking. But that could take forever.

Nick, however, had a plan, as always. It was called Oliver.

Davey was not impressed.

"Why'd he help us?" he wanted to know.

"Because he's comin' with us."

"Sez who? Any road, what's he got to run for?"

"Same as you and me."

Davey shook his head impatiently. "Oliver has it made. He gets no school. He gets no rough nasty games, everyone leaves him alone. He gets loads of sweeties and anything else he wants and all he has to do for it is take it up the arse from dear Tony Creal. And since he obviously likes it up the arse from dear Tony Creal, he doesn't 'ave a problem, does he?"

"Who says he likes it? And who says he's still getting it? 'Aven't you noticed? 'E's not been on the Flat List, lately," said Nick.

"Yer still lookin', then."

"I like to know what's goin' on."

Davey shrugged. "I wouldn't trust him with my pet hamster's peanut, let alone bringin' him in on anythin' like this."

Nick was right. Oliver didn't like the things that were done to him, or the things he was asked to do, and he didn't like Mr. Creal, either—but he did like having a protector. He liked having a bag full of chocolate and cigarettes and girlie mags on demand, and not going hungry, and getting nights away from the other boys in front of the TV in a warm flat. He liked feeling special, and Tony Creal knew how to make him feel exactly that. It wasn't love, it was prostitution; but it was the nearest thing to love Oliver could hope to get, and so he took it.

He'd had a long run with Tony Creal, but now it was coming to an end.

For one thing, his voice was breaking. Mr. Creal had wide tastes in boys of all ages, but he liked Oliver because he was pretty and young and looked like a girl. His gruff croak spoiled the effect. Mr. Creal had started to take an interest in other boys—Nick, for example. That worried Oliver, which explained the anxious looks Nick had noticed during those evenings in the flat. But a few weeks earlier, while Oliver was recovering in the infirmary, there had been a new development.

Mr. Creal had visited him regularly there, bringing goodies and treats.

"There's a new boy at the home," he told him one rainy

Tuesday afternoon. "I think you might like him, Oliver. I think you and he might have a lot in common."

Oliver saw the new boy soon enough—he watched him crossing in front of the infirmary several times with Mr. Creal's hand on his shoulder. He was slight, blond, and pale, just like Oliver, but a year or so younger. Oliver recognized him at once—not that he knew him in any way, but he knew at once what he was like. He could see in what ways this boy was like him, just as Mr. Creal had. He couldn't have put his finger on why he knew, but he did.

Mr. Creal had found a new plaything.

He knew what the new boy looked like, and soon found out his name as well. He crept out and had a look at the Flat List one day, and there it was, a new name—Jeremy Style. In the few days that Oliver had been in the infirmary at that point, Jeremy's name had already been up twice.

It was no surprise, but even so, it hurt. In fact, *hurt* was too soft a word. To his own amazement and disgust, Oliver was devastated. His head knew clearly enough that Creal was just using him, but his heart would simply not believe it. In the absence of genuine affection, he responded to the substitute, however cheap.

The weeks passed. Oliver came out of the infirmary. Nick and Davey went in. The new boy's name continued to appear on the Flat List while Oliver's visits began to die away. He wasn't dropped entirely, as yet. Creal needed some other lad around to make his new boy feel at ease, as well as a backup, in case Jeremy was slow in handing out his favors. Oliver was a good backup, but he was less use for providing a convivial atmosphere, as he had shown when Mr. Creal was trying to groom Nick. He got jealous, and he showed it. Jeremy, with a true instinct, had told Creal early on that he didn't like Oliver, and so Oliver's visits dropped sharply. In the next weeks he got up there only once, whereas before he might have spent an evening at the flat two or three times a week.

Every time Jeremy's name turned up on the list without his, Oliver felt as though someone were pushing a blunt rusty nail right through him. He had thought he had been dropped so often in the past that he'd be used to it by now, but he wasn't. It hurt more than ever each time it happened. He didn't know what amazed him more—the fact that it hurt so bad, or the fact that he was still surprised every time.

At the same time, life at school got worse. The boys noticed very quickly that he was no longer the deputy's favorite and closed in on him like wolves. It began with names, it turned quickly to blows and kicks, a familiar cycle for Oliver. When attention flagged, fear and pain followed. He knew all about that.

Oliver's life was pretty grim at the best of times, but for whatever it was worth, he was watching everything he had go down the pan. He didn't deal in friends, but he was aware that he was going to need a new protector. He didn't trust Nick, of course, but trust had long ago ceased to be an issue with him. Besides, abuse and affection was a combination he was very familiar with. Since he couldn't live without the second, he had to put up with the first—that was life. He had begun to think that Nick was different. He was wrong—so what? It was the usual, that was all. Now Nick was useful to him again, and he began to feel his way cautiously back in.

But Davey was right not to trust him. Boys like Oliver dealt in treats and favors, and there were always going to be people in a place like Meadow Hill who could provide better treats and favors than Davey and Nick.

"Soon as someone shows up who's got more to offer, he's off. He's only hanging around 'cos he's got no one else to pat him dry behind his little ears."

"I owe him," said Nick fiercely.

"You don't owe him, mate. He had it coming . . ."

"Not from me, he didn't. I owe him. OK?"

Davey lifted up his hands.

"I'd do the same for you mate, anytime."

Davey nodded. He knew it was true. Nick simply never let go.

So when the other lads started on Oliver when Nick was around, Nick stepped in. It wasn't a popular move. Davey stood back and let him get on with it—he figured they'd had enough trouble because of Oliver. But finally the inevitable happened. Nick got into a fight with a couple of lads over it. There was no choice.

"Oi! That's my mate!" yelled Davey, and there he was, back-to-back with Nick, fighting the other lads off Oliver.

They got trashed—knocked to the ground and kicked, all three of them. Davey was furious about it.

"What do you have to do that for?" he demanded. "We

could a got caught. Look! I'm bleeding!" he exclaimed, wiping his hand up his nose.

"Sorry, mate. You all right?" asked Nick, helping Oliver up.

"Thanks," said Oliver, who somehow had come out of it with hardly a scratch.

"Great," snarled Davey. "Well, you got what you wanted there, dint cha?" he growled at Nick, and he stalked off. He was right. From that moment, Oliver started to hang out with them again. It was the safest place to be.

Even so, Davey wasn't one to miss a chance. He was back soon enough to see what Oliver could help with—ciggies, for example.

"What about tabs? Can you get us any?" Davey wanted to know.

"Maybe," said Oliver doubtfully. "Depends when I get on the list," he added.

Davey pulled a disgusted face but said nothing more. Oliver didn't get on the Flat List in the next week, and he was fully expecting Nick to dump him when it turned out he had no access to any treats. He was surprised and puzzled when it didn't happen.

So it was a result for Nick, but he took Davey's point. Oliver wasn't to be trusted, and he stopped short of telling the younger boy that they were still planning on running as soon as they found a way out.

Meanwhile, Tony Creal hadn't finished with Oliver yet. It was three whole weeks after Nick and Davey had been booted out of the infirmary. A Tuesday afternoon. The Flat List had gone up and once again Oliver's name wasn't on it. So when Mr. Creal sent for him after tea, when the other boys were going out to sport, Oliver was surprised, but hopeful. He amazed himself, really, at his lack of cynicism. He just couldn't help hoping. Maybe Mr. Creal had realized how much he meant to him—maybe he had started to miss him, too. If it was true, Oliver would have forgiven him everything in a moment.

It looked good to start with. Mr. Creal received him in his office, looking delighted. He stood up and came around his desk to greet Oliver, putting his arm over his shoulder and pulling him into him while he tugged his ear.

"Where have you been all this time?" he asked, as if it were nothing to do with him. "Bruises and cuts healing nicely," he continued, turning Oliver's face in his fingers. "We'll have you back up and running in no time." Oliver stared up at him, his face betraying nothing. "You look like a little porcelain boy!" joked Mr. Creal. "Except for a few cracks that bad lad put on your pretty face. I know, I know, I've been neglecting you. Oliver . . ." He cocked his head to one side, scolding him fondly for his doubts. Despite himself, Oliver's heart leaped. "You need a bit of time to get better, you know," added Creal, gently touching the remaining bruise on Oliver's face. "We'll get you out and about soon enough, you'll see."

He sat Oliver down and gave him cocoa and chocolate biscuits, and explained what it was he wanted.

"I want you to come along for a football match at Webb Hill School tomorrow," he said, and he winked. Oliver's heart sank.

Meadow Hill was involved in various league games with some of the other local schools and children's homes. If you were good at football or running or cricket, and if you were trustworthy, you could get on the team. It was a treat—a day away from the home, a game, a look at ordinary life. Oliver had no interest in sports of any kind, so when Mr. Creal told him he was coming along, he knew exactly what was expected of him.

He began to panic. "I don't feel well, sir," he told him. "My ribs are sore."

Mr. Creal shrugged. "You'll be all right. Come on, Oliver, don't be such a wet blanket—it's a treat. The other boys would give anything for a treat like this."

Mr. Creal liked to entertain from time to time. As the virtual owner of as many boys as he liked to get, he was very popular with a certain kind of man. A number of them worked with children themselves—you could say they had a particular interest there—and so, at some of the sports days and matches, at certain schools, a group of similarly minded men gathered. From time to time, one or another of them would bring a boy along. While the other lads were out on the field playing football, Mr. Creal and his friends would be inside somewhere private, being entertained. There could be two, three, even four men present. It wasn't rough in the way they'd dealt with Nick that night—rape was a punishment—but it was rough enough, and humiliating and horrible.

"I don't want to go, sir. You know I only like it with you," Oliver begged. That was a lie. Oliver didn't like it at all. It was the disguise of affection he liked, not the man.

"Nonsense, it's a treat," repeated Mr. Creal.

"You said I needed time to get better . . ."

"This is tiresome," murmured Mr. Creal. "Come on, Oliver. I've done it all for you—more than you know." He nodded at his own words, as if there were some vast hidden reservoir of favors he'd done that Oliver knew nothing about. "Be ready at four o'clock after school tomorrow. I'll come and get you. Here, look! I've got something for you already. Just think how generous I'll be when it's over." He took one of his paper bags from the drawer and shook it at Oliver, before thrusting it into his hands and dismissing him. Oliver was outside in the corridor before he knew what was going on.

Tony Creal had long ago convinced himself that the boys he abused liked it. He and certain of his colleagues had long conversations about it—how society conspired against them, how unfair it was that children were denied sexual pleasure with a loving adult. In more enlightened times, men like them would be understood, perhaps even valued, for bringing a pleasure into children's lives that they were now denied.

Of course, nothing could be further from the truth. The boy responded not in the name of love, but in the hope of love. Creal himself had long forgotten the difference between love and power. He could not have found a better way of showing Oliver how much he despised him than by sharing him with his friends.

The following afternoon, Oliver sought Nick out.

"I want to come with you," he said.

"What?" said Nick. He'd never discussed this with Oliver so far.

Oliver made an impatient gesture with his hand. "I know you're running—everyone knows it. I want to come with you."

Behind him, Davey groaned. He could see what was coming. "Bloody hell!" he moaned.

Nick gripped Oliver by the shoulder. "Welcome aboard," he told him, and he grinned with pleasure.

As soon as Davey had Nick on his own, he had a go at him.

"He can't run."

"I owe him one," said Nick stubbornly.

"Great, and where does that leave me?"

Nick shrugged. "We need some cigs."

"Oh! Great idea! Yeah! Stupid of me. I'll just pop down the road and buy a few packs, shall I? Bollocks. Anyway, there ent enough ciggies in the world to get Andrews and that lot let 'im slip through their fingers. No one will ever believe 'e could get away from them. All you have to do is clap yer 'ands and 'e falls down." Davey lowered his voice. "Anyway. 'Ave you thought? How come he's changed his mind so quick?"

Nick shrugged. Neither of them knew anything about the sports day treat Oliver had just endured.

"He's gonna shop us," said Davey.

Nick looked away, his heart sinking. "Why do you think that?" he asked.

"Why else? To get himself back in with Creal."

"He's a mate," said Nick. "How's he going to trust us if we don't trust him?"

"We don't 'ave to be stupid about it," said Davey. "I mean, 'e doesn't speak to us for ten days and then suddenly 'e's our best friend? Come on. And when he does shop us, where are we going to be? Where are you gonna be? Back in the Secure Unit, mate, that's where."

Nick flinched and paused. "I'll keep my eye on 'im," he said.

"'E could lie for England, that one," said Davey.

He said no more, but only because the whole thing was academic. They had no bribes and no viable means of getting them, and they couldn't even try to run until they did.

18
OLIVER MAKES A MOVE

Two days later, Oliver's name appeared on the Flat List again for the first time in nearly two weeks.

He stood in front of it—and his heart sank. He knew himself too well to doubt what made his spirits fall like that. It was divided loyalties. Davey, standing by his side, guessed what was going on.

"So you an' dear Tony are buddies again, eh?"

"Leave him," said Nick. He tugged Oliver's sleeve and dropped his voice. "Now's the time, though, innit?" Oliver looked up at him and couldn't bring himself to nod.

Davey poked him from the other side. "Time to show yer colors, Oliver," he said.

Oliver studied his shoes. Davey pulled a face at Nick.

"You can pinch ciggies off Creal, Ollie, you know you can," said Nick. "When he's in the back with one of the other lads. He trusts you."

Davey snorted in amusement at the word *trust*, as if the mere idea of anyone trusting Oliver was ridiculous. Nick glared at him.

"Ollie, if you wanna run, this is it. If you're with us, this is it. What ja say?"

"I'm with you," croaked Oliver. Nick looked triumphantly at Davey. "But . . ."

"But what?"

Oliver looked at him and said nothing. The fact was, he was terrified. Creal had him like a puppet on a string. Feel bad, feel good, be happy, be sad. Fear and favor had broken his spirit.

"You'll try, won't you?" begged Nick, willing, willing, willing him on.

Oliver grimaced. "I'll try," he said.

The rest of the day passed like a slowly unfolding nightmare for Oliver. This was a turning point. If he failed to come back with cigarettes, he'd be out of favor with Nick. If he did steal them, he'd be letting down Tony Creal. In a ghastly way, the beating Nick had given him had reassured him that Nick truly had an interest in him. But Creal was something else. During Oliver's time at Meadow Hill, Creal had woven a magic knot of shame, terror, pleasure, and helplessness that left him powerless. He ruled Oliver's spirit and heart entirely.

The rest of the day moved as slowly as only time can, but it passed all the same. School came and went, tea came and went, sports came and went. Nick came to pat him and pep him up, Davey avoided him. Oliver didn't blame Davey for not trusting him. He didn't trust himself. He had no idea which way he was going to go.

Tony Creal had made a mistake in picking Nick Dane for a plaything. He was an intelligent man, but he didn't pick his victims by calculation—all his manipulation was done by instinct. He picked on weak boys, already broken, able to accept things entirely on his own terms. Perhaps his charisma, charm, and intelligence made him think too much of himself. Nick, in those first shocking weeks at Meadow Hill, gave the impression that he was beaten lower than he really was. But the boy had fought back, and that wasn't something Mr. Creal was used to. He had his way in the end, with the rape, but as one of his colleagues pointed out afterward, Nick wasn't Mr. Creal's usual type.

"Too much fight in him," said the man, a fairly senior police officer. "Take my advice. Blessed are the meek, Tony, they take what they're given." The man laughed at his own joke, and he left Tony Creal some food for thought.

Now he was reverting to kind. The new boy he was grooming, like Oliver, had been in and out of care all his life. He was pretty, blond, young, and vulnerable—just right.

The problem was the little blighter was holding out on him. He let Mr. Creal do whatever he wanted to him, like a doll in his hands. He just lay there, closed his eyes, and went limp. That suited Tony Creal well enough for a while; but the thing was, the boy wouldn't touch him. Wouldn't do a thing. It really was splendidly irritating.

It was Jeremy's way of coping with the ordeal. He simply turned himself off. He imagined there was a switch in his head which he clicked . . . and none of it was happening, or had happened or ever would happen again. Afterward, he could hardly remember a thing. It was a neat trick that served him well enough then, although in later years, when he started to try to form proper relationships, it broke the heart of whoever came near him.

That was why Mr. Creal was having Oliver along that night. If Jeremy saw another boy there enjoying Mr. Creal's attention, maybe he wouldn't take things for granted quite so much. A little bit of jealousy in the mix had pushed things along before now . . .

The evening took the usual form. Creal sat and played games with the two boys, gave them drinks—a little beer usually softened things up for later. Later, he took Oliver off and sat on his own with him—didn't do much, just fondled him a little bit and told him that he still loved him.

"You're my best boy, you know that, don't you, Oliver?" he said. "These other lads are just a bit of entertainment."

Shortly, he sent him through to ask Jeremy to come through, with instructions to wait up a bit for him. He was going to see how he got on with the new boy on his own. If he was still holding out, he planned to get Oliver in with them. See if the limp little sod liked that!

The other lad came through, rather more drunk than normal, which was perhaps a good thing. He sat him down and chatted about this and that—about his life, about being mistreated and misunderstood. Then he offered a little comfort, which the boy passively accepted, letting his limbs go limp and unresponsive as Mr. Creal slid his hand under his pajamas. But when he suggested that he could do with a little comfort too, the boy backed off. No go. Once again, Creal had to swallow his irritation. It was taking forever, the selfish little rat. But he didn't want to force things. He didn't want another Nick Dane on his hands.

"You're settling in splendidly!" he insisted as he zipped up. Jeremy looked at him with his big blue eyes—full of thanks, Mr. Creal liked to think. He went through with him to the sitting room to ask Oliver to come in and join them, but Oliver, to his surprise, had already gone.

Bugger! Creal was furious. Jealous, no doubt. It works two ways. He hadn't been giving him enough attention. Still, it was bloody rude to accept his hospitality and then slide off without so much as a good-bye or by-your-leave, leaving him angry and frustrated like this.

Disgruntled, he sent the other lad off after him and made himself a consolation whiskey to drink with his last cigarette of the day, before he went to bed unsatisfied.

19
BUNKER'S LANE

The whistle. The door bangs and Toms sticks his ugly head in each doorway and blows again.

"Up you get, you ugly little bastards! Up, up, up, you horrible little toads."

Every morning, just like the army. It was the only training he'd ever had. When a boy at the end of one of the dorms burst into tears—he'd been awoken from a lovely dream into a world of pain—Toms glared at him in a mixture of incomprehension and disgust. You never cried in the army.

"You pathetic little shit! Get up and stop sniveling," he roared. It made him want to hit the little wimp. Weakness didn't get you anywhere. When Toms had been in the army, weakness might very well have cost him and his mates their lives. Now it just cost you a beating from Toms. There was no war left but here was Toms, still having one, all on his own.

Nick, Davey, and Oliver met in the corridor along the dorms, which ran the length of the building and connected the two houses. Nick noticed at once how pale Oliver was. He hadn't slept a wink all night. He got close up to him in the press of bodies for the loos.

"How'd it go?" he asked.

Oliver nodded. He jerked his head and led Nick back into his dorm. He waited until everyone was out, then put his hand under the mattress and pulled out three packets of Bensons.

Nick was so surprised he almost yelped. He grabbed them and wrapped them up in his towel.

"Bloody hell, Oliver! How'd you manage that?"

"I know where he keeps them."

"Jesus. Bloody hell." Nick shook his head and grinned. He'd never really believed Oliver could do it. But the smile faded on his face as he looked at Oliver. He'd never seen anyone look so scared.

"It's OK," he said quietly, looking around to make sure they were alone. "You've done it. You're a hero, Oliver."

"We have to go now."

"Why now?"

"He'll know it was me. Creal'll know."

Nick licked his lips. He hadn't thought of that.

"And there's this." Oliver thrust another package at him—an envelope.

"What's in it?"

Oliver gave him a look so appalled that Nick thought better than to ask again. He brushed his hand over the younger boy's hair, nodded, and gave him the thumbs-up. He stuffed the envelope down his pajamas and went on to the loo. In a cubicle, behind the locked door—the only place in Meadow Hill where you could get on your own—he had a look to see what was inside.

He couldn't believe what he found. Oliver had stolen photos of Mr. Creal with naked boys.

"No. No, no, no. Oh, no. Oh, shit. Oh, Oliver. What have you done?"

It was simply terrifying. His throat went dry, his hands were trembling. He'd been locked away and raped for just threatening to tell. What would they do to him if they knew he had this stuff?

Suddenly he was furious. This wasn't part of the plan. This was the unspeakable. Now he had the whole filthy experience rebranded into his memory like a curse because of these stinking images, and it was all that little shit's fault.

They'd bloody kill him. Really—maybe they would actually kill him if they found this stuff on him. They'd go that far, wouldn't they, rather than spend the rest of their lives in jail?

Still trembling, Nick began ripping up the pictures and flinging the remains in between his legs into the pan. He tried to tear the lot up, but there were too many. He got through four or five before he came to his senses and sat there, panting.

Why had the little rat done this to him? But of course, he already knew the answer. It was revenge. It was standing up for yourself. Oliver was trying to reclaim his life.

For a second, Nick had a glimpse of the kind of courage Oliver had shown. To do this! To own these pictures was to own what had happened—to remember it, to keep it with you, to make it a part of you. It was something Nick was utterly unable to do for himself.

Oliver was braver than anyone he'd ever known.

Nick shook his head. Amazing! How hard had it been for Oliver, stealing these from under Creal's own nose? He'd slept with these under his pillow all night. No wonder he handed them over as soon as he could.

The little blond slip of a boy had shown them all the way.

Nick flipped through the pictures again. It wasn't just Mr. Creal—there were other men here as well. He recognized one of the men who had raped him in the Secure Unit. Got ya! You bastard. See how they liked being locked up and raped—because sure as hell that's what would happen to them when they went to jail. Nick had heard stories of what happened to nonces in the nick. He just couldn't wait for it to happen to lovable old Uncle Tony Creal.

He stuffed the photos down his pajamas, took a breath, and left the loo. He wasn't even going to tell Davey about this. It wouldn't be fair to him. It wasn't fair to Nick, either. Just to know the pictures existed was more of a weight than he wanted to carry. But he was going to do it anyway.

They were going down Bunker's Lane. They had to. If they failed now, God knows.

Davey was waiting for him outside the toilet, pretending to wash his face. As soon as Nick came out, he joined him and they walked together back to the dorm.

"We're on," said Nick.

"He got 'em?"

"Three packs."

Davey looked at him in disbelief. Nick patted his towel and nodded.

"Three packs? The little git."

"It's this morning," said Nick.

"Now?"

"Creal will know he took 'em."

Davey pulled a face and shook his head.

"What's up with you?"

"It's a setup, innit?"

"No!"

They were back in the dorm by now. Nick managed to stash the cigs under his mattress while they started to make their beds, carrying on their conversation in snatches and whispers. "Little Oliver nicks something off dear old Tony? I don't think so. Soon as we set off they'll be on us. It's just an excuse to get us."

"They don't need an excuse."

"It's a setup," insisted Davey. "It's the wrong day 'n' all. Why so quick? Why can't we wait for Friday like we planned?"

"I told you, Creal will know he nicked 'em."

Davey snorted in disgust. "It's too bloody quick, mate. You'd be mad to run on the back of his say-so."

Nick paused. It wasn't the fact that Oliver had stolen the fags that had him convinced—it was the fact that he'd stolen the pictures. But now it was time to make up the beds and there was no way he could attract attention by sneaking Davey back to the loos to show him those.

"Trust me, mate," he said, looking Davey hard in the eye.

Davey shook his head. "It's not you I'm worried about, mate."

Nick felt a surge of anger. This was the last thing he needed. "You coming or not?"

"Am I bollocks."

"Then we'll go without you, mate."

Davey shot him a glare of sheer hatred and looked away.

"Tell you what," hissed Nick. "You can stay here on your arse, wanking off old men if you feel like it. I'm out of here."

Davey didn't reply.

"Shall I tell Andrews to leave you an' all? Or what?"

The whistle blew for inspection. Davey turned away. "Tell him what you want, I don't care." He went to line up by the snooker table for Toms, with Nick following angrily behind.

The morning rush was always the same—get to the toilet, get your bed made, wait for inspection. Most of the boys didn't bother with a wash. Then downstairs, set out the tables, serve breakfast, clear up, then straight away off to school. The only chance he had to bribe the prefects was while the breakfast things were being put away.

Sixty ciggies. It wasn't bad. They stood as good a chance as anyone ever did.

He snuck up to the prefects one at a time and pushed a packet into their hand. Andrews looked sharply at him.

Nick nodded. "Twenty to leave me, Oliver, and Davey," he said.

"Three of you? And bloody Oliver? I'll want more than this, Toms'll never believe he can get away."

Nick shook his head. "That's all there is."

"I could report you anyway," hissed Andrews. "I want more."

"It's all there is. Report me and I'll tell how you got 'em," said Nick. He shrugged. Andrews shrugged. He'd known what Nick was going to say before he asked. But it was always worth a try.

"OK?" said Nick.

"Right." He looked Nick in the face for the first time and nodded.

"Including Oliver."

Andrews paused, then nodded again. "Him, too."

Nick walked off to deal with Julian and then with the third prefect, Taylor, from Oliver's side of the house. A while later, he saw the three of them together in a huddle. He would have given the world to know what exactly they were saying.

What made Bunker's Lane so desperate was the chase. They literally hunted you down, like wolves after the deer; and like all predators they were always fiercer, crueler, and harder than you were. But there were tricks. One was to do it in herds, like the deer. At least some of you would get away. With any luck, when the other boys saw three of them set off, they'd set off too and give them more of a chance.

And if you were small and you couldn't run, like Oliver—then you had to use a bribe. Use a bribe and hope for the best . . .

It was almost half a mile to freedom—half a mile of mud-sliding, chest-heaving, lung-bursting running. If you could go fast enough to convince the prefects that they weren't going to catch you, they might just give it up. It was the one thing the runners had on their side—they cared. They cared desperately or they wouldn't be running. The prefects had just their pride to lose and perhaps a beating if they didn't put up a good show. It wasn't the same.

Davey took his place next to Nick and gave him a scowl.

"I told 'em to leave you, too," hissed Nick, but Davey looked away. Nick was furious. It could never work, not without Davey. And who was going to get caught with those pictures tucked down the back of his pants? And what would happen to him then?

They lined up outside in the yard. Oliver looked as if he was about to die of fear. Nick tried to give him an encouraging smile, but it felt like a sneer on his face.

The crocodile began to move. Davey was watching him. Nick looked away. It was too late to stop now.

Calm down, thought Nick to himself. Keep your mind clear. He looked across at Oliver, who had gone literally green; it was a wonder no one noticed. Nick managed a wink. Oliver just stared, slack-jawed, like a fool.

They paused briefly as another line of kids from the other side of the building joined them, then carried on. Closer. Twenty yards. Ten.

Then they were there.

"Go, go, go!" yelled Nick. The whole crocodile jumped as three figures leaped out of the line like dogs at a racetrack, skidding on the wet grass, rushing toward the hedge that hid the mouth of Bunker's Lane.

"No way!" yelled Davey, as he hurtled like a rocket past Nick. No way was he getting left behind. Nick's spirits soared.

Yes! A shout went up—"*Oi!*" The call to hunt. Out of the

corners of his eyes he saw the prefects come to life, bodies flung forward, straining toward them. It meant nothing, they had to chase hard so long as they were in sight of the staff. Once they were behind the bushes they'd see if they were taking the bribes. Nick glanced quickly around. The bastards were going as fast as they could. And Oliver was already falling back! Please, God, let him make it to the bushes!

Nick hit the leaves and twigs in an act of faith, he couldn't see through. They lashed at his eyes and face and then he was out the other side into Bunker's Lane. The ground was broken and the cobbles were slippy, so he had to slow down. A few yards away Davey hit the ground with his arse and bounced back up with a grimace of pain. But where was Oliver? Christ!

Then the bushes parted and there he was.

"Off the path, Oliver, get off the path," gasped Nick over his shoulder. If he stayed on the lane the prefects would have to pass him to chase the rest of them—it was asking too much. He waved his hand to show the way. Oliver gasped and skidded off behind the bushes. Behind him he could hear the prefects, Andrews and Julian, shouting and cursing—shouting too loudly, perhaps, to convince the staff. Nick prayed they'd slow down or even stop once they were through the trees, but they were still coming on strong. He skidded—looking back over his shoulder like that was making him lose his balance. He hit the ground, splashing into a puddle, jumped up, and ran off again, full pelt.

They were gaining! He'd lost vital seconds helping Oliver.

He knew the prefects would have to get at least one of them. It couldn't be Oliver, it couldn't be Oliver! It couldn't be him, either, not with what he had in his back pocket.

And it couldn't be Davey because Davey was his mate. But Davey was miles ahead already. Nick could see his white face glancing back at him.

"Come on!" he yelled. Nick redoubled his efforts—but the footsteps he expected to hear behind him weren't coming. He risked another look back—they were falling back! The prefects were falling back, the bribe was working. He was as good as free.

It had just occurred to Nick that he hadn't seen Andrews the last time he looked, when he heard a shout—

"Oi!" It was Andrews. He was off the path—after Oliver, the bastard! Nick swerved, jumped over a fallen log, and ran into the trees and stopped, gulping for breath, trying to listen. He could hear the sounds of running.

"I've got you . . . !" sang Andrews.

"Leave him, Andrews," screamed Nick.

"Nick, you twat!" yelled Davey ahead, not breaking his stride. Nothing was going to make him stop running, but Nick held back. The other prefects had turned off the trail to go for Oliver, too, now. He could hear them somewhere behind him, cracking a joke.

Nick doubled back. He heard the chase—heard the thump and the wind knocked out of the smaller boy's throat. He rushed back and burst out of the trees almost on top of them. Andrews was heaving Oliver off the ground by his hair.

"Please! Please!" yelled Oliver, his face a mask of panic. Nick took a step toward them.

Andrews watched him closely. "Oi, over here!" he yelled. There was an answering cry. Reinforcements. Nick paused, unsure of what to do—unsure of what he could do. But already he could hear Julian and Taylor coming through the trees.

"You're dead," Andrews told him quietly; and he nodded his head, meaning, get out quick, run!

"Let him go," demanded Nick. Andrews smiled slightly and shook his head. Nick glanced longingly at the way to freedom.

"Don't leave me, please, don't leave me," begged Oliver, in a voice of pure panic.

Andrews slapped him hard. "Shut up," he commanded.

The other prefects thundered up and Nick's legs made up his mind for him.

"I got the package, Oliver—I'll be back. Tomorrow!" he swore. He had a flash of Oliver's white-green face; then he fled.

But now, of course, Julian and Taylor were between him and freedom. He'd thrown away his chance as far as they were concerned, and they were really after him now. He could hear them coming up fast. There was no way. There really was no way. They were bigger, faster, and stronger than him. He was stuffed. Already they were right behind him.

Nick redoubled his speed—and then suddenly crouched down in the mud and leaves. Julian couldn't brake in time and tripped headlong over Nick's back and went flying into a tangle of brambles, with a scream of pain.

The other prefect was right behind him, but Nick jumped up and seized a branch in his hand without even thinking about it. A good big stout stick a couple of meters long. As Taylor came running up, he swung it. He could see from the older boy's face that he really wasn't expecting Nick to actually do this. He froze and stood there a picture of surprise, watching the end of the stick whistle toward him. He turned his face away at the last minute so he never got it across the front of his face, but across the side. It made a sickening crack and down he went like a dummy.

Julian was back on his feet by this time. He was a big lad, but he paused when Nick waggled the stick at him. On the ground, Taylor was rolling from side to side, clutching his face and groaning. There was blood all over his hands and face.

"What have you done?" yelled Julian.

"I'll 'ave you, too," hissed Nick. Julian got down to look at Taylor, who was bleeding thickly from his scalp and ear.

"You're mad," Julian told Nick.

Nick backed off and shook the stick at Julian. "You want some, you fucker?" he asked. "You want some? I'll break your neck."

Julian just goggled at him. Nick was breaking all the rules. Men hit big boys and big boys hit smaller boys. But smaller boys never beat up big boys with a stick.

"You're mad," said Julian again; but he stayed where he was. Behind him, Andrews appeared, holding on to Oliver. He stood watching impassively among the rhododendrons.

Nick stuck the stick under his arm, and half walked, half ran toward Bunker's Lane. A second later, when he looked back and saw Julian helping Taylor to his feet, he knew he was free.

He broke into a trot. He reached a wall higher than his head and had to jump up to peer over it. There was a road, hedges, and a row of semidetached houses looking back at him. He clambered over the wall, looked around him—and there was Davey, jumping out from the cover of some overhanging bushes. He ran to him. They stood there together, looking at each other and shaking their heads and grinning.

"I'm lovin' it! I'm lovin' it!"

"Yeah . . ."

"Ran like a tornado, mate."

"Leaving like a bleedin' jet plane, wannit?"

"Oliver?" asked Davey, pulling a face.

"Bastards got him. But I got . . ." Nick patted his back pocket. It was only then that he found that the photos had fallen out of his pocket as he ran, every single one of them. They were scattered all through the woods up and down Bunker's Lane for anyone to see.

"The pictures . . ."

"What pictures?"

Nick shook his head. He didn't even want to think about it. It was too late. And Oliver was going to have to face the music alone.

20
HIDING

There wasn't time to worry about Oliver. They weren't out of trouble yet. As they stood there, the staff would be on the phone to the police. They had to get away, back to north Manchester and their own ground. So far, they didn't even know where they were.

They were hiding under an overgrown weeping willow that cascaded onto the pavement beyond the wall that marked the boundary of the home. It was early, about eight in the morning. The day was speeding up—cars, cyclists, but fortunately not many people on foot. Those that were stayed on the other side of the road, as there was no pavement on their side.

"We're bloody stuck in this bloody tree," said Davey.

He was right. They were in their Meadow Hill school uniforms, dark blue with bright yellow stripes on the jumper, blazer, and tie. Everything about it was designed to attract attention. Not only that, but the clothes were all ancient hand-me-downs. The two boys resembled a pair of badly dressed wasps looking for trouble.

"You might as well write 'On the run' on the front of yer head than go out in this lot," said Davey. So the first thing they did was chuck the lot—tie, jumper, and blazer. It was a cool morning, and they weren't at all warm in their shirts, but it was better than going around like a living advertisement for runaways.

They hid the clothes in some bushes, stepped out into the morning sunshine, and walked bravely down the road. A woman out walking her dog took a good long look at them and then turned her head away, her lips pursed.

"What you looking at?" shouted Davey.

Nick nudged him with his elbow. "Twat," he hissed.

"I didn't like the way she was looking at us."

"Everyone's going to be looking at us like that. You're attracting attention."

"Who gives a toss? We're out, aren't we?"

But Nick wasn't so sure. He hadn't forgotten the scoutmaster. The police would have their eyes peeled looking for them, and any one of the people walking past could pick up a phone and give them away. He watched them, the cars driving past, the kids on their way to school on their bikes, their eyes flicking over them and then away . . .

"This is hopeless. People know as soon as they see us," he said.

"We could nick some clothes off a washing line," suggested Davey. Back in Ancoats, that was how he and his brothers and sisters had kept themselves clothed the whole of their lives. They kept a watch on the back gardens for any washing hanging out. But it was early yet, no one had had time to do the washing and the lines hung in the morning sunshine with nothing on them but a few sparrows and pegs.

"I'm hungry," said Davey.

"Shut up," said Nick. They had to get all the way back home and they didn't even know where they were. He didn't even want to have to think about food. But a moment later, they had their first break of good luck—a road sign.

"Manchester, 5m," it said. The sign pointed down a broad, busy road.

"That'll be to the town center," said Nick. "Once we're there, we'll know how to get back."

"Oh, look at you, you big beautiful road," crooned Davey. "Oh, man, I'm lovin' this. We're good as home!"

Nick pulled a face. "Big main road, two lads walking along in their shirtsleeves, coppers going up and down it every five minutes. How far do you think we're goin' to get like that?" he asked gloomily.

Davey was getting fed up with him. "Every time somethin' good 'appens, you find the bad side to it," he said. "Anyone'd think you don't want to get away."

He was even more cross when Nick vetoed his next cunning plan. As they headed off down the busy road, they found a laundrette. Davey decided the thing to do was wait in a shop doorway till someone came out with a bag full of clothes, rush out, bang into them, knocking the clothes out of their arms, grab the bag, and run.

"Bingo! And we walk 'ome dressed like heroes," he explained.

"Yeah, or girls. Or old men. Or nurses. Or babies. Depending on what they've been washing," said Nick sourly.

Davey was furious, more from frustration than anything else, although he had to admit the fault to his plan.

"Right, well, instead of pickin' holes in mine, what's yours then, brainbox?" he demanded.

Nick turned on his heel.

"Where you goin'?" Davey asked.

"Back."

"Back?"

"We need to hide out. There's loads a places 'round Bunker's and it's the last place they'll think to look. Then when it gets busy and the rush hour comes, we can walk back and no one'll notice us."

"I can't wait that long!" exclaimed Davey. It seemed against all logic to actually go back toward Meadow Hill.

"We need the cover of darkness. We gotta give ourselves a chance, Davey."

They had an argument about it. What was the point of breaking free and then hanging around like a bunch of old men in the park?

"Runnin' is supposed to be exciting," insisted Davey.

"Yeah, an' gettin' caught's exciting too, innit?"

Davey wriggled and moaned, but in the end . . .

"I'm right, though, int I? You know it," said Nick smugly.

"You're always bloody right," snarled Davey. Nick was more interested in getting clean away than having fun—that could come later. And if that meant spending a day hiding in the bushes, that was what he was going to do. He even made them stop off and recover their uniforms from the bushes they'd dumped them in, so they could at least stay warm. Davey moaned his teeth out, but he did it anyway. On his own, he would have just run straight home and taken his chances. He didn't expect anything else but to go in and out of care, and then in and out of prison, for as long as he drew breath. But Nick was different. Once he was out, he planned on staying out.

The boys took care to hide well away from the lane itself, in the woods around it. Sitting there with nothing to do, Nick started to think about the pictures that Oliver had stolen. They'd be scattered up and down Bunker's Lane like confetti at a wedding.

What was Creal going to do? He couldn't leave them there. Maybe some of them had already been blown onto the road. If they got into the right hands and were handed in, Creal would get what was coming to him after all. And meanwhile, Oliver was still in there . . .

Nick couldn't leave it alone. He stood up.

"Where you off to?" Davey wanted to know.

Nick licked his lips. "You know how I knew to trust Oliver today?" he asked.

"'Ow come?"

"He nicked something else apart from them tabs."

"What?"

"Pictures," said Nick. "Photos."

Davey goggled at him. "What kind a pictures?" he asked, although Nick could see by his face that he knew already.

"Pictures of him with boys. You know."

"Dirty pictures."

"Yeah."

Davey looked away, then back.

"Nick—where are they?"

Nick waved his hand back into the woods. "Lost 'em. They fell out me pocket."

"Thank God for that."

"I'm going back to get 'em."

"You're bloody not!" Davey was on his feet and standing in front of him. "You're crazy! If I'da known that, I'd never 'ave gone along with it."

"That's why I never told you."

Davey shook his head. "You're not goin'. We get caught with those, we're dead, mate."

"If I can get just one," said Nick.

Davey shook his head. He was sick of this. "Stop coming on like some kind of fucking social worker on me," he said. "We're out. We're out! What more do you want?"

"I want Creal locked up."

"Oh, right. You want justice, is that it? There is no justice, Nick. 'Aven't you learned that yet?"

Nick looked away. "People like him get locked up . . ."

"People like him get away with it. Grow up."

Davey turned away in disgust and sat fuming on a fallen log. Nick stood looking at him for a moment.

"All right," he said. "What about your brothers and sisters . . ."

"Don't bring my family into this!"

"Why not? You lot are in and out of these places all the

time. How about your kid getting in here? How about Creal taking a fancy to him? How'd you like that?"

"You don't get it, do you, Nick? I'll tell you. When I was about eight, right, I was in one a those places with our kid, Sid, he was only about four. They were hitting on both of us, at night in the dorms. 'Specially Sid, 'e was quite good-looking then. So we did a runner, me and 'im both. I got us out and I got us downtown and into the local cop shop and I shopped the fat nonce that was hitting on us. And ya know what 'appened? The police listened very nicely, thank you very much, and then got us in the cop car and drove us back, thank you very much. And on the way, the copper sat in the back with our Sid had his hands up the front of his shorts. What do you think of that?"

Nick shook his head.

"The coppers are Creal's mates. Coppers, the nonces, the house tutors—they're all on the same side. So what's the point? You just have to live with it. I tried justice and it don't fucking work. OK?" Davey turned away and stared furiously off into the woods.

"You're joking . . ."

"I'm not joking."

Nick sat down. He didn't know what to say. What could he say? Davey was right. There was no point.

They sat and waited. Ten minutes went past; then he stood up.

"All right," he said. "They are all on the same side. But what about Oliver? In there with Creal."

"There's nothing we can do about that."

"And they're not all nonces. It only takes one good one, right? And if I do find that good one and I 'aven't got those pictures, who's going to believe me, then? No, mate. I'm going to 'ave a look."

"You're a twat, then," said Davey. "Be your own fault if they bloody pick you up, warn't?"

He settled himself more firmly down on his log and looked the other way while Nick went back to Bunker's Lane on his own.

He wasn't to know it, but the photos had burst out of his pocket quite early on, shortly after they had got into the cover of the woods. Oliver's panic and desperate pleas when Andrews got him were because he had seen them tumble out and scatter among the fallen leaves. But Nick didn't know this and he was scared to go close to the home, so really, he was wasting his time. He hung back from the lane and tried to spot the pictures scattered on the ground ahead, but he saw nothing. Had they all been picked up already? He looked toward the school, trying to spot flashes of white on the ground, but he wasn't prepared to risk getting too close. He crept as close as he dared—surely he'd find at least one photo. He was still several hundred yards away from the buildings when he spotted someone else through the trees.

There was a man, red-faced with exertion, stumbling about on the cobbles and among the thickets. Nick hid himself away and waited as quietly as he could, until at last the figure leaned with one arm against a tree, bent his head, and sobbed.

Sure enough, it was Creal, looking for the lost pictures. He was smeared in mud and green algae from the wet forest floor, and weeping with fear and humiliation.

He had woken up that morning without the slightest fear or suspicion of what was about to come. He still had a half packet of cigarettes left, so he had no need to look in his drawer and discover the looted packets of Bensons. When he received a telephone call from Toms telling him about the escape bid he was astonished to discover that Oliver had been among the runners. It was so amazing, it almost amused him. The other boys, maybe—although even then, he could never really grasp what it was they were running to. Their old homes? Working-class dens of misery and privation? Surely not. But Oliver was one of the privileged few, and he didn't even have that to go back to.

He told them to leave the captured boy in the Secure Unit for an hour or so. He'd forgive him, of course—he always did. But let him sweat it out for a while first. Give him time to realize the risks he was taking.

Less than an hour later, someone had stuffed an envelope under his office door. He got up and had a look down the corridor, but there was no one there. Odd. He tore the envelope open, and inside was a photograph of himself, trousers around his ankles, buggering a boy.

Creal's blood ran stone cold. He staggered back against the wall. He heard himself whimpering, like a boy himself. He ran to the sitting room and ransacked the chest of drawers where he kept these things.

Gone. All gone.

Oliver!

It pierced his heart. How could he? After all he'd done for him . . . after the times they'd had together. How could he betray him like this?

But no time for that now. There was a note with the photograph.

"Found this among the trees by the old lane."

The old lane—that meant it was a member of staff; a boy would have called it Bunker's. Mr. Creal ran straight out. He had to get those pictures back. Just one of them could ruin him. Public disgrace. Dragged through the courts. Everyone would know! Then prison. And he knew very well how the other inmates treated men like him inside. Beatings. Rape. God knows what.

And so now here he was, searching among the bushes, around and around in the mud, getting filthier and filthier, looking for the evidence. Pathetic now—but as dangerous as ever. Nick waited quietly until he passed out of sight, then crept back to where he had left Davey.

He was half expecting him to be gone, but he was still there, sitting on his log, glaring at him as he came up.

"What?"

"It's Creal."

Davey jumped up. "Where?"

"No, not here. Miles off, down the lane. Don't worry, he didn't see me."

"Sick bastard."

"Let's get 'im," said Nick suddenly.

"You what?" demanded Davey.

"Let's get 'im. Let's teach 'im a lesson. Kick 'is head in. There's two of us. Why not?"

"You want assault added to the list, do yer?" asked Davey.

"We could do it together."

"You're not listening. You want assault added to the list?"

Nick argued but Davey wasn't having it. There was too much to lose. Nick had to swallow his bile. Once again, Creal was going to get away with it.

Tony Creal did suffer some sort of punishment, though—fear. He never did find all the pictures and had to live with the thought that someone was keeping them back, Nick, perhaps, waiting to take them down to the police, or one of the other boys, or a member of staff who would use them when the time was right. For years to come, the missing photographs hung above his head, his own personal sordid doom. By the time he gave up, Creal was short, by his own reckoning, of eight or nine pictures. Two had been picked up by the prefects on their way back. They looked at them, laughed at them, handed them around their mates, and then flushed them down the loo. They were too dangerous to hold. Another was one of a pair found by an anonymous house tutor, who had pushed one under Tony Creal's door and kept the other hidden away. As Creal surmised, he thought—who knows?—that one day it might come in handy. The remainder had been destroyed and flushed away by Nick. But that, of course, Creal was not to know.

Over the course of the day, Creal's disappointment turned

into anger. Oliver was still locked up in the Secure Unit, but Creal didn't go down to see him, not yet. Let the little bastard stew in his own juice. He knew what he'd done. Another day or so. Then it would be time to pay him a little visit, one that he really, really wasn't going to enjoy.

21
THE WAY HOME

Once he knew Creal was about, Davey wanted to clear off at once, but Nick managed to calm him down. They crept off to the farthest part of the grounds to hide instead, which was little more than a thicket of brambles and alder trees growing in a bog. Neither of them had a watch, and the temptation to creep out into the streets to try and find out the time was almost irresistible. Several hissing rows later, they heard a hum coming at them through the trees. The traffic was picking up.

"The rush hour? It can't be," said Nick.

"Must be lunch, then. That'll do me. Comin'?"

Nick shrugged sheepishly. "Comin'," he said.

So the runaways dumped their uniforms for the second time and began the long walk north.

At last, the lads were on a roll. The weather was pretty good—a bit of wind but the sun was out and the air was warm on the skin. There were plenty of people out and about on the streets, other kids around, on their way home for lunch or off about some other business, in and out of school uniform, so they didn't look so odd in their shirtsleeves as they had in the morning. Cars, including police cars, came and went but no one gave two boys on a busy road a second look.

The big road they'd found was the Palatine Road, leading right out of Northenden, where Meadow Hill was, past Rusholme and the universities and on right into the heart of Manchester. From there, they knew their own way.

All they had to do now was walk.

And all around them were the things of this world, things they'd taken for granted for so long and which had then been taken from them. Chip shops, sweet shops, curry houses. Dogs, people walking them. Music, coming out of the houses from time to time—Duran Duran, Adam Ant, the Teardrop Explodes. Nick had never realized how much had been taken from him when his mother died. Music! They can even steal that from you. And cars and people and the rubbish on the streets and the dog shit and the cracked pavements. He loved it all. It was all his. He was never going to lose it again.

For the first mile or so, they gassed and laughed and did imitations of the staff, or of each other running, fell around laughing, whooped it up. Davey had a great impression of Toms trying to hit them when they weren't there, which for some reason they both found hilarious. Nick got anxious again when the lunchtime rush died down, and nagged Davey to be less conspicuous. They walked a bit longer—then the hunger took over. You were always hungry at Meadow Hill, and they'd had nothing to eat since an inadequate breakfast in the Home hours ago. They were famished.

"We need to steal some food," said Davey. He looked at Nick sideways—he suspected that his friend was a bit of a wimp when it came to this and was half expecting him to say no, it's too soon, we're too near, we're not away yet.

Nick hesitated.

"What are we going to do, starve?" asked Davey. "Listen. I have a plan."

"Not again," groaned Nick. But as it happened, this one wasn't too bad.

The plan was called runaway chips. It worked like this. You go into a fish and chip shop, you order chips, and then run off with them without paying.

"They taste better that way," said Davey.

Nick bit his lip. Davey and his brothers and sisters had more or less lived off thieving for years, but he wasn't used to it so well. He and his mates had nicked stuff, but it was all dare—sweets or a magazine, a T-shirt at the most. This was different. This was steal or starve.

"You've not got anyone to feed you now, matey," Davey told him. "You better get used to it, or what you gonna do? Starve?"

"Aren't we too close to Meadow Hill? If they catch us . . ."

"For a bag a chips?" said Davey. "Who's going to run us down for a bag of chips?"

"Maybe we'd be better off begging . . . ?"

"Begging!" said Davey in disgust. He didn't mean that begging was beneath him, just, why beg when you can get more stealing? "Anyhow, we're too old to beg," he said. "No one feels sorry for you once you're over ten. Here's a chippy! Let's go."

Nick was about to steal his first meal.

"What happens if they ask for the money first?" he wanted to know.

"Then you do a runaway nothing," said Davey. "If it was one of the chippies 'round my way, they never hand over aught without getting the money first, but they might not expect it here."

So they tried it—and it wasn't easy. The first two, the people behind the counter wanted the money first. In the third, there was a queue built up—Davey shook his head and they left.

"We'd never get out the door with that lot there," he said.

In the fourth, though, it worked. The chippy handed over the chips to Nick. He should have waited for Davey to get his, but instead he just thought, "Go for it!"—and turned and ran out the door as soon as the paper hit his hand.

"Oi!" yelled the man. Davey turned and jumped out of the shop on Nick's heels.

"Oi!" yelled the man again. The two of them hoofed it down the pavement as fast as they could. As Davey had predicted, the man wasn't going to leave his shop full of customers for the sake of one bag of chips. He stuck his head out and yelled, "Where's my money? You little bastards!" as he watched them disappear around the corner. The city opened, let them through and on their way without another thought. They made it around the corner, dodged into the ground floor of a multistory car park, and hid behind a ledge to eat their booty.

"You went off like a bloody rocket, man," exclaimed Davey. They both started laughing. "Jesus! You must have a jet-propelled arse to take off like that. Did you see his face? Oh, man, I loved the face."

Nick giggled and snorted as he unwrapped the chips. Then his face was hit by the damp smell of hot salty chips and vinegar fumes, and they both shut up and started eating. It was gorgeous. It was delicious—it was the first decent-tasting meal they'd had since they got sent inside.

"Chips," groaned Nick. He'd forgotten how delicious they were.

"Heaven, innit?" They ate and ate and licked the paper, and then the little burst of heaven was over.

"God, they're good," Nick moaned, licking the last traces of grease from his fingers.

"Right," said Davey when they'd done. "Now let's go and do it again."

On the way home that day they had runaway chips twice, runaway chocolate, runaway milk, and runaway Battenberg cake. In the last one, a security guard from the shop actually took the trouble to chase them down the road, but they soon lost him. They drank the milk out of the carton and ate the cake like a chocolate bar, big bites from the end. In that way, over a couple of miles along the Wilmslow Road, they ended up stuffed. It was fun, but it wound up your nerves like elastic every time. All Nick wanted to do was lie down and sleep it off . . .

Already, it had been a long day.

By the time they went through Rusholme, the curry mile, the smells of all that delicious Indian food hardly touched them, although Davey wanted to do a runaway curry just on principle, but Nick talked him out of it. They marched on, past the universities and on to Oxford Road. As they got close, one thing started to fill their minds: home.

Few people in care have a happy home, but happy or unhappy, it's theirs. Davey was thinking anxiously about his as they walked the last few miles into the town center. He was hoping that maybe this time it would work. Maybe this time he'd be welcomed. Maybe he'd be able to behave himself so well that his parents would love him enough to let him stay. Maybe this time there'd be enough money, or his mum off the booze, or his dad in work and earning enough money to keep him.

Fat chance—he knew it in his heart. But you can always hope.

What had Nick to hope for?

Perhaps Jenny would take him in? But probably not. He was the kid who'd made a mess at her place, that was all, and she was his mum's friend, not his. He hadn't heard from her in all the time he'd been inside—that said it all, as far as he was concerned. If only he'd known, she had been nagging like a fury to get him back. No doubt she'd have done it, too, if Creal hadn't plotted against it. But Nick didn't know that and whenever he thought about Jenny, he felt a bitter anger well up in his throat. As soon as his mum was gone, Jenny had dropped him, that's how it seemed to him. So why should anything be different now? She'd hand him back over as soon as look at him, and he wasn't going to risk that happening.

But then where? Where was his new home? Now that he had left, it was dawning on him for the first time—he had nothing to go to.

"No one's going to tell me what to do ever again," he boasted hollowly. "It's the street for me." He nodded as if he had the better deal.

"Which bit of the street are you on tonight, then?" asked Davey, cruelly.

Nick shrugged. "Stay at a few friends' for a while, till I get on me feet," he replied. Davey looked at him, regretting his jibe.

"We'll meet up," he said. "I'll introduce yer to Sunshine." He nodded. "You'll see. 'E'll help us out, mate."

"You don't need it, you've got a home to go to," said Nick.

"Maybe I have," said Davey. "But then again, maybe I don't." Nick shrugged. "You'll be OK," said Davey encouragingly. "I've been on me own before, it's fun. Sleep at your mates' for a few nights. I'll be doin' it meself once me dad gets sick of the sight of me. It's better than being at home, really," he added thoughtfully. "At least you get to keep what you steal for yourself."

"Yeah, and at least there's no one to knock you about if you say anything out of line."

"And at least your mates are on your side. You know where you are with yer mates," finished Davey.

Nick nodded. "I'll be OK," he said. "We'll meet up, yeah? Let each other know how we got on, right?"

Davey nodded. Up ahead of them, just down the road, they could see the tower of the Refuge Insurance Building, with the word *Refuge* written on it in giant red letters. Manchester town center. Home! Just for a moment, it felt like it. Now they knew where they were.

They walked together into Piccadilly Gardens and on up Oldham Street into Ancoats. They got to the parting of the ways.

"Look up a few mates," said Davey. "Mates are the thing, mate." He clapped Nick on the back one more time, and turned left up the road toward his own street, leaving Nick on his own.

Nick walked a little farther until he got to some old lock-ups and garages a few streets away from where he lived. As usual, a number of them were empty, doors half ripped off, and in one that he knew there was an old sofa, fairly dry, tucked away at the back.

Nicholas Dane laid himself out on the sofa and closed his eyes. He reflected that it was the first time he had been on his own since he got taken into care. Then he fell fast asleep.

22
HOMECOMING

He woke with a start in the dark. He'd been dreaming, he couldn't remember what, but he was left feeling scared. It was a moment before he gathered his senses together. Then he thought, "I'm out!" He didn't know whether to feel full of triumph or terrified. He truly was on his own now, with every hand in authority against him.

He was back home. He had no home. He stood up, went to the door to look over the houses of the estate. Night had fallen. The dark felt safe. He went out to see what was what.

First thing, Nick went to see his old house. He hung around by the car park at the end of his road, looking down toward it. The curtains were still up. Maybe it was empty, but it didn't feel like his anymore and he was worried about going to have a closer look. Maybe it was full of ghosts. He stood and watched for a while, but no one came in or out and he left after a few minutes.

Nick had no idea what time it was but it couldn't have been all that late, because there were still people about on the street and the corner shops were still open. Next off, he went around to see his friend Simon, his best friend from the time before. He knocked anxiously—what would they think? He was dressed like a divvy apart from anything else.

But to his huge relief it wasn't just OK—it was great. The door was opened by Simon's mum. Her face was a picture.

"Nick! Oh my God! How are you? You got taken into care. Your poor mum! What a disaster. I couldn't believe it, and we never even got to see you, just whoosh, gone, where is he?" She turned over her shoulder and bellowed, "Simon!" and carried on, hardly drawing a breath. "Look—you've changed. What are you wearing? Aren't they feeding you enough?"

Nick grinned and shrugged. She hauled him inside and ushered him through. Mrs. Simon was a big woman, wearing her work suit still. Nick had to squeeze carefully past her enormous breasts to get into the hall. The sound of the telly blaring out came from the front room.

"Simon's doing his homework—I mean, watching the TV. Eh? Same old Simon."

Simon was lying on the sofa in front of the blaring TV, his schoolwork in a heap on the floor. He scrambled to his feet when he saw Nick and then stood awkwardly in front of him, grinning. He punched him on the shoulder; Nick punched him back. He punched Nick back. Nick wanted to grab him in a headlock but his mum was standing watching them, grinning like a crocodile, and he was embarrassed.

"Well!" she exclaimed, flapping her arms like a fat old panda. "Here we are again. So what was the home like, Nick? Any good?"

Nick had to look at her twice to realize she wasn't joking.

He had to remember—no one knew. She was looking at him all eager, hoping things were OK and never guessing just how bad they could be.

What could he say?

"OK. Bit rough. Food's crap," he said brightly.

Mrs. Simon nodded. It was as if none of it had ever happened.

"The things you hear about those places you wouldn't believe, but I suppose a half-decent lad like you is taken care of all right." She laughed, obviously relieved. "You must have fallen on your feet, eh? Nick Dane, eh, Simon? Always falls on his feet, dun't he, Si?"

Simon nodded and stared at his friend as if he were some sort of a magic trick. He had huge eyes with long brown lashes—cow's eyes, Nick used to tease. He blinked and smiled in delight. Nick smiled weakly. He spread his hands.

"Abracadabra," he said.

Mrs. Simon suddenly leaned forward and gave him a big hug that almost smothered him. "Good to have you back, Nick, good to have you back," she said. She was getting slightly tearful. She stood back and looked at him. "Why've you been such a stranger? First time I've seen you since."

Nick shrugged. "They don't let you have many visits out," he said.

Mrs. Simon bulged in outrage. "Not many visits? Bastards? Are they? Are they bastards, Nick?"

Nick paused, unsure if he wanted to give her any reason to start snooping. In the end, he knew only one thing; no one was ever going to believe him, so he wasn't going to bother telling them.

Mrs. Simon helped him out. "The usual, is it? Some bastards and some not, eh?"

Nick agreed with that rather vague version of how things were at Meadow Hill.

"And you're out now, are you?"

Nick had his lie ready. "Staying with me mum's friend in Middleton. Got a few days off."

"Right." Mrs. Simon nodded. It was a Thursday. He could see what she was thinking . . . Odd kind of day to have off . . .

"Well, Nick, you're always welcome 'round here, you know that. Always room for one more. Now then," she said, looking for some treat for him. "I bet they don't feed you enough, I know they don't, they never feed kids enough at these places. So what can I get you? Celebration fry-up? Sausage and beans? I've got some crumble left, you can have that for afters. Go on, Nick, say yes. It's what mums do . . ." She got flustered again, talking about what mums do, to a boy who'd lost his. But Nick's mouth was watering already.

"I'll eat anything you can give me, Mrs. Simon," he said. He always called her Mrs. Simon, after her son. She giggled at his nerve; she didn't know that he called all his friends' parents by their sons' names—it saved having to remember who they were.

Mrs. Simon rushed into the kitchen to cook his food, and he and Simon flopped down on the sofa together.

"Sorry about your mum," said Simon. "I can't believe it."

"Yeah."

"Crap."

"Yeah."

"And they took you out of school and everything."

"Never went back after she died."

Simon blushed and looked away at the terrible word, *died*. What do you say to someone who's lost their mother, their home, their school, their mates, everything?

"We went to the funeral," said Simon.

Nick stared at him in amazement. "Funeral?" he said stupidly. Of course there would have been a funeral. No one had said a word to him about it. Despite himself, he felt his eyes filling with tears, but he fought them back. Simon was watching him curiously.

"What happened?" Simon asked.

Nick forced a grin. "I was in the cooler," he said.

"Wow. They locked you up so you couldn't go to your mum's funeral?" said Simon, his eyes goggling.

"It was a fight."

"Wow. Who was it?"

"One of the staff." Nick nodded. "They treat you like shit, so I treated them like shit straight back." He paused, unsure how to go on. "They beat you up like a man," he said.

Simon didn't reply. He just stared.

"We had to escape, over the fence," said Nick, groping to get into his role as desperado. "They hunt you down with dogs."

"What sort of dogs?"

"Alsatians and Dobermans," said Nick immediately. "I'm on the run, mate. Don't tell yer mum, all right?"

"No way. Amazing," said Simon. His big eyes opened wider than ever. He literally goggled. Starstruck.

Nick proceeded to tell his friend a lorry load of truths, half truths, lies, and exaggerations in which he was the hero of everything. Dogs, tunnels under the wire, midnight chases, cheeking the staff, getting tricks over on them. Revenge, leadership, double and dare. Well, what was he supposed to say? "Nah, mate, I got beaten up over and over again, gang-raped by a bunch of middle-aged men in smelly suits, and tortured in a bath of cold water for running away until I cried like a baby."

Nick had no money, no parents, no school, no home, nothing. But he wasn't going to be a victim in the eyes of his friends. So he made it up. He was on the run—an outlaw. He was so full of glamour, it was coming out of his ears. As he told his tall tales, Nick was suddenly certain that everything was going to be all right. He'd been scared that while he'd been in care he'd been turned into some sort of freak. But no. Instead, he was a desperado. It was like prisoners of war. He'd been tortured, he'd escaped. He was on the run. Same old Nick! It was an adventure.

The food came in and it was glorious. Two eggs, beans, three fat sausages, a heap of bacon, bread and butter. There were even a couple of mushrooms leaking juice onto his plate. Nick began to eat, steadily but so quickly it just evaporated. Mrs. Simon gawped, took the plate away, and came back in with a huge plateload of apple crumble and cold custard. Afterward, Nick felt like a python that had just eaten a buffalo—he wanted to curl up, lie down, and sleep for the next three months.

Simon wanted to go out and hear some more stories and look up a few more mates, but it was getting late.

"Nick'll need to be getting back, won't you, Nick?" said Mrs. Simon.

"Yeah . . . The buses run quite late."

"But you could stay here if you like," she suggested.

Nick looked sideways at Simon and grinned. "That'd be great."

"Anytime, Nick—there's always room for you here. You better ring your mum's friend, though," she added, and nodded to the phone in the corner.

Nick didn't even flicker. He hadn't spent four months in Meadow Hill without learning how to lie like an angel. He went to the phone, dialed a number at random . . . by sheer chance it began to ring, and then someone picked it up.

"Hi, Jenny," he said.

"I think you got the wrong number, mate."

"Is it all right if I stay over at Simon's?"

"Who's that?"

"Yeah, I'll be back tomorrow sometime. OK . . ."

"Who is this?"

"Great, no problem. See you then."

He put the phone down and gave Mrs. Simon the thumbs-up. Sorted. He had a bed for the night. He felt like he'd just struck gold.

He and Simon watched TV while she made a bed for him on Simon's floor, then they went up to bed. Nick told his stories of adventure on the high road, runaway chips, the cane, the prefects, and being on the run, and Simon brought him up to date on school, friends, boys and girls. He'd have been willing to go on till all hours, but suddenly, in mid-sentence almost, Nick fell asleep.

"Nick? Nick? You awake?" Simon didn't call him all that loudly, though. He leaned across and looked into his friend's face. Nick had changed, but he had no idea how. It was so strange seeing him lying there. He looked down into Nick's sleeping face as if he could see the past there. But he couldn't, so he turned the light off and went to sleep.

In the morning, it all happened quickly. Nick was stumbling downstairs, trying to keep up with Simon, but Mrs. Simon was wise to that and got Simon out of the house while Nick was still eating—no chance of any school if they went out the door together. She fed him a huge bowl of cereal, stuffed a tenner in his hand, made him promise to stay in touch, and pushed him out ahead of her on her way to catch the bus to work.

"'Bye, Nick," she yelled, trotting up the street at high speed on her little legs in her fat black suit.

"'Bye!" yodeled Nick back. She turned the corner and there he was, alone on the pavement. He looked up the road, he looked down the road. There was nothing there. So— what next?

Jenny? He shook his head. Jenny was all right, but even so.

Look what had happened last time. Nah, not her. Davey. Davey was going to introduce him to his mate Sunshine, who was going to help out in some way Nick didn't yet know. They'd agreed to meet in a few days, but the O'Brian house was just around the corner; it wouldn't hurt to go and have a nose.

At the house he found various O'Brians hanging around on the street and asked if any of them had seen Davey.

"What's it to you?" one of them asked aggressively.

"I'm a friend of his."

They shrugged. "Ain't seen him today" was all he could get out of them. Nick could see he wasn't being told everything, but there was nothing to do about that, so he left it.

On the road again. He had all day and no one to do it with. That's glamour for you.

The day crawled by—nowhere to go, no one to go there with. He spent most of the tenner at lunchtime just from sheer boredom after having failed to get a runaway at the local chippy. Then, more being bored, lonely, and scared. Eventually, somehow, it got to three o'clock and he went to hang around the school gates to pick up his mates and to see if he could sort out food and somewhere to sleep. Simon had spread the word—everyone wanted to meet him and to help him out, but he was alarmed to see how many people knew about him being back on the scene—all the police would have to do was ask and he'd be nabbed.

He wandered off with Simon and Jeremy to Jeremy's house, where, as he'd hoped, Mrs. Jeremy was happy to fill him up with food and ask him to stay for tea. Amanda was there too—Jeremy's sister, who had let him weep on her shoulder and kissed him. She was, he realized in amazement, pretty nearly the last girl he had spoken to for months. He would have loved to get her on her own and talk to her and tell her things, and maybe see if she'd let him kiss her again. She hung around a bit after dinner to watch telly and make chit-chat with him, but she didn't seem to have anything real to say—not like last time. When she left to see a friend, Nick was both disappointed and relieved. He had enough on his plate without having to think about girls.

Mrs. Jeremy didn't ask him to stay the night, though, so he had to go back to the lockups, where he spent a cold, scary night on his own under a damp blanket.

And that's how it went for the next few days. He talked Simon into letting him sneak into his room at night to sleep on the floor. There was no lock on his bedroom door, so Simon had to jam a chair under the door handle to keep his mum out in the morning.

"What's this locked for, you never lock this, you haven't even got a lock. Come and have some breakfast, you'll be late for school."

"I want some privacy," yelled Simon, pretending to be irritated.

"What do you want privacy for? No, don't answer that. Get up. What a boy . . ."

She left, suspecting nothing. Nick dressed himself in some of Simon's old clothes—jeans and T-shirt, the first time he'd been in jeans for four months—and legged it out the window and across the gardens to the road.

Every day he went around to see if Davey was about, but every time he'd just missed him, or he was hiding out somewhere, or something. The O'Brians wouldn't tell him what was happening, and had started to get fed up with him nosing about. He began to worry. He'd been relying on Davey to introduce him to Sunshine, who he reckoned would help them. If Davey had been recaptured, he was stuffed.

Finally, out of sheer boredom and desperation, he went around to see Jenny.

He had to walk to Middleton—the tenner Mrs. Simon had given him was long gone. He got there about four. Jenny wasn't home but Grace and Joe were already back and sitting in front of the TV, eating cereal. The house was one of those that stand right on the street, and Jenny didn't like curtains, so he was able to grab a peek in as he walked past. He walked around a bit more until he saw that her car was there. He was that scared—look what had happened last time. He had to walk past two or three times more before he picked up his courage and knocked.

When she saw him standing there she leaned out of the door, glanced up and down the street, reached forward, hooked him around the shoulder, and dragged him into the house. In alarm, Nick dug his heels in.

"Get in here, the police are looking for you, do you know that?" she hissed in a low voice. Nick let her pull him and she closed the door behind him.

"Nick, you lovely, lovely boy!" He was amazed—she was delighted! She hugged him like he was one of her own. Over her shoulder, Nick could see Grace and Joe looking at him, smiling slightly despite themselves because her glee was infectious.

Jenny spun around and pointed her finger at Grace. "You dare," she said. "You just dare." Grace scowled and looked away. "Come on, Nick—we need to talk," she added, and pulled him off into the kitchen.

"They've been 'round asking for you," she told him. He was sitting down at the kitchen table and she was busy at the stove. Everyone wanted to be his mum—for one or two nights only.

"Did they come 'round here?"

Jenny nodded. "They said I was to report as soon as you showed up. They're pretty sure you are going to show up. The thing is . . ." She glanced over her shoulder at him. "Apparently, Nick, you're dangerous."

"Dangerous?" Nick was surprised.

"A desperate character. Violent." Jenny looked over at him, trying to keep the question out of her face.

He shrugged. "There was a fight. Everyone has fights in there."

Jenny nodded encouragingly.

"It was a bad one. They'd locked me up—in the Secure Unit. Solitary," he explained. "I suppose I was a bit off me head."

Jenny gawped. "Solitary?" she asked.

"Yeah."

"Bloody hell, that sounds rough. This lad—did him a bit of damage, did you?"

"Yeah. But we're mates. We made up afterward."

Jenny turned away. "Beans on toast, double fried egg," she said, putting the plate down in front of him. She sat down with her tea and watched him eat, while she leaned back in her chair and lit a fag. "You're staying here from now on," she told him. "I don't care what Batty Batts and the rest of them say—this is your home. I agreed with your mum, if anything happened, we'd look after each other's kids. You're mine now."

Nick didn't say anything as she talked. He just ate and listened.

"Twat Face has been kicked out," said Jenny, referring to Ray, who had got drunk at the meal she'd given—only a few months ago, all told. She nodded firmly. She didn't mention Grace, since Nick had no idea of her part in the fiasco, but Grace had been rumbled and hung out to dry by her heels several times. Progress was being made.

In an odd way, Jenny felt a debt of gratitude to Nick. This whole thing had made her really focus on getting her life together for the first time. She was at college, she was working part-time, the kids were doing well at school. She was impressing herself.

She nodded. "It's all going to be done properly this time," she said.

Nick never even paused. Fork to plate to mouth. Fork to plate to mouth. Listen.

"I'm wise to the Mrs. Battses of this world, too," went on Jenny, tapping her ash. "Just because they hold all the cards doesn't mean there aren't things you can do. First thing is to get you assessed. Not everyone is suitable for those homes—they should never have put you in one of them after Muriel died, they're not for orphans. You'll have to go back for a while, of course . . ."

She looked at him to see how he took this.

"It's not a very nice place," said Nick evenly.

Jenny pulled a face. "Trouble is, Nick, if we don't do it officially, then you're just on the run, permanent. That's how it'll be. No school. Muriel wanted you to go to uni, didn't she? You won't even get a job in a shoe shop without a few O levels these days. The police hunting you down all the time. If you give yourself up it would be better than waiting to get caught. They'll get you in the end, you do know that, don't you? . . . But listen, let's leave that till tomorrow. We've got a bit of time. They're not exactly watching the house. Have to be careful, though, the local coppers have got a description, maybe even a picture . . ."

Grace appeared at the door, holding the phone, her eyes fixed on Nick.

"Is it for me?" Jenny got up and took the phone. "Hello . . . just a minute, Nick, I've got to take this . . ." She wandered into the front room and up the stairs to talk in private. It was someone from work, ringing up to discuss a case. It didn't take long, just a couple of minutes, but when she got back to the kitchen, Nick was already gone. Jenny stared at the plate of half-eaten food, then up to the back door. It wasn't closed, just pulled to. She rushed to it and opened it. Nothing. She ran out into the little paved yard at the back. The gate was ajar. She opened that and looked out.

Nothing. Once again, he'd eluded her care.

"You might at least have let me give you some bloody money!" she yelled. But there was no reply.

Nick spent another uncomfortable and anxious night in the garage. If the police were looking for him at Jenny's, they'd be looking for him here, too. He'd been lucky, but it wasn't going to last. He needed to move on.

He dozed and fidgeted on the old sofa till mid-morning, when he went around to see if Davey had turned up. He was in luck. There he was, hanging out with his brothers outside the house.

"I thought I told you to get lost," one of them said.

"He's one a mine," said Davey. "Broke out of Meadow Hill with 'im, din I?" And never again did any of them take against him.

"Where were you?" asked Nick.

"I was 'ere."

"I was. You weren't!"

"I was late," admitted Davey.

They grinned at each other. Brothers in arms—two of a pair.

"What you been doin'?" asked Nick.

"Been around," said Davey, winking, as if he'd bought and sold the world in the days since they'd seen each other. In fact, Davey had been sleeping with various mates. He was having to be wary at home. Normally, his dad let him stay for a while at least, but not this time. He'd called the police in on him right away, but his mum had told him, which was why Davey hadn't been around much.

"Bit a business," said Davey. "Bin to see my mate Sunshine. Still interested?"

"Yeah."

"Let's go."

So they went.

23
SUNSHINE

Davey led him out of Ancoats and toward the town center until they arrived at the door of an impressive Victorian brick building on Oldham Street, stained with the black grime of decades of chimney smoke, the door peeling, the windows covered in grime. They walked past the grand entrance, around the corner to a small, grubby door painted dark green, with an intercom on the side. Davey pressed the intercom button. There was a long wait. He pressed it again. There was another long wait.

Eventually, the intercom made an incomprehensible scratchy noise, in what sounded like a female voice. Davey yelled his name, and after several more scratchy noises, the door buzzed loudly. He threw his weight against it, the door flew open, and they stumbled into a dark hallway with a set of narrow stairs running up out of sight into the darkness.

It was a winding way to Sunshine's place. Twice they left the stairway to follow a corridor and then went up a different set. Nick could tell they were getting near, because of the dull, heavy thud of music coming through the walls. By the time they actually arrived at Sunshine's, Nick had no idea if they were even in the same building they had entered down on the street.

Sunshine's was a battered interior door off a nondescript corridor, that looked no different from several other doors along the same wall. It looked as if the flats had been unoccupied for years, except that the music was louder than ever. Someone had turned the bass coming from a set of big speakers right up high, and the noise was dully shaking the door, the floor underneath them, and the windows in their frames.

Davey tried the handle but it was locked, so he banged furiously. After a short pause, the door was opened, letting out a blast of music into their faces. In front of them was a skinny girl, a few years older than them, very pale, with scruffy blond hair, who looked as if she'd just got out of bed. She was wrapped up in a blanket, and Nick got the impression that she had nothing on underneath. When she saw Davey she smiled.

"Davey, you little beast," she yelled over the music, leaning forward and planting a big kiss on his face.

"Come on." She held the door open for them and they walked in.

"My mate Nick," yelled Davey—they all had to shout to be heard. The girl lazily flung an arm around Nick's neck and gave him a hug. "Name's Red. Told us about you," she said in a blurred voice. "Desperado. On the run. Fantastic."

"Where's Shiner?" asked Davey.

"No point yellin' for him, he's half deaf, anyway," she said, leading them down yet another corridor. "Lies around all day with his 'ead in the speakers. How's yer old man, then, Davey?"

Davey let out a stream of swearing that made her grin. "Sod 'im," he ended up. "I decided to hang out with my mate Nick 'ere," he said, nudging Nick in the ribs. "'E's the man with the plan, is our Nick."

"What plan?"

"Any plan."

Nick was surprised. Davey was the one who knew how to get out of Meadow Hill. But somewhere down the line, Davey had decided that Nick was the brains of the operation.

"Don't tell Shiner, then," warned the girl. "He likes to be the only man 'round here with the plan. Or anything else, come to that," she muttered. She led the way inside, through a large, greasy kitchen and into a darkened room littered with old armchairs and piles of cushions on the floor. She pointed at the cushions, and they went and lay on them, while she went over to a dark pile in the corner and whispered to it. A moment later she returned to them holding a huge glowing spliff, reeking of weed. Davey took it, grinned at Nick, lay back, and took a long drag, which made him cough and splutter.

"Not used to it, they don't supply it in Her Majesty's," he explained.

The girl laughed at him. "Yer not in nick yet," she told him.

"Matter a time," boasted Davey brightly, at which she rolled her eyes.

When his turn came, Nick sucked on it a bit more cautiously. He didn't know what on earth was going to happen in there, but if anyone wanted him to do a job, he didn't want to be so far gone that he couldn't get it done.

The room they were in was stacked up with all sorts of stuff—crates of beer, cardboard boxes, poly-wrapped goods that would have looked more at home in a warehouse. There was a pinball machine in one corner, and a road of vinyl records snaking around the walls on the floor, several hundred of them. He had a look at the ones near to him. It was reggae, all bands he had never heard of.

Sunshine's flat was an enormous, rambling thing, stretching over several floors and maybe even more than one building. No one was quite sure where it began and where it ended, not even him. Over the years he'd burrowed his way through the walls, up, down, and everywhere, opening up new places to hide his secrets. The attic, filthy with a century of dust and pigeon droppings, was full of mysterious mounds stacked up under tarpaulins. What was under them was anyone's guess—maybe electronic equipment, maybe forged money, maybe bodies cut up and set in concrete. Most likely, though, it was just stacks of rubbish he was hoping to sell one day. Shiner was a hoarder. He'd been living here for years, slowly filling the place up with anything he could lay his hands on. Old chairs, broken electronic equipment, and handfuls of cutlery he'd rescued from skips lay heaped up with antiques raided from posh shops, old newspapers and magazines, palettes for firewood, clothes, three-piece suits, and other items he'd bought under a false name from a catalogue. You name it, it was there, somewhere. It was finding it that was the problem.

Red soon gave up trying to chat to them by bawling above the music and went back to flop down in the dark corner with Sunshine. At first, the only sign of life next to her was the dull red glow of another spliff, glowing bright as Shiner sucked at it, and clouds of thick, pungent smoke. As his eyes got used to the gloom, though, Nick could just about make out a figure lying full-length on the cushions, his dread-locked head in Red's lap, smoking a big, fat spliff.

Despite trying to stay clearheaded, after only a few drags, Nick was glad he was sitting down, because otherwise he'd have been staggering like a toddler around the room. At some point, the music was turned up even louder, until it was shaking his intestines and bones. He lost all track of time, and it could have been five minutes or an hour later when the music got turned a few notches lower, and a short, stocky Jamaican man peeled himself out of the shadows and came across to meet them.

He sat down in between them and crooked one arm around Davey, pulling so hard, he was bent over sideways almost into his lap.

"Eh, man?" he said. "Eh, man? Eh?" He beamed at Nick as he did it. "Now, don't tell me, Davey, why you here? Your folk kicked you out again? You got a place to stay? You know we always have a space here for you, man."

"Me and me mate," said Davey, disentangling himself.

Sunshine looked Nick in the face. "Any friend of my friend is my friend," he said, and held out his hand for Nick to grasp.

Straight away, he began rolling up another spliff. Shiner was permanently stoned and walked in a haze of smoke. He dealt in it, breathed it, believed in it, lived it. Sitting across from Nick, he smelled like a particularly spicy fruitcake not long out of the oven.

"I love to smoke," he told Nick. "Red, get some beers for me friends. Beer's nice too, but beer is a pleasure whereas weed, that's an obligation, man. That's it, take it all right down!" he exclaimed as Nick took his turn on the end of the spliff. "Davey boy—why you been keeping this nice smokin' friend a yours away from me? Me can't tell how bad me feelings is hurt."

He put his hand on his heart and burst out in a fit of giggles.

Davey began telling the story of their escape from Meadow Hill. He really talked Nick up. To listen to him, you'd have thought it would have been possible only with Nick at the helm sorting things out.

"You won't believe Nick," he kept saying. "Plans coming out of his ears. He farts plans, Nick does—can't put two thoughts together without working something out."

"Can't put two thoughts together, you mean," muttered Nick, getting embarrassed at all the attention. Shiner made it worse by turning to him and making amazed faces.

"Man!" he kept saying, shaking his head in pretend admiration.

Red came in with a four-pack of beer in her arms, tossed one to each of them, and flopped down again next to Shiner, who put an arm protectively around her, as he finished rolling another huge spliff.

"What a life, eh?" he said. "Bastards, rapists, and thieves.

Everywhere you turn the ungodly follow you, bad wishing at every turn. You got to stick with your friends, because it's only friends make life worth living. And Jah, of course. But he's not always too much in evidence, you know, man?"

He roared with laughter and lit up, taking a few puffs before handing it to Nick, who took a few puffs out of politeness, before handing it on to Davey, who sucked enthusiastically and burst out coughing again.

"Friends, Jah, and weed," observed Shiner, who'd been thinking about the important things. He pulled the tab of his beer and tipped it down his throat. "I love me Jamaican beer too," he told Nick, holding up his can. "Red Stripe—the best beer in all the world."

Nick smiled. "Is that why she's called Red?" he asked, nodding at Red. It was just a joke, but to his surprise, Shiner nodded.

Red laughed. "My real name's Stella," she said.

"Exactly! But Stella ain't me drink. So I call her after me favorite beer because I couldn't bear to call me favorite girl after anything else but me favorite beer. Eh, Red?" Shiner hugged her till she yelped—he was more than a little rough with his affections. He lifted his beer, waved it in the air at the two boys, and they all drank.

"And the other thing is, you understand that Red for no fault of her own is a cock-a-knee."

Nick stared at him, not understanding.

"I'm from London," explained Stella.

"Oh! A cockney."

"'At's right, a cock-a-knee. I haveth me a little cock, he

croweth every dawn. But the main thing is, that makes her me little red rooster. Red! See!" Sunshine curled up with laughter until he had to wipe his eyes and take a big swig of beer to calm himself down.

After that things got squiffy. Nick had never drunk much or smoked, and of course since he'd been inside he'd had none of it, except for a couple of beers at Mr. Creal's flat. He remembered laughing a lot. He remembered drinking a few cans. He remembered playing pinball. He remembered being taken next door and finding, to his delight, a table football machine. He and Davey and Shiner and Stella all played for hours. Shiner was brilliant at it—the result of endless hours of practice—and he was able to beat all three of them on his own.

He remembered Stella coming in with a mountain of takeaways, Chinese. It felt like the first time for as long as he could remember that he ate so much, he felt sick. Finally, he fell onto a pile of cushions in a corner and slept like an emperor.

It was much, much later when he woke up, although he had no idea how late it was, since the windows were all covered in pinned-up cloth that didn't let light through. He got up and went through to the kitchen, where Shiner was sitting with Stella, drinking tea. She got up to make one for him, while Shiner gave him the lowdown.

"Now then," he said. "You see my friend Davey. He's like a little ray a sunshine. Or maybe he's like a little bird that hops out from under your feet and it's gone. Or he's your shadow. Here today, gone tomorrow. Now you see him, now you don't. He knows what's what and who's who. You see what I mean?" he asked, staring closely at Nick.

". . . no," said Nick, who hadn't got a clue, except that somehow they were talking business.

"He means, he never knows where Davey's been and he never knows where he's going," translated Stella. "And that's how he likes it."

"Sometimes I swear he don't know what his own shadow is doing. That's how much I love him. That's why he always has a place to stay here when he needs it, and he always gets a bite to eat in me house, and something to smoke. Davey is like me own son. He has a share in everything I own. Every little thing. Me weed, me food—the lot."

"And your money, eh, Shiner?" said Stella.

"Now, some things are too sacred," he replied, holding up his hand to his heart. "And me music. And me woman. You don't touch those. Everything else—well—you can ask." He laughed. "But no one ever goes hungry in the house of Sunshine, isn't that right?" He laughed and patted Nick on the back. "You just got to make me love you little bit." He nodded sagely. Nick still hadn't got a clue what he was on about.

"Now—I have to go out. Make yourselves at home. Davey knows what to do. See you later."

Sunshine got up and headed for the door, patting his pockets to make sure he had his keys, his money, and his weed.

"Can I give 'em a hand, Shine?" asked Stella, but he shook his head.

"No, you need to man the doors. And maybe I need something to warm me up when I come home."

"You'll be warm enough, I reckon," muttered Stella. Shiner shot her a sharp look, but she didn't say any more.

"What was that about, then?" asked Nick, when he'd gone.

"Payback," said Stella, and gave him a lopsided grin.

Davey didn't make any move to leave, so Nick stayed on with him. The three of them piled up a big bunch of cushions, made themselves comfortable, turned on the TV, and did nothing.

Stella was eighteen years old, although she looked younger, she was such a skinny little thing. She'd been living with Shiner for nearly a year, ever since her previous boyfriend got put inside.

"Assault, and it could have been GBH," she said with a sniff. "I'm better off without him."

Davey looked sideways at her. "'E should a gone inside for what 'e did to you long before that," he said.

"Nah, that was nothing."

"Looked like a lot a bruises to me," said Davey. "So what's going to happen when 'e comes out, then?"

"None a my business," said Stella, affecting a shrug.

"You're better off with Shiner a million times. He's dangerous, is Jonesy."

"Shiner's OK," admitted Stella. "But he won't let me out the 'ouse. Like I'm his pet dog or something. At least life with Jonesy was a bit exciting."

"No one's perfect," said Davey. He wriggled himself down deeper into the cushions. "Anyway, least it means we get someone to cook our bacon and eggs for us," he added, which made her whack him one.

The night deepened. They sat and watched TV till late. Nick got ambushed again by the sheer exhaustion of being on the run, and fell asleep in his pile of cushions. He was shaken awake sometime later, to find Davey kneeling over him.

"What's the time?" he groaned. The room was in pitch darkness.

"Dinner time, Mr. Wolf," said Davey. "Come on. It's payday."

Davey handed him a little rucksack to go on his back, and led the way to the door. Stella sat up to watch them go. "Good luck," she called. Davey waved, Nick nodded; and off they went, down the labyrinth of stairs and corridors, and out into the cool Manchester night.

The Happy Hunting Grounds, Davey called them. Later, Nick was to find out that the Happy Hunting Grounds changed every time they went out—no point in making a pattern. That night they walked north, past Oldham Road—it was too nearby and well known—and over beyond Ancoats. It was so late no one was about.

Once they got off the main road, the work began. They walked along, peering in through car windows and testing the doors. Occasionally they found one that was open, but usually there wasn't anything in there to interest them. Nick began to think they were wasting their time. "No one's going to leave stuff out 'round here," he said.

"We got all night," said Davey. Sure enough, they got their first hit after about half an hour. The door opened; Davey bent down to have a nose.

"There it is," he whispered. "The bread and butter. Look."

Nick looked inside. He couldn't see anything.

"Stereo," said Davey. He pulled a knife out of his pocket, leaned in, and used it to lever the unit loose in the dashboard. It was tight. At last he gave it an almighty tug and it broke free with a crunch.

Nick looked up in alarm—it had been quite a noise on the sleeping street, but no lights came on. Davey tucked the stereo in his bag. "First score to me," he said, and they carried on up the road.

That was their game that night—lightening up the cars. Nick had done such stuff before, but not like this. Walking down the road and peering in car windows for a lucky break was one thing; this was working for a living. They spent three hours or more out on the streets that night. They brought back four more stereos, a camera that someone had left lying on the backseat, a couple of coats, a few books, a suit still on its hanger fresh from the dry cleaner, and a scary-looking china doll in a lace frock, packed in an old box. Davey amused himself for a while pretending that the doll was alive and was going to start screaming in the bag to give them away, until Nick made him shut up; it was giving him the spooks.

Best haul of the night was someone's bag, a mock snakeskin handbag a woman had left behind after a late night. They had to smash the window for that one and then legged it down the road when a light went on. They went through it a couple of streets away and found a purse with twenty quid in it, a few credit cards, makeup, an address book, and various other bits and pieces.

"Not bad, not good," remarked Davey. They chucked the bag, which wasn't worth much, and pocketed the money. "Sunshine doesn't have to know about everything," said Davey.

By this time, there was light rising on the edge of the sky, so they called it a day and went back, sticking to the backstreets. It wasn't long before they were slipping down the road to Shiner's house with no one watching.

Stella was waiting for them at the top of the stairs. "How'd you do, then?" she asked eagerly. She nodded when they showed her their haul. "All right, not bad," she said, ruffling Nick's hair approvingly. "Right, you've earned it, I'll cook up some eggs, and I think there's some chicken in the fridge left over."

She pulled a face when Nick said thanks.

"I'd rather be out there with you guys than playing mumsie here with him," she said, nodding her head in the direction of Shiner's bedroom, not that he was in it yet. "I'm his personal bed warmer and bottle washer," she said. "Bor-ing."

"Shiner and rights for women, eh, Stella?" said Davey. "So—where's me bacon?" And he fell around laughing at his little joke, although Stella didn't find it so funny.

After eating, the two boys curled themselves up on a mattress on the floor in one of the other rooms, covered themselves with an old smelly duvet, and tried to get some sleep. Stella went back, as she said, to warm up Sunshine's bed for him.

"Sunshine thinks a woman's place is in the home, cooking and cleaning and that," said Davey as he and Nick settled down. "But her moaning about women's rights don't mean anything. The thing she doesn't like is, she ain't the only one. At least he don't knock her about like Jonesy did."

He pulled the blankets over himself, and in another minute they were both flat out.

24
SEVILLE

Michael Moberley was sitting in his kitchen in a small village near Taunton, drinking his morning coffee and reading the papers. It was the usual guff. The economy, crime, the economy, crime.

Boring. He was thinking of going over to Spain. Many of his friends had places in the south of France, but he preferred Spain. He liked the food, he liked the sun, he liked the people. He had a nice cottage with a garden in a small town outside Seville that he just adored. As the years passed by, he was spending more and more time there. His Spanish was getting better—good enough to hold a half-decent conversation these days, which was a big improvement in recent years.

It was a bit early, though. He had English neighbors near his place, but they wouldn't be there yet, and he had only so much in common with the local rurals. He'd be better off hanging around for a few weeks longer before flying south for the winter.

He needed a project, really—something to do. Find a new band and promote it, maybe. But he was far past that, really;

he had no idea what was on the scene these days. Something, though. Keep him busy.

On the other hand, he could always hang around, be bored for a bit longer, and then go to Spain and have a good time instead.

The post arrived. He wandered through to the hall and picked it up. Circulars, crap—but what's this? A letter from Greater Manchester Social Services. Must be about that boy . . .

He opened it and read.

The letter was from Mrs. Batts, who had promised to keep him abreast of any developments with his new nephew, Nicholas Dane. And something had happened—the little beast had run away.

"Finding a few new heads to break, I suppose," muttered Michael Moberley to himself. But as he said it, he felt wrong. In fact, Tony Creal had rather overdone it about Nick when he met Michael at the home. Just a bit. Not enough to make Michael disbelieve him, but enough to make him feel uncomfortable that he was taking him at his word.

He took the letter through into the kitchen and dialed the number at the top of the page. He was in luck—the last time he'd tried to ring, the switchboard had been jammed for hours. This time he got through to Mrs. Batts at once.

"So—the little thug's out, is he?" he said.

"Oooh, well. Ah wouldn't necessarily call him a thug, Mr. Moberley," drawled Mrs. Batts.

"Wouldn't you?" asked Michael in some surprise. He'd have thought there was little room to doubt that.

"Well, he certainly has had his moments, Ah agree. But Ah always felt that Nicholas was more sinned against than sinning, reeally. Conssidering all the circumstances, you know."

Michael didn't know. "That's not what that Mr. Creal led me to believe," he said.

Mrs. Batts shifted uneasily. She sometimes felt that Tony Creal wasn't telling her everything that he should—to protect her from the truth, of course. She knew that some of these boys could get up to some deeply unsavory things.

"Mr. Creal saw much more of him than Ah did, of coourse," she pointed out. "Perhaps Ah'm just bein' a bit soft," she added.

Odd, very, thought Michael. Odd enough to make him curious enough to ask a few more questions. He quickly established that nothing had been heard of the boy since he ran away some two months ago.

"You took your time getting back to me about it," said Michael.

"Ah have a lot on my plate, Mr. Moberley. This is only a courtesy call."

"I see. And no one's heard anything of him? What about that woman who knew his mum, whatsername?"

"Mrs. Hayes, yes. Weeell, she denies seeing anything of him, of course. But she would. These people sometimes don't always seem to understand that we're here to help them. Social education is one of the biggest issues in our work."

"Right." Already, Michael had heard enough to make him think that maybe the education didn't need to be all on one side. "Any chance I could have her number? I'd like to get in touch, have a chat . . . you know."

At the other end of the phone, Mrs. Batts pulled a face. One thing she hated was clients going behind her back.

"Ah'm afraid Ah can't do that," she said smoothly. "Client confidentiality forbids. Sorry."

In the end, Michael got her to agree to forward any letters he might send to Jenny. At least he could get in touch with her that way. And he fully meant to, as well. If he'd had her phone number, he'd have rung her on the spot. But he didn't. Instead, he put the letter down on the table and went for a swim. Over the next few days, he put it off. As the days turned into weeks he still didn't get around to writing the letter. Then he went to Spain and left all his cares behind him.

25
THE NOTORIOUS JONES

Apart from buying things Nick stole, Sunshine found various other little jobs for Nick. It could be anything from popping down to the shops for supplies, to carrying letters and packages around Manchester to deliver. Shiner liked having a lad he could trust nearby. Nick was quiet, quick-witted, and trustworthy, and more than happy to act as Sunshine's unofficial servant in exchange for a place to stay.

He had to be careful about it, though—Shiner was territorial and got irritable if he felt crowded in his own home— but the building was largely derelict and there was lots of space. Nick found himself a little room along the corridor from the flat and gradually started to fill it with cushions and bits of carpet, pinched from corners of Shiner's place, and a kettle, a radio, and various other bits and pieces. He spent most of his time there, lying on his back on an old mattress he found in a skip, staring at the ceiling and feeling lonely. He hated having so much time and not enough to do. He thought about things a lot—about his mother, whom he at last had time to miss dreadfully, about Meadow Hill, and also, of course, about Oliver. The fate of the little mop-haired boy was never far from Nick's mind. He felt he'd let him down. He'd promised to get him out, and then allowed him to be captured. Worst of all, he'd lost the photos Oliver had entrusted to him.

Then, a couple of weeks after they'd escaped, there was some news. Davey had been in and out of homes for so much of his life, and he knew so many people, it was inevitable that sooner or later he'd meet someone out of Meadow Hill. Apparently, Oliver wasn't there anymore. He'd been put in the Secure Unit, but after that, he'd just disappeared. No one had seen him since. The story was, he'd done another runner and this time he'd got away.

Nick was delighted. Time after time he kept underestimating Oliver. But if that was the case, if he was free, where was he now?

Nick began to use his spare time to search for his lost friend, but Manchester was a big town and he had precious few clues. Oliver had never told him where he came from—it was like he'd always been in care. He was sure he'd mentioned his own area of Ancoats to him, so he always kept an eye out when he went back there, and asked everyone he knew if they'd seen a blond-headed lad hanging around, but no one ever had. The only other clue he'd had was when Oliver had joked about going and selling himself on Canal Street. Nick started to hang out around there, too, at all times of the day or night. He asked and asked until people got sick of him, but again, there was no sign. If Oliver ever had been here, he'd gone by now. In the end, Nick came to think that he'd been caught again and Creal was so sick of him, he sent him away.

He just hoped he hadn't been given too much of a hard time—not much chance of that, though. If he was in another home, it was likely to be better than Meadow Hill, which, according to Davey, was about the worst of the lot.

Urged on by Nick, Davey kept asking, but although he saw plenty of kids come out from the other homes around Manchester, no one had any more news than that. Oliver had simply disappeared.

"Somewhere in Cheshire, maybe," said Davey. And that was it. Not a day went by that Nick didn't think about his friend, but Oliver seemed to have vanished off the face of the earth.

Much of the time, Nick was bored. Davey stayed with him a few nights a week, but he had such a huge network of friends he was always out and about. He saw Stella most days— Shiner was away a lot and she wanted the company too, so she was always popping around or calling him across for something to eat. It wasn't enough, though. There were so many sad things to think about, all Nick really wanted was to be doing—anything that stopped him thinking. There just wasn't enough to do.

He went to see his old friends back in Ancoats over the remains of the summer, but he found he had less and less in common with them these days. In September they started the lead-up to their O levels, which was about as far from

Nick's life as it was possible to get. He felt jealous of them—jealous of school! That was something he'd never expected to happen. He found himself less and less inclined to go around to see them.

He began living for those nights out with Davey, walking the streets and keeping an eye out for open cars or houses. People sometimes didn't close the door properly when they went in, or left the keys hanging in the door, or maybe the children might leave it open . . . Then you could sneak in and help yourself. They were making quite a killing. Shiner would buy pretty nearly anything—cameras, stereos, leather jackets, you name it. The idea was to sell it, but quite often it just ended up heaped in boxes in the attic along with the other stuff. He never seemed to give them as much money as they expected, that was the only thing.

Davey was frequently outraged.

"A tenner? I saw those jackets going for over a 'undred quid in the Arndale," he complained.

"There's no money in stolen goods," Shiner replied sadly, shaking his head. "I only do it as a favor for you. You know me main business lies elsewhere."

Davey moaned and grizzled, but the fact was, Shiner fed them, gave them a fair bit of pocket money and a safe place to stay, so perhaps there wasn't so much to complain about after all.

His main business, though, was selling weed, ganja, as he called it. Sometimes people came around to the flat to collect, but Shiner wasn't too happy about that unless they were old friends. He didn't want to attract attention. He was out and about himself most nights, never leaving the house before ten o'clock and not getting back till the small hours, delivering the goods to his various customers—and calling in on his other women. Pretty soon, Nick found himself helping with this side of things too, running around Manchester, first of all ferrying sealed bags of ganja, then later, great lumps of it wrapped in cling film. He could come back to Shiner's with anything up to a thousand pounds snuggling down his pants.

Shiner refused to deal in other drugs, though.

"Powders ain't natural, man," he exclaimed when one of his clients asked him if he could get some speed. "And I am a natural man. I'm here doing mankind a service. We only do the best quality, high-class ganja. It clears the lungs and lightens the spirit. A stoned man is closer to God, but speed is the devil's drug, man!"

He liked to claim he was a Jamaican Rastafarian, but according to Stella he'd been born and brought up in Bolton.

"He's only bin Jamaican since Bob Marley got famous," she said. And sure enough, when he got excited or angry, his Jamaican accent disappeared and his true Bolton accent began to show through.

Despite the other women he visited every night, Shiner simply adored Stella. He was always treating her to clothes and jewelry and other treats and couldn't take his eyes off her. Sometimes he'd just sit there looking at her, like she were made of honey.

"What?" she'd say, turning around to find him gazing at her. Shiner would shake his head and always ask her to do things for him—cook something, fetch a beer, or just come and sit down by him to keep him warm. He was more than twice her age—she was only eighteen and he wasn't far off forty. But Nick didn't get the feeling she loved him like he loved her. Perhaps as a result of that, they were always having rows. The other women were a real bone of contention. So was the fact that Shiner hated letting her out on her own. The fact is, she was suspicious of him; but not as jealous as he was of her—and with good reason.

It was a wet Manchester afternoon in October. It had been raining for days. Shiner's roof was leaking in several places and there were pots and pans on the floor to catch the drips. The flat was freezing, too—you'd need to set the place on fire to warm it up, with all those holes in the roofs and drafts blowing in through the floorboards. Shiner himself had a nice warm bedroom, of course. He heaped blankets on the bed, piled them up at the door, covered up the windows, built a huge roaring fire, got in a propane space heater, and stayed there all day, only emerging after midnight when he left to do his rounds. Sometimes he'd be out all night, much to Stella's annoyance. He was obviously staying with one of his girl-friends who had a half-decent house. He refused to see any callers unless they were very close friends, and floated through the cold weather on a pile of cushions and ganja and reggae.

For Nick and Davey, though, there was no escape. The whole place was icy, and nothing they could do could keep them warm. Stella ended up spending most of the day in bed with Shiner, but was getting more and more furious with him at nights when he was gone. He was in a warm place he certainly could never invite her to, that was how she saw it.

So that was it. A miserable Tuesday afternoon, wet outside, freezing cold inside, nothing to do but sit around and wait for nothing. Shiner was in bed. Davey and Nick were sitting wrapped up in blankets, sipping hot tea to try to stay warm, and Stella was in the kitchen making coffee for Shiner.

She was in a temper. "You should be outside," she grumbled at them.

"You sound like my mum," said Davey.

"I'm goin' mad, locked up in here," she replied. "If I could go out, you wouldn't see me."

"Why don't you, then?" asked Nick, teasingly. She jerked her head angrily at the bedroom, where Shiner slept in a glorious haze of weed. And it was at that point that the intercom made its crackly hiss.

Stella slouched irritably over to it. She bent to listen to the crackle.

She paused. She stood up straight and put her hands anxiously to her face, glancing over her shoulder at Nick and Davey before bending down to the intercom again. The crackle was louder, now, and it didn't sound very happy.

Stella stood up again and looked at Davey. "It's Jonesy," she said.

Davey sat up straight. "Shit," he said. He looked at her and scowled. "What you going to do?" he asked. But before she could answer, Shiner himself appeared at the bedroom door. One glance at Stella was enough. Evidently he knew already that Jones was out.

"Is it him?" he asked. Stella nodded. He lifted a finger to his lips. "I'm not in, and neither are you," he told her. Stella shrugged. The intercom was beginning to splutter and crack ferociously.

"You deal with him, then," she said. "Because he don't sound very 'appy to me."

Shiner walked over to listen, and Nick and Davey got to their feet and followed after him. After so many weeks of listening in, Nick was able to make out the words behind the crackle, but you had to get close up.

"I know you're in there, Shiner. You better open up for me," said a voice. There was a pause. The crackle sounded again, louder and more angry. "You're gonna open up sooner or later, you might as well make it easy." They waited some more.

"You know who I am," said the voice. "You know what I can do."

The boys glanced at each other. Shiner put his face in his hands.

"But I'm not in," he groaned to himself.

"Open up, open bloody up!" screamed the cackle. And from far away came the sound of a distant but violent banging.

"He's kicking the door in, Shine," said Stella quietly.

"Bastard, you bastard! Kicking me door down, everyone for half a mile around will hear that," wailed Shiner, flinging his hands up in outrage. He stalked away from the door. "He don't care about nothing, not even himself. Let him in, then," he snapped at Stella over his shoulder. "Which is all you want anyway, hey?"

"Not me, Shine," she said, and pressed the switch.

The banging stopped. The intercom snarled at them one more time and there was another huge amplified bang as Jones slammed the door behind him.

"Red, you and Nick go and wait next door."

"Shine!"

"Go."

"He'll want to see me," she warned.

"So you're out. Go. Not you, Davey. You stay here with me."

Davey, who had got up to leave with the others, sat back down, although he didn't look too happy about it. Stella and Nick went into one of the rooms off the big sitting room.

"What's up?" asked Nick when they closed the door.

"You'll see what's up when you see Jonesy," said Stella. She sounded so excited, Nick couldn't help glancing at her. She glared at him. "What?" she demanded. "It's all over, you know that," she added. But it didn't look like it was.

Shiner put his door ajar and went to sit down at the kitchen table to wait for Jones to come upstairs. After that noise at the door, you'd have thought he'd come up in a storm, but it was only when he was right outside the door that they all jumped when they heard the boards creak. Then the door banged open and there he was, a tall, lean man, dressed in jeans, a baggy leather jacket, a black T-shirt, and a pair of army boots. He had pale, spotty, unhealthy-looking skin, the result of months in jail. His sandy blond hair was cut so short, the gray of his scalp showed through and made him look far older than his thirty years. He stood on the threshold, his wide, fishy eyes fixed accusingly on Shiner, who immediately jumped to his feet and spread his arms with a wide smile.

"Man! The notorious Jones! Fresh out on the streets among us. And straight to the arms of your old friend. Jones, how's it? Come here, you big mother!"

Shiner stepped forward and wrapped his arms around the pale man and banged his back so hard you'd have thought they were long-lost brothers. But Jones obviously didn't see it that way. He stood there with a scowl on his face while Sunshine made merry with him, and ran his cold eye around the kitchen, at Davey, at the steaming mugs of tea on the table, and then, suddenly, with a suspicious glint, on the door behind which Nick and Stella hid. Stella stepped back as his eye fell on it—it really looked for a moment as if he could see through wood.

"You spooky bastard," whispered Stella, and she bent close to the door again to try to overhear what was going on.

Shiner stepped back. Jones looked at him for the first time.

"So! How long's it been?" asked Shiner, backing off and sitting down, still wearing his broad smile.

Jonesy stepped farther into the room and dumped his rucksack on the table. Sunshine looked at it suspiciously.

"A year or so, I'd say, thanks, Shiner. A lot of time to catch up on."

"They made you serve every second," said Shiner.

"Time on for bad behavior," said Jonesy. "You know me,

Sunshine; I don't take no shit. Now I just have to find the bastard that shopped me up, and I'll be spending a few years making him pay, when I find him."

Jones paused and looked at Shiner, who spread his hands.

"I hope you aren't accusing me, Jones," he said quietly.

"I'm accusing everyone," said Jones. "Now, where's your hospitality gone? You get thirsty twelve months without a drink."

"You haven't even had time to get a drink yet?" asked Shiner in surprise.

"I didn't say I hadn't had one. I said a year inside builds up a thirst."

Shiner waved to Davey to fetch beers from the fridge, took his tin from his pocket, and began to roll a spliff for his unwelcome guest.

Davey did his best to put the beer down by Jones without being noticed, but Jones looked up at him and raised an eyebrow, waiting for him to speak.

"Here you go, Jonesy," he said. "Nice to see you."

"Is it?" Jones turned his eye on Shiner. "Still king of the kids, are you, Sunshine?" He took a long swallow of his beer. "And I don't appreciate being kept waiting on the doorstep like that, either," he said, suddenly angry again.

"A man has the right not to open the door," said Shiner. "It's nothing personal, you understand. Rainy day. Winter. Time to relax."

"You know my voice, and you know me. You always answered the door to me in the past, Sunshine, and I expect you to always answer it in the future. You leave me standing there with a bag full of goodies in the rain? I don't think so. I really do not fucking think so!" He surged forward in his chair and stuck his chin angrily toward Sunshine, who lifted his hands peaceably.

"That intercom's even worse than it was, all the voices sound the same to me, Jonesy. I promise you! Come on, don't be like that—it's good to see you, man! Cheers!" Sunshine lifted his drink and, reluctantly, Jones raised his in return. The two men sat and drank in silence for a little bit, before Shiner lit up his spliff, took a puff, and his eyes reluctantly fell on the bag that lay on the table between them.

"Yeah," said Jones.

"How long you been out?"

"Twenty-four hours."

"Very quick. What is it?"

"What is it, he says! What do you think?"

"The usual?"

Jones nodded.

Shiner rolled his eyes. "You know, Jones, I don't do that business anymore."

Jones turned his face to him and, for the first time since he came into the room, he smiled, revealing a set of tobacco-stained teeth that had been neat at one point, before he lost a couple of them at the front. The gaps stood out like dark holes in his face.

"There are only two types of business with me," he said. "Good business and bad business. This is good business. Let's keep it that way, shall we, Sunshine?"

Sunshine shrugged and picked up the bag for a look.

"What happened to the smile, Jones?" he asked. He was referring to Jones's teeth. When he went inside, those gaps had been filled with gold.

"It was the smile got me put away, so the smile had to go. Too recognizable. I'm going to get some white ones put in soon as I get the money." He thrust his hand into his pocket and, holding out his fist, opened it up to show a pair of gold teeth. He laughed, rattled them in his hand. "I knocked 'em out myself, a few days after someone told me they planned on helping themselves in the nick. Kept them up my arse for a year. They're not going back in my mouth after that," he said, then threw back his head and laughed.

He put the teeth back in his jacket pocket, accepted the spliff from Sunshine, took a huge hit, and broke into a fit of coughing. "Need to get me throat back, everything's out of practice after a year's time." He waved his hand at the bag. "Price it up, will you? I gotta be getting on."

Shiner reached into the bag and took out a box of pharmaceutical drugs. He looked closely at the label.

"Nobody takes this stuff anymore, Jonesy," he remarked.

"What, are they all dead already?" asked Jones. "I don't think so, Shiner."

"It's not easy to sell. There are new products on the market."

"You can tell me all about that once you've paid up."

Shiner tipped the bag up on the table. Out tumbled a further array of packaged drugs.

"Where from?"

"Chemist on Blair Road."

Sunshine looked up. "That's the one you got done for in the first place."

"Serve 'em right. I've changed me modus operandi, haven't I? Always used to come in through the roof. They knew it was me as soon as they looked up."

"So what do you do now?"

"Well, now, that would be telling." Jones drew on the spliff, but in the end, he couldn't resist it. "I found the old man who gave evidence against me."

"What, the chemist?"

"Him. Once I reminded him who I was he was only too pleased to take me 'round and show me the drugs cabinet."

"But he's seen you already, man!"

"He wasn't doing a lot of looking."

Shiner stared at him, and decided he didn't want to know any more.

"It's your business." He hefted the bag. "Three hundred."

"Piss off."

"Can't do much more."

Jones banged his fist down on the table, hard. "Don't fuck me around, Sunshine. I'll find out what the street value is. Don't you take advantage of me because I done time and I'm out of the swim." Shiner looked at him from under his brows and sucked his teeth.

"It's an arguable point what the street value is," he said. "This stuff isn't often sold."

"Rarity value, then."

"And since I don't sell it anymore, how would I know? But you're an old friend, Jones. For your sake, let's call it four."

"No. Let's call it five."

"Man, Jones! I have a profit to make. You don't want no favors, do you?"

The two men stared at each other awhile. "Split the difference," said Jones.

Shiner shrugged, looked unhappy, but agreed to the deal. Jones was a dangerous man to barter with. Jones counted the money carefully and then stuffed it into his coat.

"Now then, Sunshine," he said, leaning back in his chair. "We have some unfinished business, you and me, don't we?"

Shiner gave him a sickly smile. "And what might that be, Jones?"

"I think you have something of mine, and I think you have it right here," said Jones. He stared at the door behind Shiner's back. Stella and Nick stepped back, and Jones nodded slightly at them, as if in greeting, even though he couldn't see them.

Shiner sat back in his chair and looked hard at the other man, but he had nothing to say.

"You know what I'm talking about, Shiner. Where is she?"

"I don't . . ."

"Don't play silly fuckers with me, Sunshine," snarled Jones, leaning forward. "I know what's going on. I can smell her from here. Where I come from, it's not the way things go that you pinch a man's girl when he's inside. I know men have had their balls cut off for less."

Shiner held up his hands. "Now, Jones, you and . . . and Stella weren't together when you went inside . . ."

"Me and Stella were up and down all the time. She'd have been back here in my pocket in another day or so . . ."

"Not this time, according to her."

Jones looked at the door. "If she's got anything to say she can say it to me face, can't she?"

There was a pause. Jones stared fixedly at the door. Shiner shook his head and sucked his teeth, but Stella had heard enough. She pushed the door open and walked into the room.

"Hello, Ben," she said.

"Well, well, well," sneered Jones. "What have we here? Someone who doesn't exist, eh?"

Shiner glared at her and shook his head in disgust.

"I'd already said," said Stella shakily, "I'd had enough, you know that, I said it often enough."

"Prefer the nigger, do you?" sneered Jones. Shiner flinched, but he didn't dare object.

"I didn't get together with you to work the streets for you, you shouldn't have made me do that, Ben. It wasn't part of the deal."

"It was a partnership."

Stella shook her head. "You should'na made me do that."

Jones jerked his head at Shiner. "Are you telling me it's better here with him? You're not a cage bird, Stella. You had more fun with me."

"More fun," said Stella. "And more bruises."

In a fury, Jones banged his hand on the table, and half rose from his seat. Stella stepped back and for a moment it looked as if he'd go for her. But Shiner suddenly sprang to life.

"Now, man, now! We're all friends here. Stella's free to come and go, you always said that, Jones. Let's just keep things sweet, shall we? Women, eh, man? No trusting them. You and Stella were up and down, it ended on a down note, that's the way these things often work out. Here, here, Jones, meet the crowd. Here's me new boy. Hey, Nick, come out of there and say hello to the notorious Jones."

Reluctantly Nick came out.

"Nick, a good boy, full of daring, is our Nick. Say hello, Nick. Meet Jones. Jones . . . Nick . . ."

Jones snorted, cast barely a glance at Nick, and grabbed his bag.

"You're trying to tell me he never lifts a hand to you?" he said to Stella.

"Not like you, Ben."

Jones turned to go, but paused with his back to them as he opened the door.

"Don't cross me, Stella. Or you, Sunshine."

"We haven't, man! Come on, Jones, I've done nothing wrong. It was already over between you and her. I know you had hopes . . ."

"You know nothing about my hopes, you black fucker," hissed Jones.

Shiner shook his head. "Jones, Jones, don't pick a fight over this, I'm begging you, man."

Jones paused, halfway to violence before he was able to control himself. The door banged and he was gone.

Shiner threw his hands up in the air and cursed under his breath. Stella burst into tears and fled. Davey looked at Nick and rubbed his face. "That was the notorious Jones," he said. "Fun, in 'e?"

26
PICCADILLY GARDENS

That night, Shiner and Stella had a huge row. He was convinced she preferred Jones to him.

"You've no reason to say that," she fumed.

"Only the evidence of me 'eart," insisted Shiner, laying his hand on the affected organ. Usually Stella backed down quickly enough when he was angry with her, but this time she was as stubborn as a rock. The argument ended with Stella slamming the door and rushing off downstairs.

"Now see where she runs," hissed Sunshine in a broad Bolton accent.

He waited up for her for half the night, but at two in the morning when she wasn't back, he pulled on his coat. "It's over. Me and her's finished," he insisted, and left, broken-hearted, to find solace elsewhere. But Stella did come back, an hour or so after he'd gone. She slept in the big room instead of keeping his bed warm as she usually did.

Next morning he was back in the house before eight o'clock.

"You been with him," he said flatly. Stella denied it, insisting she'd been round at her friend's place in Blackley.

There was another huge row.

"Go 'round and ask her yourself," she yelled. Uncharacteristically, Shiner backed down. They made up, but things had changed. The rows became more and more frequent. Jones made a point of turning up almost every day and sat there grinning like a rat at the tension in the atmosphere. Eventually, one day he arrived in the middle of a row. It carried on all the while he sat there drinking a beer and smoking a spliff. At last he stood up, picked up his bag, and jerked his head at the door.

"You might as well come with me."

"You might as well," said Shiner bitterly. Stella stood up and followed Jones out of the room. She didn't even stop to take her things, and the next day it was Jones who came back for them.

Sunshine was heartbroken. He went to bed for a week and came out looking thin and old. He was soon back on form, smoking his weed, doing his rounds. But he carried the memory of Stella inside him like a wound. Nick missed her too. It was more lonely than ever without Stella to keep him company.

After a few weeks, Stella started to come around again, always with Jones. All her old confidence seemed to have vanished out of her, but she was in love with Jones, no way around it. She couldn't take her eyes off him, and followed him like a dog at heel—not at all like the Stella Nick thought he knew, who always did what Shiner told her, but always with her own brand of snapping and snarling at him, despite her frustrations. Bruises began to appear too, on her cheeks, on her eyes, and sometimes she walked in a lopsided way, as if her ribs were sore. No one ever dared ask her how she'd been hurt.

It was around this time that Nick plucked up the courage to go around to see Jenny again, despite his fears of getting picked up, and her eagerness to do things officially. In fact, she'd already made up her mind that she wasn't going to get anywhere with Mrs. Batts and the social services and simply wanted to do her best to encourage him to come and see her as often as possible.

Nick was damaged—that much was very soon clear to her. She didn't understand why he was so traumatized, but something had made him very wary indeed, and that something had evidently happened inside Meadow Hill. He needed to be lured in with plates of food and a warm place to sleep, like a feral cat. As the weeks went by, the promise of a decent meal and a bed on the sofa seemed to be slowly working, and by the end of November, he was coming around once, sometimes twice a week. But with such small successes she had to be content. She was still no wiser about where he stayed or what he did to keep body and soul together, or about what on earth had happened at Meadow Hill to make him like he was. As soon as she tried to bring the subject up, he was gone, out the door and away as soon as she turned her back.

It was a fortnight before Christmas when Jenny had a letter forwarded to her by Mrs. Batts, from Michael Moberley. It came as quite a shock—she had no idea the uncle had even been found. The letter was lying on the mat inside a social services envelope, so she opened it at once, always on the alert for anything that might affect Nick. Inside was a note from Mrs. Batts, requesting that she forward on to her any information that might relate to Nick's case, and the letter from the elusive great-uncle.

It was just a few lines. He was living in Spain just now but was coming home for Christmas. He was curious as to how Nicholas was getting on. If she was still in touch with him or had any news of him, he'd be grateful to hear it. At the bottom of the page was a telephone number and a request to ring.

Her heart leaped—or was it just cavorting anxiously around her chest? Everything that had happened with Nick so far had gone so disastrously wrong. She had to shoot off to work and deal with Grace and Joe, so she didn't have time to handle it then. She put it on a shelf in the kitchen to come back to later on.

She kept picking it up and reading it through, over and over during the evening, and waited till the kids were in bed before she did anything. She didn't know what to say or how much to say, or even if she should just ignore it. She just prayed that making the call wouldn't plunge Nick into more disaster.

She ran through several conversations in her head before she thought, sod it. She sat down, dialed the number, and waited to see what happened.

It was an odd sort of conversation, hedging, fencing, probing. Michael wanted information, but she was reluctant to give it. One thing she was certain of—nothing could happen without Nick's full consent.

Where was he? Around and about, she wasn't sure. Did she see much of him? Every now and then. Was he OK? He looked well. Who was looking after him? No one in particular.

"You know, love, you're not giving a lot away," Michael scolded, rather irritated.

"I suppose. The thing is, Mr. Moberley, what exactly do you want?"

Michael thought about it. It was a fair question. "I'm not sure," he confessed. "I suppose I want to know if there's anything I can do for him."

"And what do you suppose that might be?" Jenny wanted to know, her heart beating hard.

"I have no idea whatsoever."

That was as far as they got that day. But they agreed to meet up the Wednesday before Christmas, to talk about Nick.

It was one of those blowy days, with the wind dashing about in between the buildings and throwing little handfuls of rain in the air, when Michael Moberley and Jenny Hayes, the only two people in the world with the care and the wherewithal to rescue Nick from his downward spiral to jail, met in Piccadilly Gardens by the statue of Queen Victoria.

Michael was delighted with the weather—there was something refreshing about the cold wind after a few weeks of warm air. He shook Jenny's hand, and they stood for a moment smiling at each other, while the wind pulled at coats and blew their hair.

"Lunch," he said. They headed off toward a restaurant near the town hall, chatting about Christmas, how it came earlier every year, about shopping and how crowded the town was, while the wind pushed and pulled at them, and the pigeons battled their way down to the ground to eat their crusts.

Jenny decided fairly quickly that Michael was on the right side, more or less—he certainly wasn't any more impressed with Mrs. Batts than she was. She started to tell him little bits and pieces while they were waiting for the main course and then, before she knew it, she was pouring out her heart. To her shame and surprise, she was suddenly ambushed by tears.

"I've really let him down, I've just let him down so badly," she sobbed, overwhelmed by grief and guilt. Michael was completely taken by surprise. He didn't know what he had been expecting—exasperation, a shrug, good riddance? Perhaps she was going to try and get some money out of him. The last thing he was expecting was this burst of passion and pity.

"He was always so open and now he won't tell me hardly anything anymore." Jenny wept, wiping her face with her napkin. "He doesn't trust anybody. I don't know where he's living. He's got somewhere to stay but God knows where or who with. He's stealing, I think. I'm scared it's drugs or something. I try and give him money, but when he comes 'round to my house he buys *me* stuff. He's only fifteen, he should be at school. Muriel wanted him to go to university, now look, what's he got? And it's all my fault . . ."

Jenny was inconsolable. Michael tried awkwardly to cheer her up, but it wasn't until the food arrived that she finally managed to get a grip.

"Well," he said. "He seems to have a real friend in you, anyway. He can't be all bad, then."

"Oh no," said Jenny. "He's lovely. Everyone loves Nick."

Michael goggled. He thought back to his meeting with Mr. Creal and said to himself, what on earth is going on here?

They had quite a nice afternoon, in the end. After lunch they wandered to the shops to get a present for Nick. Jenny was impressed. Michael was a nice man. She kept looking at him to work out if she could manage to fancy him—how handy would that be! And she did, too, even though he was far too old. But she had more sense than to try it on—partly, at least, because she could see he had more sense than to accept.

Rescuing people was never as easy as it looked, Michael thought as he stood in Debenhams watching Jenny rifle through the racks to find something Nick might like. He had no illusions about himself. He was a generous man, a kind man, but a lazy man as well. Taking on a damaged teenage boy wasn't something he had any inclination to try. Boarding school? The little bugger would run off. What did that leave?

He had no idea.

They ended up with a few pairs of jeans and a good coat for Nick. He insisted on getting a little something for Joe and Grace and bought a box of chocs for Jenny in the food hall while she was off doing something else, had them gift wrapped, and slipped them into her bag while she wasn't looking. They said good-bye where they met, in Piccadilly Gardens. He kissed her on the cheek and hurried away to the train station, grateful that he was leaving the problem behind him. He'd do what he could, he thought, so long as it wasn't too much. First thing was to meet the boy himself. They had arranged a date early in the New Year, a few days before he flew back to Seville. Check it out. See what could be done—if the boy managed to stay out of trouble that long, that is.

Jenny didn't want to spring his new uncle on Nick, but she didn't see him anyway until Christmas morning, when he turned up with his presents and what looked like a nasty hangover—she hoped. She needn't have worried. It was what it looked like, alcohol. One thing about Shiner, he didn't approve of drugs, hash in his eyes being no more a drug than beer to a drinker.

Jenny left Grace and Joe playing with some of their new things and took Nick to one side to tell him about his new relative.

He listened impassively.

"He wants to meet you," she said. "He's coming 'round here, all the way from Taunton just to see you, Nick, before he goes back to Spain." She nudged his arm. "He has a second home in Spain," she told him. She nudged him again. "He's loaded," she said, and grinned.

Nick looked away. Another one who wanted to help him.

He wasn't sure he wanted any more help. He was doing OK on his own.

"Say you'll be there, Nick," begged Jenny.

"I'll be there," said Nick. But he didn't nod, or blink, and she didn't really believe him.

They had the full thing that day—the roast turkey, the tree, films in the afternoon. She got Nick a Walkman and never asked any questions about where the nice leather purse he got for her came from, or the radio-controlled car he got Joe, or the makeup bag and copy of the new album by Duran Duran, which Grace was mad about. She left the package from Michael until last.

"What's this?" he wanted to know.

"Look at the label," she told him.

" 'From your uncle Michael,' " he read. He opened it. Clothes.

"I helped him pick 'em," explained Jenny. Nick nodded and put them to one side.

"Aren't you going to try them on?" she asked.

"Later," he said.

They spent the rest of the day playing games. Nick had won the two kids over, partly because he was popping in and out and not staying all the time, perhaps because of the money he spent on them. Jenny did her best to make him feel at home, but in fact, he was a bit crowded out by the end of it. He was used to Christmas with just him and Muriel on their own, and the two other kids began to get on his nerves as the afternoon wore on. On Boxing Day they all went for a walk in the park, during which Nick quietly slipped away. When she got back home, Jenny found that he'd been back and picked up his presents, from her, Grace, and Joe. But the pile of clothes Michael had left him was still tucked into the shopping bag by the sofa. He hadn't even tried them on.

27
A DEAL

It was a miserable February night Jonesy came by, when the daffodils on the municipal parks and roundabouts were poking their way through the dirty town grass. He was on his own.

"What's he doing here this time?" grumbled Shiner. He waited a bit in the vain hope that Jones was drunk and might move on, but he kept ringing the bell and banging the door. As usual, Shiner pressed the button and let him in.

He put on his usual broad smile for Jones, the bright Sunshiney smile that gave him his name, which he could turn on and off at will, and no one could ever tell whether it meant everything or nothing.

"Jonesy! Come in, man. Have a beer and a likkle smoke. Just on me way to bed, you know, but you can join us for a nightcap, eh? Nice to see you, man, nice to see you." He beamed, waving Nick over to the fridge. In this respect, serving up the beer, Nick had taken Stella's place.

"Early for you to be getting your shut-eye," grumbled Jones, perching his backside on the table and watching Nick feeling the cans for a cold one in the fridge.

"Early bird, that's me," lied Sunshine cheerfully. Jones grunted doubtfully.

"Where's Stella? Don't normally see you about without her," said Sunshine conversationally.

"Tell you the truth, Shiner, she's working."

"She's got a job?" inquired Sunshine, sharper than he would have liked.

Jones sucked down his beer. "You could call it that," he said.

Shiner said nothing but looked at Jones as if he wished him dead.

"Tell you what, you can have her back for twenty quid," said Jones. "Twenty quid an hour, that is."

Shiner swallowed hard; he never showed his temper to Jones.

"Man, shouldn't you be down there looking out for her?" he asked. "Friday night. A lot of drunks about."

Jones shook his head. "Telling me my business, Sunshine?" he asked. "She's safe enough."

"Safe as she would be at home, is she?" hissed Sunshine, unable for once to keep the hatred out of his voice.

Jones shot him a glance. "You what?" he asked dangerously, and Sunshine found his smile.

"Never mind. I'm worried about her. I care for the girl, you know that."

Jones subsided and shrugged.

"Is she safe? You left her out for the wolves. Where's she working?"

"She's on a job—that's to say, the job's on her," said Jones, watching Sunshine closely for signs of temper. "She's with some acquaintances of mine. My presence is not required to keep them in order. But I'm not here for your chat. I have a proposition to put to you, Sunshine."

"Bisniss?"

"Bisniss." Jones nodded at Nick. "You can leave us alone for ten minutes, son. Don't go, mind. This concerns you."

Sunshine paused, but only briefly. He didn't need Jones like Jones needed him, but sometimes, there was money to be made. So long as Sunshine wasn't too closely involved, he didn't mind catching a slice of it. He nodded to Nick, who had to leave and go next door, and wonder what trouble he was getting into now.

Sunshine turned to Jones.

"It had better be better than the last one, Jonesy," he said.

"Or what?" asked Jones, smiling glassily at Shiner.

"No threats, I just don't want to do bad business."

"We're old friends, you and I, Sunshine. No need for bad business."

"Then we can cope if I say no."

Jones raised an eyebrow. "Without even hearing what I got to say?"

"Now, I never said that! I never said that!" complained Sunshine raising his hands and grinning. "But there's good deals and bad deals, Jones, and last time I got my fingers burned. So, what is it this time?"

Jones leaned forward. "I want to do the chemist up on Charles Road in Droylsden. Know it?"

"Another chemist?" Shiner was disappointed. "I thought you had something more interesting."

"A lot of money to be made. Is that interesting for you?"

"Pharmaceuticals," said Shiner dismissively.

"Different. This is the place the junkies use. They keep the 'eroin in the drugs safe and I happen to have learned when the delivery takes place. And the methadone." Jones nodded. "It's happening, Sunshine. It's just a question of who's in it with me."

"And what do you want me to do?"

"It isn't what I want you to do. It's what I want you to get something of yours to do for me."

"For what?"

"A share."

"What sort of share?"

"A quarter. And you don't even 'ave to be there in person."

"I'm never there in person, you know that, Jonesy. And what part does our Nick have to play in all this?"

"I don't expect you to like it, Nick," said Sunshine later that same evening, after Jones had left. "But I expect you to do it."

"I don't wanna do it."

"It's payback."

Nick was furious. "I do things for you all the time!"

"That was out of friendship. You didn't think all this was for free?"

"Fuck you!"

"I forget you said that. Where you going to sleep—the street? You're one of mine, you do as I tell you. It's all there is to it."

28
THE JOB

Going on a job with Jonesy—Nick was getting badly out of his depth. He went around to Jenny's place, but it drove him mad there within a couple of days. He'd left that life too far behind him. He thought about hanging out with his old mates, sleeping on friends' floors, but he knew he could get away with that only for a short while. Sooner or later someone would put the police on to him and he'd end up where he started—back in Meadow Hill and the tender clutches of Tony Creal.

He talked it over with Davey, who was furious with Shiner on his behalf. He even went around to have a huge row with him about it.

"You know what Jones is like. What are you playing at? You want him to have a record?"

Shiner guffawed. "A record? Come on, Davey boy, how long do you think he's going to go without one of those?"

Davey did his best, but Shiner was immovable.

"I'm not his dad, I'm not his mama. He go leave if he like."

"Yeah, and go where?"

"Then he has to do as he's told, like every other kid that wants something for nothing."

And that was that. The way it felt to Nick was, he had no choice. And who knows? Maybe he'd make some money out of it. Maybe it wouldn't be so bad after all.

On the appointed night, Jonesy came to bang at the door. Shiner gave Nick a nod and he went down the stairs to meet Jones, who jerked his head along the road and set off, with Nick at his heels.

Jones led Nick west, up through Ancoats and out into Salford. It was a long walk in a cold wind neither of them was dressed for. Barely a word was said the whole way, except when Nick asked why they were walking.

"Good for your health," was all Jones would say.

"Is the job tonight?" asked Nick.

Jones turned to look at him. "Don't ask questions. I don't like people who ask questions. You never know what they're going to want to know next."

"Sorry, Jonesy," began Nick, but Jones snapped at him like a dog.

"I'm not Jones, Jonesy, or anything like it to you, son, get me?"

Nick cringed back. "Sorry. But what do I call you?"

That one seemed to stump Jones, who had rarely been called anything but Jones. "Mr. Jones will do," he said in the end, and gave Nick a smile as if he were joking—but he wasn't. They carried on their way in silence through the night until they got to Salford and the house where he lived with Stella, in a two-up, two-down in a warren of streets behind the Poly. Jones put the key in the door and opened it directly onto a sitting room, where a tall, red-haired man was lounging on the settee, dressed in a pair of thin, gray, stained suit trousers, a tight T-shirt with slashes in it punk-fashion, a pair of huge boots, and with a couple of rings through his nose. His hair was done up in a half-grown-out Mohawk at the back, but he was beginning to go bald at the front. He'd made a halfhearted attempt at a comb-over to conceal the bare scalp on either side of the central tuft. He had a can of lager in one hand and was watching *Coronation Street* on the TV.

"Is this the monkey, then?" he asked as they came in, looking Nick over. "Bit big for a monkey, isn't he? What's 'is name?"

Jones grunted and went into the kitchen for a beer.

"Nick, Nick Dane," said Nick.

"Surnames already! I'm pleased to know you, Nicholas Dane," said the tall man. "Surnames are for friends, and I'm going to keep mine till I know you a bit better. Best friends keep the best secrets, eh? You can call me John. Not my real name, of course," he added. "On a job like this, no one has real names. I only 'ope Nick Dane is made up as well."

Jones appeared at the door holding a beer. "We're only doing a chemist, Mr. David Manley of seventeen, Crescent Road, Salford," he said. "It's not the Cold Bloody War. You can trust Nick. He's one of Shiner's. If he's any trouble he knows he's dead, so why would he be?" Jones smiled mirthlessly at Nick, as his friend closed his eyes and sighed but didn't dare say anything. Jones took a swig out of his can. "Where's Stella?" he asked.

The other man pointed up at the ceiling. "I don't get the impression she's all that fond of me, Jones. You might get a more entertaining girlfriend next time we're in on it together."

Jones pulled a face. "She's only friendly when she's paid to be friendly," he said. He dropped himself in a chair, tipped his head back, and yelled, "Stella!" at the ceiling. Above them, the floor creaked as she got off the bed. A moment later, she came down the stairs in the middle of the house. She and Nick looked at each other anxiously over the heads of the two men slouched in the chairs.

"It's dinnertime," grumbled Jones.

Stella nodded and went through into the kitchen. Nick, glancing at Jones to make sure it was all right, followed her. She was walking stiffly, he noticed, with a bit of a limp. Her face was bruised all down one side.

"You all right?" he whispered.

"Yeah, OK." Stella straightened up and went to give Nick a hug. "Nice to see you, hon. How's things at Shiner's?"

"OK." Nick leaned up against the work surface and watched her as she got mince out of the fridge and started to chop an onion.

"What's going on?" he began, but he was interrupted by the door opening wider. It was Jones. He nodded at Stella. "She fell down the stairs drunk, the silly bitch," he said.

"Yeah, sorry," said Stella, without a trace of sarcasm. Jones nodded and went to sit down, making sure the door was wedged open, so they could see him keeping an eye on them as he watched TV and drank his beer. The TV was on loud, though, and they could at least talk without being overheard.

"You know about the job?" asked Stella.

"Yeah, but I don't know when."

She shrugged and shot him a glance. "You must be mad to get wrapped up in this, Nick. I thought you had more sense."

"So must you."

"I don't 'ave any choice."

"Oh, you do."

She chopped her onion fiercely.

"I've set up with him, I have to stick by him, don't I?"

"Do yer?"

"I do. You don't even have to be 'ere."

"Oh, I really do. Shiner made that clear enough."

"Leg it, Nick. It's not worth it."

"Where to?"

"What about that woman you told me about?"

"Jenny? Someone'll shop me if I stayed there."

"So go back into care. It can't be worse than Jones hanging over you."

Nick shrugged. "At least you know where you are with Jones," he said, by way of an excuse.

Stella looked at him irritably. "You must really hate that place to prefer to get wrapped up with this."

Nick smiled vaguely. He glanced up to see Jones staring at him through the door.

Stella saw it too. "Here, chop up some carrots. We're having mince and potatoes. He won't mind if he sees you doing something. Make yourself useful."

Nick took the carrot and began chopping. Jones settled back down in his seat.

"Just like old times 'round at Shiner's," whispered Nick, not without bitterness, and Stella gave him a hint, just a hint, of her old smile.

He didn't get much more chance to speak to Stella. Even though they were obviously both on edge, Jones and Manley were both snorting speed, which was making them more edgy than ever. Jones was ready to blow up at anything. After they'd eaten the mince, Jones insisted they all sit in the front room together and watch the TV, just in case anyone tried anything, whatever that was. Manley called him a paranoid bastard.

"I'd rather be paranoid than done," replied Jones.

So they all sat and watched a rerun cop show, with Jones glaring and watching them all like hawks. Nick did his best to stay quiet but even that wound Jones up.

"Creeping about like a fucking weasel, you're getting on my tits," he barked into Nick's face.

From his place in the armchair, Manley cut in.

"Don't break him, Jones. You've already broken the driver, there's not going to be anything left at this rate."

Jones glared at him, but Manley stared at the telly and avoided looking directly at him. Jones let Nick be, though, and the long night crept by.

It was gone two in the morning before Jones put down his beer and caught Manley's eye. They nodded at each other and stood up. Manley went into the kitchen and started rooting about in the cupboard under the sink, while Jones went upstairs and came down a moment later with something long wrapped in a blanket. Stella groaned when she saw what he had. He put the bundle on the kitchen table and began to unwrap it.

"Oh, gawd, no, Jonesy," she whined. "It's not worth it . . ."

"Don't you start," he snapped. "It's nothing to do with you. Anyway, do I look stupid? I'm not going to use these beauts. Folk sometimes need a little persuading, right, Manley?"

"Oh, definitely, Jones," said Manley. He stroked the guns with his finger. "Very persuasive little numbers, these. They have a golden tongue. You'd be amazed what people will do when they begin to talk."

Stella scowled and sulked for a moment, but then she burst out, "It's not fair getting Nick involved in this, Jones. He's nothing to do with it. And his mum died with heroin, you shouldn't make him . . ."

"Who asked you for your opinion? He has a boss and his boss has a job for him and his job's helping me and Manley out tonight. I told yer. It's nothing to do with you, so just . . . just shut it." Stella shrugged her shoulders apologetically and turned away upstairs.

Before they left, Manley delved around in his tool bag and came out with a bag of masks, all the worse for wear. There was a Ronald Reagan mask, a Margaret Thatcher mask, a monkey, and a grinning red fox. Manley claimed the Thatcher one, as he was her biggest fan, he said. He tossed Nick the monkey one—no arguments there. Jones took the fox.

"The quick red fox, that's me," he said.

Standing in the front room, they all tried their masks on.

They were big latex things, larger-than-life caricatures of the people and animals they represented—funny, but scary in a clowny sort of way. It was odd, but when he put it on, Nick suddenly felt his fear lift a little, as if he'd become someone else. They stood in a circle looking at one another. Suddenly, Nick felt a surge of laughter coming up in him. Manley snorted. Jones huffed, and suddenly they were all giggling hysterically. At least, it looked like all three of them, but suddenly, Jones pulled his mask up. He wasn't laughing at all—his face was twisted with rage.

"What are you two on, bloody acid? This isn't a circus, it's a bloody break-in. Strewth! Give me strength!"

Manley stared at his accomplice. "But you was laughing!"

"Do I look like I'm laughing?"

"Well, your shoulders were going up and down . . ." muttered Manly.

"Fuckin' 'ell," growled Jones. "The morons I have to bear. Let's get!"

They left the house and walked a few yards down the road to where a red Scimitar was parked—their getaway wheels for the night. Jones got in the front, Nick in the back. Manley got behind the wheel, started up, and they were off.

The chemist was miles away, in Droylsden. Manley parked quietly a few streets away and they walked through the lamp-lit roads into a car park and loading area behind the main road where the chemist stood. They hid in the shadows and Jones showed Nick what his job was.

"You're goin' up that drainpipe there," he said, pointing

out a black pipe running up the back of the house. "And then you're gettin' in that window there." Nick followed his finger and there, sure enough, was a small open window. "That's the bathroom," said Jones. "And with a bit of luck, there'll be no alarm. Don't matter either way. You run down and get that back door open quick. Once we're in, we're through the house and out the other side before you can count to three."

"What if they're awake? What if they catch me?" asked Nick, scared out of his wits.

"What if, what if, what if," sneered Jones. "Just do it."

"I can't get up that pipe," began Nick, but before he could say another word, Jones hiked him up by the front of his shirt, pushed him up above his head, and handed him to Manley, who sat him on his shoulders.

"Now you can," said Jones. "Right, boys. Masks on."

The three thieves pulled their masks on—the fox, the monkey, and Margaret Thatcher. Manley walked Nick over to the pipe, where he was able to reach an offshoot joining up to the main pipe. From there, it was possible to clamber up and across the bathroom window.

"Don't be long, the longer you are, the more likely you get caught," hissed Jones, gesturing down the road. Nick looked behind him—he could be seen from miles off. It wasn't much of a plan Jones had cooked up. The only thing on Nick's side was that at half past two on a Tuesday morning, not many people were about.

Nick crawled along the pipe toward the window. It was a rusty old thing that rattled on its hinges and creaked as he climbed. He got along as fast as he could and soon he was able to climb onto the windowsill and stick his head up into the open window. He was hoping the alarm would go off there and then, so he could get down quick, but all was quiet. He waited a moment, then, urged on by a hiss from Jones below him, pushed his head farther inside and began to snake his way through the narrow gap and into the room.

It was a tight fit. He was on the small size for his age, which is why they picked him, but he still got stuck halfway, squirming around like a toad stuck on its back, until he managed to get one hand inside to lean on the sill, which helped him lever his legs up and farther through. He got his hips in, then his thighs, and tried to let himself slowly down with his hands, but he was squeezing in the dark over the washbasin and a small cabinet. The inevitable happened—he caught the cabinet as he jerked about, the door opened, and down tumbled a little avalanche of toiletries and medicine.

Nick paused, three quarters in. Someone was moving inside the house.

He was stuffed. He couldn't get back so he had to go on. A board creaked outside the door. Frantically, Nick squirmed and wriggled but it was too late. The bathroom door opened—the chemist must have slept in a room right next to the bathroom. The light clicked on, and from his position upside down, Nick bent his neck up to see a fat, graying man peering around the door at him with an open mouth.

Then it all happened very quickly. Nick wriggled violently and fell to the floor in a cascade of shampoo, toothpaste, and soap. He was certain the man would go for him, but instead he backed off. Nick jumped to his feet and charged. He shoved the man in the stomach so that he fell back out the doorway, then ran out into the corridor and down the stairs. At the back door there was a tremendous bang where Jones and Manley were trying to beat the door down. As the alarm finally went off, Nick flung himself at the door, fiddling with the locks—but of course there was no key—Jones hadn't even thought of that.

Nick ran around to the back room and looked out of the window. Jones was leering in through his fox mask, clutching the shotgun, waving a hand at him, and shouting something muffled. He was trying to tell Nick to smash the window with a chair or something, but Nick had no idea what he was on about. Then Manley appeared behind him, heaving a flowerpot in his hand, which he flung through the window. The window burst with a crash and shattered glass poured down into the room. Jones wiped the remainder of the window away with the shotgun and clambered in.

The two men pushed past Nick and ran upstairs, where the chemist had barricaded himself and his wife into the bedroom.

"Open the door—now!" screamed Jones, his voice muffled by the fox mask. The chemist refused. "Open the fucking door now or I'll shoot it down," screamed Jones. The chemist refused again and Jones emptied one barrel of the shotgun into the ceiling. The chemist opened the door. Jones ignored his cries for mercy and stuck the gun barrel in his fat stomach.

"The cabinet," he growled. He pushed the poor man downstairs. By now, Nick had been in the house for five minutes. It was another five before the chemist got into the shop at the front and opened the cabinet. Jones and Manley emptied the contents into sacks, and at last, they were done. Gratuitously, Jones slammed the gun into the man's middle to make him double up, and all three of them rushed out the back and through the window Jones and Manley had come in by. A moment later, they were running through the dark streets. The alarm had been joined by the call of sirens. Nick had a hell of a job keeping up with them, and just managed to get in the car in time as they were pulling away.

Manley pressed down the gas and they shot off. They squealed around a few corners, then slowed right down. They drove down another few streets before they parked, abandoned the car with the masks in it, and got into another one, Jones's old Ford, parked on the edge of a piece of waste ground.

The drive back was slow and anxious. Every car they saw looked like a police car, but they had successfully eluded a chase. Another fifteen minutes saw them back home.

It was half past three. The whole operation had taken only one and a half hours.

"Stella!" roared Jones. "Down 'ere."

He and Manley ran upstairs with the stolen goods in sacks while Stella came down. Across the sitting room, Stella and Nick looked at each other—two kids deeply out of their depth. As, of course, were Jones and Manley.

The two men came down shortly after with some relieved chatter and laughs.

"Couple a beers, Stella," said Manley. "Drink to our success, eh, Jonesy?"

"I don't want you getting off yer face," grumbled Jones. "We could still 'ave trouble."

"What trouble?" said Manley. "We're miles away and the cops are looking for a monkey, a fox, and a prime minister. I need a drink after that."

He went to the fridge and came back with three cans, one of which he threw to Nick.

"Did you see that bloke's face?" he sniggered.

"Looked like he'd seen a ghost!"

"Yah—his own."

They laughed. Nick remembered the look on the chemist's face as he hung upside down from the window, and started to snigger himself.

"Nothing like a bit of violence for a good laugh, eh?" said Stella scornfully. She turned and went up to bed. Nick felt bad, but it wasn't the violence—it was the release from fear that was funny. It was all over now.

Jones stuck his fingers up at the departing Stella and then pulled a carton slyly from his pocket. "This is a good way of celebrating," he said. "And not too noisy for the hour, either." He rattled the box.

"Moggies," said Manley happily. Jones took out a card of little white pills and popped out nine. He gave three each to Manley and to Nick, and raised his beer to them. "Down the 'atch!"

They knocked back the pills.

"Night, night, my sons," said Manley. They went to sit down. Jones tried the telly; there wasn't much on but nobody cared. They sat smiling vaguely at one another for a while, until one by one, they all fell fast asleep. When Stella came down the next morning, all three of them were in their chairs in exactly the same positions they'd sat down in, still flat out.

29
THE OLD FOLKS AT HOME

Nick awoke a little later from a deep, seamless sleep feeling emptied out, as if he'd woken from an anaesthetic, which of course, he had. The room was full of the smell of frying bacon and for a moment he thought he was back at home with his mother, waking up on a Saturday or Sunday morning. The house he was in wasn't so different, just scruffier and dirtier. He lay still and blinked at the walls as his memory filled him in.

He found Stella in the kitchen with the frying pan.

"You've been out for the count. Eating those marbles. Those two are out, they'll be back in an hour or so. Fancy some?" she asked. Nick nodded and sat himself down at the table.

"Nice fry-up after a good day's work, eh?" said Stella, and she gave him a lopsided smile.

He waited until he had his food in front of him before he said what was on his mind.

"He's a bloody maniac, isn't he?"

"He has his good sides."

"Has he?" Nick looked at her to see if she was joking. She didn't appear to be. "Bloody hell, Stella."

She shrugged. "Don't," she said.

"But."

She shrugged again.

"Every time I see you you have another bruise or something."

"'Cos I love him?" she said. She pulled a wry smile. "Does it matter?"

"I ran away from Meadow Hill to get away from all that. It does my head in, you sticking to it like that."

"He doesn't mean it, Nick. He's always really sorry afterwards." She looked him briefly in the face. "He's got a heart, too, you know."

"Where's he keep it?"

"He just finds it hard to find it."

Nick shook his head.

"I know. But I love him," said Stella. "So that's all there is to it. I made my bed, I guess."

"I don't think all that much of being in love if that's what it means," said Nick. Stella laughed at him.

"Being in love, it's the best thing in the world," she told him, but the words sounded foolish on her lips. As for Nick, he carried that conversation in his heart long, long after it had ceased to be any use.

They chatted on and ate their food until the door banged open and Jones and Manley came in, in great good spirits. Some sort of a sale had been made.

"Now then," said Jones, clapping his hands together. "Time to have a little merry, eh?" Stella smiled and went upstairs to change. Nick stood awkwardly at the edge, hoping that he was going to be released from his service.

Jones came over and poked him in the chest with his finger. "What happened last night never happened. Not a word. Because if a word gets out, I'll know where it came from. Get me?"

"I get you," said Nick.

"Leave the lad alone," said Manley. "He did his part."

"Just so long as he knows, if a word gets out, I know who it is."

"Anyway, he's to come with us for a drink."

Jones rolled his eyes. As for Nick, it was the last thing he wanted. "It's all right," he began, but Manley had made up his mind. He came over and slapped his face playfully.

"Nah, he held his own, didn't he, Jonesy?"

"He never even got us in."

"How could he, he had no key. Nah, he done all right, he'll come with us," insisted Manley. He winked at Nick. "Don't mind old Jones," he said. "He'll be a lot cheerier with a few pints inside him. Come on, Stella," he bellowed up the stairs.

"Coming," called Stella. Jones and Manley rolled their eyes at each other, and started walking up and down with their hands behind their backs, tutting and looking at their watches comically. It was the first time Nick had ever seen Jones being playful, and he couldn't help laughing at them. Jones was delighted with it, and he turned to Nick and gave him a wide-mouthed, wobbly grin that suddenly made his hard face look weak and tired and old. Nick had to make a conscious effort not to stare.

Manley laughed at his discomfort. "Jones's smile takes a bit of getting used to," he said, and patted his friend on his back, so that Jones, still in his charming mood, smiled almost shyly at Nick, and made him think of Stella's words—that he had a heart after all but found it hard to find. Then Stella came down the stairs and they headed off in the car, Stella at the wheel, for the pub.

Jones and Manley didn't want to be seen locally with something to celebrate, so they headed off to the other side of town, a place Manley knew just outside Wythenshaw, where he used to live. They drove across Manchester for half an hour before Stella pulled up at a big, old Victorian pub on the edge of a housing estate. They went in, got a table, and Manley went to the bar.

"Now then, first one down quick to get things moving," he said when he came back, putting four pints on the table. He, Jones, and Stella solemnly downed the beer. Nick wasn't used to it and watched them pour it down their necks in amazement at how quickly it vanished.

"Get a move on," said Jones when they'd all finished and Nick's pint was still half full.

"Don't push him, we don't want him getting sick drunk, or we'll have to take him back," said Stella.

Jones muttered something about babysitting, but he went along with it for now. He went to the bar to get another one, and Manley gave Nick a wink.

"You'll see—another four a them and he'll be a different man."

"And yeah, and another four after that and he'll be another one again," said Stella, so gloomily that they both began to laugh.

The pub filled up; things got loud. Nick had a couple of beers and then a couple more. Manley and Jones were taking whiskey chasers, but fortunately they didn't force any on him. Even so, the pub began to get blurry and loud, and very, very funny. Without meaning to, Nick was enjoying himself. Like Manley said, Jones became another man—a clever, happy man, making jokes and smart remarks, roaring with laughter, wiping his eyes, smooching up with Stella, and getting all sentimental.

It carried on like that for a while, but then Nick found himself dozing off, sitting upright in his chair, and Jones started nudging him irritably again.

"I don't want you falling asleep and drawing attention to us," he hissed in Nick's ear. Nick looked across to Manley, but he was in the middle of an intense conversation with Stella. Jones looked as if his good mood was evaporating.

Nick lurched to his feet. ". . . breath of air," he muttered. Jones nodded and scowled and stuck his nose in his beer, and Nick weaved his way through the crowd toward the door. There was a beer garden outside. He was feeling sick now he'd stood up. Maybe a brisk walk around the garden, or even a brisk vomit, come to that, would sort him out.

Outside, he was surprised to find it was still day. The light hurt his eyes but it was good to get away from the fug of cigarettes and beer fumes. It was a sunshiny day, a few high white clouds, cold in the wind but quite warm in the sheltered garden. There was a patch of scratty grass with some tables set up, and a few hardy souls were sitting at them in their coats, with drinks and packets of crisps on the tabletops. There was a family group at one table, a husband and wife with a couple of small children out for a drink with some friends, two older men. Next to one of the men was another boy, aged about twelve or thirteen, watching what was going on with a bored expression on his face.

There was something about the boy Nick couldn't place. It was the poor clothes, the haircut, the way he sat . . . Everything about him was vaguely familiar.

Nick walked out past them and as he did he caught sight of the men's faces. It was such a shock to his system that he felt for a second that he was treading on air, as if his whole body left him behind for an instant. He caught himself and turned his face away quickly before they spotted him. He walked back into the pub. Suddenly, he was as sober as a bottle of lemonade.

Inside was so loud, he felt hidden in the noise, but he couldn't believe what his eyes had just told him, so he went back out for another look, even though every nerve in him told him to bury himself in the ground or run out the back door, anything to get away. But he had to see. He went out and dodged around behind the porch, so he was hidden from the drinkers in the garden. He stood there to catch his breath for a moment, before peering around to get a proper look.

The men were sideways on. One of them he'd only ever seen once before, but in circumstances he could never forget. The other one was Tony Creal.

Nick let out a small whimper of amazement. Tony Creal, out for a drink with one of the men who had joined him in gang-raping Nick in the Secure Unit.

He hid again behind the porch and lay against the wall to catch his breath before he poked his head back to have another look. No doubt about it. It was Tony Creal, wrapped up warm like your kind old uncle in his gray overcoat and wooly hat, his nose dipped in a glass of Guinness, as if him being out and loose in the world was a cozy kind of thing, something to feel happy about.

"Bum boys," whispered Nick to himself, and in his damaged heart felt a surge of hatred for both Creal and his victim.

He leaned back against the wall. He was going to go, he was off, out of there. He just needed to clear his head and wait for his moment. But before he was ready, the door opened and out came Jones, looking for him. He stood outside the door of the porch with his glass in his hand, looking this way and that for Nick for a moment before he caught sight of him flattened up against the wall like a crab, trying to hide.

"What are you up to?" demanded Jones.

"I got stuck," said Nick softly. Despite himself, he peered around the body of Jones to see what Creal was up to.

"You tell me when you want to wander off," Jones began. As he spoke, he looked around instinctively, to see what Nick was watching.

There was a pause. Then, without a word, Jones stepped back behind the porch, just as Nick had done, and pressed himself flat beside him, just as Nick had done, and twisted his head sideways for a closer look, just as Nick had done. His breath hissed out of him. It was a moment or two before Nick realized what he was saying.

"Creal," Jones was whispering to himself. "Dear Tony. It's only fucking Tony Creal."

Jones stood like that for several seconds before he remembered Nick standing next to him. He turned abruptly and looked down at him, his fishy eyes as wide and as frightened as they had been more than twenty years before, when he first discovered what Tony Creal was capable of.

Their eyes met. There was no disguising it. They both knew in an instant that they had this man in common.

Nick didn't wait to find out how he was going to react; he knew the kind of hatred Creal bred. Without a second's thought he darted out across the garden, keeping his head down to hide his face, and fled down the steps that led to the pub, up the street, and away. Jones started after him, but then stopped and pressed himself back behind the wall. He peered around once more to make sure that, yes, yes, it really was Tony Creal who sat there sipping his beer, and then went back into the pub.

30
THE HEART OF JONES

It wasn't the sort of thing you wanted to know about Jones. Nick didn't know who he was more scared of, him or Creal. He was certain that just as he had felt that unfair pulse of hatred for the poor lad sitting there with Creal, and just as he had turned on Oliver all those months ago, Jones felt the same thing for him. It made no sense, but he knew it.

He ran until his breath was gone and he was certain that he wasn't being followed, before slowing down to a walk and starting to take note of his surroundings. He was on the edge of a wooded park. He followed it around and gradually began to get a sense that he'd been here before. In fact, he was just off the Palatine Road, the same road that had led him and Davey to freedom when they had broken out of Meadow Hill months before.

He wandered about until he found his way onto the main road, then jumped on a bus. He sat there, shaking and shivering and muttering to himself, until he got back into town, and then caught another bus out to Jenny's house. It was four o'clock in the afternoon by this time, and there was no one in—she had to work late that day, and Grace and Joe were at after-school club. She'd given him a key, however, so Nick let himself in, went upstairs to Jenny's bedroom, drew the curtains, got into her bed, and fell into a troubled sleep, full of images he hadn't thought about for months—of Tony Creal, of the faces of those other two men in the Secure Unit . . . of Oliver, of Oliver, of Oliver . . .

Meanwhile, Jones wandered back into the pub and sat down with Manley and Stella.

"Found him?" asked Manley.

"Done a runner."

"What's he up to?"

"Guess who's out there having a drink," said Jones, nodding his head at the garden.

Manley cast a suspicious glance at the door.

"Only Creal."

"Creal," said Manley.

"You know Creal."

Manley sipped his beer. "I know who you mean," he said. "What's he doing here?"

"Having a drink, I'd say."

Stella looked at their faces. "Who's Creal?" she asked. "What's the problem, Ben?"

Jones ignored her. He sat awhile, tapping his finger on the table.

"Who's Creal?" repeated Stella, but Jones shot her such a glance she decided it was best to shut up.

"Want another one?" said Manley in a moment.

"Do you?"

Manley thought about it. "Will he remember us?"

"I'd a thought so, wouldn't you?"

"But will he recognize us?"

"Long time ago, wanit?"

"Aye."

There was another pause. "Come to think about it," said Manley, "Meadow Hill ain't so far from here."

"You reckon," said Jones. The two of them sat for a while, overcome with a sense of oddness that somewhere like Meadow Hill could be so near a place of celebration and pleasure.

"He's still there, then," said Manley.

"He's got a lad with him right now," said Jones. He thought about it a moment and then added, "All those years."

There was another short pause before Manley made up his mind.

"I've had enough," he said. "It's time we got back."

Without a word, the two men rose to their feet and made their way over to the door, with a very puzzled Stella following after them. At the door, Jones ordered Stella to go to the car, before slippping around the side behind the porch, with Manley close behind him.

Jones indicated the bench where Creal sat.

"It's him all right," said Manley.

"Look at him," said Jones mildly, "sitting there enjoying his pint without a care in the world."

"He must have come in to get the beers, what do you think?"

"If he saw us?"

"Yeah."

Jones thought about it. "Would he be sitting there if he did?"

"Probably not."

"I should hope not. Anyhow, what does it matter if he saw us," snarled Jones, suddenly rounding on Manley. "We haven't done anything. He's the one who should be worried."

"Worried about what?" sneered Manley. "Worried about the police? You know as well as I do, he doesn't have a worry in the world."

They peered around the porch once more at Creal and his friend, and considered how unfair it was that Creal should sit there without a worry, when he caused so much.

"The fucking nonce," said Jones. "The dirty, shitty little nonce. Look at that lad. That could be your son or my son. Someone's son. The dirty, shitty nonce."

"Death's too good for him," agreed Manley. They waited there a little longer, then got up and made their way in a circular route to the car, avoiding any means by which Mr. Creal might see their faces. Even now, years later, when they had nothing to fear from him, they feared him. In the car, they both became very quiet. They set off in silence for about ten minutes, before Stella plucked up the courage to speak again.

"Who was that man?" she asked, leaning forward in the car. "What's he done?"

Without any warning, Jones went mad. He shouted in surprise as if she'd slapped him.

"You stupid bitch!" he yelled. He shoved Stella back in her seat with the palm of his hand.

"I only . . ." she began. But Jones was beyond any control. He began hitting out at her, leaning right over into the back where she sat and punching hard as she dodged and screamed and tried to fend him off. Her attempts to avoid the blows seemed to drive him madder than ever.

Manley reached back with one hand, the other on the steering wheel, shouting, "I'm trying to drive, you twat!" But Jones had lost his temper totally. If anyone driving the other way had had time to look, they would have seen Jones, leaning over the back and beating, beating, beating something that cowered out of sight in the backseat, as if he were fighting off a visitor from hell.

If by some magic, Jones had been able to tell Stella what had happened to him as a child in care, and if Stella had somehow been able to understand the effect it had had on him, she would have held in her hand the key to all his troubles and hers. It might be difficult to believe now, with that scowl branded into his face, with his teeth knocked out, and the terrible ugliness of his violence hanging over everything he did, but like Nick, Jones had once been a pretty boy. Like Nick, he had been to Meadow Hill. Like Nick, he had come across Tony Creal. Like Nick, he had a damaged heart. Unlike Nick, his was beyond all repair.

Ben Jones had gone into care at the age of four and been in and out of it all his life. There had been not one but more than half a dozen Creals in that time, and what had happened to Nick in the Secure Unit had happened to Jones again and again. Over his years of growing, fear had become a part of every aspect of his life—fear with pain, fear with pleasure, fear with home, fear with care, fear with friendship, fear with love, fear with everything, until fear had taken root and blossomed in his heart. The root of his fear was pain, and the fruit of his fear was anger. At the center of him, buried beyond reach, locked tight into the black night of Jones's heart, was a four-year-old boy who had been crying for help for twenty-five long years.

Back at the house, Stella stumbled into the living room and Jones followed her. She tried to make it upstairs, but he was in the grip of an insurmountable fury. He pulled her backward off the stairs by her hair and the beating began all over again. Manley stood behind, crying, "Leave her, Jones, it's enough, it's enough!" but Jones was deaf to any pity. There could never be enough. So, for the first time in his life, Manley stepped in between Jones and his victim.

"Not that I care for the girl, but you're going to kill her like this," he begged. "And face it, Jones, it ain't her you want to kill, is it?"

Jones, panting in panic and rage, stood there with his hands in fists, glaring at his friend, unable to speak.

"It's not her you want to kill. Is it?" demanded Manley again.

Jones looked away, unable to meet Manley's eyes. He glanced fiercely back up in a moment, and Manley nodded at him.

"It's not her," he said.

"No, not her," repeated Jones.

Stella ran up the stairs, her face and scalp covered with

blood, clutching her side. He had rebroken the rib he had cracked a couple of weeks earlier. Jones turned away and walked to the fridge for a beer.

A few minutes later, sitting in the front room, still out of breath, he looked up. "We could do it," he said to Manley.

"Maybe we could," said Manley. "If we could find a way."

"We wouldn't have to do it on our own," said Jones. "How many men do you know who'd help us finish off dear Tony Creal?"

"A dozen or so, I reckon," said Manley. "I'm thinking . . . if there's enough suspects, it's difficult to find a culprit."

Jones stood there awhile and then said one word in a quiet voice.

"Murder."

"Murder," said Manley with a nod.

So the idea was born.

For a while longer, the two men talked. Names were suggested, characters discussed. Were they good men or bad men, strong men or weak men, singers or silent? The next day, they agreed, they'd start to make contact and feel out a few of the most trustworthy. At this point, neither was sure that this would ever be discussed further, or even that the sighting of Creal would ever be brought up again. Perhaps in the end it would be easier to do what they'd both done for twenty-odd years, and just forget all about it.

Upstairs in bed, Stella lay waiting for her lover, listening to the soft murmur of voices below and waiting fearfully for the sound of his foot on the stairs. Stella's own history was very far from gentle, but she was stronger than Jones in this respect; somehow, she had emerged from the ordeal of her childhood with a kind heart. There was so much kindness in Stella, it was a jug that could never be emptied—kindness for Nick, kindness for Davey, kindness even for Jones. There was kindness in Stella for every living thing on earth except for one, poor unforgiven soul—herself. Like Oliver, like so many before her, she was caught in that terrible trap where pain, fear, and love have become one and the same thing.

Half an hour later, when Jones opened the door and stood there, framed for a minute in dull light from the hall downstairs, she stared at him in dumb terror, unable to tell his mood. But he came to her gently, took her in his arms, laid her curled-up limbs out straight, kissed her bruises, and then, burying his head in her lap, began to weep. They were little tears at first, but quickly turned into big, heart-shaking sobs.

Cautiously, Stella laid her hand on his head and watched dully as he clutched at it and cried. It was too soon after a beating for her to feel anything but relief that it was at an end, but without even knowing it, Jones was working an ancient, terrible magic. Within a very few hours, the darkness in her heart would be lightened by an edge of pity, and before long she would feel more sorry for Jones than she would for herself. This was how he kept her heart—by breaking his own into pieces, and hers with it, time after time.

31
THE JACK OF DIAMONDS

After he had wept like a baby, Jones fell asleep wrapped up in her arms like a child. But he didn't sleep for long. He woke out of a nightmare within the hour and lay awake, tormented by flashbacks, ravaged by feelings of betrayal and guilt that turned to rage as soon as he reached out to touch them. No wonder he turned to his little bottles of calm.

"What are you doing?" asked Stella. Jones didn't answer. He got out of bed, went to the wardrobe, rattled with the key, and began to root inside.

"No, Jonesy, not tonight," begged Stella. She meant, not to obliterate himself tonight after he had been so gentle. She couldn't know it, but it was the closeness Jones wanted to wipe out. It was the hatred inside himself that he couldn't bear.

Jones flung a handful of pills down his throat and went back to bed, turning his back on her as he lay down. Stella stared at him, unable to understand, but she moved by him as always. She laid a hand on his shoulder but he shrugged it off, so she wriggled as close to him as she dared so that she could at least feel his heat, and like this, unable to touch, the two lovers fell asleep.

Jones spent a couple of days like that, full of pills and peace. The next day, he went to lie in the bath and stared at the ceiling, not thinking, not feeling much, either, as clean as a freshly washed sheet, newly pressed. He got up and sat with Stella that evening, eating the food she'd cooked him. It was a chicken roasted with potatoes, carrots, and peas, one of his favorites, and he ate with the first appetite he'd had all week.

Later that day, he called around to see Manley, and found that his friend had been spending quite some time thinking about the matter of Tony Creal. It wasn't the first time he'd thought about that subject, and over the years he'd come up with what he thought was a pretty good plan for seeing it through, although he'd never told anyone about it. It was a bold plan that meant facing down the police, and needed the company of a number of men with hearts like iron . . . if Jones was genuinely interested . . .

Jones was. Calmly now, and with mounting conviction, they began to plot the murder of Tony Creal.

As foretold, there were a great many men who dearly wished to have Tony Creal taken out of the world, and not gently, either, but not so many willing to do it. Over the next couple of weeks Jones and Manley sounded them out.

Such meetings began casually. There would be a certain amount of idle chitchat about things in the world in general, and its wicked ways, before one of the two plotters would drop into the conversation that they had seen guess who wetting his whistle down at the Old Folks at Home the other week.

"Only that nonce Creal."

"Don't ever mention him to me, I never even want to think about him again," was one reaction common enough, which ended the conversation in its tracks there and then.

But . . . "I'd kill him if I could" was another; in which case Jones widened his eyes innocently and wondered aloud if such a thing were possible.

"And if it was," Manley might remark, "and if someone had a way of polishing off dear Tony without any visible culprits, with a certainty of getting his death for free . . . you'd be there, then, would you?"

And the eyes would meet.

"Would you?" repeated Jones.

Sometimes they'd look away. Sometimes there'd be a laugh dismissing such a silly idea, or the subject might be changed. But sometimes—six times to be precise—the exchange was followed with agreement.

"I'd be the first one there with a knife at his throat," said one man, "so long as I could be sure I'd never get caught."

No more was said, no suggestions or confidences exchanged. Not every nod was taken up. But some nods would get another visit, where there'd be more chitchat, a drink perhaps, and a theory presented. Neither Jones nor Manley ever suggested that the theory was anything more than a theory, a thought, never to be put into action. Only if the nodder suggested that the theory was good enough to try, would more nods be made. Then and only then would discussion move into actual practicalities.

By the end of a fortnight, Jones and Manley had found

three more to join them. Five men. More than enough for murder.

Stella, of course, was kept completely in the dark, and Jones became increasingly distant. He began to spend long periods locked away downstairs with Manley, deeply immersed in intense conversations from which she was barred. When they were on their own he stayed away from her, snapped at her to leave him alone and stop following him around. There were long conversations on the telephone when she was ordered out of the room, and journeys out on his own or with Manley from which she was also barred.

Stella wasn't stupid. Something was going on, but what? Like Jones himself, she was caught in a terrible trap of love. Anything, even the beatings, was better than this withdrawal. At least when the violence was over, there was tenderness. Now she had nothing.

Her efforts to break through were met either with a casual dismissal or a flurry of rage. As the days turned to weeks, she became secretive herself, lingering on the stairs, coming down from the bedroom quietly and pausing outside the kitchen door to see if she could hear what was being said. She soon put a stop to that game, when Jones caught her at it. After that he took to sending her out, telling her with a sneer to visit Shiner and those kids she liked so much.

That had never happened before. Jones had always guarded her like a treasure and would have broken her jaw rather than let her be at Shiner's out of his sight. She wept bitter tears, to no avail. By now, she was convinced that whatever it was that Jones was planning, it was deep and it was dark. This was no common robbery that was being planned. It stank of violence. She had not yet allowed herself to think of death, but it was there already, on the tip of her tongue.

One month after Jones and Manley had first seen Creal in the beer garden, the five men assembled at Jones's house to discuss their final plans. This time it wasn't enough for Stella to stay up in the bedroom—she was sent out of the house. Jones gave her a little money, told her to go and get some shopping in.

He took her to the door himself. As he stood framed in the entrance, she turned to look at him, full of questions she didn't dare ask.

"Don't hurry back," said Jones, and he closed the door.

She stood there a moment, looking back at the closed curtains to the front room. What was it? What was he planning with these men that was so bad she wasn't allowed so much as a hint of it? As if his normal games weren't scary enough.

Stella was petrified, but it wasn't for herself she was scared; it was for Jones. Despite everything, there was something fearfully helpless about her lover. He was prepared to die as easily as he might catch a cold. She couldn't bear the thought that he would come to harm. His distance from her was breaking her heart.

She was certain something terrible was about to happen.

As Stella made her sad way into Manchester, Jones, Manley, and the three other men were opening a can and drinking not to health, but to death—to the death of Tony Creal. They'd been keeping a watch on the Northenden pub and knew that he was in the habit of coming out there most Mondays. The friend Nick had seen him with was a police officer on Manchester's serious fraud squad who shared his taste for boys. He'd been there two weeks in a row, but left after a few drinks while it was still light, which didn't help their plans.

A better chance was a more regular date he had at a watering hole closer to the home, a small pub called the Fox and Hounds, where he often went for a few pints, and sometimes more than a few, on a Thursday night, and walked back late, and alone. If someone watched regularly, and if someone was willing to make a phone call when he turned up and another when he left the pub, and if a group of determined men were to wait in the roads between the pub and Meadow Hill, they might very well catch Mr. Creal on his own, or with a friend or two at the most, who could easily be scared off. Once they had their hands on him, the murder could be carried out easily enough, and the escape managed, no doubt. But the difficult part comes later on. How do you elude capture and stay innocent in the eyes of the law? People would see the new drinkers coming to the pub on a Thursday night. They might notice them leaving after Mr. Creal, perhaps. And what about those who waited on the streets? Could they lurk and not be seen? Our five heroes understood very well the slow, painstaking patience the police show in a murder investigation, carefully building up a picture of a victim's movements on the day of the murder. Glimpses, even only half remembered, might help build up a trail that sooner or later would lead to the guilty door.

"But that doesn't matter," said Manley. "So long as they can't prove it, who cares?"

They would come upon Creal, all five of them, and escort him away to a waiting car, and then on to one of their homes, where he would be kept prisoner until the very dark of night. From there he would be taken to a place of execution, a small car park in a quiet part of town. The gagged Creal would be tethered to a fence and soaked with petrol. The five men would stand around him and each one would take from his pocket a box of matches. Each man would take out a match and place it head down on the box, holding box and match with one hand, thumb pressed down on the end of the match. Then, one man and one man only would flick the match, the match would ignite, followed shortly after by Tony Creal. They would all be witness to his deserved fate, that most horrible of deaths, to be burned alive.

"Only one man flicks the match," said Manley. "If we all did it, we'd all be guilty of murder. But if just one man does it, only he will be guilty. The job of the police will be to find out which one. So long as we all keep silent, that man is safe from prosecution. The police can take us in for questioning, we can admit we were there, we can admit we took him there, we can admit we were witnesses, willing witnesses to his murder. But so long as we keep the name of that man to ourselves, no one can be touched for murder."

"They can't touch us?" asked one.

"Conspiracy to murder, maybe. A few years," sneered Jones. "Who won't give a few years to see an end to Tony Creal?"

The men nodded. Well worth it, they were all agreed.

"And that man has a guarantee," put in Jones. "Because if any one of us gives his name away, he will be murdered in his turn, in the same way. Remember that," he said, glaring fiercely about him. "*In the same way.* I swear it."

"I swear it too," said Manley.

They all swore it.

"How will we choose the lucky man?" someone asked.

"We cut," said Jones. He produced a pack of cards and shuffled it well before handing it on to the next man, who also shuffled it. The pack did the rounds of all five, shuffled in every hand, before it was placed facedown on the floor.

"High wins, ace high," said Jones. He reached down, slid the pack sideways to spread it out in an untidy fan, and took a card. One after the other, all five men did the same. When it was done, they cast their cards face up on the floor before them.

Who took the highest card? It was never told, and it won't be told here, either. But it was said, by one of the five to another man many years later, that it was the jack of diamonds that won the day.

32
WHAT STELLA DID

While the five men were making their plans, Stella went to see Sunshine. She found him in, with just Davey for company, both of them wrapped up in blankets in the little kitchen, eating beans with the gas ring burning to try and keep the warmth up.

It smelled of farts.

"Bloody hell, you two, how long you been eating those beans?" she demanded.

"It's him," said Shiner, pointing at Davey.

"You were letting rip just now. And anyway, you're old. Old farts smell worse."

Shiner chuckled. "I'm an old fart, now, am I?" he said. "And beans, Stella, what else am I supposed to eat now you're gone? Have you come 'round to teach us how to do one of those lovely omelettes you used to make for me?"

Stella smiled. "I'll make you an omelette if you want, Shiner."

He smiled thinly back. "No eggs," he said.

"It's gone to pieces 'round 'ere since you went," said Davey.

Stella went to put the kettle on. Behind her back, Shiner

caught Davey's eye and indicated the door. It was the first time he had seen Stella on her own since she left him for Jones, and he wanted to make the most of it.

Davey quietly made himself scarce. Stella noticed, and smiled at Sunshine, flattered that he wanted her to himself. She made them both a cup of coffee and sat down at the table opposite him.

Shiner took a good long look at her—the bruises fading on her face, the way she held herself, how she was careful of her side where her rib was cracked. He put a hand across the table and squeezed hers.

"It's good to see you," he said.

"It's good to see you, Sunshine," said Stella. She glanced around the kitchen. "The old place is still the same."

Shiner shook his head. "Not the same."

"Yeah, it's filthy 'round here. Can't you get one of your other girls to do a little housework?" she joked.

"None of them come to live in me house. None a them is you."

"I'm sorry, Shine."

"You got your freedom now."

She threw up her hands in exasperation. "Don't go on! He lets me out of the house, which is more than you did."

Shiner tried another tack.

"Look at you. Look at your face. And I don't just mean the bruises. You're all closed up. Like the roof's about to fall in on you."

"It probably is here."

Sunshine just shook his head. Stella bent hers.

"I love him," she said stubbornly. "And he . . . he needs me."

"He needs you! What for? As a punching bag? No, don't tell me—you're going to change him! Is that it? Let me tell you something about these kind of men, Stella. Jones will never change. The more he loves you the more he hits you, the more he hits you the more he hates you, the more he hates you the more he loves you. For some men, love is full of hate."

Shiner had come very close to the truth. But Stella had other things on her mind than her own safety.

"I'm worried about him, Shiner," she said.

Shiner leaned back in his chair. "Worried about him? Eh?"

"Ever since he did that chemist's . . ."

"What happened that day? What did he do to Nick? He scared the life out of that boy. I scarcely see him these days. He's scared Jones'll come 'round and find him. Did he do something wrong?"

Stella frowned. "Not that I know of. Shiner, I think Jonesy is planning something dangerous. I think, I think he's planning on killing someone."

Having said it, Stella burst into tears. Shiner looked at her in astonishment. "Oh, man. Murder? That's not Jones's style. He'll kill you if you get in his way, but he'd never plan it. What makes you think that?"

"Nothing . . . the way he is . . . I don't know! He has Manley 'round all the time and these other blokes keep turning up, and they all look so grim. And making plans I'm not allowed to hear . . ."

Shiner shook his head. "So he's planning something he doesn't want you to know. So what's new?"

"Something's wrong, Shine. Something's going on . . ."

"Something's always going on. Who, then? Who's he want out a the way?"

"I don't know."

"When?"

"I don't know."

"Why?"

She shook her head.

"You don't know nothing." Shiner leaned back in his chair.

"I'm scared for him."

Shiner threw his hands in the air. Jones was ugly, brutal, and stupid. It was an insult to him that she should prefer a man like that to him.

They talked awhile longer. Sunshine pumped her as much as he could for information about the job. Something had happened, but Stella hadn't got a clue what it was.

"Nick," he said at last. "Go and see Nick. He knows something."

"What?"

"No idea. He won't say a word to me. Maybe he'll tell you."

Stella dried her tears. "Where's he staying?"

Shiner shrugged; no idea.

Stella nodded. She was too close to Jones. If Nick wanted to avoid him, Shiner certainly wasn't going to tell her where to find him.

She finished her coffee and left. Behind her, Shiner put his head in his hands and moaned softly to himself. He loved her still. He wanted her back, and he hadn't given up hope yet.

Jones was going to go too far sooner or later—he was going back inside, no doubt about it. Then he'd have another chance. He wasn't above helping Jones on his way, either, if only he could find a way of ratting on him and be sure of not getting caught. So far, nothing had occurred to him.

Stella left the building in Oldham Street and walked south into town to do some shopping, but before she went more than a few steps, Davey caught up with her. Unlike Shiner, Davey knew exactly what had happened that day. Nick had told him all about Creal sitting with his Guinness at the Old Folks at Home, and how Jones reacted when he saw him.

Davey had thought about it and nodded. "You mean," he said, "that Jones used to be one of Creal's bum boys?"

The two of them laughed and laughed till their sides hurt. The idea of the notorious Jones, ugly, brutal, angry Jones, bent over the back of the sofa for the old man's pleasure, was just crippling. It was also terrifying.

If she had been to see Nick, Stella would quite likely have got nothing out of him—he was far more traumatized by his experiences at Meadow Hill than Davey was and would have just clammed up. As it was, she got the information she was looking for. Tony Creal, the pub where he had been spotted; Meadow Hill, the home where he was the deputy.

"Meadow Hill," she cried. "I've heard Ben talk about it. He went there too."

"I know," said Davey, and he sniggered.

Stella got a great deal of information out of Davey—but not all. There were things you just didn't talk about, and sexual abuse was one of them. That was taboo. Davey would have felt he was letting his friend down if he so much as hinted at the kind of things Nick had suffered during his time in care. The shame, somehow, seemed to reflect as much on the victim as on the perpetrator. Instead, he mentioned the violence, and left it at that.

"If 'e wants to top someone, it's Creal, I reckon," said Davey. And he smiled at the thought of it.

Stella was horrifed. It was real? Her fears were real?

"Let him," said Davey. "Creal deserves everything he gets, and more. It'll be the only good thing Jones ever did."

But to kill a man because he knocked you around when you were a kid? It happened all the time. It was hardly a hanging offense.

Davey shrugged. "You weren't there," he said, and he smiled grimly.

They parted—Davey to run off to Nick's to tell him the news. Jones was planning on murdering Creal. Now there was a cause for celebration! Behind him, Stella wandered the streets upset, confused, not knowing what to think. She couldn't be a party to murder. If he did it, of course he would be caught, and then what? Life. Twenty, maybe thirty years inside.

She wasn't at all sure Jones could cope with being caged up for so long.

She couldn't stop him, she knew that much. Nothing she could say or do would ever deflect him from a course once he'd settled on it. And she couldn't shop him either. She could never bring herself to do that.

Around and around the streets she went, undecided what to do. Creal she didn't care about at all, although she hardly wished him dead. Her concern was Jones. How could she help him? How could she prevent this senseless act without attracting the police to his door?

In the end, she made her plan. She bought paper and pen and wrote a letter addressed to Meadow Hill—she got the address from the telephone book at the post office—and Tony Creal.

"If it is you," she wrote, "who drinks at the Old Folks at Home in Northenden, some men mean you harm. They are men that you harmed when they were at your school. You have been seen. This is a warning from someone who cares nothing for you, but doesn't want to see a good man go down for no good reason."

She posted her letter and went on her way. She did the shopping as Jones had told her, and went back home, to find her lover in a remarkably jolly mood considering the kind of thoughts that were on his mind. She tried to join in, smoked some weed with him, drank some beer, and later on they had some takeaway pizza. But she couldn't shake off her anxiety about what was being planned, or about what she had done to foil it. Jones quickly lost patience with her and went to the pub on his own, leaving her at home alone with her thoughts.

33
ANOTHER DEAL

As Stella had guessed, Shiner wasn't being completely honest with her about Nick. For the first three or four days after the job with Jones, he'd avoided Oldham Street altogether and hidden out in Jenny's house. Boredom and the need for excitement he'd developed since his mother died drove him back soon enough, but he was wary now. Knowing what he knew about Jones's past wasn't a healthy thing, and he no longer felt safe at Shiner's. He moved his room to a more distant part of the house, but he spent very little time in it after that, and from then on, he always sat in Shiner's kitchen on the seat nearest the door into the sitting room, where there was an escape hole into the attic, in case Jones turned up unexpectedly.

Bored or not, he was spending far more time at Jenny's than he ever had before.

Jenny didn't know what had happened to drive him into her house, but given Nick's recent taste for danger, she could guess it was something pretty grim. She saw it as a chance to get him back on the straight and narrow—off the streets and into a proper home, away from theft and into education . . . or into something, anyway. The question was, what? Nick scoffed at the idea of school. All his mates were well into their first exam year now; he was hardly going to catch up. What was there for a fifteen-year-old during the weekdays, if not school?

Every day she could see him itching to get away, and not daring to. Whatever trouble he was in would fade away soon enough, she guessed. Unless she found something to haul him in with, so would he.

With the social services no longer involved, she turned to the only other source of help she knew, and got in touch with Michael Moberley.

They had a long chat on the phone about what was best. His solution, of course, was to get in touch with social services, and he found it difficult to understand why she was so adamant that it was a no-go. Nick had told her a few bits and pieces over the past week—nothing about the sexual abuse, of course, but about the violence. She used that to try and explain.

Michael was horrifed. "We need to complain! That's monstrous!" he exclaimed.

"That won't help Nick, though, will it?" said Jenny.

"Well, I don't see why not. If we make a big-enough fuss, they'll make damned sure he goes somewhere pretty decent next time."

But Jenny wasn't having it. She tried to explain, although she didn't understand it herself. Nick was too shy of authority, too distrusting, and too old. At fifteen, what could they do to stop him running again? Lock him up? What good would that do?

"Sorry," she said. "I just know him. If he gets so much as a whiff of anything like that, he'll be off. Anyhow," she added, "I gave my word."

"Nothing without his consent, of course," said Michael, disappointed. Because the fact was, what else was there?

They talked a little more, but came to no conclusion. The outcome was, Michael agreed to come over and talk to Nick in person. And this time, Nick was there.

Michael Moberley took a cab from the station and got out on Jenny's road, a long row of brick terraces. He paid the driver and looked up and down. Poor area. He felt overdressed in his good coat and expensive shoes, rather too well aware that for a lot of people around here, he could be wearing several weeks' wages on his back as he stood there.

"Well, sorry, but there's not enough for all of you," he muttered under his breath. The problem was, was there enough to help Nicholas Dane? So many things can't be bought. The past, for example. We're all products of our pasts and no amount of money in the world can change that by one single second.

He knocked on the door, which was opened by a curious young girl who stared fixedly at him as she gestured him through to a kitchen diner at the back of the house, where Jenny and the phantom nephew were waiting to receive him.

It was the first time Michael had seen Nick, and he was

feeling nervous about it. Getting his eyes on him for that first look, he was left in no doubt that here was a member of his own family. The boy had Michael's old dad written all over him—although whether that was a good thing, Michael was not in the least bit sure.

He had surprised himself by how persistent he had been in tracking Nick down. It was curiosity as much as anything. There had been so many different versions. Depending on who you talked to, Nick was anything from a violent thug to a hapless victim, and he was interested to see how he came across.

There wasn't much sign of the thug, but what did he expect? To find him beating Jenny with the rolling pin and torturing the kids? The most vivid impression he got, over all, on that first meeting, was that here was someone not to be trusted. Nick's eyes were all over the place, like a pair of fried eggs slipping around a greasy plate. Victim, then, decided Michael. The boy had trouble trusting people, just like Jenny had said. But as he well knew, the road from victim to thug is a very short one indeed.

Michael had thought to take Jenny and Nick out to dinner, but she wanted to cook dinner for some reason. It was a Sunday, and she was doing a roast. The vegetables were overcooked, Michael thought, and the chicken was a battery bird and really rather tasteless, but he enjoyed it all the same—sitting in a room with a family, eating up his greens with lashings of gravy.

During the meal, he watched Nick carefully, as well as he could without drawing attention to the fact. The lad had good manners and was polite; he knew how to behave, which was a start, at least. Nick relaxed as they ate, and began chatting to the two younger children, who evidently liked him—another point in his favor. A couple of times Michael looked up and caught Nick's eyes traveling away from him, and he realized that he was being observed every bit as carefully and as artfully as he was observing Nick. The next time he looked around swiftly and caught his eye, and gave him a wink. Nick scowled, but a moment later played exactly the same trick, which made Michael laugh out loud; and to his intense pleasure, Nick laughed with him.

"Touché," said Michael, and he felt that progress was being made.

Afterward, Jenny sent her two kids away and they got down to business. Michael opened it by talking about Nick's mother—his niece, after all, even if he had never known of her existence until after she was already dead.

Nick answered his questions about Muriel curtly, which reinforced his opinion that the lad was not to be trusted. This was the first conversation either of them had had; he could at least make an effort. Then Nick stopped answering his questions altogether and sat there scowling and staring sideways at the wall. Michael was annoyed and in half a mind to leave it there, until he saw Jenny touch the boy's hand and give Michael a little shake of her head. Then he realized. Nick was crying. He was trying very, very hard not to let his tears show.

Michael's heart went out to him. "And why? Because he loved his mother, you silly old fool," he thought to himself.

Even murderers love their mothers. But he was touched anyway, and made up his mind that yes, he would help, if only he could find a way.

"Well, Nick, what's to be done?" he said, once Nick shook his head, surreptitiously wiped his eye, and looked back up. "Jenny tells me you won't have anything to do with the social services, though."

Nick shifted uncomfortably in his seat. "No way," he muttered.

"Well, don't get me wrong, I promise nothing's going to happen without your agreeing to it—no one can make you do what you don't want to. But can I ask why?"

The boy avoided his eye. "I didn't like it," he said.

"Is that a good-enough reason? I mean, there's lots of things in life we don't like," said Michael. Jenny closed her eyes and held her breath. Nick flashed him a hateful glance.

"They're a bunch of bastards in that place" was all he could say.

"OK," said Michael carefully. He got the impression the lad was about to fly out the door. Jenny was right. "OK, we can put that option out of the way then. So what? Boarding school?"

"Oh, go on, Nick," breathed Jenny. The solution to everything!

Nick moved his head to one side. "Dunno what it's like," he said finally.

Michael pulled a face. Boarding school was expensive was what it was like. He'd do it even so. But . . .

"Not many people like it," he confessed. "I thought it was

awful. And if you don't fit in, the other boys can give you a bad time. And to be honest, Nick, I don't think you'd fit in."

"Why not?" demanded Jenny belligerently.

"Class," said Michael succinctly. "He's the wrong class." He shrugged and smiled apologetically.

"Well, that just about stuffs all of us 'round here, then, doesn't it?" she demanded.

"Not necessarily. People do it. They get through and come out the other end with a good education. Qualifications. It's tough but it can be done. The thing is, would Nick stay there?"

Nick thought about it for about a minute, then grinned.

"I thought not." Michael looked at Jenny, who was furious. Such a chance! It was just being thrown away. "It's expensive," he added. "Very, actually. I'd do it if I really thought it would work, but . . ." He shrugged. He was relieved, but the fact was, Nick would last about ten minutes.

"Well, there must be something," insisted Jenny.

Michael looked at her sadly. "Is there? I wish I knew what it was. In a few years, you know, I can help with education, university, that sort of thing—when he gets to the point of wanting it. But I don't think he does right now, do you, Nick? We could take a chance, of course. But to be honest, if he's not going to make it in a school 'round here, why should he make it at one somewhere else, away from everything he knows? What do you reckon, Nick? What do you think we can do for you?"

Nick smiled wryly. "Give me a load of money?" he suggested.

Michael smiled. "To do what? Get yourself a nice little flat? Start collecting china. Nice three-piece suit and a new kitchen. We can all go out and choose the carpets. You reckon?"

Nick looked away. He was right. A few days sitting in watching TV and doing his homework, he'd go mad. Davey'd be knocking at the door, asking him to come and do a nice little job for him. And he wouldn't be able to say no.

"Maybe in a few years, if you stay out of trouble," said Michael. "But for now, tell you what. You stay here with Jenny. I'll help with money. Move in. Leave your old friends, try it at school. If it works I could help get a bigger flat. You could have your own room. Get your life back on track. But you have to do school. What do you say? It's the best offer you'll get."

Nick thought about it. He had his own life now, for what it was worth. Smoking weed and drinking beer up at Shiner's place. Doing jobs, having fun. Well, not all fun, but still . . . it was a life, and it was his life. Risky as it was, he wasn't sure he wanted to lose it. At least he was his own boss. Until he got caught . . .

But then there was Jonesy, out there somewhere. That was something else.

The thing was, he thought, nothing was forever. Why not?

"OK," he said. "I'll give it a go."

Michael Moberley smiled, and Jenny whooped and ran over to hug him and kiss his cheek. He was back on course.

And Nick thought, "For now, anyway."

34
WHAT JONES DID

Posting that letter was a momentous thing to Stella. She had named no names and had done it only to save her man from himself. But Jones would see it as a betrayal whatever her motives, if he ever found out. She felt much the same herself.

Now that it was too late, she began to doubt herself. She had no evidence. It was all instinct and superstition. To kill a man—such a thing! Jones lost his temper so violently that she believed him capable of murder if provoked enough, but to sit down and plan it and carry it out in cold blood . . . ? Shiner was right; that wasn't his style. Then, to make it worse, shortly after the letter was posted, her period began. She was hopeless at remembering the day of the month. The bleeding started, her mood lifted, and she realized the coincidence with a shock.

"That was the worst premenstrual tension *ever,*" she thought, clutching her head. Imagining people were murdering each other. What next?

Murder or not, something was up. After his initial burst of good humor on the day the plan was made, Jones sank back into an ugly mood. He hardly noticed her from one day to the next until she almost began to wish for a blow, if that's what it took. Anything was better than his blindness to her.

Of course, the plan was still afoot. Jones was spending hours at Manley's or one of the other conspirators', drinking beer and going over and over the plot. It seemed impossible that something so flimsy as a mere plan could work against blood and bone and the force of the law, or against the cunning of a man who had once held such power over them. But however often they went over it, no one could find a flaw. So long as they held true, so long as no man spoke, they were safe.

So week after week the two pubs were watched, the men taking it in turns to watch in pairs. For two weeks Creal failed to show. On the third week, finally, he turned up. A call was made. The other three conspirators came and waited on the road in two separate cars so as not to attract attention—and then the victim left in a car with some friends. Nothing happened.

Jones was enraged. Actually leaving the house to wait in the streets for Creal made it all real, somehow. Now, for the first time, he was certain it was going to happen. He was greedy for blood.

"Patience," said Manley. Creal's fate was sealed. It was just a matter of time.

For the next few weeks, nothing happened. Stella began to suspect not a crime, but another woman. Jones had ceased to care for her—what else could it be? That was where he was spending his time, with someone else. He was bored with her. Mentally, she began to prepare herself for the end. Then, four weeks after she had popped her letter in the box, there was a raid at the house. It was a Thursday. The police, looking for Jones. As usual, he was out.

Stella faced them down.

"What's he done?" she demanded.

"What do you think he's done?" one of them asked, watching her reaction carefully. Stella felt her knees quivering as if she were standing on a nerve. Carefully she pressed her hand against the wall to hide her trembling. Too late! Had he done it already?

The officers searched the house, but the gun and the drugs had all been hidden and they went away empty-handed, leaving Stella no wiser than when they arrived.

What had happened was this: Creal had taken Stella's letter to the police, and they, of course, had put a watch on the Old Folks at Home. They knew Jones, and Manley, and the other three of old—all of them had served prison terms before. Over the weeks they saw all of them in various combinations, and it didn't take them long to work out that all five had spent time at Meadow Hill. Warrants had been sought and obtained. Manley and two other men had been arrested at the Old Folks at Home and, simultaneously, the homes of all five men were raided. Jones had been taken at one of those homes. The five were arrested for conspiracy to murder and taken in for questioning.

Questions, questions, questions, all night. Someone had

given them away, that was clear. Who? Not one of them, Jones was sure of that. Held another day. Questions, questions, questions.

The police knew how to lean, and they leaned hard. The men were kept separate from one another, in brightly lit cells. Their sleep was broken, there was not enough food, not enough drink, no cigarettes. Blows, too—the police weren't fussy about how they got their results. On it went. Questions, promises, accusations, threats. It was over, their friends had confessed all, jail was opening up to receive them. On it went, for three days and nights, but it was as Manley said. No man spoke. At the end of it, the police had no more than when they started out—an anonymous letter and the presence of five men at a pub.

They were released without charge.

Who could it have been? Back home, Jones stormed around the sitting room, kicking the chairs, smashing the furniture. Stella cringed by the door, begging him to stop. Who? Not his mates—Jones would put his life on the line for those four men and they would do the same for him. Not them! But who? Who else knew?

"Maybe they watched the pub?" suggested Stella, desperate to say anything.

But how would they know which pub? Jones paused. Who else knew? . . . and then he realized. The boy. That shitty little sneak. Could have been him. Could easily have been him. He knew all about Creal, the dirty little bum boy, no doubt about that. It had been Nick who led him to Creal, standing outside, watching the old bastard as if he were a pot of cream.

It had to be. No one else knew. The little shit was protecting dear Tony. How he loved dear Tony Creal!

Where was he? Jones ran across and seized Stella by the neck. Where! She knew, she was his friend. He knew he wasn't spending much time at Oldham Street. This was why! So where was he hiding out?

Stella choked and shook her head. Jones flung her aside and went for the door.

"I'll find him anyway," he growled.

Stella knew her man. If he found Nick, he'd kill him, or not far off. Jones had been betrayed and someone was going to suffer for it. Not Nick—her friend. Jones ignored her cry. He seized a short stick, a weighted cudgel with lead poured into the drilled end of it, and rushed out in a blind fury. He was already in the street before she found her senses and rushed after him.

"Not him," she managed to gasp. "It was me."

Jones turned to look at her.

"Not really me, Ben," she begged. "Just a letter. I knew you were up to something . . . and I didn't want murder. I just warned him off, that's all . . ."

She began to babble but the pieces were falling together in Jones's head.

"Maybe they watched the pub," he said, staring at her.

"What?"

"You said it. What pub? How did you know about the pub?" hissed Jones. In two strides he was on her, pushed her inside, slamming the door behind him. He seized her by the throat and shook her like a rat. Clutching her neck in one fist, he began to beat furiously at her face and head with his fist, while she clawed breathlessly at his face. The blood spattered against him and he threw her to the ground in disgust. Stella sprawled on the carpet, clutching her injured throat, unable to catch the breath to beg for mercy. Jones kicked her hard in the face, as hard as he could, one, two, three. Look at her lying there, tears and snot and blood! Ugly, ugly! In a spasm his rage increased a hundredfold. He drew the weighted cudgel from his coat pocket, leaned over, and thrashed her over the head with it four or five times. The blood sprayed up from her broken head. Jones lifted up the cudgel and looked at it, soiled with blood, skin, matted hair, a splinter of bone. Down at his feet, Stella rolled over as if she were still alive, her arm flung back, her face before him, a mess of blood and brains. Jones screamed in rage and terror. How could anything so ugly lie there before him? How could it dare?

Possessed by rage, Jones struck again, and again, and again, over and over with all his force until Stella's head was an unrecognizable pulp. Unable to look and unable to stop, he covered his face with his arm while he beat her and beat her as if he could chase her into hell, or out of this world— anywhere, so long as neither he nor anyone would ever have to look at something so spoiled, so ugly, so awful.

The fit left him and Jones stood staring down at what he had done. He turned, ran to the door, opened it, and froze on the threshold, looking out into the street. The stink of blood was awful. The room was covered in it, pooling on the floor, spattered on the walls and the furniture. He glanced down at himself and saw that he, too, was covered from head to foot in spattered gore. He retched, backed up into the room, slammed the door behind him. He edged sideways around her, unable to look at the body of the one he loved. After what seemed an age he reached the door to the stairs, pushed it to behind him, and ran up to the bathroom, where he stripped off his clothes and ran a bath. He was still in it when he realized that the front door was only on the Yale, and had to run downstairs, dripping and naked next to the frightful thing he had made, to lock the mortice. Back upstairs, the bathwater was red, as if somehow she had bled even there, and he had to empty it, run another, and rebathe.

And there he lay, poor mad Jones, for hour after hour, filling and refilling the bath with scalding water scrubbing at his skin until he drew his own blood to discolor the water again, until darkness fell. Then he dressed in clean clothes, crept downstairs and out by the back way, avoiding the awful inhabitant of the front room. He ran around the block to the front, where he kept his battered old red Ford. He started up the engine, and with a fearful glance over his shoulder to the front of the house, put the car into gear and drove off.

He headed north first, to a lockup on the outskirts of Bolton, where he picked up the shotgun he had used on the raid, almost two months ago now, and a plastic bag containing the remains of the drugs he had stolen. He paused, then put the drugs back. He was going to need his wits about him. It was a decision Jones was going to regret a thousand times in the next days and hours, as Stella came back to haunt him.

He drove on. On the outskirts of Bolton he dumped the car and stole another one, a white Vauxhall. By now it was past two in the morning. He crossed the Pennines over Snake Pass and got onto the M1, going south. It was at about this point that his spirits suddenly lifted. His plan was to reach Harwich and cross to the Netherlands on the ferry, changing the car a couple more times on the way. Or maybe not. He was feeling unaccountably fond of the car he was driving. It had brought him luck. He patted the wheel. He felt somehow that things had at last come to a head. He was leaving his troubles all behind him, leaving his whole past on the other side of the hills—all the poison, the violence, the shame, the betrayal, all left behind. Starting a new life, a better life, a clean life. He had reached bottom—what worse could happen to him?

At this rate, he'd easily make it to the port before the news got out. Manley might come around, but he wouldn't go in without a response from Jones. It could be days before they discovered it.

Jones put down his foot and sped into the night.

35
OLDHAM STREET

When the wind blew hard, the roof on Sunshine's building in Oldham Street creaked and groaned like a tired old man shifting in his chair. It was a tall building, with a complicated slate roof that presented like sails to the storm. The groans communicated themselves down the building so that on a windy day, it sounded as if the upper stories were full of creeping strangers going about the house in their stockinged feet, setting the boards and doors creaking, while the roof above shifted and huffed and groaned aloud, as if it would be a positive relief for it to fly off into the air and never come back.

It was such a night—high clouds floating overhead, playing peek-a-boo with the stars, the house full of unseen presences, and unexpected drafts getting under the floor and appearing in all sorts of odd places, miles away from any apparent connection to the outside. The only consolation was, it was a dry night, and the southern wind was oddly warm.

Sunshine was in bed with a blond girl called Sash. Nick and Davey were sitting in the kitchen playing cards, moaning about their luck.

Nick hadn't been at Jenny's for over a week. Jones had done his worst, then he had disappeared. The first Nick knew about the murder was the police at the front door, looking for him—someone must have seen him out and about with either Stella or Jones. He'd slipped quietly out the back and hadn't been there since. He'd gone straight around to Shiner's and found Davey, who as usual knew all the news and filled him in on it.

No more Stella. It was impossible to believe. They'd smoked weed and drunk beer to mourn her, and to celebrate Jones's disappearance, and Nick had stayed there ever since. True, the police had been around here looking for him as well, but at least it was easier to disappear here—Shiner's building was full of hiding places. Behind him he left Mr. Moberley, school, and Jenny herself, more or less unmourned. Real life was here under Shiner's roof. If it led to prison and a hundred other evils, at least it was his, that's how it felt—and what else could he do but live his own life?

It was a good night for thieving. Everyone would be indoors, hiding from the wind, and no one would hear them creeping down the streets. They wouldn't be bringing the goods back to Shiner's, though. After Stella's murder Sunshine had cleared the place out as much as he could, certain that sooner or later the police were going to come and search the place from top to bottom. When there was a killing, he said, they never let go. He didn't dare actually chuck out all the stolen goods he'd hoarded over the years, in case the place was being watched. He'd got Nick and Davey to help him move it all deeper into the building, into spaces in the roof that weren't his.

They shifted an amazing amount of stuff. "It won't fool the police, though," he said anxiously, standing in front of a small mountain of car stereos, handbags, empty wallets, "lost" credit cards, coats, and God knows what else that Nick and Davey and various other people had sold to him over the years, and that he'd never parted with. He tried to convince the boys to smuggle them out of the house, but they refused.

"It's all yours now, Shine," said Davey generously, and Shiner groaned dramatically and called him a Judas.

And he kept his weed, of course. "Just a few ounces for me own personal use," he said. "No one's going to do a Jamaican man for a likkle smoke." But for now, Davey and Nick had to take their stolen goods elsewhere, or stockpile it till Shiner felt the heat was off.

It had been ten days since the killing. The police had been around asking questions several times, but they hadn't searched the place so far. Davey reckoned Sunshine was being paranoid. Jones was miles away by now, out of the country, sitting pretty somewhere—as pretty as such an ugly bastard could be, anyway.

"They don't need Jones here to want to search it," said Sunshine. "They just need to think there might be a clue, that's all. It's just a matter of time," he added, and refused to budge.

Nick gathered up the cards and shuffled for another deal.

The past week had been vile. The police were still after him, wanting to question him about Stella and Jones. What was he supposed to do? Admit he'd helped Jones rob a chemist's? Then what? It would be back to Meadow Hill and dear Tony Creal.

His nerves were on edge. He glanced anxiously at the door as he heard a loud creak from the other side. Davey laughed.

"It sounds like the bloody cops on the stairs," complained Nick, smiling despite himself and dealing out the cards.

Davey shrugged. "You're not made for this life, mate—too nervous. You should be 'round at Jenny's. Nice safe bed, bowl of cornflakes whenever you want one."

"Boring," said Nick. "Nothing ever happens."

"Too edgy for the good life, you and me both, mate, that's us. We'll be in trouble all our lives because boredom's even worse than getting caught. You reckon?"

"I reckon."

"I'll have three."

Nick dealt. From deeper in the house came a silver burst of laughter and Sunshine's throaty, smoky chuckle.

"What's he doing?" muttered Davey.

"What do you think he's doing?"

"I know what he's doing, Nick, I just wonder why he's doing it now as soon as Stella's gone."

"Not much to wait for now."

"It's disre-bloody-spectful, mate, that's what."

Nick shrugged. "She's not going to know."

"I'm a Catholic, mate. I believe the dead know everything."

"Even when you have a crap?"

"Now *you're* being disrespectful."

"I'm just asking."

"Jesus sees. Jesus knows."

"Bloody hell."

"But that doesn't mean He has to look."

"Is that what all Catholics believe?"

"I'm a Catholic and I believe it, don't I?"

"Yeah, right."

The two boys studied their cards. Across the room, the intercom buzzed. They looked at each other and waited. Nick looked up at the clock.

"Bit late for visitors," he said. Shiner had left orders that he was to OK anyone who came in.

They waited. The bell rang again. Then a voice crackled over the intercom and they both leaped to their feet.

It was Jones.

"Jesus."

"It's 'im!"

Davey ran over to the intercom and bent to listen. "Go and tell Shine. Quick!"

Nick ran down the corridor and banged on the door.

"Shiner! Shine—it's him."

"No . . ."

"It bloody is. Come and listen."

A second later Sunshine was out of the room, zipping up his jeans, with a pale blond girl following after him. Anxiously they all gathered around the intercom.

No noise.

"It was him," insisted Davey.

"Maybe he's gone."

"It'll be the first time he's taken no for an answer," said Shiner.

The bell rang again. They all held their breath. A moment later Jones's voice came hissing through the intercom.

"Open this fucking door, you little black shit. You think I have anything to lose? Open this fucking door before I come in to get you, you hear me?"

"Jesus, man!" Shiner turned and staggered around the room, clutching his hair. "What's he doing here, man? Here of all places. Thank God we cleaned the place out. Man!"

"What's going on?" demanded the girl, but no one even heard her.

"What you going to do, Shine?" Davey asked.

Shiner walked around and around the kitchen, shaking his head.

"What's going on?" asked the girl again.

"We have an unwanted visitor," explained Davey. He glanced at Nick, who was edging away to the back of the kitchen.

"Don't let him in, Shine," he said. "If he sees me, he'll kill me."

"Why's that?" demanded Sunshine. "What's he got against you?"

"Nothing . . . I can't explain it. Just don't let him in."

Suddenly a barrage of explosive bangs came through the intercom.

"Open this fucking door, open this door, open it now!" screamed the crackly voice.

"Oh, man! Oh, man!" wailed Sunshine.

"What we gonna do?" demanded Davey.

Shiner came to the same conclusion he always did.

"Open it. Let him in. What can we do? Go on, open it."

As he spoke Nick slipped away through the kitchen and into the sitting room. Just by the kitchen door there was a series of iron hoops hammered into the wall underneath an entrance to the roof space. Four steps up, and he was in the attic, tiptoeing away across a line of old cupboard doors someone had laid down years ago, to hide in the dusty darkness.

Below him, Shiner ordered the girl back to bed.

"Who is it, anyway?" she demanded.

"You read the papers? You heard the name of Ben Jones?" demanded Shiner.

"The one that did that girl in? You're joking. Bloody hell, what's he doing here?" she asked over her shoulder, and disappeared back into the bedroom without waiting for an answer. Davey began to head for the door as well, but Shiner lifted a finger.

"Two against one is better odds, Davey. Don't leave me here on my own, OK?"

Davey looked hard at him, and he sat back down. Shiner sat down slowly on the other side of the table. Like this, heads turned to the door, they waited for the coming of Jones.

Shiner picked up the cards.

"Might as well enjoy ourselves while we wait, eh?"

Davey snorted mirthlessly, picked his cards up, and they pretended to play.

The floors creaked and the doors groaned with the wind,

but they didn't have long to wait. In the end he burst suddenly in on them as usual, when they weren't expecting it, so quick, it made both of them jump with fright.

Jones looked awful—unshaven, white-faced, black rings under his eyes, his face screwed up in a permanent clench of fear and suspense. He stank—sour sweat and acrid breath. It was the smell of fear. He'd been on the run ever since he killed the girl he loved.

He stood in front of them, glaring and holding his coat around him; then he suddenly flung it open and closed it again in a moment, quick enough to reveal the sawn-off shotgun. "I've got this," he said, "in case anyone has an opinion."

"No opinions," insisted Shiner. "What, man, eh, Jones? You don't need no guns here. We thought you'd left the country, man."

"I tried."

"What 'appen, man?"

Jones grimaced in fury and humiliation before he could look at them. "Passport," he said. "I left me passport behind."

There was a pause. Jones watched them closely to see even a flicker of derision, but no one dared show anything. Indeed, no one felt anything but fear. He clutched at the gun under his coat.

Jones bustled suddenly into the room, moving like a man continually making up his mind and then changing it. He opened the fridge door and began stuffing cheese and bread into his mouth.

"Have they held the inquest yet?" he demanded, through a full mouth.

"Not that I know of," said Shiner.

"How can they bear to keep her?" muttered Jones, half to himself. Stella came to him every time he closed his eyes. In his madness, he'd come to believe that once she was buried or burned, she'd leave him alone.

Over the intercom, there was a huge crash. Jones froze. Shiner lifted his hands in the air. Another crash.

"The police!" Jones tore the gun out of his coat and pointed it straight in Shiner's face. "You rang them. You bastard, you rang 'em!"

"No, no. Jones, no . . ."

"I swear to God he never did, Jonesy," insisted Davey. "None of us did."

"They must have been watching the house," begged Shiner.

Jones glared at him and gripped the gun.

"I swear to God," said Shiner quietly. "They must have seen you come in. I knew they'd come sooner or later. Man, you brought them here yourself!"

Jones grimaced. He looked around.

"The roof," said Shiner. Jones turned and ran out of the kitchen to the iron hoops that led to the attic, his long coat swinging behind him as he climbed.

He paused halfway up.

"I'll hear every word you say," he said. He patted the gun and disappeared into the roof.

"You sent him up after Nick, you twat," hissed Davey. Above them, as if in answer, there was a scratching scuffle over their heads.

Behind him, the intercom reported the front door caving

in and there was a torrent of feet coming up the stairs. They knew the way, too. Only a minute later there was a bang at the door.

"Police," said a voice.

"It's open," said Shiner.

"You open it, Sunshine. Do it now," said the voice.

Slowly and deliberately, Shiner got up and opened the door. An armed policeman appeared behind it, shielding himself from the room with Sunshine's body, and scanned the room. Once he was sure it was empty, he pushed Shiner back into the room and gestured to him to sit down. The policeman looked to someone still in the corridor and nodded. A senior officer appeared behind him and looked at Shiner.

Above them came a voice, "Oh!" a little cry of surprise. The voice was Jones's. Shiner said nothing, but nodded and raised a finger and pointed above at the roof.

Up in the dark attic, Nick heard everything. When Shiner told Jones to go to the roof, it was like someone planning his nightmare, or death. But it didn't mean Jones was going to find him. Even though he could see hardly anything, it was as dark up there for them both. And the attic was huge—Jones could end up anywhere. Nick just had to stay very, very quiet.

As soon as the murderer was safely up on the beams, he struck a light on his Zippo. The yellow fire illuminated his face—Nick could see him quite plainly—and glinted a long bright line on the barrel of the shotgun. Nick was certain he was looking at the instrument of his death. Then the night-mare began to come true when out of all the space up there, Jones began to shuffle directly toward him.

It wasn't simply bad luck. As soon as Jones struck a light, he could see the way. Holding the lighter at arm's length before him, Jones began to creep along the cupboard doors that lay at his feet.

Nick sat stiller than he ever had in his life. As the drama below them unfolded and the armed police ran up the stairs and into the flat, the laid-out doors led Jones right up to him, until finally they were standing just inches from each other. Jones let the lighter go out before he spotted Nick, but he must have heard him breathing, or felt his heat, because almost at once he flashed it on again right in Nick's face . . .

"Oh!" gasped Jones in a fright, thus giving himself away to the police below. He swayed in surprise, then shot a hand out and seized Nick by the front of his shirt.

"You little fuck," he mouthed.

Before Nick could say a word, the police called up.

"Ben Jones!" The policeman sounded as if he was only feet away; he was. "You are wanted for the crime of murder. You are surrounded by armed officers. There is no possible way you can escape from this situation. Give yourself up. It's over, Jones," he added, more quietly.

Jones lifted the gun out of his coat, pointed it at the floor, to one side of the voice, and fired. The gun roared and flashed in the darkness and blew away a slab of ceiling. The light in the kitchen went off and coughs and yells came from below, where Davey, Shiner, and the policemen were plunged into sudden darkness and dust and plaster, and the filth of generations of pigeons fell down on them. Still with a grip on Nick's throat, Jones shuffled backward into the darkness. Below, the police, Shiner, and Davey bent to cover their faces against the falling plaster and dust.

Someone turned a light on in an adjacent room, and the borrowed light flooded up through the hole in the ceiling. Jones and Nick stared at each other in terror.

"Turn it off!" screamed Jones. "I've got the kid up here. Turn off that light."

Down below them the ceiling was still crumbling amid footsteps and a babble of voices. It went quiet at Jones's command, though. Someone barked a command and the light was turned off. Immediately, they were all plunged into darkness again.

Jones turned Nick around and pushed him away in front of him, swaying perilously over the beams that supported the dusty ceiling. In front of them, there was a small chink in the roof tiles, through which a few pale lines of light from a streetlamp below them shone.

"You wait there, where I can see your face," Jones commanded, pushing Nick down onto his haunches so the fragile light shone on his face. "And don't you move, not one inch out of the light, because as soon as that face disappears from my view, I'll kill you. Understand?"

Nick nodded agreement. Jones backed off and flicked on his lighter, still pointing the shotgun at him, casting around to see where they were. There was a wall a few yards behind him, and he carefully paced over the beams to that. He turned, still keeping the gun pointed at Nick, and gently lowered himself to the floor.

For a moment Jones held the lighter up in the air, illuminating himself, the gun, and Nick all in its little light. The gun was pointing straight at Nick's face. "So you know I got you covered," said Jones. "Understand?" Nick nodded. Jones nodded back, and turned the lighter off.

When the light vanished, so did Jones. Nick couldn't see a thing. It was the devil's own darkness, though. The next thing Nick heard was the gun being cocked.

Nick closed his eyes and prayed, although he'd never believed in anything. Around him the timbers creaked. He had no idea if it was the police, the wind, or Jones himself.

Then, in front of him, the gun clicked. Nick's eyes sprang open. It was coming, it was coming. He heard Jones sigh. He closed his eyes again to wait for oblivion, but it was almost as dark with them open. So it was that when the gun went off, Nick missed the flash of powder that might have shown him what happened.

He screamed when the gun fired and cringed back, but nothing struck him. He sat shivering in the darkness as something slid to the floor. Rapidly, the air began to fill with the thick smell of warm blood.

Nick could guess what had happened, what was lying opposite him, but he was too scared to move, or make any kind of noise at all. He sat in total darkness for several minutes more, as the policemen called and ran about below. He began to weep, then, and they could hear that. It was only when, by accident, one of them below flicked the switch that turned on the attic light, that the dreadful sight of Jones sprawled on the floor with his brains spattered on the wall behind him sprang out of the darkness at him, and Nick began to scream and scream with all his might, and the policemen came running up the stairs to fetch him down.

36
AFTERMATH

Shiner and Nick were both taken in for questioning and the police began a thorough search of the whole building, just as Shiner predicted—not for drugs, but on the off chance they might find something connected with the murder. That didn't mean to say they wouldn't act on anything else interesting, of course.

Shiner had cleared away evidence of the more illegal sides to his business, but finally his inability to do housework caught up with him. The great bags of weed he used to wheel and deal were out of the way, but under every table, all along the side of his bed, all over the work surface, and scattered generally around the place were the droppings and spillings from all the spliffs he'd smoked since Stella had gone. All in all, the police swept up over an ounce of weed, more than enough to put Sunshine in the cells for a while and to fine him several hundred pounds when the case came up in court some months later. But he was back smoking his weed, drinking his beer, and trekking around his women within a week or two. He never dealt in pharmaceuticals again, but apart from that there was not much change in the appearance of his life. He always claimed though, that his heart was broken, and perhaps it was. At least, it was several years before he moved another woman in to live with him.

Davey, despite a building full of armed police, managed to pull off one of his fabulous disappearing acts that night. He asked to go to the toilet, and once inside, cleverly forged his own peeing by tying the ballcock in the cistern so that the water was coming in at a steady trickle, and rerouting it with one of his trainers, out at the toe, into the lavatory pan. The officer in charge of him stood waiting outside the door, listening in increasing amazement to a staggeringly long piddle while Davey let himself out through a fourth-story window, climbed along a ledge at a dizzying height above the streets below to a gully on the roof, off onto another building, in through another window, down the stairs, and out onto the street and freedom, all wearing only one trainer. He deserved his freedom for a trick like that, but although he could escape almost anything, he couldn't escape his old habits and his old haunts. They picked him up at his parents' house a few days later.

There were no charges to press, though, and he was only two months off sixteen anyway by that time, so rather than send him to another home, they released him the next day. He carried on with his life of crime pretty well where it had left off.

Not much change there, either.

As for Nick, he was caught up in the attic, wiping Jones's blood off his face and weeping hysterically. He was taken to the police station, where he gave Jenny's name and address.

They drove him back there in the morning, where she wisely kept her mouth shut about next of kin and other difficult matters, but, of course, the social services were informed by the police. Mrs. Batts was duly outraged when she discovered where Nick was living, unreported by Jenny. The rules were there for a purpose, as she pointed out to Jenny over the phone. There was a disagreement, and Mrs. Batts hinted that she might be prepared to turn a blind eye so long as they could have a chat about it in a few days. But she must have changed her mind at some point, because the police picked Nick up on his way to the shops a couple of days later and drove him straight around to Meadow Hill and into the patient hands of Tony Creal.

No change there, either, you might think—but in fact there was. That sentimental old gentleman had decided somehow in his twisted heart that the letter sent to him warning him of Jones's murderous plot was something to do with Nick. After the usual welcome from Mr. James, Nick came to an interview in Mr. Creal's office, where the grateful pedophile, to Nick's astonishment, tearfully thanked him for saving his life and asked if there was anything he could do in return. Nick jumped at the chance, and suggested that they send him back to Jenny's. That wasn't possible with Mrs. Batts so much on his case, but Mr. Creal was able to offer him a place at another home.

"Anywhere that isn't here," said Nick.

"Agreed!" Mr. Creal banged his hands down on his desk and beamed. He got up from the table, and for a second, Nick thought he was actually going to come around to embrace him. But if that was his plan, the look on Nick's face put him off at once and he sat back down in his chair.

"I'll get on to that right away. Good move, I expect," said Mr. Creal, although he never explained why. The fact was, he'd had more than enough problems from Nick Dane to want to put himself in the way of any more. "I'll put you in with the Turners for tonight, and you'll be out of here tomorrow with a little luck. Bit softer than that bastard Toms, eh, Nick? Right, let's get on with it, then!"

He called in the prefect who was taking Nick around, a new boy Nick hadn't seen before, to take him off. The door closed behind him, and Mr. Creal vanished out of his life.

On the way down to America House, which the Turners ran, Nick asked the prefect something he hadn't dared ask Creal—about Oliver.

"Oliver who?"

"Oliver Brown? Small kid, blond hair. Used to be one of Creal's favorites."

But the prefect knew nothing more than Davey had already found out. "Never heard of him," he said. Later, mixing with the other boys, Nick asked around some more. Oliver, it seemed, had simply not been seen since Nick and Davey had run off. He'd been taken to the Secure Unit by the old prefects, Andrews and Julian, that much was known. After that, nothing. As Davey had reported, the story was that he'd done a runner, but at what point, no one had the slightest idea.

And that was all Nick ever got to hear about Oliver. Escaped, recaptured, transferred—there were various rumors doing the rounds. Then even the rumors dried up and Oliver was forgotten—one of many boys who came and went in and out of the homes without leaving any mark behind them.

Nick, as promised, was transferred to another home, a few miles away in Cheshire, where they ran a very different kind of regime, a genuinely kind one. He was well fed and given a room of his own for the first couple of weeks while he got used to things. Even after that he had to share with only two other boys. There were no beatings and no fences, either. He was told that if he did run, he was to remember that he was always welcome to come back—which made Nick laugh. As if!

Since it was so easy to run, he did so within a week, as much out of habit as anything. He hung around with Jenny for a few days, then, of his own free will, got bored, and, to his own surprise, went back to the home. Well—it wasn't so bad there. It fact, it was safe. He started day-release college, and when he left some months later, went on to an apprenticeship as an electrician.

All might have been well at that point, if it wasn't, once again, for Mrs. Batts. She discovered that the firm he was apprenticed to didn't know he was a children's home boy. Once again she resolutely did her duty, and told them. Nick wasn't sacked, but neither was he ever trusted at the firm again, never left on his own in the offices, never sent out on any jobs into clients' homes, and taught next to nothing. As a result, he quickly got sick of the whole thing, and left.

He signed on the dole and a few months later got a job in

a hotel, where he discovered sneaking—that is, stealing things from guests' rooms. He was caught a few weeks later and given a suspended sentence; did the same thing within a month and got another suspended sentence; took up shoplifting with Davey and the next time, he was sent to jail.

And that wasn't the last time, either.

By the time he was twenty-seven, Nick had spent four of the previous ten years inside. He had been helped on and off by Jenny and by his uncle, Michael Moberley, who had found money for various plans Nick came to him with, to buy vans, put deposits down on flats, buy tools, help with training, whatever—all of which ended up getting spent on drink, drugs, clothes, and cheap holidays. It could have gone on forever, but at that point, after a stretch of a full year inside for breaking and entering, Nick decided that enough was enough. He didn't want to spend the rest of his life being poor, drunk, stoned, and in and out of jail.

He signed on for college. He took his GCSEs, and to his surprise, found that they were easy. Then it was A levels—he got straight As. Where at school he'd found it almost impossible to concentrate, now, years later, he took to it like a duck to water. He went back to his uncle and begged for yet more money to help him go to university.

The old man was pretty reluctant by this time, but Nick had his results to show off and a job serving at a burger bar that he'd held down for over six months. It was the first time he'd come with some positive thing he'd actually already done, and Michael responded to that, rather than to his nephew's past. He provided an allowance of a hundred pounds a month—enough to keep body and soul together, along with Nick's wages at the fast food restaurant, while he was at university.

To his own amazement, three years later, Nick emerged with a first. And he'd never even known he had a brain. It was as if all the tangles of his life seemed to be somehow working themselves out inside him, because not only did he suddenly find it in him to work, he also found someone to love. There had been women before, many of them, but no one who had stayed around for longer than a couple of years. Now he wanted to build his walls and make a solid thing out of his life. Her name was Maggie; she was an older student like him, one year older. They set up house together while Nick completed his training as a youth worker; he wanted to help boys who had been disadvantaged as he had been. A year later, Maggie became pregnant, and by the time Nick was in his first full-time career job, he was already a father.

And so it was, three years after he had begun this work, at the age of thirty-five, crossing the road in a small town south of Manchester one cold December day, that he saw an old man leading a boy across the road toward him.

Something in the scene caught his eye—the way the old man walked, perhaps, or the way the lad had his head down. Without even thinking, Nick stepped back into a shop behind him and peered sideways at the two of them making their progress across the road. A shudder of recognition went through him—not at first because he knew the old man, although he did. It was something about himself.

Jones would have been perhaps a little younger than Nick

was now when he spotted Tony Creal at the pub that day, and had hidden behind a wall to watch his abuser from years before. Dear Tony had retired by now, but still liked to help out at the homes with boys who needed a little bit of extra care. Nick, like Jones, was a product of what Creal had done. In this respect, they were almost like brothers. Now, faced with the same situation, he felt closer to him than ever. All the terrors of his past came welling up inside him, and for a moment, hiding there in the shop doorway, he was unsure of his ability to avoid the same tragic path Jones had taken.

It was with a sense of utter horror that Nick understood that the old man before him had been carrying on with the same tricks ever since. Twenty years? Can it really have been so long? And how many years before that? And how many boys? How many Nick Danes and Olivers . . . how many Joneses had this wicked old man driven to destruction?

Nick was still unsure that he had truly escaped himself. He felt sick to his stomach as he watched the old man and his current victim walk away down the road. As soon as they were out of sight, he went to the nearest pub and got rapidly and soundly drunk.

The next day, and the day after that, and the day after that, Nick put off what he had to do. Finally, he plucked up courage and went to talk to Maggie, and, for the first time in his life, found the words to tell the story of Meadow Hill and Tony Creal, and Oliver and Jones and the whole thing. Upstairs, his two sons slept the sleep of the innocent while below their father wept and cursed and stormed. Was it possible that even now, in this day and age, they too could fall to the likes of Tony Creal? Of course it was. It could happen to anyone at any time.

Maggie was amazed. She'd had no idea he had such a history or so many hidden tears.

"You have to go to the police," she told him.

That, Nick refused to do—he was too aware that at least one of the men who had raped him in the Secure Unit had been a policeman. But the next day, with Maggie by his side, he went to see a solicitor and gave a statement. He cried like a baby when it was done, and kept bursting into tears for days afterward; but the ball was in motion by then, and nothing was going to stop it.

Only a few years before, nothing would have happened. People were so disturbed by abuse of that kind that they didn't want their institutions or even the courts polluted with it. But times had changed. There had by this time been several other cases up and down the country and it was becoming understood that sexual abuse in institutions designed to care for children was far more widespread than anyone had once believed. In Manchester, as in other places around the country, a process was begun of getting in touch with the men who had been boys not just at Meadow Hill, but at other homes, to see if their experiences there had anything in common with Nick's. The records were examined, old cases were turned over and reopened. Three years later, the first prosecutions were begun.

It would be nice to report that Tony Creal got what he deserved, but by this time he was seventy-five. Although he seemed in good health when he was arrested, his solicitor advised him well, and when he appeared in the dock, he had aged dreadfully almost overnight. The shock of the accusations, the wearisome questions, the hatred of him this affair had brought about in his own community had all taken their toll, as his solicitor movingly explained. The judge deemed him unfit to stand trial.

Amid screams of rage, the case against Tony Creal was dropped, although a number of his colleagues, including Toms, were eventually sent to jail.

Creal lived another five years. He moved south to finish his retirement in Nottingham, after a few too many bricks had come in through his window, a bit too much dog shit and the odd burning rag had been pushed through his letterbox. He was an active member of an organization founded to defend innocent and dedicated workers at children's homes who had been unfairly accused by ex-inmates, jailbirds to a man, who had obviously made such allegations only to get compensation. In this enterprise he was well supported by the likes of Mrs. Batts and others who refused to believe a word against him.

He died as he lived—unloved. And with him died any number of secrets, and fates. Perhaps, even, including Oliver's. Nick spoke to the police about him when the files were opened and tried to find out what had happend to him, but there was no record of him at all. Records at Meadow Hill were badly kept, boys came and went with very little in the way of a paper trail behind them. Oliver disappeared without a mention.

Nicholas Dane was not one of those who pursued his

revenge outside the courts. In his view, nothing could happen to Tony Creal that would change what had gone before. The only important thing was that he had helped to put a stop to abuse on the most vulnerable members of society that left victims dumb with shame or mad with rage, and turned victims into some of the most violent men in the country for decades to come.

Love comes to us all, if only we can recognize it and hold on to it. Jones had it and destroyed it. Nick had it, too. He recognized it in Maggie, but during Creal's trial he went through such a turmoil that he lost sight of everything he had gained. Dreadful years followed, but in her, Nick had at last found something every bit as precious as love itself—a full answer to that old Nick Dane loyalty. When he emerged at the other end, there she still was, waiting for her Nick to come back to her. And back he came, and there he still is. He lives in a Pennine town north of Manchester. As much as anyone could have, he has laid his ghosts to rest.